TIME GATE

ASCENSION AT AECHYR

Book I

By Evan J Kuder

Contents

I

A False Start

It all happened in a single moment.

As the embers circled in the smokey night air. As they lived their little loops and then flickered out. As they were quenched by winds drifting in from the sea. The waves lapped at the bloody sands and stained rocks, whose patchy outcroppings grew thicker as one went inland. Or tried to.

The unmoving bodies wrapped at the bases or foisted on the peaks of these stones were unholy testimony to the difficulty of such a journey. The approach to the cliff face was precarious even in open sand because of *them*. The enemy skulking in the crags of the sheer rock, pelting bullets down into the beach. Some lay in waiting inside caves and tunnels. Some scuttled to better vantage points to ensnare incautious men below. And some manned cannons—great bloated beasts belching fire at the scrambling soldiers below.

But at that moment, they were silent. Their absence made the beach seem almost quiet, at least for a second. But soon the air would be alive with screams. Shouted orders, cries for help, or shrieks of pain.

I wasn't listening to them. That particular symphony was already too familiar to me. I was fixated on a point in the distance. At a crater just in front of the cave carved into the rise. A deep red light burned from below and spilled out ominously onto the scarred sand. But the cave, the gullet of a sleeping dragon, wasn't the thing I was staring at. I was staring at the nothing just in front of the mouth.

They had been there just a moment ago.

I caught a glimpse of another squad to my left. They were preparing another assault. *I should go to them,* I thought. I was all alone otherwise. But as soon as I considered this, I finally saw something stir in the space I was staring at.

A shadow picked itself off the ground slightly. The form had lost most of its gear, enough so that it was almost recognizable. It was a woman, lying under the lip of the cave, silhouetted against the flickering bloom beneath. She was wounded, but safely out of sight of the attackers above. At least for the moment.

I looked back towards the other squad. They were closer. They would need all the help they could get. In the relative quiet, as the world seemed to catch its breath, nothing was certain. Every direction promised danger. But I fixated.

In that one moment, I acted.

I leapt over the rise and my boots hit the sand. I charged forward, right towards my wounded comrade.

And after two steps, the sand exploded in front of me.

The ground was ripped from me, and for a moment I was weightless, and everything was truly silent. It was nearly bliss. But the stinging shock stabbed back into my brain as I slammed into the sand.

When the dust settled, when my vision faded back in, I saw the cold moon staring down on me. It was wreathed with a scattering of circling embers. I watched them flicker out with detached disinterest. I almost forgot where I was.

Then the pain set in. Like burning oil poured into a vessel shaped like my body. My bones blistered. My shoulder splintered in agony. It shattered. And somehow, as my senses returned, it kept getting worse. The pain burrowed into my brain. I let out a scream.

And then I shot up in my bed.

A cold sweat drenched me and a vice crushed my shoulder. Gasping for breath, I tried to see where *he* was, but I couldn't see anything. My vision was entirely bleached. I could only stare into a uniformly murky white. Gulping down a few lungsful, I shivered. The heat of the battlefield had disappeared, replaced with a hollow cold. I realized the clamp on my shoulder was my own hand. For a moment, I couldn't remember how to ease my muscles. I pried my fingers in spasms from my body. I almost panicked as my hand, even free from my shoulder, kept its muscles locked tightly.

But slowly, they relaxed again. I could feel every tendon, primed from exertion, for minutes after that. But relief shuddered through me. Relief and a sick feeling. I wasn't on the beach. I was safe in my dorm. Everything was normal. Even my blindness was normal. But the dream's emotions had congealed at the bottom of my stomach. Like they did every night.

I felt the nausea from getting worked up, even as the details of the dream began to dissolve. The compulsion to save every detail jerked me into action. I reached over towards the nightstand, fingers fumbling for my glasses. My hand clumsily slammed into several shapes, one of which I recognized as the alarm clock. I was close. I moved my hand right, towards the glasses and—

They clattered to the floor. I cursed myself. Every second, the dream was becoming less vivid.

I leaned over the bed to feel around and misjudged the edge of the mattress. I tumbled and banged my wrist. Finally, I found my glasses and carefully placed them over my eyes. Everything finally swam into view. My academy dorm room, in the middle of the night. Exactly as it should have been.

My wrist throbbed as I looked around for my notebook. I saw it on the floor immediately. I had shoved it too off the nightstand in my fumbling. I started to reach for it, then stopped. My aching hand wasn't exactly in writing condition, and my sudden re-introduction to the real world had already obliterated some specifics of the landing from my mind. I could afford a moment to wake up a little before I did something else stupid.

I slowly crept into the bathroom. Splashing water on my face helped ground me in the moment. I looked at myself in the mirror, and some of the sickness settled. My face was still pale, paler than its usual sandy tone. And I had gotten some of the strands of my dark blonde hair wet. They hung to either side of my face, parted down the middle into two short curtains ending near the temples of the sunglasses.

The sunglasses. I pulled them off and wiped water droplets away with my T-shirt. Once more, I was plunged into a world of white until I put them back on my face. I felt like a tool wearing them at night, but what choice did I have? Polarized, photochromatic, UV protected, and most of all, just really dark, they were the only thing that let me see anymore. They wrapped around my face, giving me as large a field of view as possible, and always marked me apart from everyone else.

I certainly felt apart. And not just because I was probably the only one up at that hour. These dreams were telling me something. Something impossible, but there was truth in there, I was sure. If only I could figure it out.

Almost every night, I would wake up in the middle of the same dream. Over and over again, it played in my head. Every night, it felt so real. But it couldn't be. I had never been a marine. I had never stormed any beaches. I had never even been in a real fight.

All things considered, I was a screwup. A screwup who had been swept up into something incredible, but nothing like my dreams. In reality, I had run away from home, only to be recruited into some interdimensional agency. Basically. They had the time gate—a portal to another world. Just what I had needed. Or so I thought, until I stepped through and lost my sight. They told me it was a freak accident and made me my sunglasses to compensate. After that, they shipped me here.

Nowhere in there did I become a marine. Nowhere in there had I nearly died on a dirty beach. So why was I remembering it?

If there were answers anywhere, they would be in the dreams themselves. I walked back into my room, towards the notebook where I charted every detail of those visions. Usually, I scrambled to get the fleeting glimpses of my dreams onto paper as soon as I woke up, hoping that one of these nights I would remember something new that would solve this riddle. It was my hopeless ritual. It was the only thing I could do.

I picked the notebook up from its spot next to the camouflage bedspread spilling onto the floor. In the morning, the bedding would be a claim to the identity I thought I lost. In the dim blue light, it looked like a joke. My jumbled thoughts were reaching back for unreal memories, like twisted déjà vu, and what I found made the pattern on the bed seem childish.

I took a deep breath. The real thing was waiting. If it was real at all. I sat behind my desk, opened the journal, and prepared to dive back in. I concentrated on finding the earliest thread of the last dream. It was always so hard to find the beginning. Eventually, I found the earliest part I could remember, and started writing.

Rolling. I remembered the rolling motion. A surging upwards, then a stomach-churning fall. We crashed into the next wave, a slow-motion collision. The cramped transport pushed its way through the roiling seas.

Inside, there was barely enough room to breathe, and the atmosphere was thick enough that I didn't want to. The marines were packed in tight lines, facing the firmly sealed door. The smell of oil and sweaty anticipation soaked the air. Red light bathed the faces of the troops in front of me. I was near the back, with only a sliver of a view of the rest of the compartment.

We hit another swell, and a trickle of water swung back towards me. As the boat pointed into the air, the stream splashed across my helmet, dribbling down on my face. We reached the top of the wave and plunged down again. The stream angled away from me, just as my stomach lurched into my throat. With a shudder, we reached the bottom, and we started the whole process again. I tried to adjust, to lean out of the way, but there was no space. We were shoulder-to-shoulder in there. Add in our gear and rifles and there was nowhere to go to avoid the next splash.

I gritted my teeth and wiped the salty droplets off my face.

"Doin' all right, son?" someone asked from my right side. I looked over to Thomas Madding. He was big, standing six feet to the dot, and with a hearty amount of muscle. His skin was rough, coffee-colored, and hairless. I kept imagining I would see a gray bristle, but nope. He didn't even have any stubble around his jaw. It made it extremely hard to tell his age. He was young enough to outperform all of us in all the drills, but he had an air of experience around him. Maybe it was the deep, commanding voice.

"A-OK," I said loudly over the roaring engine. It sounded too loud to me. Surely, the baying motor was betraying us by belting out our position. I started to anticipate that something might tear through the landing craft, splintering it to bits.

"I hope we get out soon," I added to Tommy.

He leaned in closer. Only to me, he said quietly, "You'll be eating those words pretty quick."

He looked me in the eye seriously. I didn't have an answer, but I didn't really need to give him one. He probably knew exactly what I was thinking. He had an uncanny ability to befriend everyone in the squad, and I was no exception. Of the few friends I had, he automatically added himself to the list.

All at once, something changed in the air. I heard a radio squawking, but the words were gibberish. Someone replied intensely, and a ripple ran through the marines. You could hardly see it; everyone was still stoic, ready for the order to charge out. But you could feel it. Something was deeply wrong.

A man signaled for us to ready ourselves. Everyone did so with solemn dread. Any foolish eagerness had been quashed. Something had gone sideways for sure.

As I checked my things, I whispered to Tommy, "Who screwed up?"

"Don't sweat it," he said, but for once, his words weren't much comfort. The atmosphere quenched the spirit in them. Tommy saw this, looked back to me, and added in a louder voice, "Must be the boys upstairs again. Once again, someone was too busy pushing papers to certify the obvious. Once again, something

wasn't filed in triplicate, and slipped through the cracks. Once again, someone was too busy calculating to think. Once again—as per standard procedure. So it's just another day at the office, son. Just like always, it's up to the boys on the ground to pick up the pieces, carry the load, and punch our way through. And just like every other day, we'll do it, and we'll do it in style. And when we get back, we'll give the boys another complaint for them to lose. So no sense moanin' now. Another day, another disaster."

"And another drink," another of our squad, Happy, chimed in.

"You're buying," Claire insisted from behind him.

"Sure thing, sweetheart," Happy replied. "It's a date."

Claire rolled her eyes as we heard the man upfront call out again. Our lines stiffened. Tommy glanced over his shoulder one last time.

"Alright, kid. Ready to jam?"

Behind his grin, there was a warning. Not all of us would be coming back.

I nodded and gave him a joyless grin in return.

We heard thuds from outside. Something rattled. The booms became more and more regular, like a cacophony of fireworks.

The boat levelled out. I felt the deck suddenly rise. It was sudden, almost violent. Not like the waves had been. The boat never jumped towards the sky. It was a shallow rise, and I could feel the craft slide up the plane. It was solid ground. We were there.

The light flashed green, turning all our skin sickly. The giant hatch at the end of the room heaved open. With a thud that shook the deck, it dug itself into the sand. Immediately, the front lines drained out of the craft.

The columns advanced, slowly, as we disembarked. I could just make out the first glimpses of the landscape between the heads of those in front of me. I saw a mountainous rise beyond the beach. We had landed in a cove, a cave opening onto the sea at one point. Many more opened to the sand. One was directly in my line of sight. It glowed, like there was a deep fire inside it.

The line moved forward again. I could hear the gunfire now. It rattled off from different directions. Occasionally the rapid staccato was punctuated by a deep boom of a heavier shell being fired, or a thunderous tremor as it struck the ground. I saw a plume of sand shoot skyward outside and felt my stomach shrivel with dread. How much longer until our landing craft was targeted?

Another group of marines charged out. We were inching closer. Just inching. The ship rattled, but it hadn't been hit yet.

The line shortened. It was painfully slow. But there were only a few men left before it was my turn. My turn. Would that be worse than the waiting?

Finally, Happy dove out of the transport. He vanished from my sight as he zipped out. I lost track of him and tried to bury my worry.

Claire was next, right behind him. She ran down the ramp into the maw of chaos opening in front of us. Before I could mentally wish her well, the line moved again.

The man in front of me charged out. It was our turn.

Tommy rushed in, shouted something to me, but I froze. It was the most terrifying moment of my life. Just inside the familiar walls of the transport, I stood on the precipice of static fear and the utter insanity of the open world ahead.

Fire and salt assailed my nostrils as I watched the streaming lines of marines rushing towards the impenetrable rock.

The rocky cliffside loomed at us threateningly. Marines searched for cover in the frantic hailstorm. Some laid motionless on the sand, near splintered shells and guns.

In that fraction of a second, I also saw Tommy. He was charging in undaunted. Something made a decision for me. I started running forward, my legs moving on my own. While my conscious mind reeled at the assault of sights, sounds, and smells, my training kicked in. The endless drills made it instinct. I didn't think, I acted.

I pounded down the deck, my heart slamming in beat after beat. It was like it was making up for every one it would never get. Adrenaline pushed itself through my veins. I forced myself into the fray, as fast as I could.

And then it all exploded in front of me.

I dropped the pencil. My hand was seizing up in pain. I leaned back, looking at my furious scribblings. I had been writing in a frenzy, and my hand couldn't take any more. I set it aside and tried to relax.

But another headache was on me. I wasn't sure anymore if a shell really had exploded in front of me as I ran out of the landing craft. That hadn't been the moment when I had to choose between running towards the marine at the cave and joining another squad. But it was suspiciously similar.

Both times, everything seemed to be in slow-motion. Both times, I was getting ready to run out onto the beach. And both times, I was cut short by an explosion in front of me. Though, charging out of the craft, I was sure I hadn't actually been hit. It had looked closer than it had been. But still, I wondered if I was getting it right.

That was a problem. Even though the dreams seemed the same each night, when I jotted them down, discrepancies started to emerge. One night, I remembered Claire jumping out before Happy. Another time, Tommy was in front of me, not beside me. Sometimes, we were closer to the door. Other times, farther away. A hundred little changes, enough to eat away at my certainty.

Panic rose up in me again. In those moments where I wasn't sure of anything, of what was real or what wasn't, it got worse. My mental defenses collapsed, and a roiling wave of confusion washed over me. Hideous howling winds ripped away my sense of self, until I was dissociated fragments of awareness, tumbling in a lose pattern through an unforgiving world.

Stop. Stop it, I told myself.

Breathe. Focus on what you do know. Anchor yourself.

I am Kennedy Frost. Serial number... No, I didn't have a serial number.

Yes, I absolutely did, another part of my mind resisted. It was struggling to find the numbers. It was sure that I could do this on instinct, and yet, nothing was coming to me. As if something had been cut out of me—a phantom limb of a past life.

Forget the number. What do you know for sure?

I am Kennedy Frost. I am eighteen years old. Is that old enough to enlist?

Focus.

I am currently in my dorm room. I am enrolled in Aechyr Academy. My dorm is in Aechyr Academy West. I had to resist telling myself, "Duh" after that. *I know it's obvious, that's the point of the exercise. Now keep going.*

Aechyr Academy is in the nation of Aechyr. Aechyr like "acre." And Aechyr shouldn't exist.

I sighed and went to my window. Opening it, the smell of the ocean wafted into my room. For a split-second I thought about diving to cover. As the smell hit my nostrils, I was back at the cove, assaulting the beach. But after a few seconds, the difference became obvious. This time, the scent was somehow cool, calming. Pure salty spray. No hint of burning, or gunpowder, or death. Just the waves.

No, as I looked down, a much friendlier beach met my eyes. In the distance, pure white sands glistened in the silver moonlight. Dark blue waves gently lapped at it. The rhythmic shushing sound soothed me, even as I thought about how this place shouldn't exist.

Aechyr was an island nation, roughly the same size as the UK. But back home, in my world, you couldn't find it on any map. In this world, you could spot it easily enough—just look for that little pocket between the Carolinas and Florida, and you'd find Aechyr nestling up to the lower United States. I was pretty sure we didn't just miss this landmass back home. No, Aechyr only existed in this one alternate universe.

I looked at it. Towards the capitol, Thysiopolis, and the mountains rising behind it. Towards the rest of campus below. And in the opposite direction, towards the flat forests beyond the city. I drank in all the sights, just thankful to see again.

I stood there for a while, my mind clearing. Everything was quiet. I could believe everything would just stay like that forever, nothing ever changing. As if I was alone in the world.

I realized I had been zoning out when a sleek black car crawled through the still landscape. As it pulled out of the campus and towards the capitol, I wondered how much time I had lost.

Looking back inside, I saw my alarm clock dimly display 4:42 a.m. I shook my head. No one in their right mind would be up at this hour. I would have thought about going to bed, but I would never be able to fall back asleep. For as long as I could remember, whenever I woke up, even if it was the middle of the night, I would stay up. The dreams hadn't changed that.

I felt at my wrist. It didn't hurt quite as much. Just a little sore. I had to get down the rest of my story, what little I could remember of it. Even if what I had just dreamed didn't match the other dozens of versions I had jotted down, I had to save what I had relived. Anything could wind up being the clue I needed.

I walked back to my desk but left the window open. I might need a calming influence.

Picking up the pencil, I continued where I had left off.

The sand shot up in a fiery pillar. The shockwave ran up my legs. A split-second later, it thudded against my chest.

When I realized I was still standing, I dived for cover. Only once I had ducked behind a piece of debris did I let myself look for the rest of my team. To my shuddering relief, I saw Tommy and the others had also taken shelter. They were huddled far ahead of me, and Tommy barked something to Claire and Happy.

I edged closer, ready to run up to them as soon as it was clear. But as I peeked around the corner, Tommy spotted me. He held up a hand and shouted back to me. But he was too far away and something roared overhead. A huge explosion rocked the beach from behind us. I tried to ignore it, focusing on Tommy. I cupped my hand to my ear to signal to him I hadn't heard.

He glanced towards the cliffs. As if shushed by his glare, there was a lull in the pounding gunfire.

Tommy quickly turned back and shouted, "Our comms are down. Get the backup and—"

Another explosion cut his words short. I saw sand plume behind Tommy, but it wasn't close enough to throw shrapnel into him. Still, he reflexively ducked. Someone else shouted in the distance. Tommy glanced back at me one last time.

"Get to the comms, that's an order!" he barked.

Then he turned back to the others, and they leapt back into the fray. I felt it as they ripped themselves away from me. I had to root myself to the ground to not follow after. I tore my gaze away from the beach as it was chewed up around them and looked back towards the landing craft.

It was burning, half in the water, half in the sand. It looked like the waves were on fire. And spillage littered the sand. Strips of metal. Equipment. And somewhere in that mechanical gore was the backup comms.

Suddenly I had control over myself again. I rushed into the minefield, eyes darting across the wreckage. My mind was racing, processing the information I was seeing too quickly to put into words. It didn't take me long to find what I was looking for.

I slid down next to the half-buried metal box. It flashed to life as my hands scrambled over the controls. Soon, I was shouting into it over the noise behind me. I turned back and saw my squad rushing from cover to cover.

The fight wasn't going well. If we couldn't push into their stronghold, we would be wiped out. I shouted this into the mic. Someone on the other side issued a placid reply. It was lost on me in a muddle of emotion, but I heard something about backup.

Finally. Before I could get details, though, another shell exploded to my side. I buried myself in the sand, and when I sat back up, saw I was unharmed. The spare comms was another story.

Shrapnel had lodged itself into the back of the transmitter, gutting its usefulness. No sense staying here. I darted forward, careful to cling to any concealment I could find. I was heading straight for my team when it happened.

A shell landed right in the middle of the group, and they were swallowed by fire and sand. Ducking behind a rise, I waited, nerves electrified. But as the dust settled, no one moved.

I stared. My muscles coiled and uncoiled again. I didn't believe what I was seeing.

I saw the other fireteam making their way up the beach. I remembered the overall situation. Our odds of winning this were already near zero.

And then, with one motion in the distance, it was all real.

Claire stirred at the mouth of the cavern. The red glow surrounded her, as if she was on fire. Feeling kicked back in, right down to my toes. Claire was moving gingerly, haltingly.

I pushed aside the other fireteam. I had to help her.

My guts roiling, I leapt into action. I wasn't calm. I wasn't controlled. But I had a goal. Clarity. Peace of Mind.

Almost.

I was knocked off my feet almost as soon as they had gone over the ridge. I landed on my back and shock numbed me. I saw the pale moon, and the slowly circling embers. And finally, the pain set in. It burned through me and took my mind.

And yet, I was sure that somewhere in there, I heard footsteps. Crunching sand and broken metal underneath.

I set down the pencil. If there was anything concrete to these visions, I had lost it by now. The early morning haze had rolled in over the memory of the dreams. I could have just been making this up now.

My headache, my unease, started to creep back in. Even though I finished putting down what I had relived, I was still wallowing in uncertainty. Or was it dread? Did that last part of the dream dredge up the fear that came with the end of the memory?

I had been spared that final scene that night, but every other time I revisited the beach, it ended the same way. With *him*. I shuddered. He seemed the most unreal part. But if the rest of the dream was real, he had to be too. Given the choice, I wasn't sure which I'd take.

As the doubt built up in my chest, I looked for some sort of anchor. I turned on the TV, hoping for some mild white noise.

"...missile program may even rival America's. Testing is scheduled for the end of November," the newsman said, ending a story. "In more somber news, the Queen's condition continues to deteriorate. Despite the best care being made available, doctors tell us it is only a matter of time. Joining us is Dr. Hardwick to discuss the situation. Doctor, what are looking at in terms of time?"

It wasn't helping. A queen was, quite literally, a foreign concept to me. I was still trying to sort out my two lives. One where I had been sent, uneventfully, to Aechyr. Another where I had been gravely wounded charging into battle. I shook my head and turned off the TV.

I saw underneath stacks of old movies. Movies from another dimension. Cheesy flicks that would love that label. I thought about putting one of them on instead but realized that wouldn't be much better. They would wind up being familiar, but different. In the day, that made them wildly entertaining. But they were given to me to be educational—to get me acclimated to this world. Tonight, they would be neither. Just confusing.

Instead, I tried to bring the day closer by getting ready. I cleaned up and slipped on my usual white T-shirt and camouflage pants. The sun still hadn't cracked the horizon.

And still, the nagging in the back of my head persisted. I looked back to my notebook. I had a sinking feeling that the only way out was through. The rest of the memory, what would be the rest of the dream on any other night, was waiting for me. Maybe to exorcize myself of the dread clinging to me, I would have to read the other entries. Relive it just once more.

I didn't have anything else to do, so I sat down once more. I paged to the last entry. Skimming through it, ignoring the inconsistencies, I found roughly where the most recent vision had ended.

And I leapt in to finish it.

I was lying there.

I was wounded and I couldn't do anything. I was on one side with shrapnel in the other. I was drained of all my energy. Exhausted. Adrenaline did nothing anymore. It was all over. No more screams left in me. And all I had done was rush forward and get killed.

Then he stepped through the ash.

He walked toward me calmly despite the war raging around him. His stride was unworldly, serene, but his body was as real as the dead around him.

He was tall and bone thin. His alabaster skin hugged his skull just a little too tightly. His mouth curled slightly at the edges,

17

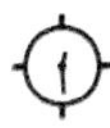

making a thin smile. He had a pointed nose, which he might have been holding it high in the air, but that could have been my angle. His eyes literally shone in the dark—a bright eerie green, like two burning ghosts floating through the air. His hair was long and white, the only part of him paler than his skin. At one point, it might have been kept in line. Now, strands blew freely in the breeze. He wore a perfectly black suit. There wasn't even a seam to break it up. His shoes and gloves were equally black, though the shoes glinted in the moonlight.

They, and the rest of him, were spotlessly clean. It was as if he had taken considerable effort to remove any trace of filth. On this battlefield, where dirt seemed to seep into every crevice, that was quite a task. But his neat appearance did nothing to make him seem friendlier. I had the impression that his job back in whatever dim realm he had come from would be to extract the worst fears and weaknesses of his victims. Then, he would systematically use these discoveries against them.

As he carefully stepped forward, avoiding anything that might stain his boots, I noticed his hand. It was cradling some sort of silver sphere, but it was hard to make out. An impossibly bright, piercing light burst out of an opening, already stabbing into my eyes. The light seemed tinged blue, but it was so intense it dimmed everything around it.

He reached me and kneeled down, right next to me. I tried to squirm away, but my body didn't cooperate. I couldn't say anything. Exhaustion and fear kept me pinned. As did his mere presence. He briefly scanned over my body. I thought he must have been inspecting my wounds. It was like he was a doctor examining a terminally ill patient. No, it was as if he were a coroner examining a corpse.

He grabbed my face with his hand and forced me to look him straight in the eyes. The green glow faded slightly and his pupils started to shimmer. I felt like I was looking into two obsidian mirrors. Then, I felt him extract every ounce of my experiences and emotions and understand them fully. I was mortified. Had I been right? Was he now going to use my greatest fear against me? What would it be? Could I handle it? I had a sickening feeling that I couldn't. At that moment, I became convinced that my greatest fear, of everything in the world, was him. He didn't even have to do anything. I was already terrified.

He started to bring up the silver device and I tried to look away, but his hand gripped my head firmly. I was frantic, desperate. Then I saw his eyes change. The green was drowned in circulating blood red. Blood circling two black holes, only hatred escaping their pull.

I glanced up at the stars and moon, at anything but the white glare that was overtaking my vision. It wouldn't stop, and in desperation I closed my eyes as tightly as I could. It didn't matter. The light penetrated my eyelids and burned straight into me. It seemed to irradiate every synapse of my brain and consume my entire consciousness. It bore into my brain, into my very soul. Nothing remained except whiteness.

I waited for it to clear.

It never did.

The sky had been the last thing I ever saw with my own eyes.

II

Aechyr Academy

It was a bright, beautiful day. The sun was out, birds were singing, and I hated every moment of it. What I wouldn't have given for gray skies and a light drizzle.

I was up long before most everyone else. Typical college students don't like waking before the crack of noon, which was fine by me. If the elite students wanted to surrender the space to me, I was more than happy to decompress.

I fell into my morning run. My path took me right into the heart of Aechyr Academy—a huge courtyard in the middle of the campus. It was outlined by red brick paths, dotted by a few tables along the edges, and broken up by shady trees every couple dozen feet. The very center of it all was marked by an elaborate fountain, already bubbling happily along.

I shook my head as I passed it. I still couldn't believe Time Peace—the interdimensional agency that recruited me—put me here. The reason Aechyr Academy could so boldly claim the name of the nation it belonged to was because of its prestigious history and its ongoing mission. It produced a remarkable number of senators, judges, high-profile businessmen, and all-around important figures. And that wasn't by accident. The country invested a lot in making sure the Academy found potential and cranked out real skill. It was practically a public service, both the schools and the students.

So what in the world was I doing here?

I passed one of the towering pillars which marked the corners of the courtyard. This one was topped with a wolf pointing southeast to the quadrant for Political Theory and Business. The roots of all evil, as the students said.

Time Peace insisted I pay attention to my class in this wing. Intro to Aechrian Civics. Whatever they would have me doing in this timeline, I must have needed to know how its unique country worked.

Professor Martinez, while comparing and contrasting the virtues of a monarchy and democracy, liked to try and catch any dozing students off-guard. My sunglasses probably made me look like I was slipping into a morning snooze, so it wasn't too surprising he had a tendency to call on me unexpectedly.

"Mr. Frost, please tell us one benefit of a democracy over a monarchy," he had instructed on one such occasion.

"You get the leader you deserve," I said, only half-thinking. I realized that snarky sentiment was probably inappropriate for the class, brought on by another night of bad dreams. I snapped my mouth shut. But Professor Martinez waited, expecting me to elaborate. Cautiously, I said, "If the candidate wasn't trustworthy, it was still your choice to elect them. If you're lazy about it, then you can't be surprised who you wind up with. If you give away your power, your vote, you have no one to blame but yourself."

"An interesting insight," Professor Martinez... complimented? To the class, "Keep in mind the implications of where political power comes from. Someone else, what is a counter argument in favor of monarchy? Miss Criss?" he asked of someone behind me.

A dismissive voice replied, "In theory? That the people deserve better."

I didn't listen to the rest of the answers but glanced around with my eyes safely concealed. No one was looking at me like I was an idiot. They seemed too busy eagerly explaining the virtues of having a symbolic monarch. Maybe they were too busy patting themselves on the back to notice how basic what I said had been.

Now I was selling them short, I thought. I ran past two guys deep in discussion over a pile of papers, their eyes baggy with exhaustion. They hardly paid attention as they walked down the stately staircase sloping up to a building whose pillars subtly reminded me of a capitol building. Even so, the taller guy glanced up and nodded as I passed.

That was the thing. You would think such a successful university would be pretty snooty, right? Not Aechyr Academy. I couldn't tell you how they had done it, but somehow, there was very little boastfulness around the place. From the teachers to the students, it was all... well maybe not down-to-earth, but close enough.

I passed the northeast pillar, topped by a posturing hawk. Posturing—perfect for the Law and Philosophy quarter, I thought. If you didn't say precisely what you meant to these people, in exacting detail, they would often twist the conversation in an unexpected way. And cut down any attitude that would sour the atmosphere of the place.

Last week, during Professor Perry's Intro to Philosophy class, another student thought their play on the words *a posteriori* was too hilarious not to share aloud.

"Thank you for sharing, James," Professor Perry had replied with an easy, if thin, smile. "I hope we'll be hearing just as much from you in our discussion groups."

James shrugged this off, seeming to think that was the worst coming his way. He was wrong.

"And that brings us to synthetic versus analytic," Professor Perry said minutes later. "James, let's have another witticism, if you will. Something better than the obvious, if you can."

James was, in fact, winding up for another lowball when the professor beat him to the punch. His request took the wind from James' sails. James' quip was delivered a lot less impressively and got a far less enthusiastic chuckle.

"Two out of ten," the professor said sadly. "Let's hope your quiz scores are better."

As I continued to run, the statelier red-brick buildings turned to simple, modern buildings. A lot of white walls and big glass windows. This was the northwest, the quarter guarded by a sleek fox where the departments for Arts and Sciences were. The Science department tended to soak up much of the Academy's resources, and it dwarfed the jealous Arts wing. Still, it seemed strangely appropriate that the two shared a quadrant.

As if to prove my point, a small pack of excitedly yammering students nearly got hit by a frisbee. They had their heads in the clouds and had totally missed the ultimate frisbee team coming out for early practice. I tried to guess what had distracted them from the real world: a fascinating scientific idea, or a new artistic aesthetic?

"Heads up, Candlestick," the guy who tossed the frisbee said, laughing in embarrassment.

Candlestick. Arts, it was then. I remembered a story going around about how someone nearly burned down a theater set after knocking over a lit candle that had been intended to make a set look more "authentic". Authenticity became a bit of a dirty word in the department after that, I heard.

It was hard to figure out the nicknames that flew around sometimes. Like a particular guy who partied too hard and passed out on a pile of jackets and woke up with creases all across his face. He was soon dubbed Leather-Face. Bonus points there, since he thought he was something of a tough guy. But was that an endearing nickname or reminder to shape up? Hard to say. Maybe the test was if a professor started picking it up. "That's what the kids are calling you, aren't they?"

Yeah, that was definitely the line. It might sound kind of awful, but punishment was public, while praise was private. At least when it came to the professors. As for students... glancing back, it seemed Candlestick was smiling at Frisbee Guy now. Sometimes taking a few lumps brought the students closer together.

And no group on campus was more tightly knit together than the Navy cadets. I passed the pillar supporting the Bison, which marked the way to the Naval wing. Other Academies would train the Army or Air force. Here, it was the Navy. I should say that the Aechyr Academy I was describing was actually one of four Aechyr Academies. We were in Academy West, on, you guessed it, the West Coast of Aechyr, which housed a healthy-sized dock for passing naval vessels.

As soon as I stepped over the imaginary boundary into Navy territory, I felt the atmosphere change. Somehow, the air was crisper, more intense. I hesitated. And then I turned back towards the courtyard. Whatever my dreams and inner convictions said, I felt wrong being there.

By now, more students were starting to mill about. I recognized several of them in a particularly thick group. There was Isiah, tall, dreadlocked, always with a grin and a helpful attitude. Denisha, still on her phone even as she talked with the group, no doubt keeping a close eye on her schedule along with the other conversations she was having in cyberspace. Scarlett, hair matching the name, off to the side, quiet, yet capable of gently steering the conversation when she did speak up. Michael, eyes always half-closed like he was about to fall asleep, chiming in on some technicality in the conversation, one hand making sliding gestures, while the other was stuck in his pocket. And then there was David.

David Greene. David was friends with everyone. He had a friendly face, warm, green eyes (appropriately enough), and his brown hair was left kind of shaggy, wavy. Despite his young looks, he was by far the most mature freshman on campus. I, unfortunately, was subject to his gentle, yet iron will all too often.

Because David was team leader.

David was in the middle of the overlapping conversation in the huddle of students, and yet, he still noticed me pass by from across the courtyard. He managed to pick me out, meet my eyes, and nod in just such a way that I knew meant "come talk to me." He did it all without missing a beat. Of course he did.

I won't lie, I resented having to report to David. He hadn't done anything to me, he was easy to get along with, and I wasn't jealous. He just irritated me. And he irritated me because I had no right to be irritated with him.

When I hated David, it was because I could see the ghost of a familiar pain. But his didn't linger, it didn't fester. It had

forged him. I resented that he had come out of his suffering whole. It didn't leave me room to make excuses for myself.

I changed my course slightly and stopped in front of a small unoccupied table within sight of the large group. I took a sip from my water bottle as I waited. David didn't come up immediately, of course. Although it was no secret that our little group associated with each other, we didn't play up our ties. To the contrary, we preferred to go our own ways when we didn't have to be together. Usually, this was just fine with me. Right now, when I had to pretend to take a rest while waiting for his conversation to finally end, it was less so. But he didn't make me wait long.

"Meeting tonight," David said when he arrived. He wasn't trying to talk in a whisper or to speak in code or anything. He disguised any importance in the message with an air of casual conversation. Sometimes that was the best approach.

"On campus?" I asked. We had met a few times in the dorms to go over some very, very basic information. I had never liked that idea. The rooms were fine, but they were small, and cramming four people in was never pleasant.

David was way ahead of me. "Nope. Pick you up on the corner of 4th and Arbor. Bring Blake."

"You'll have Randy?" I asked.

"Yep," he replied. "We'll get you all caught up."

He looked more closely at me for a moment, deciding what to say, or if to say it. Finally, "You hanging in there?"

"I'm fine," I answered. It was a bad lie.

David thought carefully for a moment longer.

"Give it time," he suggested. "How about the campus? Getting familiar with it?"

"Yep," I said curtly.

"Good. We take things one step at a time. Soon enough, you'll be bored. It's just the change at first that gets you."

"Yeah, sure," I said skeptically.

I regretted taking that tone. I had just invited him to pry further. If I had a mind for social stuff, I would have latched onto the excuse he provided. I would have agreed and he would have to drop it.

I think. I couldn't be sure how a conversation with David would go. Despite being no older than me, he was already a spook—a spy. Everything he did, nice as it seemed, might have more than one meaning.

David nodded. "Okay then. See you at six." He rapped the table once with his knuckles, turned and walked away.

Not what I had expected. Was I being too harsh on him? Or was I overthinking everything? There was too much I didn't know. Tonight should help. 1800 hours. Good.

I immediately set off on my jog again. The crowd David had been a part of had dispersed, and there were many more students in the courtyard now. It seemed morning had reached a critical mass. Classes were about to start for most students. Not for me just yet. I pounded the pavement, keeping my thoughts from circling each other faster and faster.

And just as I started beating away the distracting mind clutter, I ran straight into someone.

Stumbling back to my feet, I muttered, "Sorry."

"Watch it," the guy I had bumped into said. When I finally tore my eyes from the ground to see him, I was kind of surprised. He stood next to two other figures; all three of them were wearing the unofficial school uniform.

Hardly anyone actually wore the "uniform." It was just a convention for job interviews or if you were out representing the school. But these guys had bucked tradition. In the exact same way. The usual navy of the blazer and slacks was replaced with a dark gray, and their dress shirts were black instead of white. They kept the tie dark, but now it was nearly invisible against their shirts. No club or team pins, though the school patch, a modification of the red and pale gold flag of Aechyr, was still prominently displayed. The black eagle set against the bright quarters of the flag somehow looked more ominous on them than it had anywhere else.

The only difference between them was that first guy had rolled up his sleeves. That, and his hair was slightly longer than the severe cuts of his pals. The black locks were swept back casually, but his affected attitude couldn't maintain the carefree illusion.

"Well, no wonder you can't see where you're going," he said, seeming to relax a little. "You trying to be a trend-setter?"

He was gesturing towards my sunglasses. Of course he was.

After my mistake, a little ribbing was justified. Didn't mean I had to like it. Deciding to get this over with, I lifted the glasses to my forehead, revealing my pallid eyes.

"They just help me see," I explained simply.

"Not very well, apparently," Sleeves replied. "Maybe next time you should lean into the blind schtick and get a walking cane instead of worrying whether your Ray-Bans were in season. At least then if you're still clumsy enough to run into people, your tap-tapping along will be a warning to those considerate enough to mind their own business."

Huh? That wasn't right. Sure, you were supposed to be ridiculed for doing something ridiculous, but not for being something different. Not for something you couldn't help.

I'm not always good with reading a situation. But I should have trusted my gut as soon as I thought something was wrong. Because in the next moment, a hand snapped away the glasses.

"Let's see these, Slick," Sleeves said. "Very American. Ostentatious and tasteless."

Some comeback about matching outfits caught in my throat. My brain had just gone from shock to lockdown. I was completely blind, only seeing a thick fog of white before me.

When my mind finally whirred back into motion, it flooded with hate and determination. But I remained perfectly still. I couldn't do anything without my sight. For now, I couldn't let any of my feelings show.

"Here," I vaguely heard Sleeves say as the others snickered. I focused on where the voice came from. It was close.

I felt the hand approach my face again. That's all I needed.

Like a striking snake, my arm shot out, grabbed his hand and squeezed. He yelped in surprise. That was just the start.

I grabbed his collar with my free left hand. Pulling on this new anchor, I released my right and brought it around. My mental picture was right on. I felt my knuckles connect to his jaw. And then the others collided into me.

The fight devolved from there. It wasn't some martial arts exhibition with crisp moves and decisive strikes. It was a scuffle. Our bodies awkwardly collided as we piled together, throwing punches and throwing each other around. It was more wrestling than anything, and Sleeves and I hit the ground early, and hard.

I wasn't letting go. I had Sleeves, almost by the throat, and that was all I cared about. I focused on the grip more than anything else. I could have bent iron with that grip. In the blind haze, that grip was more solid to me than the ground, which sloped up to hit me again and again. The tangle of limbs and blows didn't

make anything clearer, either. I was moving to add energy to the scuffle in the hope that something would come back around to hurt them.

I heard a new voice. Something else was kicking and pulling at them. Good. More ammo, I thought.

For a moment, I was freed from the mass of limbs. Just enough to launch into a new assault, swinging at the collar I still held tightly. My hand was starting to seize from the force of my grip.

And then a bellowing roar cut through the mad scramble. Its raw authority shocked me to my senses. I finally let go.

As I got to my feet, dusting myself off, I realized I had no idea where my glasses were. But then, I felt someone gently pressing them against my arm, with just enough force to let me know they were there.

"Here," Blake whispered.

Blake Anthony. My best friend. He had been the one to jump into the fight. It had been a stupid thing to do, of course. But I had already lowered the bar. Even if his charge hadn't been effective, I would have still owed him for that. For the sentiment alone. Especially since Blake couldn't fight to save his life.

I slipped the glasses on and he came into focus. He didn't look banged up, actually. He seemed like his usual self. He was a couple inches taller than me, though his hair was several inches shorter. The black tuft was vaguely spiked upwards, though that was less out of a sense of style and more the natural state of those bristles. It had always stuck up in some fashion for as long as I could remember. It was only now when it was cut shorter and as we were growing up that it started to look, well, good. His long face was tense and serious at the moment, but his dark blue eyes sparkled as usual. *We got 'em, buddy*, they seemed to say.

For a second, at least. Suddenly, they lost a little of the hidden triumph. And then I noticed it, too. At first, I thought my eyes were just adjusting after the fight or something, but no. The dark blobs in my vision didn't go away. Something was on my lenses.

I turned away from the small crowd I could hear gathering. I pulled off my sunglasses and wiped them against my T-shirt.

"What is it, blood?" I asked, suddenly realizing that a white shirt might not be the best tool for that job.

"They wrote something on there," Blake answered. "Kind of silvery ink."

I scrubbed harder, then threw the shades back on.

"It's still there," Blake said, twisting his mouth in awkward embarrassment.

"Is it permanent?" I hissed. I wasn't mad at him, of course, but suddenly the humiliation of the moment had doubled. I was already wiping at the lenses again.

"It looks like it's on the inside," Blake noted, faintly curious.

I wiped at the inside and then slapped them back on my face. Even before he could speak, I could tell by his relieved expression I had gotten it this time.

Dourly, I asked, "What did they write?"

He grimaced. He was never good at hiding his emotions, and I could tell this time he was feeling confused about the meaning, but he was sure it was embarrassing. "It said 'student driver,'" he explained.

Ha. Ha. Very funny. I hope they found my fist doing a head-on into their leader's jaw just as riotous.

No time for catching up though. The uniform club had finished getting to their feet, and while the instructor (definitely former military) had waited for us to recover, his patience had run out.

"All of you," he barked at us with undertones of disappointed outrage, "should be ashamed. You call yourself Academy material? Is this Academy standards? I don't want to hear it!"

One of the uniform club had started to open his mouth to protest. Big mistake. The instructor's gaze was terrifying enough to wither even the cocky arrogance of the three thugs.

"All of you are reporting to the dean, and tell you the truth, I hope some of you didn't finish unpacking," the instructor roared on. "I dare say it would save some of you time. Now move!"

He swatted the air with his hand, indicating the way to the dean's. He made sure we were separated, a couple of witnesses between our groups. Still, there was a moment where the gray-suited students passed right in front of us as we set off.

"Keep your eyes open, Slick," Sleeves said, the taunt left in an undertone, but still obvious enough. "Here there be monsters."

Here there be monsters. That was something of a motto in Aechyr. Apparently, they had a rich folklore of various monsters that would stalk the night, and that led to the saying becoming so common. It was a strange statement of pride from the people of the country. We fought monsters, it usually meant. We fought monsters, and we won. It wasn't supposed to mean "we are the monsters."

I was sitting in the waiting area outside the dean's office. The space looked like it belonged to an old courthouse. It was all polished, elegant woodwork, from the secretary's large desk, looking uncomfortably like a judge's podium, to the hot benches where I was sitting. The stark sunlight shining through the tall, arched windows on the right was gradually warming the stale air. And it did nothing to cheer up the place. When Aechyr Academy handled discipline quietly, you had to worry.

We were being taken into the dean's office one at a time. Everyone but me and one uniform had already gone back into the large dean's office. Even the witnesses had been questioned.

The door to the office opened, and Blake was shooed out towards the waiting room's side door, conveniently away from those of us waiting. From me. Not that we had tried to communicate. We were on the same wavelength. *Let's not make it any worse by inventing a lie.*

The last uniform was summoned past the large desk and into the office. That just left me alone in the room with the secretary, who was now burying herself in her work. She didn't need to keep an eye out for conspiracies anymore.

I sat back and waited for the time to pass as my gut tightened. David was going to kill me. All I had to do was lay low until tonight. All I had to do was lay low, period.

I heard someone else walk in from the hallway that fed into the waiting room. My head shot up, and I turned around. It was Scarlett, the red-haired girl from the courtyard. *Oh, another witness,* I thought. I looked back at my knees, embarrassed, again.

"He'll be right with you, after this matter is finished," the secretary told her.

I guess maybe she wasn't another witness. Great. Even better. If I was holding up a meeting because of my screw-up... well, even better. I really needed to trade the glaring sun for rain.

After an eternity, the uniformed guy was let out, and the dean called, "Frost?"

I let out a deep breath, trying to exhale my tension, and stepped through the door. Inside the woodwork was darker, more somber. The light wasn't as glaring and sound didn't echo hollowly like outside. In theory, it was more comforting.

In theory.

Dean Foster, a smallish, older man with only the faintest halo of hair left, sat behind the wide desk. He had the typical wiry professor glasses perched on his thin nose, which itself was slightly out of place on his round face. After a couple of quick clicks on his computer, he leaned back in his chair and steepled his fingers behind the piles of file folders covering his desk.

"Mr. Frost, please tell me what happened," he instructed. "Don't leave anything out."

I obeyed. When I got to the part about throwing the first punch, I hesitated. I had an impulse to throw in a bit about them striking first, but I quickly realized that would never hold up. I braced myself internally and told him the plain, simple truth.

When I had finished, he sat for a moment thinking. Finally, he flipped open a file and turned up a page.

"I understand you've had this condition for a while," he said.

"Yes," I lied, remembering my cover story.

"Don't misunderstand," the dean said, entirely flatly, "we are taking very seriously the way the other students behaved towards you. We take mistreatment based on disability or other characteristics very seriously."

I bristled slightly but didn't say anything. Obviously, what he was saying was in my favor, so I wasn't going to interrupt. But disability? I hadn't thought of myself as having a disability. I didn't like that.

"Having said that, I find your response disappointing," he continued. "Aechyr Academy students are held to a higher standard, and you don't dispute the accusation that you struck first."

I really hoped that didn't mean this had all been my word against theirs. *Please don't tell me I could have just lied. Shoot—maybe no one else actually saw the start of the fight.*

"We take this very seriously, and we'll have to look into whether or not you're still a good fit for this Academy. However, before a final decision is reached, you will be notified, and have an opportunity to request a review of the decision before a disciplinary committee. Do you understand?"

"Yes," I said numbly. It was as bad as I had feared.

"Is there anything else you would like to say now?"

My mind went blank. I wished I could have thought of some brilliant speech, like a dramatic closing statement in a lawyer movie. Or some straight-from-the-heart plea to change his mind. Or anything, really.

But all I could say was, "No."

The dean considered for a moment, looking like he wanted to press on, but he didn't.

"Very well," he said. "You will have my preliminary decision within twenty-four hours. You're dismissed."

I got up, feeling like I had just missed a big opportunity. The secretary didn't bother to look up or show me out from the waiting room.

"Hey," someone said.

I blinked. Then I remembered that there had been someone else in this room.

Turning back towards Scarlett, I said, "Uh, hey," like an idiot.

I don't think we had exchanged two words before this point. The only other time we were in a room together was in the Civics lecture hall. And now here she was, walking right up to me. Her red bangs were frayed over her heart-shaped face, stopping just short of her faint blue eyes. They almost paled into gray, like an iced-over lake, but they weren't as cold as that sounded. Does that make sense? Well, it was true. Somehow, the wispy blue was warm.

"How are you? Are you alright?" she asked.

"Uh, I'm alright," I answered automatically. That wasn't true, of course, but that's what you said to people you didn't really know. Then a couple moments later, I realized she was asking if I had been hurt. In that case, I had more or less given the right answer. I was sore, but no real damage had been done.

"Right, that's good," she said. "What'd the dean say?"

"So, I—" I rubbed my neck. Oh, what did it matter? Odds were I'd never see anyone at the Academy again. "I messed up," I admitted.

Scarlett tilted her head and glanced away. "I guess," she said. "I saw what happened—honestly, they were looking for a fight."

"I threw the first punch," I pointed out.

"Yes, technically. But those guys kind of had it coming."

I raised an eyebrow. "You know them?"

"Well, you know Charmies," she replied with a shrug.

She must have seen my blank look, even with the sunglasses. She smiled slightly.

"Sorry," she said, stifling the grin. "It's an Aechrian thing. You're new here right? American?"

It always surprised me how Aechrians could somehow tell I was from the States. To my ears, they didn't have an accent, and neither did I.

"Yeah," I said, trying a smile myself. "Just got here. Not exactly a great start."

Scarlett shrugged. "Do you mind if I ask you something?"

"Sure, go ahead. I'm an open book." I nearly slapped myself for that one. Why did I say things that will get me in trouble?

Scarlett bit her lip for a moment before pressing on. "I don't mean to pry, but do you really need those to see?"

"These things?" I asked, taking the sunglasses off for a moment, flipping them around, and sliding them back on. Why was I acting like such an idiot? If Sleeves had seen me then, his impression of Americans would surely have been validated. "Yeah. It's a rare condition. Head injury."

If you asked me, that part was kind of true.

"Sorry to hear that," she said.

"Nah, don't be," I replied, waving her off. "It happens. You know, with a guy like me, always bonking my head." I mimed doing just that. "Bound to be a little brain damage," I joked.

She half laughed at that, but in an awkward, I'm-just-going-along-with-this sort of way. "Don't say that," she insisted a moment later, pulling my arm away from my head. I felt an electric shock where her fingers touched my skin. "I doubt you've done that much. Honestly, you don't seem like the type."

"Miss Foster," the secretary interrupted the conversation. "Alan will see you now."

"Okay, thank you, Miss Clarkson," Scarlett answered before turning back one last time. "Well, if you do decide to stick around, why don't you come by this Saturday? Some friends of mine are throwing a welcome-slash-welcome-back party now that everyone's settled in. It's something of a tradition. You'd have to try really hard to get in trouble there. You can make some new friends, see that not all of us bite."

"Uh, sure," I said. I didn't really do parties. "But I don't really think it's up to me whether I stay."

She looked at me kind of funny. "Isn't it?" she asked.

Before I could think of an answer, or even figure out what she had meant, she walked towards the dean's office. As the door closed, I shook myself back to my senses. I think I had made myself look like an idiot yet again in that conversation. But I felt a little better. I think someone was actually on my side.

I was taking the long way out when the secretary called back, "Mr. Frost!"

My heart dropped. But I walked back.

"Dean Foster would like another word," the secretary informed me. Yeah, I had figured.

I nodded and entered the office again. The dean was still behind the desk. I didn't even see Scarlett at first; she was off in a corner.

"I have a proposal," the dean said, sliding a piece of paper across the desk. I sat down and picked it up tentatively. It was a standard form, a waiver or something. A large section in the middle had been scrawled in hastily by hand.

Before I could read the details, he continued, "In light of the circumstances, if you agree to waive arbitration, we will reduce the disciplinary action to a one-month suspension, along with an agreement that any similar infractions that may occur will be grounds for immediate expulsion. This would be the same punishment for all parties involved. No favoritism."

Huh? I mean, wow. That was good—that was great! I didn't believe this. *How—?*

"Do you understand what this means?" the dean asked, perhaps thinking my stunned silence was confusion.

"Yeah, yeah," I said hurriedly. "As long as I don't do the committee thing, this is the punishment I get."

"That's correct," he agreed. "What do you think? Do you agree?"

"Yes," I said immediately. "Absolutely."

The dean looked a little annoyed at my eager agreement, but said nothing, instead handing me a pen. I quickly scribbled my signature and handed the form back. He didn't look me in the eyes. I didn't really care.

"That will be all," the dean dismissed me. "I hope I won't hear you bragging about this incident, Mr. Frost," he added, this time looking up at me as I was rising from the chair.

In all seriousness, I replied, "No, sir. Not a chance."

"Good," he said. "Remember, not a toe out of line," he added, and then returned to his papers.

I had just stepped outside the Administrative Building, wondering what had happened, and what I should do with my day, when Scarlett stepped outside.

"Right. I hope, then," she said, placing a note in my hand, "you'll be there this Saturday. Celebrate some school spirit."

My brain only locked up for *half* a second this time. "Yeah," I said. "Sounds good."

She smiled. "Cool. Bring some friends." And then she walked off.

Scarlett Foster. At long last, it clicked in my mind.

"Hey," I called after her. She turned back for a moment. "The dean—Dean Foster. Is he—?"

"My uncle," she answered, smiling again. "I don't get many favors, so don't come asking for any more."

"Got it. Thank you! I owe you one," I said.

"That's what the invite's for," Scarlett answered coolly, and turned away once more.

I looked down at the short note with the address. To my mild disappointment, her phone number wasn't on there. But really, I had no idea what I would've said. The only thing that mattered right now was that I'd somehow gotten out of this one intact. Despite it all, things were turning out all right.

Guess the day should be sunny after all.

III

The Road Ahead

Gray.

White noise.

Rain.

Kennedy didn't see the suburban world as it was smeared away around him. He didn't see the gray sky, or the yellowing leaves of the trees. He just walked onwards, feet pressing into the wet grass, papers held tight against his chest. The rain had soaked his clothes and hair, but at that moment, he couldn't care. At that moment, he could only think of how long it had taken him to get to this point. How much he had just let pass by, thinking that it would get better.

He didn't even look up to see what was ahead. As he rushed away from his old home, he slipped on the damp grass and fell face down on the ground. He hurriedly scrambled to stand up, slipped again, and splashed into the mud.

He wiped aside the filth smudged across his face, feeling humiliated. At first, he didn't know why. He thought he couldn't be ashamed anymore. Except in front of one person. The one person following him.

He finally decided he'd have to address Blake. He was standing several paces behind Kennedy, holding a soccer ball. The rain was even soaking through his jersey.

But Kennedy didn't have words for him. He didn't know how to talk about real life. Its mundanity precluded it from conversation. Over the years, the pattern became a taboo.

Kennedy clenched his fist in the mud.

"Why are you here?" Kennedy finally asked—almost shouted—back at Blake.

"I mean," Blake answered. "I'm worried."

Kennedy bit back the urge to scream. He couldn't decide if Blake was a loyal guard dog or lost puppy.

"I need to be alone," he finally said through clenched teeth.

"And what if I do leave you alone?" Blake asked. "What then?"

Kennedy kept his back to him, not daring to look at his friend. Not daring to stand up.

"I know you're not turning around," Blake said. The heavy rain made it impossible to tell if either of them were shedding tears.

Kennedy clenched his fists. "No. I'm not going back," he admitted.

"I don't blame you," Blake said. "But you're not going alone."

That made Kennedy pause. He turned back. "What did you say?"

"I'm coming with you," Blake replied, straightening up, as if to prove his determination.

Kennedy swallowed. "No," he finally managed to say. He held up his hand as he searched for the right words. "You have things good. I mean—you have things to lose. I don't. You shouldn't follow me."

"Too bad," Blake said.

Kennedy ripped himself from the ground and started to run. He had no destination except away from Blake. But his friend followed at a respectful distance.

The mowed green grass turned into rough sidewalks. Kennedy's bare feet began to sting. He eventually had to stop, right next to a bench, panting. He stuffed the ruined papers roughly into his pocket. All that was left was to stand there, leaning against a bus stop sign. Blake stood a couple of feet away, ready to run after his friend at any moment.

The rain fell.

A mist matted everything.

The sound absorbed them.

Time slipped away.

Kennedy and Blake stood in the middle of a faded world.

And then...

There was a clack. And another. They were distant, but they cut through the drizzling patter. The rhythmic sounds were determinedly growing louder. Soon a faint silhouette appeared, indistinct at first. Within seconds it had seized its form, that of a young woman, and cut through the mist.

She could only have been a few years older than Kennedy and Blake, and yet could hardly be more different. From beneath her black, newsboy cap, there flowed long, pure white hair. It was a sharp contrast to the rest of her black attire, including the leather jacket and boots, whose hard bases and slightly raised heels had made the clacking sound. And the pouring rain didn't seem to affect her as it did everything else. Her rosy cheeks still held their color, and her hair didn't seem as sopping wet as either Kennedy's or Blake's. The drops simply rolled off it as it were wax.

She stepped in front of the two of them and offered a small, knowing smile.

"Long time, no see, boys," she said.

Kennedy and Blake exchanged glances. After a bit, Blake took the initiative.

"Do we know you?" he asked.

"Not yet," the girl with the white hair said. Despite her somber eyes, she radiated a confidence that seemed to push back the gray.

"I've come to help," she continued. "To give you what you want."

"And that is...?" Blake asked, raising his eyebrow in polite suspicion.

The strange girl pulled out two tickets from her jacket pocket. "A way out. A place to go. Whatever you want to call it."

"How do you know we want to go anywhere?" Kennedy asked, finding his voice again.

It was the girl's turn to raise her eyebrow. She nodded towards the sign Kennedy had been leaning against. "This is a bus stop, isn't it?"

Neither Kennedy nor Blake seemed impressed by this answer.

The girl shrugged and explained, "This has all happened before, and it will happen again. With luck, for the last time."

"That doesn't mean anything," Blake protested. "You're speaking in riddles. How hard is it to give a straight answer?"

She smiled. "Harder than you might think. Technically, I'm not allowed to tell you until you've at least accepted my offer to think it over."

"To think what over?" Kennedy was getting frustrated again.

"Take these tickets. Get onto the next bus that drives up. If you want to get away from this place, you'll get the chance. The bus will take you to someone who will explain more. They'll take you to a new world. It won't be like this one, for better and for worse. But I promise it will be different.

"Like I said, this has all happened before. You both accepted once, and I expect you'll do it again. You," she nodded at Kennedy, "want to get away more than anything. I can give you somewhere to go, Kennedy."

"How do you know my name?" That had startled him. More than her knowing what he was doing here.

"I wasn't lying," she said simply. "I've met you before, even if you haven't met me. And because I've met you, I'd bet you'll find what you're looking for. You did last time."

"You'd bet?" Kennedy shot at her. "Shouldn't you know for sure?"

"And what do you mean, 'last time'?" Blake asked.

"That I can't tell you," she said seriously. "I can only answer with another question. If you had a chance to do everything in your life all over, knowing all of the mistakes you made before, would you do it differently?"

Kennedy and Blake exchanged glances again. They understood the question, of course (this being the sort of hypothetical they would casually ask each other), but they weren't sure what she was getting at.

"Let's say yes," Blake replied.

"There's your 'last time'," she said to Blake, and then turned to Kennedy, "and there's your reason why I can't know what you'll find."

"What are you going to change?" Kennedy asked.

"How does that work?" Blake added.

"I'm giving you a chance to change something you haven't done yet," she explained to Kennedy. To Blake, "And because you haven't done it yet, you still have time to change it. How do I make this simple for you? Think of me as your guardian angel, like in It's a Wonderful Life."

Both Kennedy and Blake blinked at her blankly.

"I forgot how uncultured you were," she murmured to herself. "Listen, if you want the why's and how's, take the tickets and find out. Right now, you don't need to worry if it's possible. Right now, you need to worry whether or not you'll take the chance. Like I said, you want to get away, Kennedy. And Blake, you will follow him wherever he goes."

Blake was startled. Kennedy felt uncomfortable.

She continued, "So, you decide. Do you want to go somewhere? Or would you prefer being stuck—"

She looked around at the curtains of rain pointedly.

"—nowhere?"

She held out the tickets, their thick, glossy paper repelling the rain. The three stood in silence, neither Kennedy nor Blake really trusting this stranger. But curiosity lingered.

"If we take the tickets," Kennedy finally asked cautiously, "we get more information. We don't have to go anywhere?"

"Nowhere you can't get back from," she replied.

Kennedy thought long and hard, weighing the options. But at the same time, he knew part of his mind was made up. The more he thought about it, the surer he became. Perhaps this girl had been right about him. He would have always accepted the offer.

He took the ticket. A moment later, Blake did the same.

The girl smiled. "See you on the other side," she said, and started to walk off.

After a few steps, her silhouette slid back behind the gray curtain of rain, and it started to lose its shape. As it did so, a question popped into Kennedy's head.

"Wait!" he shouted over the pouring rain. "Who are you?"

He could just make out the figure pausing, as if to think. A moment later, she raised her right hand, perhaps as a wave, perhaps as a salute, and he just barely heard the answer.

"Mira. Call me Mirabelle."

"Should we tell him?" Blake asked.

"I mean, we don't have to?" I said, more as a question than a statement. "It shouldn't affect our training, right?"

"It doesn't blow our cover, does it?" Blake wondered.

"Maybe it does," I admitted.

"We could ask him."

I laughed. "Hey David," I mock-asked, "would getting suspended for a public brawl blow our cover? No? Forget I asked."

Blake shrugged, grinning. "Fair enough. We tell him?"

I sighed a little. "I don't think we have a choice."

We waited at the corner for David to show. It was a cool evening, the sun not having set just yet, and the wind blowing away the last traces of warmth it had provided. I was just about to suggest finding someplace inside to wait when the car pulled up.

It was an unimpressive black vehicle, which made it clear to us who it was meant for. David merely confirmed this by rolling down his window and nodding for us to get in.

Blake and I hopped into the plush leather seats in the back. But before we could get comfortable, I noticed who was driving.

Randy. Randy O'Neill. Randy was, uh, how should I put it? Abrasive. Randy was abrasive. He wasn't nice, and he wasn't cheerful. When he was happy, it was usually at someone else's expense.

Randy wasn't that big, but he had broad shoulders, especially for his wiry frame. His face was a little pointed, but meaty, and it was topped off with a dash of red hair that he kept combed back and up, tapering to a point behind his head. Had his cool green eyes not been so sharp and piercing, he might have looked comical, like an evil gnome. Instead, he often looked like a shark.

"Leather-Face," I greeted.

Randy saw through the front. "Relax," he told us, holding back a thin smile. "you've got seatbelts."

"I'd rather not have to use them," Blake countered. "You can drive, right? Safely, I mean?"

Now his smile was nasty. "They teach safe driving now? I'll have to get my license renewed."

"Ah-ha," Blake laughed nervously. "That's not funny."

"Relax," David interjected. "We'll be there in no time."

David, for reasons I could never understand, seemed to trust Randy. While admittedly, Blake and I were new to all of this while David and Randy were old hat, I still couldn't fathom how the two could get along.

We started driving and David pulled out a tablet, hooked it to a jointed arm on his seat. He turned it to face us.

"Today," David said, "you learn the whole truth. The time gates, the timelines, everything."

"I thought we were told everything when we signed up," Blake put in.

David shook his head. "You were told the bare basics. Enough to make an informed decision. Today, we look at the full picture."

He tapped the monitor and an image of several lines appeared. At regular intervals along the bottom of the screen, there were years marked off.

"You were told that there were several parallel dimensions the time gates had access to," David continued. "This is almost true. In reality, these dimensions are splits from the timeline." He tapped the screen, and the lines changed. Where once they had all been distinct, parallel lines, now many intersected with the central line on the left of the screen, before branching off towards the right. Some broke off earlier, some broke off later, but most stemmed from a single main line. The main line, the stem, had its first branch shortly after 1900 on the scale.

"We are the Timeless," David continued, looking Blake and I directly in the eyes. "We traded our old lives for the ability to travel the timelines. If we were to go back home, back to our own timelines, we would find that it's as if we never existed. No one would recognize us, no one would know our names. We can never go back to the way things were. We've been erased from the timelines.

"But what is a timeline?" David asked rhetorically. "At any moment, there are infinite possibilities of what could happen. An infinite number of decisions you could make. Every possible choice anyone could make, every possibility in the universe exists as information somewhere out there. But most possibilities don't matter."

"But why not?" Blake suddenly asked, curious. "Why aren't there infinite timelines, one for each choice?"

Blake looked intensely fascinated by the suggestion, but it made my head hurt. I didn't like the idea of an infinity of Earth's with an infinity of me's or Blakes. Or anyone else for that matter.

David smiled patiently. "Are you going to stab me right now?" he asked.

Blake was completely taken aback. So was I.

"No way," Blake said, offended.

"But you could," David insisted. "There are sharp objects in here you could find. It is physically possible."

"Blake could do that, but he's not going to," I said. "Why would he?"

"Oh!" Blake exclaimed. "You're saying that with infinite possibilities, there should be a version of me that does."

"Uh, run that by me again," I prompted.

"Because it's possible, given an infinite amount of tries, eventually, it'll happen," Blake explained unhelpfully. Even through my sunglasses, my blank stare must have been obvious, because he continued hurriedly, "If you play the lottery, you're probably not going to win, right?"

"Right," I answered. "The odds are against you."

"Exactly," Blake agreed. "But what if you played it a lot? Like a million times?"

"Then you're probably not going to get your money back," I quipped.

Randy laughed uproariously. I felt a little annoyed, like I was being condescended to.

"I get the lottery thing," I said emphatically. "Play enough and eventually you'll win, no matter how small the chance. But forget that. That's a game. We're talking about people. You wouldn't stab David because that would be completely random."

"Yeah, exactly!" Blake said happily, as if I had just gotten it. He, however, didn't seem to be getting my point.

"Exactly wrong," I countered. "People aren't random. We make choices for a reason."

"You're both right," David interjected.

I looked at him sideways and felt my head start to throb again.

"To address your point, Kennedy," he went on, "there's an element of chance to everything. To make it simple, let's say that it's possible that something in Blake's brain suddenly misfires and that makes him stab me. It's a one in a trillion-trillion-trillion chance, maybe even less, but it could happen."

"Okay, I guess, technically," I said, slowly processing that. "But one in a trillion-trillion-trillion or whatever might as well be zero. That's like saying, 'what if a million dollars fell into my lap?'"

"That's it," David said approvingly. "It would be so unlikely that we can safely ignore it. These timelines," David said, gesturing back to the diagram, "represent what is most likely to happen on planet Earth. Yes, there's a small chance that anything could happen, but if the probabilities aren't high enough, those possibilities don't become real timelines. They only exist as information. They are either swallowed up by a more probable timeline or are so unlikely as to be intangible. They are a possibility, not a reality. There's a difference."

"Uh..." I started to say, but Randy cut me off.

"Unless you want to take a deep dive into pointless geek stuff, just roll with it," he said.

I shrugged. If it would make the headache go away, fine. At least for now.

"Most of the time, the big picture remains the same," David continued, attempting to clarify. "Put it like this—when you woke up today, you didn't know what was going to happen. But look back. You actually did things for a reason, like you said, Kennedy. Most things are logical consequences of factors we just didn't know about. And that is a timeline."

I considered that. He had no idea how right he was about how my day turned out. But looking back, could it have gone any other way? I was suspended because I fought Sleeves. I fought Sleeves because he had stolen my sunglasses. Because I ran into him. Because I wasn't paying attention. Because my nightmares had kept me up.

All that led me to talking with Scarlett. It made sense, but it bothered me. And of all the things that bothered me, the one that bothered me the most was the implication that I was always going to have babbled like an idiot in front of her. And then I was bothered by how pathetically shallow that made me.

Blake interjected with the thought I wish had occurred to me.

"But then," he said, "what about free will? You're making it sound like we have no choice in the matter. That things will always play out in one specific way."

David smiled ruefully. "You'll have to talk to a philosopher about that. But there are theoretically infinite splits in timelines—different possibilities. I don't know if that means anything to individual people, or to free will, but I will say this: There have been moments, few and far between, when I've felt a pull. A real pull between two options, both weighing heavily on me, neither the obvious choice. I can't actually prove that we have any ultimate choice, but in those moments, you can feel it. If you really want to show that you're more than the sum of your past, that you have a choice, wait for one of those moments. Then, when you figure out which is which, take the harder path. The one you know you should, but you normally wouldn't. If you can do that, well, maybe you still have a choice after all."

Something rang true in those words, but I wasn't sure. My thoughts were still muddled. And I wasn't sure I had lived up the challenge he had just laid down.

I changed the subject.

"But if the timeline is what's most likely to happen, why does it split?" .

"Most of the time, history follows trends," David explained. "But there are moments in history where everything hangs in the balance. Flashpoints in which the smallest act can change the world. Where a few seconds will shape all of the future. The probabilities are just right, and things could change so quickly, that if a Timeless appears in that timeline at that moment, he could change everything. The timeline wants to follow a path that's 51% likely to happen, but this person that shouldn't quite exist—a Timeless—interferes. He pushes history down the 49% path, and the timeline disintegrates, fractures, splits."

"So we don't change the future?" I asked.

"Sadly no, not at a flashpoint. There, we create a new one," David said. He pointed to one of the branches at random, where a new timeline split off from the old one. "The old timeline still exists, but because events could have gone either way—because we forced a change that very quickly changes the entire world—the timeline splits in two. A Timeless in a flashpoint doesn't change the old timeline, they create a new one."

"So," I said tentatively, "what if we, say, stop Pearl Harbor? There's the one timeline that we know, where it happens, but there's another where it doesn't, and things happen differently? Maybe America doesn't join the war, or something?"

Randy snorted.

"We can't choose any point in time," David explained, briefly giving Randy a dirty look. "The events also have to be very quick and very decisive. Planning an attack like Pearl Harbor would have taken a lot of time, so there probably wasn't one single moment where the decision was made, and it certainly wouldn't have been right before the attack. But to answer the spirit of your question, yes. If there was such a moment, and someone convinced the Japanese leadership not to go with the risky Pearl Harbor plan, the world would have changed, and we would see a new timeline."

"Hang on," I said. "If the time gate connects the different timelines, why can't they go to any point in time? Why can't we time travel?"

David tapped another button on the screen and several dots appeared on the timelines. I noticed the dot on the Aechrian timeline was one of the few dots furthest to the right, near present day. There were some even further to the right, but most timelines had dots in the past. They were scattered all about the map, some closer to the start point of 1900, but there wasn't really a pattern. The main timeline had three dots that I could see, and some of the others had two. None of them were at a flashpoint, though.

"These," David explained, "are the temporal locations of the time gates. In other words, you can take a time gate and travel to one of these times, on these timelines, but only these times. You can't choose when you pop up. It's always 'now' when you step through a time gate. Doesn't matter if you step out into 1941 or 1989 or 2030. Five minutes passing in one means five minutes pass on all the others."

"You and I can't make extra time," David added mysteriously.

"You and I?" Blake repeated. He was sitting at the edge of his seat, and I could practically see his mind spinning with possibilities.

"You're not a Tau," Randy added unhelpfully.

"Different Time Peace agents have different roles," David elaborated. "Ours won't involve anything like time travel. Kennedy, did you have a question?"

I did. "Each of these timelines is a whole Earth, right?" I asked. He nodded as I had expected, so I continued. "So, the time gate we came out of here in Aechyr isn't the same as the time gate we went through in our world, is it? Just how many time gates are there on each world?"

David nodded. "Good question. No, you jumped from one time gate to another. There's a different number of gates in each timeline. In some timelines, we just haven't discovered and activated as many. In others, we've discovered many more. Some timelines have had gates destroyed. But on average, there are about twenty gates in each timeline."

"Twenty?" I asked, impressed.

"That's not a lot," Randy interjected. "Remember, that's twenty across the world. Over the seven continents, that would mean about three on each. Think about North America—if they were distributed fairly, that might be one in Canada, one in the U.S., and one in Mexico. Then think about the size of the U.S.—if the time gate is on the East Coast, it would be a pain to get to California in a hurry, and vice versa."

David nodded again. "It's true. And time gates aren't always distributed fairly. Sometimes, you might get a country with two or three, and have a whole continent without anything. And that's not mentioning when some timelines have useless gates, like ones in Antarctica, or under the ocean."

"Or ones controlled by Anarakia," I guessed, referring to Time Peace's hated enemy.

David nodded grimly. "Like I said, some have been destroyed. It usually happens when we fight over one."

"But then, what if Anarakia controls all of the gates in one timeline?" Blake suddenly asked suspiciously.

David zoomed out the screen, returning it to the tree diagram of all the timelines. Another click, and a couple of branches turned bright red.

"You're not getting in," he explained simply. "A gate's a literal gate. All you have to do is put enough guns pointing at it, and it's going to be pretty much impossible for us to get through."

"So what we—what Time Peace—does," I said slowly, "is find these key moments and change them for the better."

"No," Randy scoffed. "Weren't you listening? If you change something at a flashpoint, you don't change the timeline, you create a new one."

"Whatever. That's what I meant," I growled back. "We make better timelines."

David held up a hand, cutting Randy's "Wrong again!" short.

"Not quite," David explained calmly, glancing, but not quite glaring, at Randy. When Randy remained silent, David tapped another icon on the screen and a new image appeared. It was the symbol of Time Peace, which, ironically enough, was shaped like crosshairs mixed with the face of a clock.

"The mission of Time Peace is to preserve the timelines. More specifically, we try to remove Anarakia's influence. The people of each timeline can decide for themselves how things should play out, but they deserve to be free from Anarakia."

He tapped the screen once more, and a new symbol appeared. This one was less polished, less formal. Instead of the gold clock/crosshair combination, this one was made of sharp, dark red lines that formed a stylized spider. As I looked closer, I saw that the body of the spider was actually an hourglass. The shape was also mirrored by its legs—four pointing up, four pointing down.

"Anarakia," David explained, "is a multi-headed beast. Their members may be fanatics, fascists, or freaks. Greedy mercenaries or devoted madmen. The only thing they have in common is that they want to exploit as many timelines as they can. Whatever they want, it never ends well for the people of the timeline they invade. So we fight them. But we don't do it at those key moments—not at the flashpoints. Do you know why?"

It hit me all at once. "Because if we create new timelines, that would mean we'd need even more people, more Timeless to fight Anarakia. We'd need some in the 'good' timeline, and some in the 'bad' timeline."

"Exactly," David agreed. "More timelines means we'd need more personnel to monitor and protect them. We want to free the timelines that do exist. The question is, how do you do that?"

When we didn't immediately answer, he went on. "Imagine a dirt road, one made by cars constantly driving over it, until it became a path. How do you move that road?"

Neither of us had any suggestions.

"Gradually," David explained. "If you lead a bunch of cars off the path all at once, sure, you might make a new road, but the old one's still there. But if instead, you get everyone to drive a little bit more on one side than the other... then a little bit more... then a little bit more..."

"Eventually, the road moves," Blake said. "You pave a new road while the old side becomes overgrown or worn away."

"Exactly," David said. "Just a little influence. And that's what we do in the timelines. We don't tell everyone what to do,

we just influence things. If Anarakia is creating or infiltrating a dangerous group, maybe we slowly weaken them, or warn people of the danger. Maybe we offer advice and help to the right people, who can really make a difference."

"This isn't hypothetical," I realized. "You're talking here and now."

David nodded grimly.

"There is a group in Aechyr called the People's Front Nine. It's a secret movement that wants to shake up the power structure. If they have it their way, power in Aechyr will be taken from the Queen and given to senior government officials, and only the ones they like. They're going to start building up a military presence, upgrading and advancing their nuclear arsenal, and from there, focusing on influencing world politics as they see fit. Aechyr won't be just an out-of-the-way, peaceful nation, it's going to get its share of empire that it never had."

"And we know this? How?" Blake asked.

"The People's Front Nine do have some obvious associates. Plus, we have spies who have confirmed all of this. They're very much a real threat."

"Well then let's do something," I urged. "If we know where some of them are, let's just take care of them."

"Hold on there," David said warningly. "They haven't done anything yet. Just because they're not nice people and they *might* be a threat, even *probably* will be a threat, doesn't mean we can just start hunting them down. For one, you might expose that Time Peace is even here. For another, that would make us just as bad as them, if not worse. We don't just kill political opponents because of what they *might* do. We have better options than that."

"But then Aechyr—the government—they don't know Time Peace is here?" Blake asked.

"Not yet," David answered. "Time Peace prefers to leave timelines as they are. It's not our job to tell the world how it should work. But with Anarakia sniffing around, it's almost inevitable that we have to get involved. Our people will make contact with Aechyr, carefully, diplomatically. If all goes well, we'll have something of a minor, informal alliance. But not for a while."

"Okay," I said, feeling chastened by David's rebuke. "So what are we doing about People's Front Nine or Anarakia or whoever?"

"We're trying to find the right person to talk to," David answered vaguely. "Someone who will realize what the Front are, but who won't overreact." He didn't look at me when he said that, but I still felt a bit singled out. "Someone who can handle the situation delicately and appropriately and lead Aechyr on a more peaceful course."

"It sounds like you have someone in mind," Blake observed.

"We do," David confirmed. "If we can find her."

"Her who?" I prodded.

"Aechyr's timeline is nearing a flashpoint," David said. "Aechyr and the United States have had friendly relations for decades now, but that's about to change. The question is just how this change happens. Senator Charles Becker and his allies have engineered the expansion of Aechyr's military, which includes several upcoming missile tests. There's a high chance that the U.S. will suddenly reevaluate their little ally. They might even overreact. But Aechyr would overreact, too. Some of Aechyr has a bit of an inferiority complex, and could see the United States' response as bullying, and feel the need to show their strength. And without a strong voice to ease the country through the crisis, suddenly, the People's Front Nine goes from a fringe group to a palatable alternative. And the world notices, and the entire geo-political landscape shifts. Flashpoint."

"That is, without a strong voice," he repeated. David tapped the screen yet again, and a picture of three people appeared. In the center was a woman wrapped in regal attire and adorned with a small crown. On either side of her were two young children, presumably hers. Neither of them could have been older than ten.

As David picked up again, another photo appeared. It was the mother, but she looked like she had aged a couple decades since the first picture. "The Queen is dying. But her daughter, the Crown Princess Sophia, is missing. The only other surviving member of the royal family is the Queen's second child—Simon."

Another image popped up. It was the boy, but almost grown up. I might not have recognized him, except that his bright blonde hair still curled the exact same way.

"Unfortunately," David continued, "he, like the People's Front, thinks Aechyr and its military should have a larger say in the world. He, too, wants to leave a permanent mark on history."

"But I thought the People's Front Nine hates the royals," I put in. "It's not like they'd be working together. Would they?" I added, suddenly anticipating one of David's twists.

He nodded. "They might, actually. Both want an empire. Sure, one hates the monarchy, and the other is royalty. But if they decide the first point is more important, they might just work out a deal rather than tear each other, and their country, apart. Especially if they see a common enemy that was preventing the glorious expansion of Aechyr."

"So we find the Princess?" I asked.

"Too dramatic, and we might not have to," David explained. "The Princess hasn't been seen in the public eye since she was ten." Sure enough, no new photo appeared next to the girl, whose blonde hair wasn't quite as brilliant as her brother's. David went on, "And apparently, she renounced her claim to the Crown at the age of thirteen. Except that decision isn't official, as she was a child. But as of this year, she is eighteen, and can either confirm or go back on that choice. With her mother dying, she might already be reconsidering. If she becomes Queen, all we need to do is slowly show her the true danger of the People's Front. Or better yet," he added mischievously, "show her before she ascends to the throne."

"But if she's missing..." Blake began to ask, then his eyes widened. "You don't know where she is, do you?"

"Nothing solid," David cautioned, "but if she is considering taking the Crown, she'd probably be the type to have prepared herself. To teach herself as best she could."

I realized what he was implying. "She's at Aechyr Academy."

"Maybe," David said cautiously, but he had the slightest grin. "If we're lucky, and if we're right—if she has changed her mind, and if she is at Aechyr Academy. Those are some big ifs. Even if we're right about that, there's only a quarter chance she's at Aechyr West. But even so," he grinned thinly again, "I've got a good feeling about this. Call it a hunch."

This all started to get very exciting. My mind was racing with the possibilities.

"But this is only if she wants to become Queen," Blake said skeptically. "She already renounced it once, what if she doesn't want it?"

"That's the bad news," David conceded. "We don't know exactly why she left the royal family. The official story is that she didn't do well in the spotlight. That could be true. Maybe she wasn't cut out for politics. Maybe there are other secrets we don't know about. There's no guarantee that Sophia would even take the Crown. Or it could be worse than that. Simon has been seduced by the thought of empire. Sophia, too, may find herself siding with the People's Front Nine on that issue. She did leave her family. Kids do stupid things, and she might share some of their anti-royalist sentiment, as odd as that may seem."

Kids do stupid things. *Not just kids*, I reflected. I thought back to David's words about the harder path, and Mirabelle's about all this happening again.

"So we change her mind," I declared, already taking this as a personal challenge.

"No," David said sternly. "Not if she doesn't want the throne. Remember, Time Peace doesn't have the people to fight a war on two timelines. You change her mind at the flashpoint here, and you'll ensure that happens. Anarakia outnumbers us four to one. The only thing keeping us in this war is their infighting. If they ever gathered around a leader..."

A very dark look came over him, but he pushed it back down quickly. "If we split this into two timelines, that'll be two victories for Anarakia. If the Princess doesn't want to come back, then we'll find another way. We work the problem. We always do. And soon, so will you."

I nodded, but I was getting antsy again. Everything he was saying made sense, but it wasn't my style. I liked things clear and simple, not all this subtlety.

As I mulled that over, I glanced back at the screen, which David had returned to the image of the timelines. One, I noticed, was separate. Unlike most of the others, it didn't connect to the stem around 1900, but stayed by itself the entire time. It was its own stem, without any branches.

"Why's this one separate?" I asked, pointing to it.

David smiled knowingly, irritatingly. "Can't you guess?" he asked.

It took me a moment. Duh, I realized, feeling even stupider than before.

"Aechyr," I answered. "In this timeline, Aechyr exists."

David nodded, satisfied. But I wasn't.

"But if these are all possible timelines, likely timelines," I said, "why does Aechyr exist at all? Shouldn't that be one of those nearly impossible timelines?"

David smiled again, though this time, thinly, and without as much joy in his eyes. "That's the mystery, isn't it?" he replied simply.

"I suppose the timeline diverged eons ago to create a whole new landmass," Blake mused. "But if it broke away so long ago, you would have thought everything was different. Countries, history, even the species on the island. I could just imagine an entire new class of animals evolving because of this isolated landmass."

Thankfully, David held up a hand. Unfortunately, Randy also piped in to cut him off. "Stuff the know-it-all routine," he called over his shoulder. "Nobody knows why it is, so you're sure not going to be the first one to bust the case open."

"Hey, shut up, Randy," I called to him.

Randy briefly let go of the wheel to hold his hands up in fake fright at my words, before returning his grip. David gave him a side-eye that stifled any more mockery. He turned back to us.

"Randy's right that no one knows," David said gently. "For now, that's not important. The important part is you understand the basics of timelines."

"At certain moments, where world-changing events are decided very quickly," Blake summarized at once, "a Timeless can make things play out differently than they would have. If that happens, a new timeline is created, but the old one, where things happen as they would have without us, still goes on. Otherwise,

Timeless can gradually change timelines by influencing people who are already in those timelines."

He looked at David eagerly, who smiled and nodded. "That's the gist," he agreed.

Blake leaned back in his seat, grinning, satisfied at his own understanding.

"We've been dancing around the big question," I put in, voicing something I had been wondering for a long time now. "Where do the time gates come from?"

"And that," David sighed, "is another mystery, actually. The truth is no one knows. Forgive the pun, but the history has been lost to time. All that remains is the fable."

He let the comment hang in the air for a moment, but before I could ask him to elaborate, Blake piped up.

"Wait a second, just where are we going?" he asked.

Randy had turned off the freeway. I had barely paid attention, but we had long since left Thysiopolis and were now headed further out. Fewer and fewer buildings dotted the sides of the road, and more and more trees popped up instead.

"We're going on a little camping trip," David explained.

"Um, it's the middle of the week," Blake pointed out. "And we didn't pack any of our things."

"Surprise," Randy said sadistically.

"I've decided to bump up some of the training," David said, suppressing his own smile. "I figured now would be the perfect time, what with you being suspended and all."

Blake and I groaned.

Of course he had known. The spy always knew.

IV

The Legend of Anarakia

The time gate stood twenty feet tall, made of two intersecting ceramic white rings. They crossed through each other at their vertical axes, where they were inset into a wall. At first, there was nothing behind the crossed halos besides a maintenance tunnel. But then, a technician flipped a switch and the gate sprang to life.

The circles turned, closing together like curtains being drawn. And then they opened on a new sight. The eggshell-colored loops passed through each other, and between them one could see the passageway had vanished. Instead, there was a brightly glowing turquoise film over the round entryway. Floating within it were large round and oblong shapes. Most were several feet across with crisply defined edges and centers even brighter than the rest of the surface. They looked like bubbles, except that they didn't protrude from the gate—they were perfectly flush with the surface of the bluish substance. They shifted, grew, and shrank very slowly, giving the gate an ominous quality—like it was a window into a world of giant cells.

The gate came to a rest, the rings once more slightly angled into the room. Some recruits jostled to get a view through the wedge between the wall and the gate. To their confusion, this smaller opening still showed the access tunnel. When viewed from the front, they saw the glowing film, but from the side, it was completely invisible. The phenomenon was inexplicable, but the recruits were getting used to mysteries.

The recruiter hadn't explained everything; he couldn't have. He hadn't promised glamor or safety. And he had assured everyone that stepping through the time gate was a one-way trip. He had answered questions from the recruits as best he could, but none of that mattered to Kennedy. He had already made up his mind. The Time Peace soldiers practically had to hold him back from stepping through the gate. He would have signed up for much riskier ventures to get as far away as they promised.

When he finally stepped up to the gate, the mysterious substance in the middle began to change. The turquoise glow grew warmer, brighter. The hues shifted as the edges of the bubbles became fuzzy. They merged together as the color changed, and by the time it became a bright golden light, there were none left. The edges of the gate continued to cycle through the hues until they became a rich, pinkish color. Finally, the surface, once clearly defined, had become fuzzy until it appeared as if the time gate was an entrance to a long tunnel into puffy, heavenly clouds.

All that was left was to walk through it.

Stepping in, Kennedy felt the ground fall away. The colors changed again, eventually fading until only white remained. He floated in the white void, alone. While hovering between realities, motionless, he felt something. It was as if he was being stretched outward, his arms and legs extending as far as they could. He didn't choose to do this, it just happened. And it went on. It felt as if his soul was being pulled out on either side, his consciousness extending painfully. And then, all at once, it compressed. He slammed into himself over and over and over—a *million times in the span of a heartbeat. A snap, and then he was back to himself. Only then did he fall out the other side.*

Except he never saw the other side of the time gate. He tumbled out, still only seeing pure white. The reality took a while to dawn on him.

"A one-in-a-billion side-effect," someone explained later.

"A freak occurrence, couldn't have expected this."

Shortly after, the dreams began. And once they did, Kennedy never again quite believed their explanations of his blindness. Not when the green-eyed man prowled his sleeping mind.

"You're part of Time Peace now," David reiterated as we hiked deeper into the forest. I couldn't help but notice that he and Randy had rather large packs with them. We, on the other hand, had nothing but the clothes on our backs. There was no pretense—Blake and I were being trained, not them.

"There are a lot of roles within Time Peace. Right now, you're just recruits, but Alpha Control has you scheduled to become an informants, and that's the focus of your training."

He stopped in a clearing and nodded towards Randy. They shrugged off their packs and Randy began to set up camp. David dug out a small cloth and unfolded it. There were several pins in them, some of them letters I recognized, others took a moment. Greek letters, I realized. They were stylized, and the first of them was a stylized *A*. No—an Alpha.

"There are several branches of Time Peace, and each has their own symbol and specialization. Alpha is the symbol for Alpha Control, which are those who direct the entire war effort, including the War Marshall—the commander-in-chief—The Hawk."

David said the last as if it were a name, which made me wonder just what kind of commander let themselves be named after a bird.

"So, what are we?" Blake asked.

"You," Randy said, halfway through tossing out a tent, "are nothing. You're just a recruit. You don't get a letter. You have to earn it."

"Letters are given out based on what training you complete, and you get them when you get your tab," David explained in a more even tone than Randy's. "Right now, you're on track to become an Omicron."

He pointed to the symbol, which just looked like a regular *O* to me.

"Omicrons are observers. They're the small O's—not operatives, not Omegas, just observers. Their job is to feed Time Peace information while living their life within one of the timelines. They keep tabs on how things are shaping up, getting a firsthand account of what is happening in that world."

"They just live regular lives?" I asked, a little disappointed.

David shrugged. "Not entirely. The best Omicrons are those that know the most, so we prefer to have those who live well-connected lives. People in government, for example. But otherwise, yes, they mostly live their lives as they see fit. We keep the risk minimal."

"What are the other branches?" Blake asked. He didn't seem quite as disappointed as I was about the sound of this career choice, but still.

"Most of them you won't have to worry about or run into, but there are a few you should know," David continued.

"Like the Thetas." He pointed to a symbol like an *O*, but with a horizontal line inside of it. "Theta is the symbol of death, and Thetas are the military wing of Time Peace. We don't bring them in unless we have to, as more often than not, using them means splitting the timeline. But when push comes to shove, they're our last line of defense. Our first is the Deltas."

He revealed a triangular letter. "Delta means change, and the job of the Deltas is to change the timelines, slowly, for the better. They are our operatives. Deltas come in many different forms, with many different specialties, but their mission is the same. Go into a timeline and influence the world to keep it out of the hands of Anarakia. Sometimes that means politics, sometimes that means espionage, sometimes that means combat. Deltas are precision instruments that have to change the world, one way or another. Often, they have to do it by themselves."

That little speech had caught Blake's and my attention.

"So they're super spies," Blake said.

David shrugged. "Something like that. It's not glamorous. It's hard, and it's dangerous. But to sum it up, yeah, they're kind of spies. That's why we call them operatives."

"Okay, so what if I didn't want to be an Omicron?" I asked. "If I want to be something more than the little O?"

David smiled faintly. "Well, you'd have to complete the appropriate training. If for example, you were the types who wanted to be an operative, a Delta," he looked up at us and my eagerness must have shown because his grin widened, "you'd have a lot to learn. How to gather information, how our technology works, how to fight, when to run, how to survive."

And at the last, he looked back over to Randy setting up the tent.

I understood and I was suddenly grateful for David. I was sure I was still going to hate this little trip, but he had called it right. I didn't want to be an Omicron, I wanted to be on the front lines. I wanted to be a Delta, and David had clearly anticipated that.

"So, do we get a tent?" Blake asked nervously.

"No way," Randy said, smiling maliciously again.

"You better listen up," David said seriously now, "because you're about to get a crash course in survival. After that, you're on your own."

"And if you're still kicking by then," Randy added, "we start the combat trials."

"Combat trials?" Blake and I asked simultaneously. I had said it eagerly, Blake... less so.

"Sure," David said. "Best way to learn is by seeing all of your mistakes, then we can build you up from there. And if you want to be a Delta, you have to know how to fight."

"So what does dragging us out here without warning teach us?" Blake asked sullenly.

"Isn't it obvious?" David asked, surprised.

"Be ready for anything," I guessed.

"Look out for surprises," David agreed, and then added, "always have a go-bag ready, and never relax around your superiors."

My gratitude towards David dried up quickly. His idea of training was a two-hour lecture on survival, and then making us fend for ourselves. We had to remember everything we were told in order to find or build shelter, catch food, and purify water. We had paid close attention to the lecture, but it made everything sound so much easier than it was. And to top it all off, he and Randy just sat there, in front of a tent and a blazing fire.

Despite being right there, when we tried to ask for advice or a refresher on what he had explained, David would ignore us. Instead, we had to try and fail, and then he might point out one, and only one, mistake we had made. Problem was, we rarely made just one mistake. Everything was slow and meticulous, and if we didn't get it perfect, it would fail. If we did get it perfect, we got mediocre results.

After a couple of days in which we were constantly hungry, David either took pity on us, or decided we had reached the minimum requirements to pass. They gave us a hot meal, set up a second tent, and let us fall asleep under some real shelter for once.

The thin sleeping bag was paradise to my tired body and I immediately fell into a delightful sleep. I felt like my head had just touched the pillow when David burst in and tore me from my rest. To my horror, only a hint of the rising sun could be seen in the lightening sky. Not only had the night passed by too quickly, but we had been woken far too early.

"Run," David said, pushing paintball guns into our arms.

"Run from what? The rising sun?" Blake asked. "Can't we go back to bed?"

"Randy is hunting you down," David said seriously. "You have to make a break for it, don't get hit or you're dead."

His voice was so serious, and I was so tired that I really believed Randy was going to kill us. As David pushed us towards the trees, I clutched the paintball gun tightly and signaled to Blake. We plunged blindly through the forest, running fast, until we were thoroughly lost. A spray of yellow paintball pellets shot out of nowhere, assuring us of the danger. If Randy hadn't fired from a distance, we would have been splattered. We fired back

blindly and kept running, only for a burst of yellow to splatter against my shirt. The stinging pain set in a moment later.

Blake, who had always been faster than me, shot off ahead and vanished into the distance. I sat down where I had been hit, slowly coming to grips with the fact that I hadn't suffered serious harm. A moment later, I saw Randy appear out of nowhere, darting after Blake in an impossibly quiet sprint through the woods.

It was some time after that when the two came to collect me, a couple of yellow spots on Blake's shirt and knees indicating the results of that skirmish. Randy's clothes were noticeably clean.

"This one didn't quite get the rules," Randy said to David when we had reconvened. "Had to hit him in the knees before he stopped moving."

Blake scowled, rubbing his wounds.

"What's the big idea?" I asked irritably.

David folded his arms. "I thought I told you to be ready for anything. And not to let your guard down."

Our scowls got deeper. I still felt it was playing unfair, but I didn't want to say that. Exchanging a glance with Blake, I could see he was thinking the same thing. In what must have been the first recorded incident of telepathy, we mentally told each other, "Don't tempt them."

And boy was I glad that we didn't say anything, because the rest of the tests were brutal enough as is. In the morning, David would allow us a little real food (read: canned crap) before reviewing a survival lesson, this time with hands-on tips. Then, in the afternoon, we had combat drills.

They were virtually all the same, and yet Blake and I lost consistently. Randy would be at one end of the woods and Blake and I would be at the other. We were given our paintball guns, mine red and Blake's blue, and told whoever was left at the end was the victor.

Randy was an unstoppable beast. He was quick, he was quiet, he was precise, and he loved every minute of this. It was his personal little hunt, and after each one, we would come back with a few more yellow stains on our skin.

At first, it seemed like hitting our heads against a brick wall. I had been excited when combat trials first started because I figured my dreams of the marines would give me an edge. Well, I was certainly a good shot, but that was about it. The first few times we encountered Randy, I would rush forward, determined to shoot him down. I'd get him alright. A split-second after getting hit myself. Meaning my shots didn't count, and Blake was lunch meat.

Blake wasn't a bad shot either, he just didn't have an instinct for this sort of thing. He would plan things out in his mind, see what he wanted to do, but get lost when the rubber hit the road. He would fire wildly, or try a messy retreat, or generally get off-balance and off-guard.

After a half a dozen humiliating defeats, it really sank through my head that the two of us needed to get on the same page. Before, I had just expected him to deal with Randy while I was distracting him. To think and act like I would. It was only when my pride was finally worn down that I started actually talking to him.

That was a big breakthrough, even if it didn't turn our little franchise around. Blake was the better scout and tactician, and I was the better combatant. So, we quickly developed a very basic strategy of hunt and kill. Blake would scout, and I would hide. He'd distract Randy, and I'd flank him.

In practice, there were several problems. One, we didn't always find Randy. More often, actually, he found us. Two, we

rarely could perform an effective flank. That simple tactic proved too fanciful for us when the action started. Which led to three: we still couldn't outfight Randy.

One time, we were sneaking through the woods, and Blake spotted something.

"Right," he whispered quickly.

I looked to my right, but Randy was already gone. He was shifting aim from Blake, who gasped as he went down. Before I could line him up, Randy had splattered me, too.

In total frustration, I simply demanded, "How?" from Randy.

"Blake made too much noise," he answered. It surprised me that he wasn't holding back like David had with the survival tips. Then I realized this was the first time I actually asked him about what had happened.

"Blake said 'right'," Randy continued, "So not only did I know where he was, I knew you were facing the same direction. That gave me enough to guess where you were. So, I made sure not to be where you expected me."

"One more go," I insisted. Randy only nodded.

Blake was looking tired, but he perked up when I explained.

"Hand signals," I said. "We have to work on hand signals."

"Absolutely," Blake agreed.

Soon we were back in the game with a few simple signs worked out. A held-up fist meant "wait" or "hold here." Waving forward meant "come here." Shading your eyes with your hand meant "look," often followed by a point, as in "look there." We would simply point to each other and then to a location for "you go there." That one was mostly used by Blake. And of course, the signal for Randy was our fingers held out like an *L* against our forehead. Make an *L* and point to say "Randy is there."

We were improving, but still not winning. David applauded our decision to use hand gestures.

"This is why we do this," he said. "When you realize by yourself why things are useful, you'll remember them better."

"The hand signals help," I said begrudgingly, "but they're slow."

"That's not the problem," David said. "You just need a larger vocabulary. You only have about five signals for a complicated problem. Let me add a couple."

He introduced them one at a time, and they all helped. But by the end of the week, we still hadn't beaten Randy. He was just too skilled for us. We had gotten better, but he kept stepping up his own game. Before we had even thought about trickery, he started shooting us on the ground if he didn't immediately see yellow spots. We had noticed some of the paintballs didn't splatter all the time. These were the especially painful ones, but it explained why Randy made sure to shoot us even if we were "dead." We quickly learned to love the ones that splattered and left evidence. And that wasn't the only evil trick he had.

For instance, we learned to be careful grouping up when he tossed a paint balloon that left us completely splattered. We had to wash our clothes extra thoroughly in the dirty river that night. You couldn't have seen any new hits on us after that trial.

All this time, in the evenings, David would take us aside for a new lesson.

"If you graduate, not only will you earn a letter, but you will get your tab, too," he said, procuring a small metal bar. It was about four inches long, and it was split into five equal boxes.

David slipped on a black tunic-like uniform top, then carefully pinned the shiny bar to the left side of his chest. The box furthest to his right on the tab was a deep gold, whereas the other four were a brass so dull they were near stony gray.

"A tab tells other Time Peace personnel your rank. These would be yours," David continued. "So you need to know what these mean. Each tab tells you two things. It displays your rank, obviously, and your access to classified information."

"Rank is easy to determine. The larger the gold bar on your tab, the higher ranked you are. Simple, easy, you can read it at a glance."

"Let me guess," I said, non-plussed, "this is the lowest rank."

"No, actually," David replied. "This is second-lowest. There are non-combat personnel with lower ranks. In an emergency, they defer to the people on the ground. Even to Omicrons. Omicrons are technically field agents, so they need some authority in an emergency."

"Alright," I said. "So what about the other bars?"

"That's slightly more subtle. It reflects what level of information you have access to. There are five classes of information classification in Time Peace. Class 5 is Fundamental Information. The basics of the war with Anarakia, how timelines work, or even the existence of the time gates themselves. Information known to anyone within Time Peace, but not the general public of the timelines. Class 4 is Formation Data. That is, information about the movements of squads, individual missions, and logistics. Stuff that could do damage if Anarakia got ahold of it, but that field supervisors need to know. Class 3 is Threat Assessment. This is a bigger picture within a fight over a timeline—what our strategies are to win a battle over a flashpoint, for example. And just above that is Class 2, Temporal Factors.

Predictions about timelines, how we connect our time gates, our rabbit hole calculations, and any information about arcane technology. And of course, the grand strategy to win the war."

"Five is Fundamental, Four is Formation, Three is Threats, and Two is Temporal," Blake repeated, testing the alliteration.

David nodded.

"That seems to cover everything," I noted. "What's left for Class 1?"

"Unspeakable," David replied with a grimace. "Information so secret, we foot soldiers can't even guess as to what it is."

"I don't like secrets," I muttered.

"If it's any comfort, rumor has it that there is almost nothing that falls under the Unspeakable category. Some people say only one file is actually labelled Class 1," David assured me. Or at least he tried. He didn't look too comforted, either.

"So," Blake said, "five bars means we only have access to Class 5 information?"

"Exactly," David confirmed.

"Only the fundamentals," I noted. "Good to see we're still on top."

And speaking of being on top, we still hadn't tagged Randy out by the time the last day came upon us. With only one trial left, Blake and I were in complete, determined agreement. We weren't leaving these woods without at least one victory.

"We need to cheat," I whispered in our dark tent.

"But then we won't really beat him," Blake replied. "Besides, he's ready for that. I have the welts to prove it."

"Well, we can't fight him," I pointed out. "So we're going to have to do some kind of trick."

"That's what's called strategy in the biz," Blake agreed lightheartedly. "I just don't know how we'd pull anything off. We just don't have time. As soon as he sees us, he hits us. We—oh..."

"Yes. Yes," I said, recognizing his expression. "We've got something, don't we?"

"Just a chance," Blake said slowly.

"That's a lot more than we've had all week."

"But you'll have to hit him hard. And maybe go down hard, too."

After so many defeats, I didn't have enough pride to object.

"Let's do it," I declared.

It was a chilly, but sunny day, the warmth not quite making its way through the canopy of leaves above us. My aching bones and tired muscles seemed to promise another defeat, but I steeled my mind as we walked into position on our side of the forest. By now, we had learned that Randy's starting point could be anywhere, so we had to be careful.

We began our usual scouting, Blake leading the way while I stayed in cover, hoping for a kill. By this time, we were both reasonably quiet, and extremely alert. We knew which rustling leaves were normal and which twig snaps meant there was an intruder in the forest. Randy still had the edge in stealth, but the margin was narrowing.

Blake held up a fist. I quickly took cover behind the tree I was at. I made sure to be more concealed than normal, sacrificing my line of sight. But that was okay.

Blake fired, and immediately there was return fire from Randy.

"Hit!" Blake announced, and slowly laid down on the floor, all the while keeping his gun held above his head.

I let Randy advance slightly before taking a couple shots at him. I didn't have a clear angle and missed by a wide margin. Randy took cover and returned fire, but I had my own protection.

Even so, there were a couple close calls. I started my retreat, firing back a few times to keep his head down.

Randy took the bait. I saw him walk towards Blake, see he was hit, and kick his gun away. It splashed into a nearby stream. Randy wasn't taking any chances.

I took the opportunity to fire at him, but at this distance, the paintball guns just weren't accurate enough to hit. Randy vanished immediately, and I knew he had started to stalk me. I immediately shifted into listening mode. I couldn't stay where I was, he would find me too easily. I was hiding behind a fallen log, but it was an easy landmark that would draw him towards me.

I quietly dashed from tree to tree, listening intently for Randy. If I could hit him, then it would really prove—

Three paintballs exploded against my chest. I hadn't heard a thing.

"Hit," I announced sullenly. Or at least, that's how I made it sound.

Randy only came out after I had set my paintball gun on the ground.

"Honestly, I'm kind of disappointed," he said, though he was grinning. "I mean, I know I'm good, but I thought that if there were two of you, you could have beaten me once."

"Has anyone ever told you you're a cad?" I asked him.

He snorted. "No. Usually I'm called worse. And the insults are from this century."

Suddenly, I heard the splattering against his back. He spun around, revealing to me the back of his shirt and head which now looked like exploding blue and red fireworks.

"You're a cad," Blake said. "That makes twice now. A new record."

"What is wrong with you?" Randy howled. "You're already out!"

David emerged from somewhere.

"What's going on?" he demanded. He didn't look happy to have seen Randy splattered by a dozen paint balls at once from behind. Blake dropped the bag he had been holding. Before the game had started, we had emptied several paint balls from both of our guns and put them inside before hiding the bag. Then, Blake threw a handful at Randy at the right time. We agreed on several in case some didn't pop the way they would when shot from the guns.

"I shot Blake, he's out," Randy explained angrily.

"Actually, you never hit me," Blake said, grinning.

"Do you think I'm blind? I can see my paint," he said, pointing at a prominent and visible yellow splotch just under the collar of Blake's shirt.

"Oh, that?" Blake said. "That was me. I did that. I just pretended to be hit."

"What?" Randy was staring at him like he was crazy.

I pulled out one of the unexploded yellow paintballs. "We picked up a few of these. You gave us a lot," I explained. "We just waited for the right time and then..." I pressed the paintball hard against a clean spot on my shirt until it burst. "Ta-da!"

Randy shook his head. "That's the dumbest thing I ever heard. But hey, if you want to get yourself out, be my guest. I say I hit you, the paint's there, end of story."

David was frowning. "It sounds like a convenient lie," he agreed. "The paint splatter is supposed to be the proof of a kill, so like Randy said, even if you set all this up, it's pointless. Unless you can prove you did this yourselves."

"Oh, but we can," Blake said happily.

I grinned at Randy's disbelief. Blake flipped his shirt inside out and pointed to an X drawn on the exact point where he had popped the paintball on the other side.

"Now, either Randy has X-Ray vision," Blake crowed, "or we planned this all out."

"He drew that in after the fact!" Randy declared desperately. He was grasping at anything as the realization of what happened sank in.

"You can check the tent," I said. "We left a note, not just explaining our plan, but describing the exact spot where Blake was 'hit.'"

"You didn't shoot me," Randy insisted. "This doesn't count!"

"The proof is in the paint," I said, glancing meaningfully towards David. "Unless Randy can prove he did this to himself, right?"

He slowly shook his head. "If this were the real deal, real combat, this would never have worked. But..." He slowly cracked a smile. "...this kind of thinking is just what a Delta needs."

Blake and I cheered and high-fived as Randy muttered under his breath. It might have been cheating a bit, but it was a win we desperately needed. Tomorrow, we rode home in victory. A winning record of 1-13.

That night, we were sitting around the campfire, Randy glaring daggers at us. The paint on his clothes was already washing out, but the paint in his hair was another story. It was stuck and it was drying, and based on how he muttered and complained, it was uncomfortable. But after everything he had put us through, Blake and I didn't really care.

"Good work," David said, passing out some soda bottles to us. Randy already had a bottle of a different sort. "I think we've covered a lot this week."

"We did?" I asked incredulously. "I mean, we learned some survival stuff and some hand signals, but aside from that, mostly we just got shot."

"Really? Is that all?" David asked.

"We learned some tactics?" Blake guessed. "Look, don't keep us in suspense, the training's supposed to be over."

"First of all, it's never over," David said. "There's always something more to learn, even if you become a Delta. But to answer your question, you've learned a lot. The importance of communication and working as a team. The importance of communication security when Randy overheard you. The importance of chain of command when you decided to let Blake make the decisions. You learned to keep strategies flexible, and that no plan survives first contact with the enemy. I could have told you all of that, but—"

"We learn better through failure," I guessed, not disagreeing, but not approving either. The experience was too fresh for that.

"Add it to the list," David agreed. "These are the basics from which everything else flows. You can know facts, strategies, tactics, how to survive, how to negotiate, how to sneak, or a million other things, but without these lessons, you wouldn't get anywhere in this war."

Blake was staying quiet, staring into the fire.

"Something wrong?" David asked him.

"Well, I was just thinking about this war," he said. "There's so much we still don't know. Like who exactly are Anarakia? We only have an outline."

David took a sip of his drink before answering. "There's the facts, there's the official story, and there's the legend."

"You sound like you doubt the official story," I observed, sitting up straighter.

"The facts about Anarakia's are true," David said flatly. "It's a fact that they have time gate technology, exploit other timelines for their gain, and aren't afraid to destroy anything that gets in their way. It's a fact that they are bandits, thugs, tyrants and thieves. It's a fact that they will despoil any timeline they come across. You haven't seen Anarakia in action just yet and be glad you haven't. When they get serious, the planet burns. For now, it should be enough to say that they've led two Earths into nuclear annihilation instead of giving them up."

I let that sink in for a moment.

"But?" Blake prompted.

"The details around their origins are... muddy," David said heavily, "The official story is that they stumbled across the time gates and simply let their greed get the better of them. Then a few brave individuals learned the truth and found the remaining time gates, forming Time Peace to fight Anarakia."

"Sounds pretty simple," I said. "And that checks out with their M.O., right?"

"Mostly," David said. He looked as if he was debating what to say next, bringing the bottle up to his lips. He stopped, lowered it. "There's also the legend. And it fits too."

The fire crackled in the silent dark. David took a deep breath, steadied himself, then began.

"The legend says that in the far, far future, there was an advanced civilization. A civilization of peace and harmony, one where hatred and war had long since become relics of the past."

Randy snorted.

"Shhh," Blake silenced him.

"The legend says that people there were better than us," David continued. "Maybe in morals, but definitely in strength and intelligence. They say they were like unto angels. And yet, this Society of Angels fell.

"Maybe they overlooked something in their Great Society, maybe a disaster tore them apart, maybe humans weren't meant to live in a utopia. One way or another, a New Generation grew up different. Something was wrong with them. They were heartless, sadistic, and destructively ambitious. While they were as clever and successful as the rest of the Society, their dreams were not to build, but to destroy. For some reason, having everything in the world just made them want to see it break. So, they began the Eternal War.

"Some say the time gates were made because of the war. Others say they already existed. Either way, both the Society of Angels and the New Generation used them in the conflict. They knew how to use the time gates to their full potential. Unlike us, they could travel through time in any way they wanted.

"Needless to say, the war was complicated. Every time one side would make a move, the other would jump back further in time and stop them. Entire timelines were created and destroyed at the drop of a hat, and the New Generation loved it. This was the glorious war they had always wanted. It destroyed everything, including themselves.

"Eventually, nearly all of the people of the Great Society were killed off or erased from existence entirely. As they continued to jump further and further back in time, reaching back hundreds or even thousands of years, they eventually reached the twentieth century. And when they did, only two of the angels remained. The last general of the Great Society and the last fanatic of the New Generation faced their final battle, armies of recruits from various timelines on their sides. The battle raged, leaving the world a barren husk. Smoldering radioactive clouds covered the surface of that Earth, leaving the few humans left huddling for shelter.

"The wounds of the Great Society's general proved to be fatal. He only left behind fragments of his knowledge and wisdom. The last man of the New Generation hardly fared better. But he lived. His wounds were great, and he was forced to seal himself in a hibernation chamber until he could one day return, healed once again. But before he hid himself, he rallied the last of his fanatical army. He appointed his lieutenants to carry out his mad dream in his place, to prepare for his return. This army is Anarakia. The man is called the Ashen Phoenix.

"Whether Anarakia follows his mad vision or not hardly matters. He gifted madmen the keys to his former kingdom. Anarakia has access to the time gates, and only cares for gaining more power. Some of us believe they are doing so for the Ashen

Phoenix, waiting for him to rise again. Others think they are just abusing the opportunity given to them.

"As for the remnants of the general's army, well, there were too few to carry on the fight. But as Anarakia savaged the timelines, there was always resistance. Men from different timelines eventually found what was left of the general's troops, and from them, learned the secret of the time gates. They united and formed a new army. One dedicated to preserving their homes, their timelines, and fighting Anarakia. And that is Time Peace. And thus, the Eternal War goes on."

I let the story wash over me. The camp was silent for a moment.

"So how come we don't know for sure about the legend?" Blake asked. "A Timeless doesn't exist on a timeline anymore, right? Once you step through a time gate, you never existed back then. Or you only existed in a timeline that once was, but isn't. Whatever the right grammar for that is."

I felt a churning in my stomach that had nothing to do with my fizzy drink. Despite what David said about the nature of timelines, I still wondered if Blake's absence would change his parents' and siblings' world.

"Let's say I'm an Anarakian agent for a moment," David replied. Blake and I exchanged a glance, dreading some new bizarre test. "I want to go back in time and kill you before you join Time Peace. What happens?"

"You can't," I immediately replied. "It's like Blake said, we don't exist back on the old timeline. We never did. So you'd never find us, even when we were kids."

"Why not?" David asked mildly. "You were once kids, weren't you?"

"Yes...?" I began tentatively.

"...and no," Blake finished, equally puzzled.

"So at one point you did exist on your timeline, and at another, you didn't," David summarized. "At one point in what, though? Time?"

"At one point in time, the timeline had us in it, and at another point in time, it didn't," Blake echoed, trying to tease out that puzzler.

"Well then it's not really time," I said. "Time is on the timelines. You're talking about the time of the timelines. The, uh, timeline of the timelines," I suggested, feeling a headache coming on.

"A meta-timeline!" Blake exclaimed, clearly happy to dub the new phenomenon.

"Exactly right," David agreed. "Apart from all of the real timelines, the other Earths, there is a separate pocket dimension where Time Peace Headquarters is located—Iterant Point. The meta-timeline is the timeline for the Timeless. We were recreated on it when we first went through a time gate. It's our present. It's always 'now' in the meta-timeline. And the clock is always running there."

He held up his silver watch and twisted a dial. The face changed, the hands suddenly changing positions, but still ticking away. David tapped the crystal.

"Universal Time," he explained. "On 39.17.7.13 Universal Time, you existed on your home timeline. The next day, on 7.14, you went through a time gate. By 7.15, you never existed on that timeline. By 7.15, if I go back to any point on the timeline to kill you, it would be too late. Like I said, the clock's always running at Iterant Point.

"Unless," David added slowly, "you open a rabbit hole. Despite how impossible it sounds, despite the fact that it should

absolutely create a paradox, some rare Timeless can travel along the meta-timeline. They can even change meta-history. This is why it's called the Eternal War. Whenever Time Peace or Anarakia gets close to beating the other, we undo the whole thing. We fight each other, competing over the time gates, over the timelines, leaping back and forth in them when we can. Then when Time Peace has almost beaten Anarakia, or more often, if Anarakia is about to wipe out Time Peace, we send someone back down the meta-timeline. The meta-time-traveler then says, 'the Talhesian flashpoint is a trap' or 'Anarakia's hacked the Digital Beach' or whatever. They tell us how Anarakia won, what mistakes we made, and so we don't do that again. We keep fighting. The war goes on all over again. And it's not like there's any end in sight. But what are we going to do? We can't give up and let Anarakia win, but we can never defeat them."

Something was frustratingly familiar about what he was saying. Like an itch I couldn't quite scratch.

"Only some Timeless can go back in meta-time?" Blake asked, interrupting my thoughts. "Into the rabbit holes?"

"That's right," David nodded. "They need to have a particular level of mental fortitude and are treated with a variety of drugs to withstand the effects. They call them white rabbits."

Suddenly, my pulse quickened as something in my mind clicked into place. I glanced towards Blake, who seemed to have had the same, wild thought. We both were thinking back to the same moment. Back to something said to us, something the conversation about meta-timelines had echoed.

"This has all happened before," she had said, "and it will all happen again."

The girl who called herself Mirabelle. She stood out so clearly in our memories because of one striking feature. One unnatural trait that was impossible to miss as soon as you laid eyes on her.

David didn't seem to notice our added interest as he finished his thought.

"They call them that because no matter their age, their hair turns white."

V

A Lesson in Civics

"Ken, do you realize what this means?" Blake chattered excitedly from behind the rotting door. Despite the fact that we could easily break them down, we were supposed to get through these doors with subtler means. I tilted my head to hear better as I fumbled with my own lockpicks in a room across the hallway. "If we actually met a white rabbit—"

"Then my dreams are real," I announced yet again. And no matter how many times I said it, I couldn't be less enthused. A perfectly shaped puzzle piece had fallen into our laps, and Blake and I couldn't stop ourselves from marveling at how it fit into place. "I must have fought for Time Peace in other versions of the Eternal War, too!"

"Or it could be, you know, a dream," Randy added sarcastically from behind me.

Blake didn't seem to notice. "The time gate must have reached across meta-timelines for some reason. But if they can create rabbit holes, that should be possible."

"No, it shouldn't," David said. He stood in the hallway, waiting for either Blake or me to escape our mock-prison cells in the abandoned apartment. "Timeless don't get memories from other meta-timelines. And even if you had something to support your wild theory, it doesn't change anything."

"It doesn't?" I asked skeptically.

"Unless you can remember the overall strategies used last time around, no," David said. In a more sympathetic tone, he added, "If this is what's going on, then I'm of course glad that you've figured it out, but I don't want it distracting from what's important. You don't remember anything useful, do you?"

I rattled my lockpicks furiously in the door, to no avail. "I'm sure it's real," I said sullenly, avoiding the question. "I've felt it—they're real."

"Are you really such a baby?" Randy mocked. "Do you actually think that feeling it means it's real? Do you actually think you're so special that Time Peace came back just for you?"

"Randy," David said warningly. Randy held his tongue for the moment, casting his glaring eyes to the side, and scoffed.

"Listen," David said with a sigh, "Travelling through a rabbit hole is a last resort, a rare resource, and a white rabbit would need something extremely special to hop through one. white rabbits go back to change the course of the war. Recruiting one person is not going to do that."

"Why not?" I asked stubbornly, ripping the lockpicks from their place. The words weren't even out of my mouth when I realized how silly the thought was. Maybe someone could change

the course of an entire war by themselves, but I didn't expect that to be me.

David didn't bother to answer, but let my words hang in the air. I slowly picked up my little pins and leaned over again to continue my task, silently admitting to everyone how silly my outburst had been.

"Okay, so maybe Mira had other steps to her plan," I whispered to Blake from behind a stack of books. We were in the library back on campus, trying to catch up on some of the lessons we had missed while we were gone. Just because we were suspended didn't mean we were going to let ourselves be unprepared come time to rejoin our classes. Neither would David.

"If she didn't come back just for us," Blake said absentmindedly as he flipped through a textbook on Aechrian politics, "then what else did she come back for?"

"How should I know?" I retorted, trying half-heartedly to spot what page he was on. "I'm just saying that it's possible. But I'm sure you were right about the dreams."

"Well, you can't be 100% sure," Blake said diplomatically. "You said yourself that some of those visions felt more like nightmares. I mean, we don't have any proof."

"Okay... okay. How are we going to get that?" I asked, anticipating a hare-brained scheme Blake had surely cooked up.

"I don't know," he replied instead, taking out a notebook and scribbling down a date. "Any proof has to be super-top-secret, like Class 2—Temporal Factors, right? And that's if it exists in the first place. We can't get to it, and it's not like David's going to tell us."

"So that's why I'm asking we brainstorm," I persisted.

Before Blake could reply, Quincy rolled up to our table. Quincy was a wheelchair-bound girl who shared several classes with Blake. Her hair was now, as always, in an elegant bun atop her head, and her eyes were kept behind large, squarish, black glasses. She was always polite, if a bit distant, though she was quite helpful towards us as we tried to catch up.

"These should be all the reference books," she said, offloading a distressingly large stack onto the table.

Blake scanned the books apprehensively. "Thanks," he said.

Then he shot me a strange look. When I couldn't figure out what it meant, I gave him a puzzled one in return. He nodded towards Quincy.

I wasn't getting it.

Then he said in his most casual of voices, "So life must be pretty grand with queens and princesses running around."

I cringed immediately as understanding hit me like a ten-ton truck. Blake was doing "espionage." Somehow, he thought he could get useful information out of a random classmate.

"I'm sorry?" Quincy said, glancing up from one of the large volumes.

"What Blake means is," I said, trying to salvage the situation, "this is all kind of new to us. The, uh, culture and everything."

"Exactly," Blake agreed. He still pressed on, "I was wondering about the local festivities, the traditions and rituals, the..." he trailed off.

"If you need help in Civics, you can always ask," Quincy offered.

Blake and I caved at the same time. "Yes, please," we said together.

"It's really quite simple, believe me," Quincy explained knowingly, as she pulled out yet another book. "The Queen is technically the seat of power but has constitutionally deferred the vast majority of it to the prime minister and the senate, who attend to the day-to-day needs of the nation. Everything from the maintenance of public services to making legislation. The Queen simply retains the authority to intervene in emergency matters."

"That's where you lose me," Blake said, returning to normal speech patterns, "what exactly is an emergency matter? Everything I read makes it sound like the Queen has the ability to do anything, but she just doesn't? Why? Isn't anyone worried about that?"

"No, no, I'm afraid you have it all backwards," Quincy said anxiously. "The Queen wouldn't assert her power needlessly. That's simply not how it works. There are charters with the senate which defer—limit—her power. Most of the time. Of course, there are exceptions, and ultimate authority still rests with her. But really, it's against the station itself to assert dominance like that."

"Against the station? I don't even know what that means," Blake confessed.

"You see, it's... just not something that a Queen would do," Quincy tried to explain. "That wouldn't be acting like a monarch. Doing so would tarnish the dignity of the position. There is a propriety, a way of acting, manners and all that, that a Queen needs to maintain. It would be an insult to the country if a Queen didn't act with all the virtue imbued within the title."

"Okay, that sounds great and all, but I just have this nagging problem. Is there anything, anything at all, firmly stopping her from going full tyrant if she wants to?" Blake asked, trying to hammer the point in.

"Tradition," Quincy said matter-of-factly.

"That's not—Okay, what if she breaks tradition? What then?"

"She wouldn't. That's just not how the monarchy works. Any Aechrian knows that."

I was getting a headache, too, when I noticed a new group of students walk into the library. It was some of the popular crowd, Denisha and Scarlett among them. Scarlett.

"Oh no," I said, suddenly clapping my hand to my forehead.

"What?" Blake and Quincy asked together.

"I forgot," I replied. I glanced awkwardly at Quincy, feeling uncomfortable sharing this information in front of her, though I wasn't sure why. Deciding that it would be stranger to hide it from her now, I pressed on. "Scarlett invited me—us—to a party a couple weeks back. But we were gone. Out on that... trip."

"Oh," Blake said. He shrugged, almost relieved. "Big deal. It's not like we would have known anyone there, really. Probably not worth our time."

"Yeah," I said tentatively. Blake didn't look like he remembered what I had told him about Scarlett getting me off the hook, and I didn't really want to say anything in front of Quincy. I felt like I had owed it to Scarlett to show up. Hadn't she basically said as much?

Scarlett had taken a seat by herself and had just opened a book when she glanced up and caught my eye. I hurriedly looked away, feeling my face suddenly grow warm.

Quincy sighed. "Just go up to her," she said.

"Huh, what?" I said unconvincingly. Even I cringed at that performance.

Quincy looked at me, unimpressed. "Really, it's like no one knows how to socialize anymore," she lamented.

"Okay," I said defensively, "maybe I don't. Maybe, even if I wanted to say something, I wouldn't know how to start. Maybe I'm especially awkward after skipping town all at once."

"Do this," Quincy instructed. "Start by walking up to a chair and asking, 'Do you mind if I sit here?' Then—"

"Woah, woah," Blake said, suddenly looking as if he was the one doing this. "What if she says no?"

"Yeah," I echoed. "What if she says no?"

Quincy stole a glance towards Scarlett. "She won't say no."

"How do you know that?" Blake and I both asked skeptically.

"Children," Quincy declared exasperatedly. "I don't have time to fill in your woefully inadequate knowledge of social cues and body language, just trust me."

"But—" I started.

"If she doesn't want you to sit by her," Quincy interrupted, "then she will say something like 'actually, I'm waiting for a friend.' But she won't. If she does," Quincy hurriedly added before my protest was fully formed, "then just say the following anyway, and then excuse yourself. Say, 'I just wanted to apologize for missing the party. I was in this club that had a mandatory meeting out of the blue. I really tried to get out of it, but it was impossible. Is there a way I can make it up to you?' Or something fairly similar, fill in the details as appropriate. But emphasize that you tried and ask if you can make it up to her."

Blake and I exchanged unconvinced looks.

Quincy continued, "Just talk to her. Either she'll have a real conversation, or she'll give you short, curt answers. If that happens, you'll say, 'see you around' and leave. And everything will be fine. Believe me."

"What if she says, 'you jerk, I don't want to talk to you'?" I asked.

"She's not going to say that," Quincy said dismissively.

"How do you know?" Blake and I asked again.

"Because she's not rude," Quincy exclaimed. "Honestly, do you know anything about how polite conversation works?"

"No, I've never tried it," I said jokingly.

Quincy rubbed her forehead. "Children, I tell you. I'm surrounded by children. If you're going to go," she added. "Do it now before it gets to be too long."

"Like right now?" I asked, suddenly feeling like a spotlight had lit up above my head.

"What, do you need a script?"

"That would be nice, yes," I nodded fervently.

But Quincy had grown tired of the conversation and knocked one of my books off the side of the table. "Whoops," she whispered as I scrambled to pick it up. It had fallen to the side closest to Scarlett, and I couldn't help but peek up, mortified that she might see me fumbling around. Sure enough, our eyes met again.

I glared at Quincy, but now I had no choice. It was follow through or chicken out for all of eternity. If for no other reason than to wipe off Blake's stupid grin, I couldn't back out now. I stuffed my books in my bag and stood up.

"Knock her socks off," Blake said, still smiling like an idiot.

I bared my teeth at him before turning and wiping my expression blank. My heart thudded and I felt like I was already

slipping back into moron mode. My feet seemed a lot less coordinated all of a sudden. Honestly, it was embarrassing that I was this embarrassed. But I trudged forward.

I stood awkwardly by the chair next to Scarlett, and she looked up.

"Uh, do you mind if I sit here for a moment?" I asked, clasping my hand on the back of the chair, hoping to squeeze away any trembling.

She glanced around a moment, and I panicked, thinking she was looking for her friends. "Not at all," she answered politely.

Relief washed over me. I sat down, putting my bag under the chair. She watched, waiting for my question, and I nearly panicked again as everything Quincy had told me suddenly slipped away.

"I wanted to say, uh, that is," I stuttered. She tried to keep a polite straight face, but the corners of her mouth were twitching upwards, threatening to break into a patronizing smile. I felt hot and a little angry, like I was being mocked. I determined I wouldn't make a fool of myself. "Sorry for missing the party. The one you invited me to. I had this meeting, couldn't get out of it. I tried. Is..." I stumbled over this part, but I couldn't let myself stop now that I had started. "Is there any way I could make it up to you?"

Scarlett looked a little surprised, but pleasantly so. "Sure," she said, stifling a little laugh. Then, glancing back at our table, she asked mischievously, "Tell me something, was Quincy coaching you?"

I froze.

Scarlett suppressed another laugh. "Relax," she said. For just a second, she placed her hand reassuringly on my arm. An electric tingle shot up to my shoulder at the gentle touch. "I was just teasing. It just sounded like her. She's a little old-fashioned."

"I, uh, guess so," I said, smiling weakly and wondering if there was an "uh" switch I could turn off in my brain.

"She's lovely," Scarlett said, hurriedly covering for any possible unintended offense. And all at once, the nerves nearly vanished. I was talking to someone who had doubts and insecurities just like me. And that made all the difference. "The phrasing," Scarlett continued, "it—well, it was unique."

"'Making it up to you'?" I guessed.

"That's the one," she confirmed.

"Well, it might not have been my words," I said, plunging ahead, "but I meant it. I don't know what you did, but I still owe you for that whole Charmies incident."

"Don't worry about it," she said, shaking her head. "Really. But if you want more practice stepping out of your shell, I have a friend with a Halloween party next week. And everyone will be at the Crystal Ball."

"Sounds great," I said. "Wait, Crystal Ball?"

"November Ninth? Traditional Aechrian holiday, kind of a formal occasion?" That didn't ring any bells. She must have seen this because she continued, "It's a big deal in Thysiopolis. Pretty much all of the Academy is invited to the basilica. Haven't you seen the signs?"

"Must have missed them," I admitted, feeling a bit oblivious. As much as I wasn't usually a fan of parties, I was even less of a fan of formal ones. It was definitely a subject I wanted to avoid.

"Right, like I said, most of the school's invited. It's a good chance to meet new people," she went on.

"Yeah, sounds like it," I replied lamely. Meeting people wasn't much more of a welcome topic than formal parties were.

My lack of enthusiasm killed the momentum of the conversation. I didn't know how to pivot back to a real topic.

I searched desperately for something else to talk about. My gaze fell on a folded open notebook sticking out of her bag. That wouldn't have caught my eye by itself, but the crisp dark lines on the pages did.

"Do you draw?" I asked out of the blue, irresistibly curious.

"Oh. Yes," she said, somewhere between sheepish and quietly eager to share. She unfolded the pages in front of her, revealing a composition of several line drawings. The black ink swooped around, starting hair thin and flourishing into heavy lines at key points. A blossoming flower sat in the lower foreground, a string of other symbols arrayed in a complex pattern behind it. A crescent moon, a hidden sword, and a little doll were all intertwined amongst other curious items in the branches of thick forest trees.

"It's just some doodles," Scarlett said. An elegant black pen had appeared automatically between her fingers, apparently without her noticing. She gestured in affected casualness at the images, saying, "Just some symbols, I guess. I thought they looked cool, and I like playing with these pictures that are supposed to have some meaning attached to them."

My eyes stuck on the little doll. Maybe it was just me, some deep quirk of my personality, but the innocuous doll struck me as hopelessly tragic. I saw shadows that weren't there, an absent sideways light accidentally illuminating a forgotten flash of delight dirtied in the woods. A conglomeration of simple materials imbued with a desire to spark joy. A patchwork of worthless components that never could.

I stared at it, wondering. The tracings took me back to another sheet of paper that had moved me just as much. Scarlett cleared her throat awkwardly.

"I guess that's kind of weird, isn't it?" she said.

"No, no," I hastily said, snapping back to the moment. "It's good. Really good. Just reminded me of something else."

"Right, anyway, that's not all I draw," Scarlett said, shifting the focus, and flipping the page. "Just one of the weirder ones. Most of this is just sketches, characters, costume ideas."

I didn't know how to convince her that I wasn't judging her first drawing. Instead, I latched onto her last comment.

"For Halloween? I take it next week's a costume party," I guessed.

"In Aechyr?" Scarlett smiled, the notebook sliding back into her bag. "Always. Here there be monsters."

Feeling an upturn in the mood, I made a leap of faith. "Well, maybe you can give me some pointers on which traditional Aechrian monsters are a good choice?"

"Sure," she agreed. "A group of us are going costume shopping this weekend. I could show you around while we're at it. You'll let me know if there's a sudden appointment, right?"

"You don't have to worry about that," I said quickly. "This weekend it is. Promise."

She raised an eyebrow sardonically. "I'm going to hold you to that."

"Good. Magnificent," I said. I wasn't sure how to leave. "Well, uh, 'til next time?"

"Of course. Take care," Scarlett said happily. "You can tell Quincy she gets an A plus."

"Hey, she's the teacher," I said as I rose to my feet. "I'm the student. What's my grade?"

"Show up on Saturday, and then we'll see," Scarlett said, the mischievous glint back in her eye.

A group of friends, huh? Well, it could've been better, but it was a good start. I walked back to Blake and Quincy's table, trying hard not to let the spring in my step overpower me.

"Well?" Blake asked.

"We're meeting Saturday," I said. "With her friends. But she invited me to a Halloween party."

"Right on," Blake cheered softly, offering a fist-bump under the table which I quickly accepted.

"Also," I said, turning back to Quincy, "she said you were an excellent teacher."

Quincy looked mortified. "She knew?"

"Relax," I said, teasing. "It's just polite conversation."

Both Quincy and Blake rolled their eyes.

Blake and I strode against the crowd. David had picked the perfect day for on-campus training. There was a visiting speaker, and the event was distracting many of the students. Even if we hadn't chosen a secluded spot, the chances of someone stumbling upon us were...

Apparently pretty good.

Blake and I turned a corner, just coming into view of the buildings that made up the Box (our destination), when we saw them. Sleeves and the other gray-uniformed students. The Charmies, as Scarlett had called them. They were standing right in front of the entrance we were aiming at, discussing something. It was only a moment before Sleeves noticed us.

Immediately, the group went silent, and all eyes turned to us. Muscles tensed. Feet inched towards fighting stances. Faces hardened.

"Easy there, boys," a voice cut in from the pack. A tall, athletic girl with long, steely blond hair pulled herself out of the background. She wore the same uniform as the rest of them, though it hung from her with a hint of casual style.

"No one owns the place," she continued. "Besides, the bloodshed would be pretty hard to cover up."

The pack of Charmies eased their formation slightly but didn't look any friendlier. After a moment, the new girl stepped towards us in a crisp, yet mildly graceful way.

"Avery Criss," she introduced herself. Something clicked, and I realized I had seen her before. She was in my Civics class, usually lounging in the back. We had never spoken.

I eyed the hand she extended, and then her companions again. "You have class here?" I asked.

"Yeah, Loitering 101," she replied coolly. "Are you going to take my hand or head back to the dean?"

Slowly, I reached out and shook her hand. "Kennedy Frost," I said.

"Blake Anthony," he said when Avery turned to him.

"I'm glad to see you weren't expelled, by the way," she continued. There was a warmth in her grin that reached to her deep brown eyes. They seemed to smolder lightly, like a bonfire after a long night's party. Her crisply defined jaw and pointed chin were softened by the barest hint of freckles across her glowing cheeks. "I know we can step on some toes, metaphorically speaking."

"And literally. I don't suppose your friends care to apologize themselves?" I suggested. I had said the words before my brain could stop me.

"Given the circumstances, I don't think they'd mind volunteering me as a spokeswoman," she said without missing a beat, but she did step a bit closer. She leaned in almost conspiratorially, keeping herself turned just enough to allow me a clear view to her friends. "We wouldn't want to stumble into any inflammatory remarks. And if you don't mind my saying, concessions are usually best proffered after the cessation of hostilities."

She looked me over carefully. I did the same. Her response had caught me by surprise.

Avery looked like she was satisfied and straightened. "Call it a truce?" she asked.

Still examining her, I nodded.

She glanced back over at Sleeves, who stepped forward. He extended a hand stiffly. "Call it an even fight?" he suggested. He didn't look terribly happy about it, but he also didn't seem to be looking to stir up trouble. Reluctantly, I accepted the gesture of reconciliation. We both squeezed a bit harder than necessary. Neither of us broke eye contact.

Avery relaxed. Only then did I realize that her shoulders had been tensed.

"You did pretty good, American," Sleeves complimented.

"You just had to say something, didn't you, Brooks?" Avery complained.

"It's a joke, Ave. We're cool," Sleeves—Brooks, I guess, assured her.

Avery rolled her eyes. "Nothing to bond two men like getting into a fistfight," she said under her breath. There was some truth to that idea, I thought. Most of the time.

The other Charmies relaxed, and the no-man's-land disappeared. As they gathered around, Brooks nodded to Blake.

"Guess I owe you a thank you," he said.

"For what?" Blake asked.

"Not pinning this on us," Brooks replied. "How'd you manage to pull down this deal anyway?"

"Oh, that wasn't anything special," Blake said sheepishly. He seemed unsure of what exactly to say. "Not like we did anything, really."

"Sure you didn't. Come on, you've got to have friends in high places for this one," another Charmy commented wryly.

"Not us," I answered for Blake. "I figured you guys for the types with connections."

"Not a chance," Brooks scoffed. "If anything, we have enemies in high places."

"The highest," the other Charmy chuckled.

More seriously, more passionately, Brooks said, "We worked hard just for the chance to step foot here. This isn't some birthright. We're going to make the most of it while we're here, and we'll show everyone else just how committed we are to that."

He gestured at the uniform, as if his comments had explained why he wore it. Then he added, "I'm not about to have a bunch of rich kids laughing at me."

"Let them laugh, they'll just make fools of themselves," yet another of the group said.

"That won't be hard," a fourth chimed in.

Blake rubbed his chin. "Most of the people I've seen here aren't rich," he commented.

"They're not," Avery interjected. "The rich are made here. You can see the superior attitude being drilled into them. Every tradition, every nicety, every arrogant thought is taught to them here. You can feel 'the society' if you know what you're looking for." She said "society" with the scorn of the too familiar, I thought. That tone, and the way she had become negotiator all of a sudden started a couple of gears turning in my head. It would be very convenient, but the pieces seemed to fit with what David had said...

"Most of them already have too much brains. Enough to think they're better than you," she went on.

"We got in the only way regular men and women can," Brooks added proudly. "We're Naval Academy. It gives us access to the same resources as these elites but keeps our feet on the ground. How about you—what's your major?"

"Undecided," I said coolly. I was still testing my idea in my mind, hardly paying attention.

Brooks nodded. "For what it's worth, you don't seem like one of the snobs. If it weren't for the American thing, maybe you could've been Navy material."

"Speaking of, how did you wind up at the Academy, anyway?" one of the other ones—I couldn't tell two of them apart—chimed in.

"My parents," I said on a whim. Suspicion nudged me in this direction, and experience helped me down the path. Kids do stupid stuff. I channeled my memories for my performance. "If I had to stay in that same old house any longer, or anywhere near it, I was going to suffocate. So I went as far as I could make it."

I directed my remarks to the entire group but made sure my gaze ended on Avery.

"This place—the Naval Academy—can be good for that sort of thing," she commented carefully. "Leaving the baggage behind."

"Are you speaking from experience?" I dared to ask.

"I'm not in the Naval Academy," she answered evasively.

I waited for a moment.

"Yeah, I'm speaking from experience," she said.

"So you guys are Charmies?" Blake asked, plowing straight through my moment. Still, I held Avery's gaze for a second longer. I caught a hint of something more in her eyes. As I wondered how to spot colored contacts, our attention was pulled back to the larger group.

The crowd laughed at Blake's comment, but Brooks answered.

"If you insist, you can call us that. We like Charlie, why hide it?"

"Who?" Blake asked, suddenly lost.

One of the identical Charmies slapped his palm against his face and cried out, "oh noooo!"

Brooks shook his head. "You don't even know where the term 'Charmy' comes from? Maybe you shouldn't sling it around. It's from Senator Charles Becker. Elitists tried to smear him by calling him 'Charming Charlie.'"

"Don't know how they thought that would work out," another Charmy snarked.

"For real," Brooks agreed. "But they started calling those of us who are also skeptical of the monarchy 'Charmies,' like we're his lapdogs or something."

"But then, he is your leader?" Blake pressed.

"Yeah, and I'm president of the fan club," Avery interjected sarcastically. She continued more calmly, "We're not a team. We don't have a roster or rules. Becker's one of the few officials who will actually say what we're all thinking. Most people are too afraid to suggest that we can do without royalty. For a long time, if you even suggested abandoning the monarchy, you would be shouted down for being unpatriotic, even though nothing could be further from the truth. Even though he had everything to lose, Charlie Becker still spoke out. So, yeah, we respect him for that. I respect him."

"Is this really that big of a deal?" Blake asked skeptically. "I was under the impression that the Queen didn't actually interfere all that much."

Blake was taking a position in stark contrast to the line he had taken with Quincy. Now, he was dismissing his own concerns. He was working Avery for information, I realized. And he was doing a lot better than he had with Quincy. But he was still one step behind me if my suspicions were correct.

"Why don't you come with us and find out?" Avery suggested, derailing Blake's line of questioning. She gestured back towards campus. "We were just about to head out anyway. Why don't you come see the man himself?"

"Right now?" Blake asked, surprised.

I cut in, "Sure, let's go."

Blake glanced towards me, leaving the obvious question unspoken. I nodded as slightly as I could, and he nervously looked back to Avery. She got the Charmies moving, and we started walking towards the southeast quadrant. But she lagged behind the group when she saw I didn't fall in as quickly as Blake.

"Problem, Shades?" she asked. "I promise it's not the lion's den."

"Hope not," I said. I hesitated a moment, then realized I had to plunge ahead or miss the chance. "I don't really want to wind up with People's Front Nine or something."

The smile drained from Avery's face. But she answered calmly and politely. "None of us are People's Front. That's straight-up slander, and if you had said that to Brooks, he'd have stopped caring about how obvious blood would be. If you want to call us 'Charmies,' that's fine. But don't spread around a lie. Too many people try to tell us that we're something we're not. Or that we're not something we are, for that matter."

She held my gaze a moment, undaunted by my black visor. Her eyes told me she wasn't to be tested on that point. I could almost feel the weight of all the mistruths hanging over her. Or the weight of something else.

"Like an important voice?" I suggested.

She looked at me a bit differently. "We all have an important voice. But some people can forget that because of the company you keep." She nodded towards the crowd we were approaching.

A crowd was spread out before a podium, like it was an outdoor amphitheater. Many of the students in the crowd had the uniform of the Charmies, but none of the students at the edges did. They weren't looking on in rapt attention like the rest. Many had their arms folded, and a couple were holding signs over their shoulders.

"We'll stick towards the back," Avery said. "Then you can pretend you were never here."

"I wouldn't do that," I said.

"Maybe you should," Avery suggested. "No one needs to know everything about you. They rarely tell you everything in return."

"You're speaking from experience again."

"You noticed again."

A man walked up to the podium. The seated crowd stood and applauded. Some on the periphery booed. The man, Charles Becker, didn't seem to notice. He was a clean-looking gentleman in a trimmed gray suit, which matched the gray streaks on the side of his otherwise jet-black, crisply combed-back hair. Blake and the other Charmies were just a little ahead, listening intently as the senator began his speech. Avery only seemed to be half-listening.

After a few sentences, I said, "Your folks—if you don't mind me asking—you had some friction with them, too?"

"You could say that," Avery conceded. "You could say we fought like cats and dogs. They didn't exactly approve of my misadventures."

"Misadventures?"

"Believe it or not, I wasn't always the sweet angel before you today," she said sarcastically. "I had a tendency to run off and... 'explore,' let's call it. No details, you haven't earned those. Anyway, I split years ago. It's tough, but you manage. Good way to really shake things up, by the way. I put the whole 'you're making the worst decision of your life' thing they told me to the test. They couldn't have been more wrong. Family is who you choose, Kennedy. Don't let anyone tell you differently. And we've got a family. One that won't hide things from you or turn away because they don't like your attitude. No matter how bad it is."

She stared through the stage a moment, weighing up her last words. After a moment, she seemed to notice the crowd, and a look crossed her face. A quiet satisfaction as she lost herself in thought. And at that moment, as a light breeze blew through our hair, I felt a deep pang of envy.

She noticed me staring and snapped back to the moment. "Your attitude, I mean," she clarified, though in a way that I was sure was intended to move past the moment than to actually explain her feelings. "Sometimes you need something as hard as yourself to straighten you out. The Charmies are rough, but they'll quickly teach you to be responsible for yourself. It takes longer for some to learn, but hey, even Brooks can do it. If you slap him around a bit."

I nodded. The conversation was drifting, and I had lost focus.

"That's a joke," she added flatly when I didn't react appropriately.

"Right. You ever think of patching things up with your folks?" I asked, opting for the direct approach. My favorite.

Avery scoffed. "That would be difficult."

"I get it," I said truthfully, but she interrupted.

"I don't think so. My parents are dead."

She held a deadpan look for a moment, daring a comment. A surprised "oh" died on my lips. Her mouth twitched in distasteful amusement for a moment at my discomfort. When I didn't make another move, she patted my shoulder.

"Relax, Shades," she said, starting towards the other Charmies. "It's no big deal. But if you ever want to see if you measure up, stop by again. Who knows? You might even find a real friend."

As she joined the rest of her group, I tried to piece together the conversation. For a minute there, I had been convinced. I thought David had been right, that the Princess had leaned into rebellion from her family and had ironically become anti-monarchist. But I wasn't so sure anymore. I wasn't sure about a lot of things.

"—we ask that experts evaluate those critical decisions," Becker was saying. "Experts chosen by Aechyr, who serve Aechyr. I hope you'll agree that we have done quite well in creating institutions like this Academy. In turn, these institutions create quite capable, electable leaders. So let them serve our country unhampered by mere ceremony or outdated tradition. Let our strength of character, tested in the fires of experience, be the strength of our nation."

He was quite a good speaker. A brimming passion seeped through his professional demeanor—a potent, tangible desire backed by a force of will. But his speech had already faded from my hearing. Everything began to fade away. Everything except one person.

"Who is that?" I said, suddenly next to Avery again. My hand was gripping her shoulder, and I had cut in between two of the Charmies.

Avery, cut off mid-sentence, blinked, then turned to the far end of the stage. She squinted at the figure I was pointing to. She shuddered.

"I don't know," she said. "He has a unique—ah—presence, though."

"If you mean his creepiness borders on terror, then, yeah," Blake added.

"You can say that again," Avery muttered agreement.

Their comments came to me from the end of a mile-long tunnel. My eyes were glued on the pale figure with the long hair. Even as a small figure in the distance, shrouded in shadow behind

Charlie Becker's posse, I could easily recognize the man with the skull-like face.

The man with green eyes.

The man who had blinded me.

VI

The Iron Mosk

"It's real. It's all real," I declared before David had finished setting down his briefcase.

We were in the Box—a little courtyard formed by four of the Academy's lesser-used buildings. And only one of these buildings had a backdoor into this secluded spot. Since the four buildings made a complete seal, cutting it off from the rest of campus, it was a great place to train in secret. Randy made it better by grabbing some plywood from the junk heaps and using it to block the tinted windows, while David had already jammed a rubber wedge under the door. Yet again, he was casually teaching us another simple and effective trick, but I wasn't in a learning mood.

"I saw the man who blinded me," I continued, accusation seeping into my words. "The one from my dreams."

"Not this again," Randy moaned.

David held out a hand to quiet him. "Go on," he said.

More calmly, I explained, "He was with Becker, the senator, at his speech. This guy with long white hair, tall and gaunt."

David glanced towards Randy. "Could be Sainne," he muttered.

"Who?" I asked insistently.

"Director Sainne," David explained. "He's an Anarak—a general of Anarakia. Time Peace knows he's on the island, working with Becker. We have eyes on him."

"I've seen him before," I repeated.

David looked me over with newfound appreciation. "We'll look into it," he said. "Maybe there is something to these dreams after all. We'll have to ask the specialists—temporal mechanics and Psi's. Those are the experts in Timeless psychology. I'll pass it along."

I nodded to him, and relaxed. I had been prepared for a fight. I was pleasantly surprised I wouldn't have to have one.

"Until then, we still have training," David began again and pulled out something from the briefcase. "Today, we talk about temporal combat."

David held out his hands and showed us two large watches The bands were thick silver links, nearly as wide as the watch itself. A black rubbery stripe ran down the middle of each band. The watch face appeared blank under a glass lens. Around that lens, a black ring was inlaid into the silver body.

"These are your time gauges," David explained. "Get used to them, because you'll be wearing them from now on."

"Are they broken?" I asked, taking mine. Blake was already strapping his on the way David was demonstrating. "There's no time here."

"Not yet. Twist the top crown," David instructed.

I did so, and it clicked sharply. In a blink, the watch face suddenly materialized a pair of hands and several dashes around the edges. Astonished, I tilted the back and forth, trying to see how the illusion was made. It looked like the hands were three-dimensional, not just displayed on a screen. It didn't glow either. It really was an impressive trick.

I twisted the crown another notch, and the face changed again. Numbers appeared on the notches. Another twist, and a third hand appeared—ticking away the seconds. Each click added or removed features, sometimes even adding more tiny watch faces within, like one showing a 24-hour clock, or one displaying the day of the week.

"As you might have seen," David said, interrupting my experimentation, "this isn't just a watch. This is arcane tech—future tech. Technology Time Peace has uncovered and reverse engineered. If the legends are to be believed, you're holding just the tiniest example of what the Society of Angels was capable of."

I stared at the watch with newfound appreciation and wonder.

"Other features include monitoring your vitals and communicating with other time gauges," David continued. He lifted his watch to his mouth and pressed in the bottom crown. "Can you hear me?" he asked.

His voice emerged from our own watches simultaneously.

"Right on," Blake said. "What else can it do?"

"It can save your life," David answered. "Randy?"

Randy took out a tennis ball and tossed it up and away. Just as it reached the top of its arc, heading towards one of the roofs, David ordered, "Now. Press the big crown."

Both Blake and I looked down to see what we were doing and then pressed the middle of the three dials. The air seemed to shimmer for a split second. Then, the world vanished. The walls and floor of the Box remained around us, but beyond it, the blue sky was gone. Instead, a black dome appeared and encased us.

Except it wasn't just a black dome. Looking into it felt like staring out into infinity. Swirls of semi-random color poured just beyond the black surface. Specks of light, like stars, littered the background, but they were by far the least interesting apparitions. Streaks of teal auras, magenta spirals, blue half-fireworks, half-galaxies all stole my attention. Brilliant, slow-motion yellow flashes blossomed like cosmic flowers before folding in on themselves and disappearing. Vague reddish clouds, an eternity away, swirled into vaguely familiar shapes before being blown apart across the stars. And on and on, an endless series of strange, beautiful forms appeared before my eyes. And none of it quite strange enough to be terrifying.

But I didn't have time to dwell in the infinity.

My head shot around. I didn't see David; I only saw a threat. I dropped to the ground and rolled away as the gun spat. I had dived out of the line of fire, but Blake was too slow. Still gazing at the stars, he was struck in the chest. I saw the spray of liquid against his shirt from the corner of my eye.

I locked onto David. My heels dug into the pavement and I sprang at him.

A moment before impact, a blurred shape cut in front of me. I felt someone grab my arm and twist me around.

"Good instincts, Flash," Randy said, "but pay attention a little more, would ya?"

Holding my arm behind me, Randy had forced me around to face Blake. He was perfectly alive, though splattered in green paint.

Randy reached to my watch, still in my view, and pressed the middle crown.

The cosmos jerked to the side. I felt as if my mind flew off a cliff, sputtered, and then finally regained traction. It was as if reality was a video tape that stuttered to a stop one moment, only to be running smoothly again the next second as if nothing had happened.

We were all standing as we had been before David's random outburst. Standing under the dome of the endless void. Including Blake, who was looking down at his clean shirt, touching it as if in disbelief.

"It doesn't hurt," he said, astonished. "But then—what did you do? It was like you rewound time?"

"More or less," David agreed. "we've all been reset back to the moment when we clicked on the time gauges."

"But I thought time travel wasn't something you could just do," I said as I carefully watched David put the paintball gun back into the case. I had to tell myself to relax.

"It's not time travel," David replied. "It's a reset. We don't control how far back in time we go. We can only reset back to the first moment. But it will reset you physically, no matter how injured you are. Also, it only works in a small arena—inside this dome."

"So, what's outside it?" I asked.

David gazed out at the distant stars. "What can I say? No one knows that either. In here, we're in a quasi-timeline called hang time. We're cut off from the regular timeline. Given that, maybe we're seeing possibility itself."

I stared out at the endless black, sprinkled with wondrous images that came and went.

"Better not look too long," David warned. "You might never stop."

I pulled myself away from the enticing imagery with some difficulty. I forced my mind back to the conversation.

"Each reset of hang time is like a rough draft of this place in the timeline," David continued. "When we resync, the last reset, the last draft, becomes real. Follow my lead."

David hit the middle crown and I felt reality snap again. I was suddenly yanked back to where I had been casually standing, looking down at my watch after pressing the middle crown for the first time. I glanced up to see David pull the crown this time, popping it out slightly. Blake and I echoed his motion.

Reality rippled back into order. The cosmic dome vanished in an instant. We were once more firmly planted in Aechyr Academy, the sky back to the correct color.

And then the tennis ball struck the roof, falling as if it had just been thrown.

"See?" David asked.

"I think so," I said, my mind catching up to the miraculous technology.

"To the outside observer, all that happened was we fiddled with our watches," David said. "They only saw that last reset. That's the official history of this timeline now."

"Sweet," Blake said. "So we could basically have infinite time. We could, as an admittedly lame example, study for hours in the arena while only a few minutes pass outside."

"Not a chance," Randy piped in, "the watches don't have infinite charge. Every second in the arena drains some of it, and it

takes real time to recharge. The longer in the arena, the longer the recharge. So if you do something stupid like use it to study and then an Anarakian hit squad rolls up, you're out of charge. They can still use their time gauges to find just the perfect way to kill you, but hey, you'll die knowing a little more calculus."

"Jeez," Blake said, taken aback. "Just a question."

"Wait, even if we don't press the middle crown, Anarakians can create an arena? We don't all have to press the button?" I asked.

"It only takes one person to make an arena," David confirmed. "It takes everyone to end it."

"But no charge means no resets," Randy added. "At least for you."

"Okay, so if anyone can rewind the arena, then how do you win?" I asked. "We wait until everyone runs out of charge?"

"There are two ways," David answered. "First, the two teams agree to end the battle. All the participants pull the middle crowns on their time gauges, and the arena ends."

"How often does that happen?" I asked skeptically.

"Not often," David admitted. "But if you get killed a few dozen times, you might get tired of it. Eventually, you'd rather negotiate than fight. More commonly, someone breaks the arena."

David picked up another ball and activated the arena. Once more, the black dome blocked out the sky.

"Like this," David said, and threw the ball straight up.

It rose and slowed, almost at the top of its arc when it kissed the top of the dome. As soon as it crossed the barrier, the arena collapsed, flashing out of existence.

The ball fell back into David's outstretched arm.

"Touch the edge, and the arena breaks," Blake mused.

"That's it," David nodded. "Arenas can't be created anywhere because of this. They can't be in a place where they'll be broken from the outside."

"That's what makes it a duel," Randy said knowingly. "You see an Anarakian hit squad in a crowded street and you don't start shooting. You pick an abandoned warehouse, and if they agree, you see who's got the chops to come walkin' back out."

"But why?" Blake asked. "If we're just going to kill each other, then why would we agree on anything?"

"Because both sides want to get their people out alive," David explained. "Even if we win in one iteration, we might lose one of our teammates. They're dead, and we don't want to accept that. So we run it again until all of us are alive, and all of them are dead. Or we go crazy."

"Everyone wants a perfect run," Randy explained. "It never happens. But hey, you gotta try."

"Outside the arena, we have other tools," David interjected. "Some non-lethal. Like these."

He reached back into the briefcase and pulled out a reflective silver rod with a handle at the end. It was a gun of some sort, though it didn't look like any I had ever seen. Instead of a hammer at one end, there was a sort of cap, kind of like the crowns on our watches. Other than that, the only distinguishing feature were two switches above the thin trigger.

"This is an arcane tech electro-pulse gun," David explained. "or ATEP gun for short. Gauge guns if we're feeling informal. It fires an energy beam that carries electricity. It disrupts the nervous system of the target. It stuns them. Every time."

"Every time?" I asked, interested.

"Every person is different and requires a different setting to stun them, but when you attach it to your watch..." David said, demonstrating. He pulled the black strap from the metal band of his watch and looped it around his thumb. It snapped into the handle of the ray gun resting in his palm. "...It will use a variant of the arena. It creates a mini-arena around the gun and the target. It fires, checks if the stun worked, and if not, resets the mini-arena and tries again. If it used too high of a voltage, it'll lower it for next time. If it did it too low, it'll try higher. And it'll try again and again, a million times until it has used just the right level of energy to stun the target. We, outside the arena, only see the one that worked."

"Of course, you can also choose the power setting manually," David said, clicking a switch and flicking his thumb across the cap on the back.

David pointed the gun at a cinder block resting in the middle of the Box. As soon as he had his shot lined up, he pulled the trigger. A brilliant bolt of blue-white light shot from the tip of the gun and scorched the surface with a sharp crack.

"But if you really want power," David began as Blake and I noted the pit in the block, "there's one other gadget."

David set aside the gun, twisted the black ring atop the watch like it was a cap, and removed the crystal lens. He then put it in the palm of his hand, snapping it to the black strap still wrapped around his thumb.

"The time gauge will send power through the crystal, and there's about a .1% chance that a critical reaction will take place," he explained. "But we cheat."

He carefully aimed his hand at the cinder block. He twisted a dial that had been hidden underneath the crystal lens, apparently upping the power.

"Just like the gauge gun, the watch will reset a million times if necessary until it gets the perfect reaction. Just like this."

David squeezed the watch. In a brilliant white flash, a jolt of energy vaporized the entire cinderblock, scattering the little dust that remained into the air. It was gone as quick as it had appeared, leaving only spots in our eyes, my sunglasses doing little to dim the light.

"That," David announced. "Is the crystal ray. Weapon of last resort. It really drains the battery, but if you really want something gone..." He shrugged modestly.

"But there's a catch," Randy warned. "You can never use it in an arena."

"That's right," David said somberly. "You can't have an arena inside an arena. So if you try to use the gauge gun on stun or any level of the crystal ray inside an arena, the whole thing resets. Constantly. In split-second increments, a million times, until the gun or the ray works. If you thought the arena could make you crazy, imagine what getting looped could do."

Suddenly, the gauge gun, which had seemed like such a safe alternative a moment ago, now seemed far more terrifying.

"You said you could adjust the ray's power," Blake said slowly. "How high does it go?"

David considered, then looked to the north building. He held out his hands, measuring its entire width.

"Maybe that big," he said.

We gaped at him. I looked down at the small piece of equipment on my wrist, realizing just how much power was entrusted in me.

"Righteous," Blake breathed.

***

The lessons continued as the days passed by. Since Blake and I didn't have classes, David had taken it upon himself to fill up our time. As promised, we were taught a smattering of, well, everything. Tactics, history, engineering, codebreaking, and on and on. We got just a taste of each, and I was pretty sure I wouldn't be able to remember most of it, but I tried my best.

The one thing I couldn't get out of my mind was the thought of Sainne. The man who had blinded me haunted my nightmares more than ever. It seemed like every night I got a little less sleep, and every morning I asked David if he had heard anything from Time Peace. Each time, he would tell me patiently that he was still waiting. And each time, I would get a little more anxious for answers.

Finally, one chilly morning, when we were all assembled in an empty field, he had news for me.

"Good morning, everyone," David greeted us from in front of a line of four-wheelers. "Kennedy, I finally heard back from the Psi's."

I immediately perked up. As much as I could while still bundled up in my jacket.

"And? What'd they say?" I asked.

David shook his head gently. "I'm sorry. They looked back over your earlier evaluations. Obviously, you saw someone with long white hair and green eyes in your dreams. But there were clear distinctions between him and Sainne. Memory has a way of playing tricks on people. We remember things that didn't happen or forget things that did. Things that happen after the fact change how we look back on events. Even important ones. Crimes, tragedies, disasters, all these can get confused despite how important they are. And it seems like the man you first described wasn't Sainne."

He handed me a file.

I was numb. I flipped it open, but only glanced.

"No, I've seen Sainne. Sainne specifically," I insisted.

"Yes, of course you've seen him now," David said. "After you saw him in real life, he's replaced the original man in your dreams. That's how it happens sometimes. If you see in the report—"

"No," I insisted. "That's wrong. I know what I saw. If anything's changed, it's these papers."

"I told you this was how it would go," Randy smirked.

That was it. That pushed me over the edge.

"Forget this," I said, throwing the file to the ground. "You're lying to me. Either you or Time Peace."

"Give me a break," Randy muttered.

"I'm serious," I said defiantly. "I want some answers, and I want them now."

David had already given Randy a look, and his expression was still souring. Randy rolled his eyes and sidled away as David turned to me. He lowered his shoulders, but I still caught a tightness in his jaw.

"Kennedy, it's not like I know everything that's going on in Time Peace," he began. "But if there was something you needed to know—"

Just then, Randy slipped up behind me and I felt my back pocket lighten. I spun on my heels and saw him waving my wallet. He was holding it tauntingly, but without the usual grin to match. Instead, his lips were twisted into a snarl.

"What are you doing?" I hissed at him. I snatched at my wallet, but Randy held it just beyond my reach. He stepped backwards and easily mounted one of the ATVs. With a quick twist of the throttle, he was off. I could just catch a glimpse of him stuffing my wallet into his own pocket before the swaying grass swept him from view.

He spun the vehicle around expertly, his upper body reappearing to loom over the green tufts.

"What are you waiting for?" he called out.

"Randy, what are you doing?" David asked tiredly.

"He wants his stuff back, he's going to have to catch it," Randy stated plainly. To me, he barked, "Get on the ATV."

"This is a lesson," Blake muttered to me. His frown deepened at the deteriorating situation.

"Okay, fine," I said. I was sick of being jerked around by these two. David knew more than he was letting on and I wasn't going to let Randy bail him out.

I leapt onto one of the ATVs. As soon as it rumbled to life, I gave the throttle a test twist, and shot off faster than I expected. I barely clung on long enough to point the wheels towards Randy. He was already speeding away with a delighted smirk splashed across his face.

I twisted the throttle again, catching up to him. I aimed straight for him. But suddenly, he wasn't there. He had zipped aside with incredible ease and speed—faster than I could track while keeping an eye on the ground whizzing past.

I tried to turn after him, but I could feel the machine start to tip. I reversed sharply and it threatened to tip the other way. I pulled the machine back under control, but I had lost Randy.

Slowing and holding a steady course, I glanced around. I saw him to my right. I turned towards him, this time smoothly. But I paid a price for my control. Randy, who was watching me this entire time, zipped out of the way once again.

"Almost!" he taunted. I hadn't been anywhere near him.

He led me in a game of cat-and-mouse, and I quickly realized how right Blake had been. Each move he made was just a little bit more difficult for me to follow, giving me plenty of time to get used to the machine. I was picking up more little tricks as we went on.

I felt a heat rising inside me, but I suppressed it. *Let him teach me*, I told myself. He was just making it easier for me.

Finally, I swerved in on him aggressively again. He dodged, of course, but this time I didn't let up. I turned in sharply, barely keeping the wheels on the ground. Randy looked irritated, but not stressed. His student was misbehaving.

I tried to cut him off again, but he vanished. I glanced around fitfully, finally spotting him over my shoulder. He was right on my tail. He wasn't just proving his superior driving skills; he was playing defensively.

He underestimated my resolve.

I let go with one hand and slapped the middle crown of my time gauge. Immediately, a black dome descended on the field, trapping Randy and I inside our little racetrack.

Randy's head shot around. By the time he had pulled his eyes back from the blooming blackness, and towards his target (a mere split-second), I was already making my move. Before my better instincts could protest the absurd idea, I had placed my right shoe on the seat, and turned back.

I locked eyes with Randy. His widened in surprise as realization dawned.

I released the handles and pushed off. I didn't get a chance to see what happened with Randy. I hadn't leapt cleanly. My ATV swerved and tumbled.

I landed brutally a second before and the machine tumbled over me. The burning engine pressed heavily into my exposed skin,

melting through the surface. But even through the pain and my spinning head, I had enough presence of mind to hit the middle crown again.

In a snap, I was back on my ATV. Randy was quicker to tear his eyes from the dome, even as his mind was slowed slightly by processing my plan. In contrast, I was quicker to make my leap. I dove clumsily from my ATV and hung terrifyingly in the air for a second. Rushing ground below, a sprinting monster ahead.

Randy, on instinct, swerved out of the way. I was doomed to slam into the rushing ground beneath me. I hit as my fingers found my watch again.

On my ATV, my limbs shook. But it wasn't from the rough terrain. The pain from each jump could be erased alongside any physical injury, but a different scar persisted.

I grunted, exhaling my terror, and hit the watch again. I didn't wait for the shakes this time. I jumped again.

Once more I hung between the four-wheelers, the ground whizzing violently below. Once more our eyes locked.

Randy glared in outrage. He saw the trap he had been forced into. If I couldn't reset the arena; he'd have to. Randy was sick, but not a psycho. He couldn't let me be seriously injured or killed. But resetting would lead us right back here, where I would just jump again. So he had to let me land. When I came up with it, I couldn't have laid it out that clearly, it was just a wild idea. A gut feeling. But that didn't stop Randy from glaring, and I could understand his seething resentment.

"You didn't beat me through skill," his eyes said. And if we had still been in the woods, shooting paint at each other, I wouldn't have cared. But hanging in midair, in that millisecond, some self-loathing crept in through the adrenaline.

And before that thought could linger, I landed. I immediately grabbed on to Randy's shirt. My body hit the front of the ATV, but as I slid, my grip pulled Randy's arm to the side. He fought to keep the ATV from tipping. I splayed to the side, my feet finding themselves planted against the flank of the vehicle. Now it was Randy holding onto me. He pulled at my shirt as I dangled off to the right.

He heaved the four-wheeler in a turn to the left, pulling me away from the ground, and pointing it towards the wall of the arena. He drove through it and the dome vanished, folding in on itself at a point in the middle of the sky. He had me. I couldn't reset, and I was at his mercy.

But I couldn't go quietly. On another wild whim, I grabbed at Randy's wrist.

"What—?" I could hear him start, but I had already found the clasp and clip of his time gauge. Randy was stuck with one hand on the handles of the ATV, and one holding me up. He slowed, but I had enough time to unclasp the metal bands and release the rubber strip strapping his watch to his arm.

As soon as the four-wheeler reached a crawl, I forced myself free and fell hard into the tall grass. Randy was off his mount in a heartbeat, and I was on my feet a second later.

"What do you say we trade?" I suggested even as I slipped into a fighting stance, holding the watch behind me.

Randy casually adjusted his footing before scoffing. "Forget that. Take it. Like this."

And in a blink, his relaxed crouch exploded into a frontal assault. He had covered half of the ground between us before my coiled muscles could react. But at long last, this one time, I was fast enough.

I didn't retreat, I didn't turn and run. With as little movement as possible, I tossed Randy's time gauge at his face and twisted aside.

Randy's arms shot up in surprise and lightning-fast reflexes. He caught it without breaking stride, even pointing his elbows towards me for a sharper impact. But I wasn't there.

His legs caught on mine as I twisted around. He stumbled, hit the dirt with his knees, breaking his fall before he could sprawl out helplessly. In a moment he twisted back, reaching out to try and grab me, but I had already darted in and slipped back out.

"Like that?" I asked, tightly gripping the prize I had snatched from his pocket.

He stared at my repossessed wallet for a moment, apparently trying on different emotions to see which best fit.

"Fair trade?" I suggested again, a little more hesitantly. Randy could still spring up and knock my teeth out if he wanted to. But after a tense moment, I could have sworn I heard an amused chuckle start to bubble up, about to burst into a belly laugh.

But it was cut short.

"What is wrong with you?" David shouted at me. He grabbed my wrist with the time gauge and held it up in front of my face. "This is not a toy!"

"I wasn't playing," I countered, the peace within me dissolving. My jaw set, but I said calmly, "I don't know what you're getting at, but I know for a fact there's more going on here."

"I'm not lying," David replied, some of his own calm starting to return. He put a hand on my shoulder. But his mood was still ragged. "But Kennedy, you're just a trainee. There are things you aren't qualified to know."

"Fine," I said coldly, and pried David's hand off of me. "You don't have to tell me. But I don't have to keep doing this. Forget the trainee, operative, whatever thing."

"You're just going to quit?" David asked incredulously.

"I'll put it on pause at the very least," I retorted. "You want an agent; I want some information. Fair trade?"

"Oh don't be such a baby," Randy said. "You signed up for this. You—"

"I didn't sign up for my mind getting scrambled!" I suddenly snapped at him. "You—Time Peace—were the ones that brought me through the time gate and did this to me!"

I pointed directly at my eyes, obscured by the dark lenses. They didn't react. I took a deep breath and forced my voice calm.

"Or is there more to the story?" I asked again.

David looked away. A pained, frustrated expression had developed on his face, and his breathing was a little shallow.

"So what?" Randy spat. "You just think you're going to lounge around on Aechyr? You're here because of Time Peace."

"I got here because I ran away from home," I replied. "I can handle being on my own again."

"Kennedy," Blake said softly.

"Forget it. If they want to talk, they know where to find me," I said. I waited a moment, but when even Randy seemed to have run out of taunts, I took a step back and turned to leave.

If anything good came out of my confrontation with David, it was that it distracted me from the mixed emotions as my outing with Scarlett and friends drew nearer. Normally, I would have spent too much time sweating it. But Saturday afternoon came before I knew it, and I only had to be a nervous wreck during the trip over to the capitol market.

Of the many traditions Aechrians proudly held onto, it seemed the open-air marketplace was one of them. But it hadn't just been left alone. It had been expanded and modernized while clinging to the spirit of the original agora.

I heard Scarlett's voice as I waded uncomfortably through the sea of people. "Kennedy, over here." I craned around, peeking through a passing crowd and saw her next to her friends.

I lifted a hand in greeting and tried to smile as naturally as I could. Before I knew it, Isiah had grabbed me and was introducing or re-introducing me to Denisha, Michael, and some others whose names slipped through my mind in the blur of activity. It was a few minutes before the group turned in on itself, chatting about plans. Only then did I get a chance to say hi to Scarlett.

"How's it going?" I asked.

"Hanging in there," she replied. I couldn't quite tell how serious she was being. "You?"

"Every day I die a little inside," I lied. I mean, I thought I lied. I said it like a joke, anyway, but I had no idea what prompted me to say something like that.

Scarlett laughed anyway. Just like when she answered my innocuous question, I couldn't quite tell what her laugh meant—if she was laughing at a perceived joke or reacting in sympathy. If she meant "that's so funny" or "I feel that." Maybe both.

"What would you say to a bite to eat while we head out? Something life-affirming should cure you," she suggested, again in that tone of either imperceptible irony or secret sincerity.

"Couldn't hurt. Lead the way," I said, relaxing despite myself.

We walked down the snake-like street. It began dotted with booths, but a quarter of the way in, it blossomed. The street widened into a plaza, fountains arced water through the air, and on all sides, rising like giant steps, were three levels of shops and amusements. It felt like standing in the middle of a large amphitheater, or a coliseum.

I gaped at it all, trying to take it in.

Scarlett smiled broadly. "Well, come on," she said. "You won't see any of it if you stand here gawking all day."

"This is a monster? It looks like a ghost," I said as I polished off my lamb wrap. We were standing in front of a display in a cramped little store, which smelled an awful lot like incense. Somewhere deeper within, the rest of our little party had gotten lost looking at costumes. The display in front of us had two mannequins, one covered in a white sheet, and the other in a black one.

"A white sheet is a ghost, a black sheet is a monster," Scarlett explained simply.

"I thought monsters were like werewolves and vampires," I replied, positive that I had the right definition of the word.

"Well, those are monsters, but these are *monsters*," Scarlett said unhelpfully, gesturing at the black sheet.

"I don't get it."

"I guess it's an Aechrian thing," she mused. "It's kind of like if you saw a floating white translucent Abraham Lincoln, you'd say that's a ghost, right? But so is someone in a white sheet. There's the basic ghost, and then a specific ghost. A black sheet is a generic monster, but there are also other monsters, like zombies or mummies."

"Sure," I said, not really seeing the point. "Is that really a popular costume?"

"Oh, that's not the whole costume," Scarlett explained more animatedly. "See, if you wear a fun, happy, costume, like a princess or a superhero, you wear the white sheet over it, and if you wear a scary costume, you pick the black sheet. Then, when you show up to a party, you say, 'trick or treat' and everyone there has to guess who's under the sheet."

"Like who I'm dressed up as?" I asked, wondering how in the world anyone would be able to figure that out.

"No, I mean you. The real person under the sheet. The hosts and whoever is there has to guess from your voice. Then, if someone gets it right, you throw back the sheet and show everyone what you're dressed as."

"Mmm, fun," I said, unenthusiastically. I wondered if this would be less awkward or just more obnoxious if I arrived early for the party.

"Don't be such a grump," Scarlett said, lightly jabbing my arm. "It's not that big of a deal. Being around people, I mean."

I stopped and looked at her quizzically.

"Well, you're almost always by yourself," she said, shrugging. "I know it's stupid, but people will start to think you hate everyone."

"I don't hate anyone," I said immediately. Though that wasn't entirely true. Sainne came to mind, but I didn't hate anyone on campus. Not even the Charmies. I didn't like them, but Avery was alright, I guess. I didn't hate them, I just wanted to avoid them.

"I believe you," Scarlett said sincerely. "Some people just think it's strange you're always by yourself, even if it isn't. I know from experience."

"I hang out with Blake," I muttered. "Quincy, I guess, too."

"Right, it's just you're always jogging around by yourself. We'll see Blake chatting with the physics guys or in a café with Quincy, but—"

"Wait, what?" I asked, snapping my head around.

Scarlett blinked. "Blake and Quincy. Sometimes they meet in the café on Third, studying or something."

I quickly picked up that "something" was the real answer.

"You didn't know?" she asked.

"No," I mumbled. She was looking at me a bit oddly, and I suddenly felt I had to justify that. "That's not the kind of thing we talk about, really. It's not that weird, is it?"

"No," Scarlett said quickly, then stopped, as if catching herself.. "Well, maybe. But if that's what works, then who cares what everyone else thinks?"

"Yeah," I said. Still, a knot in my stomach refused to loosen.

"But," Scarlett said tentatively, "if it would help you to have *someone* to talk to about those things... we could find someone."

"I—" I wanted to acknowledge what she was saying, but I couldn't. It was all too locked away. No, it was barricaded. Barricaded against the awful possibilities that could come spilling in if I opened up.

"Take a look at this," Scarlett said softly, and gently led me to a new display. A series of masquerade masks were on four racks. Each rack had a series of slightly different, but similarly styled masks.

"For the Crystal Ball," Scarlett explained. "It's tradition to pick one that represents a native Aechrian monster. So, if you had to pick one…"

She glanced over the four. Her hand hovered for a moment over the masks on the first rack. Their noses were tipped black like a dog's, and the upper cheeks seemed to curl upwards, as if it anticipated the wearer to smile broadly.

"This is the Lyarch," Scarlett explained. Her voice was distant, like she was recounting half-remembered childhood stories. "Two mouths and six legs. One mouth speaks human language and the other is for singing. It howls a song which lures travelers without purpose into a river where it drowns them. The lesser hunts in packs, while the truly powerful hunts alone. Mmm, not quite right for you.

"Then there's the Rawbeak," she went on, pointing to the next group of masks. These had sharp, pointed noses, and decorative false eyes above and below the eye slits. "A giant, proud bird the size of a man with six eyes and four legs. It walks like a dog but flies like a hawk. It sees the lies that stick to you, no matter how old. Liars are its favorite prey. I don't think that fits, either.

"The Silent Maw," she continued, pointing to a mask with heavy black around the eyes and decorative thread hanging down from the bottom. "Half-racoon, half-fox, it can turn invisible and weave anything into a spell circle. There's a spider living in its mouth that spins the thread. It gets wrapped around the Maw's snout, nearly sealing it. But the Silent Maw feeds on stolen dreams, not on physical sustenance. And that's definitely not right.

"But I think this…" her hand flittered about through the final row. The masks here were slightly larger, and flourishes like curved horns dominated either side of the eyes. "I think this fits. You could be the Iron Mosk."

She held the mask up to my face and turned her head side to side. It wouldn't sit well with my sunglasses already perched on my nose, and it must have looked funny to see glossy black instead of eyes behind the mask. But with it held an inch out, there wasn't any discomfort, and Scarlett didn't seem put off, either.

"Yes, I think so," she said, handing it to me.

"What's the Mosk?" I asked, flipping the mask back over to examine it closer.

"Half bison, half man, kind of like a minotaur. Its horns and its hooves are made of unbreakable iron, and its footsteps burn cold fire. Once it chooses its prey, it never gives up the chase, though on occasion they can be bargained with. A deal with an Iron Mosk, though, is dangerous, as no trickery works against them. They only acknowledge the spirit of the agreement, not the letter of the law. The only thing that soothes them is gentle music under the light of a full moon. Usually a fiddle, but sometimes, the voice of a young woman works too."

I looked up into Scarlett's eyes. I placed the mask over my face. I could see she now held a Silent Maw's mask over her own.

"What might you say?" Scarlett asked soothingly. "If you had someone to tell a secret to, what might you say?"

The thin paper mask somehow eased everything. It was a bridge, a gate out of my barricade. When I spoke, it wasn't me, but it was this creature. The Iron Mosk.

"I might say... I don't know what I'm doing," I admitted. I wasn't thinking of what the words meant, they just flowed forth.

"How so?" Scarlett, the Silent Maw, asked kindly.

"I've put a wedge between me and... not quite friends. Associates, I guess. I think they're lying to me, but I might have gone too far. And now I might not even be at this school much longer. And I don't know what to do about it. Really, what to do with my life."

Scarlett paused, taking that in. Thinking.

"Do you *know* if they're lying?" she finally asked.

"I don't know anything," I admitted. "It's complicated, and I'm not allowed to tell."

"Do you believe they're lying?" she rephrased.

"Yes," I said firmly.

"If you have nothing else to grab onto, then I'd say grab onto that until you know," she suggested slowly. "If you have to fight yourself and the world, you're already doomed. Later, if you're wrong, you can always change your mind."

I nodded, but words were only so much comfort.

Scarlett considered me quietly. Her eyes showed pained sympathy. She lowered her mask and bit her lip, looking away. I slowly pulled mine from my face. The silence ate at me, and I had to cut it short.

"Say," I asked abruptly, "I've been wondering. How come everyone here can immediately tell I'm American?"

Scarlett suddenly stifled a laugh. "It's the accent," she explained simply.

"I don't have an accent," I protested. "You don't have an accent."

"Of course I do," she said, fighting back the laugh. "You really can't hear it?"

"You don't have an accent," I insisted blandly.

"You're the one with an accent," she poked back. "I can hear it every time you talk—it's your *O*'s. That is not how Aechrians talk."

"You're making this up."

"You asked me how we could tell," Scarlett protested.

"And now you're lying to me. I must have a star-spangled banner tattooed to my forehead, because I do not have an accent."

"Now you're really being bullheaded."

I held the Iron Mosk up again and snorted comedically. My stomach did a somersault as Scarlett burst out laughing. I pulled off the mask, re-examining it.

"So what even is this Crystal Ball thing, anyway?" I asked lightly.

"Well traditionally, it's a dance," Scarlett answered, stifling her giggles. "But it's a full-on party these nights. It's on November Ninth, the supposed anniversary of when Prince Alexander the First won his first victory against the monsters of the island. After the battle, a wise woman prophesied he would found the country—be the first person to tame the island. You know, silly superstition. But it's the symbolism that matters. It's a psychological safety net, I think."

"Like the royalty?" I asked.

"I suppose," Scarlett said, a little less enthusiastically. Then she shook her head. "But those symbols have people behind them. And people... well, there's a reason I, too, need a break from people every once and a while." Then she said, with a twinkle in her eye, "But we were talking about a masquerade."

I felt a twinge in my stomach. It was the moment, I immediately knew. And I almost let it slip by. But before my worse instincts would let me, I reached for the mask. Scarlett mirrored my move.

"About the Crystal Ball," I began from behind the Iron Mosk. "People usually have dates, right?"

"Yes," Scarlett said, very calmly.

My mouth felt dry. "Have you—"

"Not yet."

"Would you—"

"Wait," she said, and pulled off her mask. "Now ask."

I lowered my own mask.

"Would you go to the Crystal Ball with me?"

"Sure," she said, still smiling that soft, small smile. "Sounds like fun."

VII

White Rabbit at Iterant Point

The spectral image of Becker danced over the passing students. Inside, they could hardly have noticed the pale reflection. If they wanted to watch the senator, all they had do was look out and across into the dining hall in the opposite building. They would be able to see the TV itself, playing the public channel's broadcast of Becker's speech. But from the sunken stairs between the two buildings, I only got the mirrored image.

The sky was threatening to drizzle, but the stairway down to the basement levels of the student center was sheltered by a lip bridging the two buildings. I leaned against the wall of the dining side and continued to scan the window of the entryway for the ghostly Sainne. His intangible shape was still recognizable, even cast through one window and reflected on another. But it resisted taking solid form, teasing at becoming the shape I swore had been in my dreams.

"Kennedy," Blake greeted plainly.

I glanced towards the top of the stairs.

"Hey," I said, and turned back to the broadcast.

Blake trudged down a couple steps, then followed my gaze.

"I bet you could find an unfiltered view," he commented.

"Didn't feel like being seen," I replied.

Blake had a point about the view. A corner of the screen was blotted out by the head of a diner. I could just make out the cut of a navy cadet uniform. Inside the dining hall, more cadets were watching the broadcast carefully. Across in the student center, other cadets passed by, but these guys didn't even glance over. They strode out of the building with purpose. They had somewhere to be.

"You're still wearing your watch," Blake observed.

I looked to my time gauge and back to him. He seemed mildly hopeful.

"Safety," I answered ambiguously.

He nodded. And finally, "David wants to see you."

"I'll bet."

"Something new this time. He says you'll get answers."

I tried to read Blake's expression.

"He's said that before," I noted cautiously, but listened.

"This time it's not from him. It's from the white rabbit herself."

I raised a skeptical eyebrow. Blake shrugged. As an ambassador for David, he wasn't exactly selling his case. And as I tried to figure his angle, it finally clicked. Blake was trying to figure mine.

Blake stood against the gray sky, waiting to see what move I'd make. Just over his shoulder, I could make out the bison on top of the southwest pillar, pointing the way for the steadfast cadets. Wild thoughts flitted through my mind as I pondered the two silhouettes.

There were always options.

"Where are we meeting?" I asked at last.

Blake cracked a very slight smile. "Where else would you meet a white rabbit? Time Peace headquarters."

David drove Blake and me into thick woods again. This time, though, Randy would be staying behind to complete whatever work David was missing on the trip. The dark trees thickened around us as the road turned to dirt. It narrowed as we travelled on into the night.

It was only after I felt the last rays of the sun vanish, blotted out by the towering trees, that I saw it in the distance. The alabaster white of the time gate peeked out from between the trees, and a moment later, I saw the blue glow of the strange fluid within.

"Let's keep moving. There are Thetas in here guarding the time gate," David said as we left the car.

"I don't see anyone," Blake noted.

"You wouldn't," David replied. "That's the point."

He stepped forward towards the time gate. This gate wasn't inset into a wall or chunk of rock, but standing upright on its own. One of the ceramic-like rings was partly buried into the dirt, and the other was free to turn if it needed to. But the buried ring was already projecting the flat turquoise surface I had seen

before. We followed until the large glowing opening of the gate ate up our entire field of vision. David held up his wrist and twisted a dial on his time gauge.

The gate's interior swam to life. Once more, the bubble-like structures widened and grew, most shoved to the edges or absorbed by others, until one took up the entirety of the glowing surface. Its interior, already brighter than its edges, had continued to glow warmer and warmer until the hazy pink-gold had melted away all the other hues. The surface surrendered to the expansion and became hazier, almost like fog, threatening to collapse and spill out of the gate, but never doing so. Instead, the faded border invited us to step through, blurring the line between this reality and the next.

David glanced over his shoulder and nodded for us to follow him, and then stepped through. As he walked into the warm light, his sharp outline seemed to distort as well, and he transformed into a blurry silhouette. Within a few steps, he had disappeared entirely.

Although we had done it before, Blake and I still glanced at each other. Each of us was a little unsure, each of us a little hesitant. And each of us deciding not to let that show. Too much.

We stepped forward at the same time. Once in motion, we never broke or slowed our stride. We walked firmly into the waiting ethereal nothingness of the time gate. As before, the glow turned to white as I felt myself become weightless, the ground fading away from under me. I panicked a little as I turned and could only see blank space; Blake was nowhere in sight despite being beside me a moment ago. It was just like before. Would I lose something this time as well?

But before the thought could take root, I saw the circular shape of the exit gate. It cut a harsh shape into the endless white, its borders clearly defined. As it grew close, I felt weight slowly returning to me, and I carefully aimed my feet. Soon, ground was underneath me again, and I had stepped out on the other side.

After the all-encompassing brightness, my eyes felt relieved to see anything else. I glanced to my right and saw that Blake had reappeared as well, apparently at the exact same time as me.

I caught my breath and looked up, only for it to be taken away again. The first time I had arrived at Time Peace's headquarters, I had been blinded, and I spent most of my time in the hospital. This was the first time I got an undistracted look at the place, and boy, I had missed a lot.

The complex was a little city of the future stuffed into a bottle. A huge dome made of deep indigo metal arches and riveted rafters replaced the sky. Enormous octagonal patches dotted across the ceiling looked like they might have been some complicated stained glass of light blues and clear whites. Light beamed in from these massive windows, but where it came from, I wasn't sure. The windows seemed hazed, and the light seemed all-encompassing beyond them.

The sight didn't get any less impressive as my eyes lowered. At the center, the complex rose up to a sphere made of hundreds of little triangles. At first, it seemed to be floating. Looking closer, I could see that the metallic gray ball was held aloft by dozens of thin metal spokes and a squat pillar in the middle. The ground of the entire city extended out from this core in a series of platforms, like a giant concrete snowflake. The further out you went, the spindlier the platforms were, until they were just bridges to the perimeter of the dome.

Here on the edge, a combined set of roadways stretched out like a multi-story highway. Each led to a single time gate embedded in the dome wall and sitting some twenty feet above a gravelly pit which filled the whole place. Below the platforms, more bridges connected the whole place, so big black jeeps and transport trucks could run between any two points in the complex.

"Welcome to Iterant Point," David said mildly.

He hailed an electric transport, boxy except for the tapered front, and we got in. We sped silently through the city, past more shuttles and bustling personnel. Many people we saw were uniformed in black tunics with rank tabs. All of the activity was carried out with a sense of purpose, but not pressure. It was a great garden of girders, steel, and knowledge, calming and enlightening those who visited. A reflecting pool of aluminum.

I was torn from my thoughts by a familiar sight. Stretching five stories into the air, it was an arced glass building, topped with a golden sign reading Square One Medical Center. We pulled up to it on a roundabout, which was shielded by a large overhang. As we stepped out of the car, I saw a huge golden mural of cherubim and angels painted on it, watching over us as we walked to the entryway.

Inside, a semi-circular entrance hall reached up all five stories. Curving ramps lined every floor, each leading to the next. Directly across the marbled floor from us, there were a series of glass elevators stretching down a large hallway. We passed by several interactive displays and a couple of help desks, underneath a gigantic chandelier hanging far, far above us on our way there.

"Slow day?" Blake asked to David as we reached the nearly empty elevator hall. The massive structure felt decidedly emptier than it should have been. Only a dozen or so people were wandering about the foyer. Each of their voices and footsteps echoed impressively, barely masked by the size of the room and the bubbling of small fountains running along the inner walls.

"Thankfully," David said. He glanced towards a large clock hanging two stories above us at the end of the elevator hall. With a jolt, I realized it was actually the Time Peace logo, but with moving hands.

"It usually gets busier in an hour or two," David continued as we stepped into one of the elevators. "Visiting hours," he explained.

The doors behind us slid open after we reached the fourth floor. Blake and I turned and followed David out and down the hallways until we found ourselves in a warmly decorated waiting room filled with plush chairs. David walked up to the receptionist, a woman with blonde curly hair in an old-fashioned nurse's outfit blowing pink bubbles with her gum.

"Heya, Kate," David smiled at her. "Is our room ready?"

Kate seemed entirely unmoved by the greeting, her heavily shadowed eyes still half-closed in apathy. I noticed a small silver *K* on her uniform. All the medical staff had *K*'s, I recalled. What was that symbol for? Kappa? Yeah, that was it. Medical was Kappa.

Just as David was beginning to pry some conversation out of Kate, Blake elbowed me in the ribs. I looked over, wincing in pain, only for Blake to give me an "act casual" look. I tried my best while rubbing the painful spot where he had hit me but didn't see the big deal at first. He jerked his head towards one of the comfy-looking armchairs.

There was a bald man in the chair, holding a book in his left hand as he waited, and at first, I didn't notice anything. Then, without warning, his right arm shot out in a burst of motion, extending as if drawing a pistol and taking aim. The man hardly seemed to notice, save for a twitch in his eyebrow. Then his arm relaxed and fell back to his side. Suddenly, it sprang up again, in the exact same motion, identical in every way. His lip twitched this time, and I thought his expression looked pained behind his forced calm. The impression was only strengthened when his arm shot out a third time.

"Come on," David said, snapping us both from our spying on the man. "This way."

As he led us down the hallway, I finally asked, "Why are we at the medical center anyway?"

"For your records," David explained simply. "They have a lot of the answers you're looking for. Along with your white rabbit."

He held out his hand towards a door.

"Are you not coming with?" I inquired.

He shook his head. "You don't need me in there. Besides, I've got some other things to take care of."

Whatever they were, he clearly wasn't looking forward to them. I nodded to him curtly and walked to the door. Putting my hand on the handle, I took a breath, then opened it. Inside, sitting on one of the three chairs of the office, was the white-haired girl Blake and I had met on a rainy day so long ago.

"Hello, stranger," she greeted us casually. "I hear you've just been dying to talk to me."

It felt surreal. There she was, dressed all in black, but capless this time. She also had a silver Omega pin on the high neck of her shirt. Omega. The big O. The end. It was the symbol of our last resort. Of whom we would turn to when all was lost. I walked in, Blake following right behind.

"You're the white rabbit?" I asked as the door shut behind us.

"White Rabbit I am," she said. "White Rabbit the Twelfth."

"The Twelfth?" Blake asked, startled.

"Yup. There are another eleven of me walking around Iterant Point."

"You're kidding."

"No way. I'm from the future, remember? Jumped back in meta-time to prevent an Anarakian victory. So have another ten versions of me. Add on top of that the original version, who in this meta-timeline, hasn't had to jump back at all (yet), and that makes me number twelve in this place."

"Are you saying Time Peace lost in eleven other meta-timelines?"

"No, I'm saying they *nearly* lost in *at least* eleven other meta-timelines."

"Is Time Peace that outnumbered?" Blake asked, horrified.

"Come on, think a little," White Rabbit scoffed. "We're not including the times Anarakia has used their own rabbit holes. Or Time Peace's other white rabbits, I suppose. Point is, the win-loss is probably around 1-2."

"Oh, so nothing that bad, then," Blake said sarcastically.

"Exactly," she replied, either missing or ignoring Blake's scathing tone. "Clearly, it would be much worse if it was just a numbers game. By the way, I hope that you appreciate all this. This is at least Class 3 information."

"Good to know," I interjected. "What would be really great to know would be the truth. The whole truth."

"About what?" White Rabbit asked coyly.

"You know what," I pressed, resisting the urge to pace. "You came to recruit us specifically."

"Well, obviously, I recruited you. Duh," she said with a wave of her hand.

"So we were right," I said excitedly. "I have been remembering a past meta-timeline."

White Rabbit shrugged. "Probably. Weird, but probably. You'll have to ask the Psi's about that. And yeah, you were agents before. You bet I recruited you again."

"But why? Why did you come back just for us?"

"Oh come, come, come," she chided. "I didn't go through the rabbit hole for you two. I came back to fry bigger fish. Don't ask. It's Temporal Factors stuff, and you're not wheedling that out of me. You two just happened to be in the neighborhood, and you hadn't been recruited yet in this meta-timeline. I was killing two birds with one stone. Sorry you don't get approached by chicks that much, but it really was only a convenience on my part, nothing special, nothing personal."

She adjusted her positions slightly, now looking a bit embarrassed, but apparently trying to hide it. "Actually, I do owe you a tiny apology. Like I said, what I do is Class 2 from the start. So even if all I do is say hi to you cats, it's wrapped up tight." She shrugged ironically. "You try to do someone a solid, and the system locks away their whole story. My bad."

I was flabbergasted. "That—but—but what about that Director Sainne? He blinded me! There has to be a reason that he did that!"

For the first time, White Rabbit dropped the sarcastic act. Instead, she looked at me pityingly. "You bet there is. You saw him during a battle?"

"Yeah," I promptly agreed.

"Well, to be frank, you were a good soldier, but it was mostly coincidence. That device Director Sainne was using? That's a Talhesian torture device."

"A what?" Blake interjected.

White Rabbit winced. "You know how an ATEP stun gun or crystal ray works?" We nodded tentatively. She continued,

"Same principle, much crueler. Instead of finding the right frequency to stun someone with, it loops time until it finds the right pattern to inflict the max pain with the least damage. It's Sainne's favorite form of interrogation. To be frank, he was probably going from soldier to soldier, extracting as much information as possible. You were unfortunate enough to be in his way."

"No, no that's not right," I insisted. "I was in the middle of the battlefield. There were still soldiers up and running around."

White Rabbit shook her head. "Kennedy, you know your dreams have some details jumbled up. It's no surprise what with the trauma and all. Plus how you're remembering stuff from a whole 'nother meta-timeline."

"No. That doesn't make sense. If Sainne was using this device, then how come he blinded me? You said it was supposed to minimize damage!"

"Sainne wouldn't consider blinding you to be damage," she grimaced. "As long as you could still think and speak, he wouldn't even notice. If he did, he'd think it was funny."

"But this Talhesian torture device," Blake said graspingly. "How could it affect Kennedy in another meta-timeline?"

"It's future tech," White Rabbit replied simply. "It's designed to torment the Timeless. Kill them if necessary. It can alter the information pattern that time gates recognize as 'you,' so that as soon as you enter them, any injuries inflicted in previous meta-timelines are carried over. Probably why you have the dreams in the first place. It's a very nasty weapon. We're lucky they're so rare. Sainne has the only one we've confirmed so far. Sorry, Kennedy, but you just happened to have crossed a particularly sick cat."

"You're lying!" I shouted abruptly. Immediately, White Rabbit became frosty. Her hard eyes watched me as I approached, fists clenched. "You could have told me all of this before! You're lying again!"

"What am I lying about?" White Rabbit asked coldly. "I told you why it was classified."

"You aren't telling me anything! You're just covering it up again!" I accused.

"Kennedy," Blake cautioned, "cool it."

"She's lying to me!" I shouted towards Blake.

"All of this was Class 2 and you haven't even finished training. I'm doing you a favor by telling you any of this. We're trying to make up for this even after your tantrum."

"You—"

"And you're still throwing one," White Rabbit observed, refusing to rise from her chair. She still held her relaxed pose, but her muscles were taut. I suddenly realized I was looming over her, hands gripped on either arm of her chair, knuckles white.

A horrible cold feeling clutched my stomach and crawled up my skin. I held my face neutral but recoiled in disgust at myself. I couldn't let myself show my self-hatred at that moment, I was still half-convinced there was more to the story. But I couldn't form the words. My mouth opened and closed twice.

"Tell me there was more to it than that," I finally asked weakly. "Tell me it was more than just chance."

White Rabbit slowly relaxed but remained silent.

I sank into one of the chairs. I couldn't believe this. My head fell into my hands.

"What did you expect to hear?" she asked quietly.

"I don't know," I confessed. "I guess I just hoped... I had hoped for something. Some reason."

From the corner of my eye, I saw her shake her head slowly. "All Time Peace has is the mission. If you wanted something more than that, sorry, but that's up to you. It's not going to just get handed to you on a silver platter. You want meaning? That's on you."

I clenched my fingers behind my head. I didn't need to hear this now. I had pushed ahead so pig-headedly convinced there was a big secret behind it all, and instead, there was nothing. Mere happenstance.

Someone else entered the room, dropped something off, and then shut the door as they left.

"Here's your file if you want to look at it," White Rabbit said. "The Psi's reports are in there. They'll back up everything I've said."

I took the file numbly. I stared at it but didn't process any of the words. My eyes glazed over the same sentences again and again, none of the jargon reaching my brain.

"So," Blake said awkwardly, switching to an academic comfort zone, "do white rabbits—Omegas—have to see the Psi's? I mean, does rabbit hole travel have any psychological side-effects?"

"Not if you're prepared. A little treatment and you're fine," White Rabbit replied. "The travel itself isn't psychologically damaging. It's not like doing a *Groundhog Day*."

"Pardon?"

"*Groundhog Day*. Trapping yourself in an arena loop. How do you not get that? Are you really that uncultured?"

My brain locked. A domino tipped.

"What's your name?" I asked.

"Hmm?" White Rabbit asked, glancing back towards me.

"Your name," I repeated. "What is it?"

"Now, now," she teased, "I don't know you that well. And no angling for Class 3 information."

The domino fell.

"What was the name you gave us?" I sat up. "When you recruited us, what did you say your name was?"

She stared at me blankly for a moment. The next domino was struck.

I rose to my feet again. My anger was cold in my veins this time.

"What did you call yourself?" I repeated.

Blake was suddenly looking skeptical as well.

"I don't remember," she said with an attempt at her usual casual attitude.

"You told us a name, what was it?" I demanded, but I didn't wait for her to give an excuse. The dominoes were all toppling over. "You're not the same White Rabbit, are you?"

Her expression hardened, and it told me everything I needed to know.

"Where is she?" I asked quietly.

The door clicked open behind me again. At first I didn't turn, but after noticing the amazed expression on Blake's face, I glanced back.

A powerful-looking Asian man, around thirty-five years of age, stood framed in the doorway. His sharply maintained black hair matched his crisp black uniform. Slight brass bars on his shoulders glinted, as did a stylized letter A on the neck of his outfit. A single long, rectangular gold bar was placed prominently on his chest. Top rank, Class 1 access.

The Hawk's energetic eyes looked across the scene, just barely softening his stern features.

"Mr. Anthony, Twelve, would you mind giving Mr. Frost and me some room?" he asked.

Blake nodded, and White Rabbit casually slid to her feet. A moment later, and The Hawk and I were all alone in the room, which suddenly felt much smaller.

"Sit down," he requested calmly, gesturing to the chair I had just vacated, as he took one behind the desk. I didn't move. When he looked up, he gestured again. "Please," he said.

I hesitated a moment, but finally did as he asked, pulling the chair up to the other side of the desk.

"So," The Hawk said, still calmly, "you have some issues with Time Peace."

"You lied," I stated.

"Yes," he answered plainly. I was taken aback, suddenly struck off-course from the rant building up inside me. The Hawk continued before I could reassess. "And I'm not going to give you the answers you want."

"Why not?" I managed to ask.

"We deal in time travel, Kennedy. Can you not think of a reason why I would withhold information?"

I stared at him a moment, not quite sure what he meant. But as I slowly worked over the question, one thing did come to mind. I mulled it over and over again, not quite believing what he was suggesting. But it fit.

"If you told me, it would change the future?" I half-asked, half-suggested. "But you can't know the future of this meta-timeline, can you?"

It was his turn to stare at me.

"You have a guess," I figured, working it out aloud. "You're hoping things turn out a certain way."

"That is one possibility," The Hawk replied ambiguously. "As I said, I can't give you the answers you want. You're at a personal flashpoint. You've suggested that you would like to leave Time Peace, and I'm sure you're capable of finding your own path. We won't stop you. We won't chase you. But I don't think that's what you really want."

"No?" I asked, bristling slightly. "How do you figure that?"

"I think there are two very compelling reasons for you to stay," he explained. "First, Director Sainne. You hate him enough to have torn through half of Time Peace looking for answers about him. If you abandon your commission, you'll be abandoning your best shot at him."

I didn't say anything.

"Second," The Hawk continued, "you want direction. You want something concrete. And if you've taken to Aechyr as much as I suspect you have, then you'll want to finish your mission."

"What mission?" I scoffed. "Blake and I are just trainees, remember?"

"Yes, Omicron trainees," he agreed. "And yet, you've taken to Mr. Greene's—David's—unscheduled, unsanctioned, and unofficial Delta training with gusto."

I glanced up, semi-guiltily, but I thought I saw the barest of smiles cross his lips.

"Aside from the drive and desire that suggests, it also helps justify your candidacy for this." He pulled out another folder and placed it on the desk, but held the tips of his fingers on it, holding it away from me. "While Dark Eye Squadron—your team—is in a convenient position to act on this, many of my staff think it a leap of faith to entrust you with it. But as always, Time Peace is short on available personnel. Yours is the only team in the area ready to deploy. If you are a team."

"What is it?" I asked cautiously.

"The alternate identity of one Princess Sophia," The Hawk said. This time, he really did smile at the evident surprise, maybe even eagerness, on my face.

"You know who she is?"

"We will, if this data is retrieved," The Hawk replied. "Our observers and researchers have discovered an anomaly. With a potential succession crisis on their hands, the Aechrian government has scrambled to retrieve all the data they have on the royal family, and especially the Princess. And yet, in the rush, it seems this data drive never finished its move. Overlooked in the chaos, perhaps. As I said, your team is uniquely positioned to retrieve it."

"Really? Why?" I asked, reaching for the file.

The Hawk pulled it back an inch. "This time, the answers aren't so easy. This time, I need a commitment from you. Make no mistake, this is crucial information. If I am to trust you with it, I need something in return."

"What?" I asked suspiciously.

"You promise to complete your training, you agree to follow orders, and of course, you are sworn to secrecy with the information granted to you."

I thought about it carefully.

"You're still not going to tell me anything about my past?" I asked.

"No," The Hawk said. "I will say that I won't lie to you any more than absolutely necessary, but I know that you have no reason to take that seriously."

"You can say that again," I mumbled. Still, he had played me well. I was interested in the contents of that file. I had a hunger to see this thing through, and while I couldn't explain why, I still had to.

"If I finish my training," I said tentatively, "what if I quit afterwards?"

"I would be disappointed," The Hawk replied, "and we do require a year's service after training. But I have to confess, we don't have much of a way to enforce that. As determined as you are, I'm sure you would have no trouble finding a way out."

I wasn't sure I believed him about that last part. But it was good enough. An escape plan.

"Fine," I said. "You've got a deal."

"Glad to hear it," The Hawk said seriously, and then slid the file over to me. "You'll find everything you need in here. I suggest handing it to David. He still is team leader after all."

I had already opened the file and was skimming over it. I noticed a couple words right away.

"The Crystal Ball, sir?" I asked, glancing up as The Hawk was standing to leave.

"Indeed. You'll find the drive is in the same building. As students of Aechyr Academy, you are in prime position to get in with minimal suspicion," he explained. "Is there a problem with that?"

I shook my head. "I look forward to it."

Outside, I met up with Blake, promising to explain everything later, and then we tracked down David. Eventually, he made his way down from the far end of the hallway. I handed him the folder and briefly explained the mission as we rode the elevators back down.

"Real super-spy stuff," Blake said excitedly.

"Dark Eye Squadron's first mission," I agreed happily.

David's head snapped up from the folder. "What did you say?" he asked.

"Dark Eye Squadron," I replied, a little unsure. "That's what The Hawk called our group."

David, who a moment ago had started to relax, grew distant again.

"What? What's wrong with that?" Blake asked.

"Nothing," David muttered in reply. The doors of the elevator opened before him, and he marched towards the exit without looking back. Blake and I hurried after him.

When we hit the fresh air outside, David paused a moment.

"Look," he warned, "don't advertise the whole Dark Eye Squadron thing."

"Why not?" Blake asked. "Sounds cool. We could all get sunglasses to match the theme!"

Disgust flashed across David's face for the first time I could remember, but he spoke calmly. "It's not something to be proud of."

"What do you mean?" I asked.

"I wasn't going to tell you," David admitted, "because frankly, you didn't need to know."

"I'm getting awfully tired of hearing that," I grumbled.

"Not like that," David corrected. "It's not classified. It's not secret. But I didn't see any reason to bring either of you down."

Blake and I exchanged confused looks. David looked frustrated again.

"Dark Eye Squadron is a remedial unit," he spat. "It's where you put the has-beens and losers. The people you want to watch closely, because they're a threat to you almost as much as the enemy. Haven't you noticed? We've got a hot head, a psychopath, and a washed-up wannabe as our crack team. Sorry, Blake, you don't deserve to be saddled with us."

My jaw dropped open, and I glanced from David to Blake, and suddenly a pit in my stomach formed again. I hadn't realized it, but David was right. I had dragged Blake down into a remedial squadron because, no doubt, someone thought he would keep me in line.

"No way," Blake said adamantly. "I don't believe it."

"It's the truth," David said irritably. "Dark Eye Squadron is the black eye on Time Peace's reputation."

"So what?" Blake said. David blinked, unsure of what to make of that. "Dark Eye is just us four right now, right?"

David nodded.

"Then what's the problem? Randy is a jerk, but he's a monster in combat, and an expert in sneaking around. Nothing can stop Kennedy when he sets his mind on it, and in a couple of months, I bet he could even show Randy up. Meanwhile, you've taught us everything we know, doing double training and you're still running circles around us with infiltration and espionage stuff. And even you can't find anything to complain about me, so obviously, I'm good."

Blake finished with a big smile that must have been for show, but it still squeezed a grin from me. His optimism was contagious, and soon, we were both staring David down, waiting for him to tell us that Blake was of course right about all of this. Instead, he just glanced back at the folder.

"This mission is easy enough that we might just have a shot," he finally conceded. "You don't get it yet, Blake. But you're right that we can try this."

David was still shaking his head as he made his way towards the time gate. He didn't notice Blake's expression of intense relief, but I did. I nodded to him and whispered, "Good job. You almost had me believing."

He looked at me a couple of seconds, struggling to say something.

"What?" I asked.

Blake twisted his face up trying to get the words out or decide what to say. Finally, he said, "It's not your fault, Kennedy."

I turned away. "I don't know what you're talking about."

He didn't clarify, but as we stepped towards the glowing gate, I felt the pit in my stomach loosen just a little bit.

VIII

The Crystal Ball

The slender figure slipped out the door. In the dark of the night, her black ensemble was barely visible. Less so as she slipped into the long shadows cast by the moon. Within minutes, she reached the small watery tunnel no one ever entered or paid much attention to. The campus police were also instructed to avoid it, so the figure was the only one to ever visit the damp, concrete underpass.

There, the black car was waiting for her. She slipped off her silk gloves and slid inside. The engine purred to life as if it had been expecting her. A sleek display glowed softly, offering up-to-the-minute traffic data, and the option of automating the usual route. As always, she tapped the decline option. The car recognized her touch and surrendered control to it.

The vehicle crawled quietly from its cave and took its anonymous place among the handful of others that were prowling the streets at this hour. As it entered Thysiopolis, it became even less conspicuous, lost amongst a throng of lights. Even its tinted windows were not so rare as to draw attention, and while sleek, it was not so fashionable as to turn heads.

But soon it left the crowded comfort of the city and took an exit rarely used by the civilian populace. Once more, it found itself on a quiet road, this one bordered by trees. But this time, it wasn't unwatched. The car passed several invisible checkpoints, none of which reacted, all recognizing the authorized traffic.

Only after a mile of this hidden surveillance did a visible checkpoint appear. When the driver pulled up to the stiff marine stationed there, he only needed a cursory glance at her credentials. If it weren't for his default thoroughness, he would have let her through the instant he saw her. There was no chance this was an imposter, and he had become more and more accustomed to her increasingly frequent visits.

Once waved through, it was only a short drive to the Crown Royal Hospital. Though she had unofficially revoked her title and privileges long ago, there was always space reserved for Crown Princess Sophia Phile Tiscardia in the small, private garage. From there, it was only a short elevator ride, one which bypassed much of the hospital administration, to the ward she was looking for.

She knocked softly, and at the sound of a muffled answer, she stepped inside. The room was not as opulent as one would expect. In fact, it looked rather mundane, save for the giant bouquets that were piled against one wall. Sophia's plain black clothes didn't seem as out of place in here, away from the opulence outside.

"Mom," she said, approaching the woman who had aged another twenty years while bedridden.

It took a moment for the Queen's eyes to find the face of her daughter. She smiled weakly. "Sophie. It's been so long."

Sophia kneeled down next to bed. "Mom, I was just here two days ago."

"Mmm," the Queen said. "Yes, but that is so long ago. Each day feels longer and longer."

Sophia couldn't tell whether her mother was being honest or if she was drawing on her deep wells of composure to quickly cover up a momentary weakness.

"How have you been?" the Queen asked, smiling at her daughter. Despite her deteriorating condition, she seemed to glow as she asked it.

"I should be asking you that," Sophia replied, somewhat guiltily.

"Nonsense. I only have a few minutes with you each visit, I want to hear about my daughter. I want to hear something happy."

"Well, you'll have a lot more time soon."

"You're not going to be neglecting your schooling, are you? You've always been adamant—"

"Mom, I can't leave you like this. I'll be here, by your side."

"Don't interrupt, dear. But I'd like that," the Queen smiled again, a little more faintly. "After, will you return to school?"

"No," Sophia replied somberly, fighting back tears at the implication.

"You're doing what you want, aren't you?" the Queen asked with genuine concern.

"Yes, Mom, I am. And I'm coming back. For you, and," she choked a little, "and after."

The Queen patted Sophia's hand. "You'll do fine."

The tears really did start to fall now. "That's not what I'm worried about."

The Queen continued to hold her daughter's hand. "You'll be fine."

***

"Trick or treat!" Blake said enthusiastically from under his black sheet. My own simultaneous greeting wasn't quite as energetic.

We were standing in the entryway to Isiah's spacious apartment. Only a few people were milling about the place so far.

"Well, well," Isiah said, looking us over. "Early birds. And it sounds like at least one new voice, but if I had to guess..."

He pointed towards Blake. "I think I recognize you from Physics. Is it... Blake?"

"Nailed it," Blake said, pulling the black sheet off to reveal his Frankenstein makeup.

"And I know Kennedy," he said to me.

I pulled off my own black sheet to reveal my pirate costume. David had actually done me a solid and ordered a custom shaded monocle I could use. Turning it into an eyepatch, I could see without detracting from the costume. The colored contact in my other eye I had snagged myself. It didn't help me see, but it prevented the uncomfortable gawking I might receive otherwise. Still, keeping the eye bare made me feel a little exposed.

"Man, you made that look easy," I told Isiah.

Isiah laughed. "It's a gift," he said easily. "Now, come on in, join the party. It should really get swinging here in just a couple minutes. You can hang your coverings up over here. Got your names on them? Good."

He led us past the closet and gestured towards one half of the apartment.

"We got snacks over there, music over here, and these are my roommates."

He cordially introduced us to his friends but had to leave us as more people showed up. Slowly, we fell out of the conversations, and as I had anticipated, we found ourselves at the edge of the room, by ourselves. The living room, or whatever room it was, had its furniture all pushed aside or taken somewhere else, leaving the bare wood floor open for dancing, though no one had yet taken to it. Strung about were the usual decorations: pumpkins, bats, strings of orange and white lights, everything you would expect. And on a ledge, a stereo was pumping out suitably spooky tunes.

I tapped my foot nervously, wondering what I should be doing in this situation. Blake was disguising his own nerves by helping himself to the nearby tray of snacks. I quickly copied him, but soon we were just two guys awkwardly munching on chocolate-dipped pretzels.

"So," I said eventually, "what do we even do?"

"Have fun, I guess," Blake said.

"Doing what?"

"Socializing."

"Having fun or socializing, pick one," I countered. Blake laughed, but looking around at the crowd, didn't look much more eager than I was. He fell back on business instead.

"So, have you told her?"

For a moment, I thought about pretending I didn't understand the question. Yeah, fat chance. Our first mission at the Crystal Ball was looming nearer and nearer.

"Well, no," I finally admitted.

"You're setting yourself up for trouble," Blake warned.

"Okay, so what am I supposed to say?" I finally complained. Really, I was just didn't want to admit how hard of a time I was having breaking the news to Scarlett that I would have to leave early.

"You can say what I'm saying," Blake immediately suggested.

"To Quincy?" I asked pointedly.

"Yeah," he said off-handedly. He awkwardly brushed over the fact that he had never mentioned taking Quincy to the ball. I couldn't help but shake my head. He ignored my gesture and barreled forward.

"It'll work better with the two of us anyway. We're supposed to be attending through the school, right? Let's say it's a condition of our suspension that we leave early."

I looked at him with exaggerated skepticism.

"Did you forget that Scarlett's uncle is the dean? There's no way she'd buy that."

"Oh yeah," Blake said thoughtfully. "I suppose you could say Randy fell over drunk and you need to go help him."

"One, I hate Randy," I said. "Two, what's stopping her from coming to help?"

"Now you're just looking for excuses," Blake said dismissively.

Before I could counter, we heard a familiar voice at the door putting on a cackling witch impression. "Trick or treat!" she said from under the giant black veil draped over a pointed hat.

"Always a treat, Scarlett," Isiah replied along with his friends. Scarlett threw back the veil as she blushed slightly to reveal her blue-black costume, which matched the voice she had put on. After a quick hello to everyone, she skittered over to the corner where Blake and I were standing.

"You weren't kidding about beating the crowd," she observed.

"You arrived plenty early yourself," I deflected.

"I'm allowed," Scarlett protested, mock indignant. "I've been through enough of these to be properly over them. You haven't gone through the torment yet."

I couldn't help but grin a little, even as I observed, "You were talking about this tradition like it was a big deal. You never said anything about hating it yourself."

"I guess now you know me a little better," she said. "And speaking of, it's Blake, I take it?"

"That's me," Blake said, shaking Scarlett's extended hand. Scarlett knew his name, of course, but the act was a form of politeness, I supposed.

"I'm Scarlett," she introduced herself.

"I had guessed," Blake grinned, eyes flicking to her hair.

Scarlett rolled her eyes. "Yeah, yeah. I know. Parents must have had a really cruel sense of humor to stick the redhead with the name Scarlett."

"No, I think it's cool," Blake said honestly.

Scarlett smiled, but said, "You haven't lived with it. But thank you."

She glanced around at the guests. A new group had just arrived, and those around the door were tripping over themselves to guess who was who, laughing uproariously among the tangled threads of conversation.

"Is Quincy coming tonight?" Scarlett asked Blake.

Blake shifted uncomfortably. "Uh, no. She's been really busy recently. Working on a project, or something. And she's not really a party person. I think," he added on the end unconvincingly.

"No," I added quickly. "When we were all working in the library, she said something about parties being a waste of time.

And I think she's overworked. She looked exhausted last time she was catching us up."

That was all true, actually, but I would have said it anyway to help ease over Blake's unease. Sure, it was silly, but if Blake wasn't quite comfortable having him and Quincy thought of in the same breath, then I was happy to help cover for him. As it was, I didn't quite know what I would think of all these strangers seeing Scarlett and I together for most of the party. Happy. I should feel happy. Instead, I felt that squirming nervousness in my stomach again.

Scarlett nodded, gracefully taking the cue. "It gets crowded enough at these things; it must be genuinely claustrophobic from her vantage point."

"Hey, I think that's David," Blake said abruptly, indeed spotting our team leader in the entryway. "Think I'm gonna say hi."

And as he slipped past, I exchanged a quick glance with him. We each said a silent "thank you" to the other. Blake soon joined the mob at the front of the apartment, leaving Scarlett and me in that out-of-the-way corner.

She leaned a little closer and asked seriously, "I didn't chase him off, did I?"

"No," I quickly replied. "No, of course not."

"Okay, good," she said. "I didn't want to break up the party."

"Nah, you're fine," I repeated.

She nodded and we fell into silence. I immediately regretted my short answers and dug around for any topic of conversation.

After a moment, I said, "I—"

"Did you—" Scarlett began at the exact same moment.

We laughed. Laughed much harder than the moment deserved. The mutual relief was more easily expressed without words.

"You first," she said.

"I don't even remember what I was going to say," I admitted. "I was just trying to find anything to talk about."

"Well then, what do you say to getting the rounds out of the way first?" Scarlett asked, gesturing to the exuberant crowd. "It'll at least give us something to moan about later."

"First the costume thing, now talking with people, you don't hate everything you insist on doing, do you?" I asked jokingly.

She lightly jabbed my arm while suppressing a smile. "Hate is such a strong word. 'Overexposed to' is much better. Now if we do this quick, we can avoid being overexposed to the crowds. Unless you'd prefer that?"

"Not a chance." I quickly replied. "I *would* hate that."

"Then let's go," she said, and she dragged me into the mess of costumed students.

The faces flashed past in a blur as Scarlett weaved us through the room. I recognized some, like Denisha, rocking the classic vampire look, and Michael, wearing a Santa outfit that he must have thought was ironic or something, but most were new to me. Scarlett, I noticed, was practiced in giving warm greetings to everyone, but detaching quickly, usually by excusing herself to say hi to someone else. I had a vision of her doing this in every student assembly, debate tournament or volunteer group she had naturally been expected to attend. Pretty soon, I was admiring her technique. She had turned social nicety into a defensive shield. Maybe one day I could get her to teach me. Or I could continue hanging out in corners. The latter had always been quite effective for me.

After what felt like an eternity, we had greeted all of her seemingly endless friends and acquaintances, so we took a seat on the windowsill at the back of the living room. Scarlett pulled her legs up and pried off the high-heeled, buckled boots she was wearing.

"Good grief, these things hurt," she said, wincing.

"Then why'd you wear them?" I asked, having genuinely wondered about this masochistic behavior for ages.

"Aesthetics," she replied, elongating the word defiantly. "I took a lot of time to get this costume just right. See?" She held out her arm to show me a carefully crafted bracelet with little charms, like crescent moons and black cats on it.

"Or," and she held up the silver star necklace.

Scarlett was probably about to demonstrate how her skirt was properly ripped when I interrupted, "I see, I see, it's great."

She raised her eyebrow and gave me a look somewhere between skepticism and indignation. I coughed awkwardly and hastily added, "Just seems like a lot of work just for looks."

Now she really did stare at me incredulously, tilting her head while arching that eyebrow even further. "I'm sorry, is that a custom contact in your right eye, mister?"

"That's different," I stated firmly. I knew I had no case, but continued nonetheless. "Piracy is a lifestyle. This is no costume."

"Oh really? Do I need to call the coast guard? Are you going to plunder Isiah's apartment?" Scarlett asked.

"Nah," I said. "Modern piracy is about freedom, not the looting. Besides, not even the navy could stop me. I've already infiltrated this apartment's defenses."

"Well, someone's confident," she replied, amused. "So you really want to be a pirate?"

The question caught me a little off-guard, so I replied automatically, "Yeah. Who doesn't?"

"Probably someone really boring," she conceded. "But tell me something. There are other choices out there. What makes 'pirate' yours?"

"Well, as you know, I do my best work outside the rules," I said, attempting a roguish grin.

She considered me a long moment, cruelly letting my smile wilt. Then she shook her head. "I don't think so."

"Don't think what?" I asked, then quickly tried to recover my pseudo-swagger. "Do you doubt my swashbuckling abilities?"

"I don't think you're nearly as much the rebel as you pretend."

"Really? What part of nearly getting expelled did you miss?"

She rolled her eyes. "Drop the macho thing. You don't pull it off as well as you think. No, I think, and correct me if I'm wrong," she said seriously, "but I think you'd be just as happy sitting inside, thinking and watching the rain."

I shook my head. "I think you got me confused with Blake. He's the brainy one, not me."

"You're not stupid," she said firmly. "I've heard you in class. And that's the second time you've done that."

"Done what?"

"Pretended you were. Back at the dean's, you were joking about getting hit on the head. I can tell you're not dumb, Kennedy. Why do you think you are?"

I turned away. "I don't think I'm dumb."

"Then why do you do it? What do you think?" she asked carefully.

Having turned away, I became uncomfortably aware of how many people were around us. For a few minutes, I had happily forgotten where we were. My poofy pirate shirt suddenly felt much scratchier around the neck.

I could feel Scarlett stir next to me, pondering something. She must have been looking out at the crowd. Maybe wondering why she was here.

"I'd rather be reading while it rains," Scarlett said softly. Her quiet sincere voice drew me back in. "As opposed to half the things we have to do now. I used to do it all the time, just sit inside with a good book. Escapism at its purest. When real life wasn't enough, and as a kid, it's never enough, there was always another time and place to escape to. Nowadays," she laughed lightly, "I fantasize about curling up on the couch again with time to read."

I smiled a little. "I never had something like that," I admitted. "I guess I was too restless to sit still and... indulge."

"So what did you do?"

I ran, I wanted to say. All too often, I just ran. I ran when I couldn't stand being in that house any longer. I prowled through the woods or drifted through the park. I ran to Blake's. I tinkered with things. And then I forgot them.

"You know," I said vaguely, "kid stuff."

Scarlett looked disappointed but didn't push. She glanced out at the party as well, still massaging her feet.

"Nice thing about talking to you," she whispered to me, "no one is rude enough to interrupt. Sometimes, it's nice to be alone in the crowd."

She glanced towards me, but I wasn't sure what she wanted me to say.

After a moment, she seemed to accept that I wasn't going to find words. She shook her head, then stood up, not bothering to put her shoes back on. She turned on her heel and held out a gentle hand toward me.

"Come on," she said.

"What?" I asked, alert.

"Come on," she repeated.

"Where are we going?" I asked.

"Take my hand," she insisted.

I was thinking of protesting again, but those light blue eyes cut short the outburst. Pale, yet warm, an unmistakable signature, uniquely hers.

I cautiously took her hand and rose. She led me, gently but forcefully, towards an open space on the dance floor.

"No way," I immediately objected.

"Just look at me," she said.

"No, I don't dance," I reiterated.

"That's fine," she reassured, or at least tried to. "Let me teach you."

"What, here?" I asked, mortified.

"If not here, then where?" she retorted, a little pompously, as if reciting from one of her favorite books.

"I can survive without learning to dance," I said flatly.

"Kennedy," she sighed, "we're going to the Crystal Ball, aren't we?"

"Well, yeah," I admitted. I suddenly felt another pang of guilt.

She continued with a slight knowing smile. "I know boys hate learning to dance, but—"

"I hate being watched," I explained hastily. "And I do mean hate."

"Kennedy, listen," she said, a little more intently. "You might not be here next semester. If you aren't, you won't have to worry about being embarrassed, you might never see any of us again. But if you don't try, you will always look back and wonder what if, right?"

"I kinda like what-ifs," I mumbled, half-jokingly. Scarlett didn't smile. She continued to look at me with her bright eyes.

"Who doesn't?" she whispered. "But I think now... now I'd rather have memories. And if we look back on it and laugh at ourselves, then that's a good story to tell. You always have to start somewhere, and you can't be ashamed to learn. But, again—"

"You can't look back on what-ifs?" I suggested.

She nodded fervently.

I took a chance. I leaned in a little closer. "Please, let's make this one a good memory," I implored. "Maybe I'm full up on the other kind."

She smiled, gently, but with incredible reassurance. A deep, calming feeling radiating from it. A cautious confidence that promised each step would be its own reward. "Just keep your eyes on me, and we will," she promised.

A little of my anxiety melted away. "Now who's confident?" I teased.

"Don't sass me now," she admonished gently, and began the first steps. I followed clumsily. But after a bit, I managed to ignore

the rest of the room. Soon, my embarrassed mistakes were just another joke in an evening of laughter.

My feet found the floor, and I learned how to dance.

In the next week and a half, I barely had a chance to see Scarlett again. Dark Eye Squadron was preparing for its first mission, and David was monopolizing my time. In one way, it was fortunate that Scarlett was busy too. She was part of a committee for the event that organized something about the student body and the planning of the event. I hadn't quite followed when she hurriedly explained it to me. Her being busy was great in that it meant I didn't have to make excuses for my own inability to make an appearance. It was awful in that it meant I didn't get a chance to explain why my upcoming appearance would be cut short. In that way, it was a serious problem. But David kept us so busy with our own planning that I could hardly consider what I would have said.

As we walked into one of our daily meetings, Blake commented, "Nice suits."

"Check the tags," David instructed as he unpackaged several gadgets. As I looked at the four formal outfits hanging next to each other near the longest wall of David's apartment, I noted they indeed had each of our names on them. Mine was written in red. Blake's was in blue.

"We're not getting color-coded ties, too, are we?" I asked.

"Quick and easy codenames. Get used to them," David explained. "Short, easy to identify over comms, and easy to remember. Mine's 'Green.' For obvious reasons."

I remembered the paintball colors we had used before. "So that makes you Yellow," I said to Randy.

"Gold," Randy corrected with a smirk.

"What makes you so special?" Blake asked.

"How long do you have?" he replied. "You might want to get something to jot it down."

"It's a single syllable," David interrupted. "Also, it doesn't share any vowel sounds with Red, Blue, or Green. You can't mistake it if the comm is unclear."

"That too," Randy said casually as he grabbed his own suit and started trying it on.

Blake and I followed his lead, and soon discovered that these were far from mere formal wear. For one, they were way easier to move in. For another, they had multiple pockets that I was sure weren't standard. And those pockets were unique to each suit.

"Blake," David said, tossing a thin tablet to him, "you're the data specialist. I'm your backup."

He placed an identical tablet into his suit coat, demonstrating for Blake how to perfectly hide it. He passed a lockpick kit, a rubber wedge, and a nylon pry bar to me. We each were assigned a specific role in the mission. David leading the team, Blake watching cameras, Randy keeping watch, and me working the doors. In all reality, we would perform whatever task was necessary. On top of that, we were each carrying one of the gauge guns, sewn carefully into the backs of our suits.

They were hardly easy to reach back there, but that wasn't the point. The final feature of our wardrobe was its ability to be converted in just a few minutes into an all-black getup far more useful for sneaking around, and whose pockets were much easier to reach.

"Got it?" David asked as we practiced for the third time changing them into stealth mode. We nodded. "Wonderful," he

said, then wrapped a blindfold around Blake's eyes and took off my sunglasses. "Do it again. And in reverse."

Even Randy grumbled, but we all followed through with it. And more. We practiced every conceivable scenario we could think of. We practiced marksmanship in the Box, even though we shouldn't have to use our weapons on the mission. We memorized maps, we verbally rehearsed endless escape scenarios and backup plans. But most of all, we played hypothetical games. David would present us a scenario and demand we come up with a solution as quick as possible. He ran through it so many times, trying to surprise us in new and creative ways by springing questions in abrupt places. He would spring it so fast and so suddenly that his usual, "what do you do?" eventually became an abbreviated "what do?"

But finally, as the night approached, whether out of exhaustion on his part, because there was no time left, or even—heaven forbid—because we were actually prepared, David turned to us and said, "We're ready."

The four of us strode up to the steps of the Bridgehead Borough Basilica in our identical suits, calm and composed. Throngs of people, young and old, gathered throughout the square in front of the towering, lavish cathedral. Bathed in blue and purple spotlights, adorned with similarly colored banners and streamers, the grand old building looked positively mystical. Deep shadows seemed to hold cryptic mysteries, even as the sculpted angels, painted with the modern lighting, promised an assuring ethereal wonder within.

The square was surrounded by stately hotels, each hosting their own dancefloors for the great celebration. Some of these celebrations would be more prestigious, and private affairs. But the main show would be in the basilica. Some dignitaries and celebrities would make an appearance, as would a lucky random sampling of the populace. And us schmucks.

David nodded at us as we approached the group of Academy students awaiting entry. Blake and I nodded back. David walked off to the left, Randy wandered off to the right. Blake and I scanned the crowd for Scarlett and Quincy. None of us had cars, and both Scarlett and Quincy had elected to meet us here. Now we just had to find each other.

It didn't take long. I saw Scarlett first. Her deep red hair stood out right away against the sea of cool colored suits and dresses. She waved to me, and as I approached, I tried not to let my jaw hang open. She had mastered an effortless less-is-more look, with a simple black halter dress, a ribbon around her waist, and her hair done up beautifully.

"Hi," I said.

"Hi," she answered, beaming.

"You look gorgeous," I said before I could even think. Probably for the best.

"Thank you," she said happily. "You don't look too bad yourself."

Blake rolled up with Quincy, who was almost unrecognizable. She had ditched her usual glasses and had apparently swapped hairstyles with Scarlett, letting her hair down for the first time that I could remember. The bags under her eyes had nearly vanished, and instead I saw a happy glint for the first time in weeks. Her flowing green dress transformed the rest of her. She looked like a blooming flower on a padded pedestal.

"Let's not just stand around here," Blake said, "there's a perfectly good line made for just that."

We chatted, Scarlett and Quincy giving us yet another crash course in Aechrian culture. They pointed out various local celebrities, a few of the traditions surrounding the event and even some of the architectural details of the Bridgehead Borough Basilica. Blake was very interested in this topic, happily asking questions about history and myth. I found myself instead slowly slipping out of the festive mood. It was getting harder and harder to look at Scarlett. At some point, I was going to have to tell her about our early exit. But I didn't want to interrupt their conversation. Soon, I was feeling like an outsider among friends.

We slipped through security easily enough. None of our gadgets showed up on the quick scans, and no one patted us down thoroughly enough to find them. Soon, we were inside the massive domed hall of the basilica. As outside, blue and purple lights cast a beautiful and ephemeral glow across the place. A live orchestra was already playing, and the dance floor was filling fast.

Scarlett elbowed me. I turned to see her putting on her Silent Maw mask. Blake was donning his own mask of the same kind, and Quincy was putting on her Rawbeak one. I hurriedly grabbed my own mask. An Iron Mosk to finish our incomplete collection, just a Lyarch short.

"What do you say?" Scarlett asked when Blake and Quincy went off for refreshments.

"What are we waiting for?" I said, a catch in my throat.

Scarlett must have taken it for nerves, and she took the lead in dragging us onto the floor. I was determined now in showing her a good time before having to break the news. At least one blissful dance before I ruined it.

But I couldn't do it. In the midst of the mass of masked dancers, all swaying serenely in time to the spellbinding music, I felt more and more out of step. I tried to fall into the same mesmerizing movements as everyone around me, but I only half-succeeded. I felt as if somehow, I was the only one unmasked in the crowd.

"Can I talk to you?" I finally asked, leaning in towards Scarlett after our third dance.

"Of course," she said, some of her own energy dying. I had drained it, I knew.

Stepping off the dancefloor and to the side, I once more tried to rehearse what I would say as the moment approached. I internally kicked myself for waiting so long to do this. Was it really so hard to have done it earlier? Apparently, yes, as even now I was avoiding going over my lines and was instead beating myself up.

"Uh, Scarlett," I said, still searching for words. She looked at me patiently, but I could tell she wasn't excited for whatever I was going to say. "I haven't... that is... I have to tell you something."

She continued to look at me in that same impassive way. She didn't chide me for babbling or stating the obvious, but that was almost worse.

"I have to leave early," I finally stated.

"What?"

"I have to leave the ball early," I repeated. "I'm sorry, I don't want to, but it's Dean Foster. It's part of my suspension."

"Why didn't you tell me this sooner?" she asked. Her voice was level, but there was no mistaking a brief flash of anger in her expression.

"I don't know," I admitted. "I'm an idiot."

"You—" she cut herself off, not affirming my statement, but struggling with something internal. And just maybe resenting me for foisting that struggle onto her. "I would have talked to Alan," she finally said, the forcing calm back into herself. "We could have worked something out. Why couldn't you just tell me sooner?"

Her frustration squeezed through her defenses in the last words, slipping out in a near patronizing tone. Automatically, defensive anger boiled up within me in a well-trained response.

"I thought you were out of favors," I said harshly before I could moderate my tone. I immediately regretted it. "No, you're right," I started to say, but she joined the escalation and cut me off.

"You *thought*? Did you really?"

"No, I—yes, I did. I didn't know how to—I'm sorry. I'm really, really sorry."

"Forget it," she said, but she didn't look like any of the tension was relieved. "You're not an idiot. I didn't mean—But this... All you had to do was talk to me, or think ahead, or—"

She took a deep breath and closed her eyes.

"I don't want the rest of the night ruined," she said tensely. "When do you have to leave?"

"Nine," I said sheepishly.

"So before the ball drop and everything," she said irritably. She sighed and as the breath left her body, she appeared more morose than mad. "Fine. Let's just try and have fun before it's time."

I tried to apologize again, but she shushed me. I wanted to hide under a rock. I wanted to do everything I could to lift her spirits. I wanted her to tell me to just disappear, or to bring her the world, something besides just "try to enjoy yourself." It was the one thing I couldn't do.

Halfway through our last, clumsy dance, it seemed too much for her as well.

"Right, look, I need to be alone," she said.

"Scarlett, I'm so sorry. I should have—"

"Please stop," she said abruptly, not even looking at me. "I just need some space. I'll see you later, okay?"

"Okay," I said, hoping she meant those last words.

"Bye, Kennedy," she said, and slipped off into the crowd.

I skulked to the perimeter of the enormous room. I had blown it. And not tonight. There was no way I could have broken the news well tonight. I had sabotaged myself days before. I had known what I was doing. Why couldn't I have just gotten it over with?

I had to push the thoughts out of my mind. There was a job that needed doing now. I needed to go in with a clear head. Even as I recognized the logic in that statement, I chastised myself for trying to skate around my own mistake. I stewed in the grip of these roiling thoughts and emotions for an hour.

Finally, Blake walked up. He looked at me a little sadly, a little disappointedly. I stood up, waiting for him to say something. It was a testament to our friendship that he didn't say "I told you so." Instead, he gestured towards the meet up point. I nodded.

There was work to be done.

IX

The Enigma

The music had changed. Instead of the bouncing waltzes, the orchestra was now playing a rising tune that announced something was about to happen. Right on schedule. As the crowds were drawn into the next room, Blake and I met up with David and Randy and we stole up a back stairway.

Several stories above everyone else, we slipped under the cordons separating the public access from the historical section, high in the steeple. I glanced down, and I could see everyone from my shadowy perch. The mass of partygoers all gathered around a large circular cap in the middle of the room, directly under the tip of the tower. A group of men were ceremonially removing that heavy lid, as the eponymous crystal ball was being brought in for a traditional reading. I tried scanning the crowd for Scarlett, but at this height, she was just another dot.

Randy smacked me on the back of the head. I turned back, and he gestured into the small room the others were in, swapping around their suits for their mission gear.

Right. I quickly entered the small room myself and joined them. The alcove was little more than an excuse for a large, mostly decorative, window high in the steeple tower. And that was perfect for our purposes.

"Careful now," David said as he and Blake slowly tilted the old window so the bottom swung out into the night air.

"I am being careful," Blake retorted, straining. The winch clicked into place, suspending the window at an angle. He and David sighed with relief as they released it.

"Masks," David instructed, but Randy and I had already traded our paper masquerade ones for the concealing black cloths.

"Heads up," Blake said. "The ledge out there looks really thin, and this is a historical site. I—"

"Yeah, yeah, move aside," Randy said in his usual graceful tones. He pushed past Blake with ease, slipping out onto the ledge below. "You're burning moonlight."

"Excuse me for valuing your life," Blake mumbled.

"People did this for years. How do you think they used to clean these things before the renovations?"

"Well I, for one, am not a window washer," Blake reminded him.

"Enough chatter, let's move," David ordered.

Blake, then David, then I each slunk out onto the ledge, grasping for any purchase on the elaborate ornamentation. The ledge we were standing on wasn't even a foot wide. Randy may have been confident when speaking to Blake, but we were all silent once outside.

Randy and Blake were already descending towards the sloped roof, moving slowly and carefully, making sure to keep to the north side of the steeple. There, we were less likely to be seen as it didn't face any of the streets below, just more of the basilica itself. Still, we had been instructed to hurry, which was hardly an easy feat.

The autumn air was a cutting gale up here. I tried to refrain from shivering as David once more gripped the window. He would hold it open while I undid the winch. Only then could he carefully set it back into place. I was reminded of how hard it had been for him and Blake when there was room to maneuver. Somehow, he was going to hold it open while balancing on the ledge.

I turned to David and shook my head. He glared at me, but I pointed to my time gauge. He was immediately mollified and nodded. The window still latched open, he let go and fiddled with the controls of his watch before clicking the middle crown.

We were engulfed in a small bubble, streaming prismatic stars rushing past.

"Let's still try to get this right the first time," he said in a natural voice, which took me by surprise. A moment later, when he reset the arena, I realized no one outside would hear the comment. That hypothetical version of us in the arena would never be part of the real timeline. That draft would be erased.

David grabbed the window, and I reached in. I pulled, but the latch didn't budge. I yanked hard. If I broke it, we could try again. But it had been just enough force to get the old latch to disengage. David nearly stumbled as the window came free but caught himself so quickly that even I hardly noticed.

I pulled my arm out and together we lowered the window back into place. David clicked off the arena, and the vista of the city lights returned, stretching up towards the mountain at the heart of the island. Below us, Randy and Blake were still climbing as they had been a second ago. Now it was our turn.

We descended, painfully slowly, down to the roof of the basilica. If standing on the thin ledge had been bad, rappelling down was far, far worse. Because we had emphasized speed, at least we had a line to hold onto and weren't downclimbing. Still, every moment of the descent was hair-raising. Every little drop, no matter how controlled, set my stomach fluttering. Finally, mercifully, I arrived on the sloping shingles.

I lay flat with the others as David acknowledged that we had all made it. With a click of a button, our rope unlatched, clattering onto the roof before David could wind it back up. As he struggled to reel in the cord, he signaled to Randy and Blake. It was what they had been waiting for. They immediately crawled to the next point.

They slipped through another small window, this time well within the restricted section of the basilica. David and I were only moments behind, with him refusing to let the snag with the cable hold us back. The room beyond the window was another small empty affair, and it gave us an excuse to catch our breath before setting off again. The break was short, of course, but thirty seconds was something.

Blake snaked a small flexible rod out below the door as he watched his tablet screen. When he confirmed that no one was in the hallway outside, he pulled the camera free and we carefully stepped out one by one.

We weaved through small access corridors, making our way back, funnily enough, towards the big steeple tower. We had basically done a long and complicated loop around, but in doing so, we had evaded virtually all of the security. Now, we only had to stop every once in a while for Blake to tap on his tablet and program a loop on some of the cameras we passed. The advanced tech Time Peace had provided us made it a cinch even for our inexperienced team.

We were almost to our final obstacle when things went awry. One of the guards was out of place. He had left his patrol route and was looking down a corridor to another landing which was open to the steeple. Someone was saying something down there, reciting a long speech. Her voice was deep and ponderous. The ceremonial reading of the future, I guessed. It sounded dull enough to put me to sleep.

But the guard seemed interested. He was standing in the corridor, between us and the door we had to reach. We were all at the intersection of two corridors, our squad in the east corridor, the guard in the one running south. He had his back to us, but he was standing just a couple feet from the door we needed to make. There was no way we could sneak past him. If he turned for even a second, he would spot us.

Randy raised his silver gun. David pushed it back down nice and easy. He nodded reassuringly and reached into his pocket. I watched curiously as he drew out a little black rubber ball.

David sat, listening for a while as the speaker below continued. Only as she finished did he raise his hand with the ball. The guard leaned forward a little bit, toward the tower interior. Someone announced something from the base of the steeple. David tossed the ball.

There was a great shattering down below. At the same time, the ball smacked against a door in the west corridor and bounced around a corner.

The guard jumped, guilty panic crossing his face. He quickly scrambled to find the source of the sound, and to return to his post. As soon as he had turned down the west corridor, back to us, David waved us forward. The applause from below easily covered our already soft footsteps as we reached the door and bustled in.

A few tense minutes later, and I squeezed myself out of the dumbwaiter. It had led us down into the subterranean levels—our final destination. From here, it was an easy walk to the last access corridor where the files had been forgotten.

A quick tiptoe through dark and dusty corridors and we found it. It was the narrowest passageway yet, barely visible between two piles of abandoned pallets and crates at the end of an alcove in a long hall. It seemed these underground levels hadn't had the same loving restoration as the rest of the basilica.

We stood guard as Blake squeezed into the tiny corridor, which was hardly more than dust and cobwebs. We were so close. I gripped my gun tightly in anticipation.

"Ugh, they could've put a hazard warning on the map," he complained.

Randy rolled his eyes. I chuckled and let myself relax.

Soon, Blake re-emerged, a thin gray coating on his black suit. He handed a black box to David. "It was in a crate with some paper files. I suppose we should confirm."

"Yes," David said, hands almost trembling as he cradled the object. He took out yet another small device, the size of a phone, and held it above the black box. I recognized it as a universal data reader, which displayed for him what was inside. He immediately began scrolling through the listings.

"Yes," he whispered. "This is it."

"Hands where I can see them," a voice ordered.

We all froze.

David nodded slowly, slipping the devices up his sleeves as he raised his hands. I couldn't perform the same trick. I raised my

free hand and slowly, clearly, laid my own gauge gun down as I turned.

Quincy stood at the end of the black stone hallway, a gun pointed at us.

If adrenaline and instinct hadn't been gripping my mind, I would have openly gaped. As it was, I only processed what was happening in the most utilitarian way. A new threat had appeared, and she had the jump on us. But she only had a single weapon, there were four of us, and she was hardly dressed for combat. And she was standing. Standing. Something was wrong about that.

It took a moment for the combat instincts part of my brain to connect to the friends-and-acquaintances part. The realization was like an egg cracked on my head. A sudden shock, then slow, seeping comprehension.

"Quincy?" Blake asked in disbelief.

David made a minor gesture to quell Blake. He didn't pay attention. He pulled off his mask—a dangerous move, I immediately thought. *Don't make sudden moves*, my instincts tried to remind him psychically. Blake obviously wasn't seeing the threat.

"Quincy, what is going on?" Blake repeated.

"Don't move," Quincy repeated. "And I'd ask you the same question."

Now Blake finally did glance towards David, who had made no motion to remove his own mask. He slowly shook his head. With my senses sharpened, I noticed Randy slowly adjust his posture, positioning himself to quickly draw a second, hidden gun at his back. A real gun.

I focused my mind on options but couldn't think of anything fast. I needed more time. And there was only one way to get it.

I shifted position slightly, wondering if I would have time to reach over and grab my wrist while my hands were in the air. Neither Blake nor Quincy seemed to notice Randy's move yet, though Quincy's eyes were darting between us. Her tired eyes. Eyes tracking too many targets.

"You can walk?" Blake finally said, unable to give her anything else.

"Yes," she replied simply. She was clearly falling back into professional habits. She looked practiced with the pistol, and her posture was ready and alert. But with an edge to it.

"Then, what—why? How?" Blake stammered.

Quincy gave the obvious answer. "I always could. This was part of my cover."

"Cover for what?"

I could see that Randy was nearly ready. He was tilting his body slightly to help mask the movement once it started. I couldn't tell when exactly he would make his move. If I wanted to beat him, I would need to grab my watch. But I had to worry about Quincy. If she fired before I reached my watch, none of this would matter.

"I was planted in the Academy," Quincy explained coldly. "I'm Royal Guard."

Blake exchanged a glance with David. It seemed our leader's gamble really would pay off then. Blake, however, didn't look too celebratory. Instead, he seemed focused. I recognized his expression: This had become a problem for him to overcome.

"Quincy," he said slowly. He couldn't see Randy lower his hand slightly. I raised my own hands higher, bringing them inches closer to each other.

Don't do it, Randy.

"Quincy," Blake repeated. "We're not here to cause any trouble. We don't mean you or the Princess any harm."

"Is that why you're sneaking around here? Something to do with the Princess?" Quincy asked, still emotionless.

It would still take Randy a heartbeat to grab his gun, raise it and fire. He had to know that. I waited for his twitch.

Then I noticed David's face pale. I wanted to follow his gaze, to see what he saw. But if I tore my eyes from Randy, I might miss when he—

I couldn't help myself. I glanced back towards Quincy. And I saw it too.

Distant, in the hallway behind her, there was a silvery tentacle descending from an open accessway. I blinked. I couldn't understand what I was seeing at first. It was made of segmented metal, and it seemed to just be suspended in a dull, dusty shaft of light.

"Quincy," David said suddenly. "My name is David Greene, Delta agent of an organization called Time Peace, serial number 113-497-87214, and I'm formally surrendering to you and handing my team over to the Royal Guard, but please listen to me right now."

The fear emanated off of him in waves. He didn't tremble; his voice was only slightly tense. But coming from him, he might as well have been shrieking. I suddenly remembered Randy and glanced back to him. He looked startled as well, suddenly focusing on the tentacle, his gun forgotten.

I looked back and I saw the thing begin to descend. Two, then three, four more of those same metallic tentacles descended behind her. Then I saw some tattered black cloth lowering as well.

"There is a threat to you down here. I know you have reason to doubt," David hastily added, seeing the highly skeptical expression on Quincy's face, "but I have to warn you. We will obey any order you give us, but I'm asking, begging you to step as far away from the access shaft behind you as you can."

Blake was looking more and more apprehensive. Randy was looking like he was going for his gun again. I could have killed him right then. Quincy noticed.

"Hands in the air, high!" she ordered to Randy.

The thing came fully into view now. It was hanging in midair, slightly larger than a man, but nothing like one. A tattered black cloak was draped over something round—head or body, I couldn't tell. Only the mechanical tentacles, snaking out from under the cloth, were exposed. It was as if it the rest was too hideous or twisted to be viewed by human beings. The grasping fingers on the ends of the tendrils were disturbing enough, opening and closing, pulsating like a breathing organ as they searched or sniffed the air like metal snakes.

"Your 'threat' will have to wait for my backup," Quincy said to David, though her eyes didn't easily leave Randy. They darted to each of us. Her finger was on the trigger.

The silent sightless thing floated ponderously towards Quincy, hovering effortlessly three feet off the ground.

"Quincy, he's not lying," Blake said carefully. He looked like he wanted to say more, but he glanced towards David.

"Quincy, I've surrendered, and I will answer any questions you have," David said as calmly as he could manage. "It will do us no good if you got hurt now. But there is a danger to you here, and it is close. I know it sounds silly, but there is a threat behind you. Thirty feet behind you, your five o'clock. We will do whatever you ask, I only want you to be safe as well."

"I'm not turning my back on you," Quincy answered simply.

The strange technological creature floated closer. I wanted to scream that this thing that should not be was right there. I wanted to describe it, to tell her she was being stupid. But I couldn't. I couldn't afford to screw this up. This was David's game. I had to have faith in him.

"I told you who I am, you know Blake Anthony, this is Kennedy Frost and Randy O'Neill. You were right, we were here looking for information on Princess Sophia. There is a hostile fifteen feet behind you at your five o'clock. Please, we'll turn around, or drop to the floor, or anything, but please believe me."

"What is it?" Blake couldn't help but asking.

Maybe it was something in his voice. Maybe Quincy could sense something. But her expression changed subtly.

"Turn around and lie flat on the floor, hands above your heads, now!" she instructed.

I only hesitated a split second to see if Randy was cooperating. He wasn't, until a furious glare from David changed his mind. The four of us quickly dropped to the floor, clasping our hands together over the backs of our heads.

I took the chance. I reached for my wrist and pressed the middle crown.

Nothing happened. The arena didn't activate.

Quincy gasped.

The shock of my time gauge failing had set my entire nervous system on edge. I had to act. It wasn't a choice. I turned to see what was happening.

The creature seemed to tower over Quincy's frame. She was frozen in shock. The bulbous shape raised one of its tentacles from under the black cloth. The fabric draped along the spine-like appendage as it raised itself lazily towards Quincy's suddenly frail-looking form. A single mechanical finger stretched out towards her, nearly touching her nose.

And then reality popped. Like an electric shock to my brain, my mind seized for a moment. It wasn't painful as much as it was startling. I felt as if an elastic cord in my spine had been snapped. As if my body was afraid to return to its previous position after something inside had cracked. But it wasn't inside me. It had been the world around me.

Mostly I could tell because Quincy was gone. One second she had been there, and now she wasn't. There was only empty space, and the monstrous machine's tendril, still outstretched.

"Run!" David shouted.

Randy disobeyed immediately. He grabbed his second gun and started shooting. The blue beam seared through the ratty black cloak but vanished within. If it had any effect, it was invisible to us. The monster only reacted by seeming to shift its intent towards Randy.

"Quincy!" Blake said. "Where's Quincy?"

"Blake!" David shouted, already on his feet, as was I, "grab your stuff and fall back, that's an order!"

I didn't wait for my friend to get the hint. Even with my neck still cringing, I had to get up. I saw everyone's equipment, including our guns, grabbed as much as I could, and kicked the rest back to the group. I dashed away as the thing began to float forward.

David scooped up two guns, Randy a third.

"Back, back, back, now!" David was saying.

We all hustled backwards, not letting our eyes drift from the thing even as it began to follow ominously, still unhindered by anything Randy tried.

I nearly dropped one of the pads I was carrying. Blake ran up to me, trying to grab as much as he could. It was slowing us down. I dumped half of my load into his arms and began to stuff what remained into my pockets, whether it fit or not.

We rounded a corner, but David had ground to a stop. We heard voices descending a nearby staircase. David swore.

"Priority is the mission," Randy reminded him. "Get out safely and quietly."

"I'm well aware," David replied. "You got that, right? Kennedy, Blake?"

"Get out safely and quietly," I repeated. David was thinking. Buying time with talk. Time we didn't have.

"It's getting closer," Blake warned.

"It can't clip you," David hurriedly explained. "It can hurt you, but enigmas can't clip Timeless."

"Clip?" I asked.

"Kill you like Quincy," Randy shot at me as fast as he could.

"Quincy is—?" Blake began to ask but cut himself short.

David nodded. "Focus. The objective is clear. We get to the rendezvous. Silently. No matter the cost."

I suddenly understood. The footsteps we heard. The other guards. Quincy had summoned them, or they had heard the commotion. This enigma, or whatever it was, could "clip" them as it had done to Quincy. But we couldn't care. We shouldn't.

"There are hundreds of people up there," I said.

"We can't risk exposure," David repeated.

"Done," I said, a wild thought flitting through my mind.

"What? What's 'done'?" Randy spat.

"It's done. No exposure. You get the data out, I'll meet you there. And if I'm caught, well, I don't know enough to tell them anything useful. But it won't come to that. I can kill this," I insisted.

I twisted off the crystal from my time gauge and palmed it. David saw. He didn't tell me it wouldn't work. He looked conflicted. But there was no time. The footsteps were approaching.

"Do it," he said. He turned to the others, "we're out."

He and Randy immediately peeled out, and I darted towards the corner hiding the enigma. And realized I wasn't alone. I glanced back at Blake questioningly. He had stayed right at my side.

"Thought you'd like some backup," my friend said, preparing his own crystal ray. "Besides, I know as little as you do."

I nodded appreciatively. In truth, this really did make us both idiots. But if I was going to do something this suicidal, it was nice to once again have Blake at my side. Call it superstitious, but with us together, there was a chance that a dead end would suddenly open up into a never-before-seen shortcut.

"We're going to lure it down, give us some space to really open up," I explained quick. Blake nodded. "Try to keep up."

"I always do," he said, and then suddenly raised his hand and fired a small beam.

The creature had just turned the corner, two of its tentacles raised and sniffing towards us. It had appeared all at once, no warning, no sound. I leapt backwards and fired as it approached.

I felt a wave of pressure, the air around me becoming thick and dry. It was harder to walk. As if from across time itself, I could distantly hear the sound of a dozen footsteps approaching. They were coming from behind.

I waved Blake forward and charged.

It was ludicrous, but it was that or let the enigma take the Royal Guard. We zapped it and dived under its tentacles. I ducked below the tattered fabric and immediately regretted every decision that had led up to that single moment.

A billion screams and cries pierced my ears, drilling into my head. My bones seemed to cry with sound of it all. Only sheer panic kept my legs automatically stumbling over each other. I couldn't even tell if my muscles were still working as the soul-rending cries burrowed into the deep recesses of my memory. They were there... every loss, every heartbreak—they were there.

I almost didn't notice when I emerged on the other side. I was snapped back to the present, though, when one of the tentacles wrapped around me and I tripped. It slithered around my stomach. My head was still ringing from the screams which had been suddenly silenced seconds ago. I didn't react fast enough as it lifted me into the air.

Blake, beside me, leapt over a sweeping tentacle that nearly caught his leg. He didn't even pause to take in the situation. He ran up to me, cranked the power up on his crystal ray and pressed it against the tentacle.

I felt a searing heat for just a moment, but the tentacle loosened its grip. I tore myself free, scrambling away from the demon.

Blake was just a second too slow. Another tentacle lashed out and wrapped around his chest. Even from a distance, I could feel it burn. Blake bit down a scream as it melted through his clothes. I quickly repeated Blake's stunt. Pressing my crystal ray against the tentacle, I fired.

It tore away, but not before burning away his shirt. As Blake pulled back, it revealed a segmented scar creeping up towards his neck like a serpent.

Then we stumbled. All at once, gravity had tripled and it became hard to breathe—almost impossible. The air was practically solid. Three more tendrils were reaching out for us, snaking towards us in midair. We shot at them. Poorly. We weren't as quiet or as subtle as we should have been. We couldn't think about that now. Now it was do or die.

We scrambled and fired until the air thinned just enough to breathe. I pulled myself to my feet. I yanked Blake to his. We rushed to put more distance between us and it. It followed regardless. But we could breathe again.

"Go, go, go!" I said unnecessarily. Blake wheezed along right behind me.

It was on our trail but appeared to be in no hurry. But its lethargic pace was an illusion. Its floating path covered a lot of ground, and Blake and I had to maintain a jog at the very least to stay safe. He was still stumbling a little.

We rounded a corner. I heard another squad of guards approaching that way.

"New route!" I whisper-shouted to Blake.

"Uh," he said, apparently scanning his mental map for another path downwards. "This way!"

We had to retrace our steps—undo the turn we had just made and rush down the other forking path. For a moment, we crossed into that aura of choking air. We tripped. It was just behind us. We felt a pull, as if invisible arms were grasping at us. I held Blake up.

We turned, we fired, we ran.

It was a blur from then on. We stumbled down a flight of stairs somehow. I don't know how we had the coordination. It didn't matter. All that mattered was that we got to the bottom.

We raced towards the final door. I sprinted ahead and threw my full weight against it.

I crashed through, Blake racing shortly behind, though he quickly skidded to a stop. He had nearly run into a pile of shattered crystal scattered across the floor. Right below the round cap, directly beneath the steeple.

It was dark, the cover was back in place, and that was just what I wanted. No one would be looking in this room. Blake spun, turned up the power on his crystal ray.

"The door," Blake said. I nodded, a pit forming in my stomach. As soon as that thing was through, I would have to leap in and shut the door so no one else would see the flash.

"If this isn't enough, you'll have to take the second shot," Blake told me, wincing as he tuned the setting on the ray.

I nodded again and set my watch even higher than Blake's as I skidded to the side, trying to stay out of sight from the door. I hoped we wouldn't be caving ourselves in here.

The spine-like tentacles slithered through the doorway. Blake raised his hand. I leaned in, ready to make my move.

The tattered cloak followed, draped over the unsettling appendage.

We waited.

The air became choked. My body felt leaden—and then like it was melting. A dry, claustrophobic heat infected the air.

The body, the main mass of the thing slowly pulled itself through the threshold. The tentacles were snaking their way through the air. One sniffed out towards Blake. He stepped back, arm still raised, ready to fire.

Almost there.

The last tentacle followed the domed body.

But I could still feel the heat, the gravity bearing down on me. It was too close to the door. I couldn't make another sprint through its field. I couldn't get that close to its tentacles again. I could hardly stand. I needed it further in the room.

It hovered towards Blake. He backpedaled, eyes never leaving the thing's central mass.

The heat dissipated just a little, but it wasn't enough. I would still fall to pieces if I broke into a run.

Blake's foot skittered across glass. "Kennedy!" he shouted.

That was all I needed. I dashed forward and immediately felt the oppressive atmosphere engulf me. But I had to push through. Even as my legs turned to molten iron, I had to push through. I reached the door, heaved it shut.

As soon as I heard the latch click, I shoved myself off the wall. But I was so much slower now. My legs wouldn't pull themselves off the ground. But I needed to get out of Blake's line of fire. The tentacle was nearly on him.

With whatever remained of my strength, I leapt to the side.

Blake clicked his watch.

A burst of pure energy flooded the room. I could feel the walls rattle, bits of stone raining down as it bathed the enigma in sheer, raw, power.

As quick as it had come, it vanished. The clogged air had cleared of the enigma's influence, but now dust and smoke swirled through the circular chamber. I could hear Blake coughing. I was choking myself, but desperately scanning from my position on the floor. I was worried now that we had gone overboard. That we would be discovered.

And then I saw it. The faintest outline of a shape in the hazy smoke, but it was there. That round bulge with the black cloth hanging from it. The mechanical monster was still there, though judging by the flickering orange light, some of its cloak was burning.

And yet, something was different. I couldn't quite tell what, until the shape began to dissolve. It wasn't falling apart. It wasn't wounded. It was simply vanishing. More smoke filled the room, but then quickly folded in on itself. As if the smoke were being sucked into a vacuum. Soon, only a thin haze of dust was left.

The room wasn't as damaged as I expected. There was a thin layer of disturbed stone particles on the floor, but otherwise no obvious damage. David should be happy.

"Was that it? Is it dead?" I asked, still hacking a bit.

Blake considered a moment. "No," he answered honestly. "No, I don't think so."

Our eyes met, and at that moment, I was sure a chill ran down his spine as it did mine.

"Come on," I said. "Let's get out of here."

I pulled on the green sweater. The chilly night air was still, but it slowly stole away my body heat. The sweater was a welcome relief. Stuffing the black gloves in my pockets was less so, but it was important. We were to appear as casual as possible. Completely unrecognizable as those who were sneaking through the bowels of the basilica.

Blake and I had rushed to the designated point, finding the garbage bags we had planted next to bins beforehand. Naturally, no one had bothered to steal what seemed to be trash, so our casual, civilian clothes had been left untouched. We saw, to our relief, that David and Randy's bags were already gone.

Blake had a harder time changing with the burn across his chest, but he managed. He stubbornly refused my suggestion that we find some bandages before we rendezvous with the others. So we tossed the bags and continued on. The first wave of partygoers were returning home, and we joined them in retreating from the city center. Soon, however, we had put enough distance between us and the basilica that the thin crowd had dispersed entirely. We were all alone in the silent streets, the flickering lamps above our only company.

Blake and I crept around the corner of a small diner, one of the few buildings that still had lights on at this hour. I glanced around anxiously. The little square we were in seemed entirely vacant. The four faces of a block-shaped clock standing in the middle illuminated the dusty space. We were all alone. Then someone grabbed my arm.

I jumped and spun around. Randy had emerged from the shadows.

"Were you followed?" he hissed.

"No, we got out clean," I replied, a little surly at being caught by surprise.

Randy nodded. He waved over at someone across the street. David walked out, glancing around at the street, but he relaxed slightly.

"Are you alright?" he asked Blake and me.

"That thing got Blake—burned him or something," I immediately answered.

David looked concerned, glanced around. But we were alone. He waved us deeper into the shadows, next to a wall and pulled out a first aid kit from... somewhere.

"Let's see it," David ordered.

"It's not that bad," Blake lied, but he started pulling off his shirt. The burn was bright red except where the seams in the tentacle's segments had been. There it was a nasty black. Blake had to be in agony, but he looked too dazed to show it. David immediately handed him some sort of cream and started unrolling bandages.

"And the mission?" he asked, even as he worked.

"No one saw us," I reported. "That thing didn't get anyone else."

"What was it?" Blake demanded.

"An enigma," David replied, wrapping the bandage around him. "If we had known there would be one there, you can bet someone else would have taken this mission. I guess we know why the files were abandoned."

"What do you mean?" Blake pressed.

"Enigmas erase people from existence," Randy said grimly. For once, his tone wasn't sharp or condescending.

"What... what does that mean?" Blake asked. Randy's words had been shocking, surreal, but they had been clear.

"We call them enigmas for a reason," David said quietly. "It's just another mystery. They're future tech, obviously, and very advanced future tech at that."

"Anyone can see that," Blake snapped. "What do you mean they erase people?"

"They can manipulate the timeline," David said, a little more firmly, but without shouting. "Remember the infinite possible timelines?"

"Yes, but most of those are improbable," Blake said, trying to suppress his anxious irritation. Or just his pain.

"Some are extremely similar, to the point where they're almost as likely as the real timeline. But they still aren't 'real' to us. If you had pancakes versus waffles for breakfast, for instance. Pancakes are 51% probability, but waffles are 49%. And yet, we only see the pancake timeline on the time gate network. The waffle timeline doesn't become real. It's overshadowed by the pancake timeline because it's so similar."

"I don't see..." Blake began, but the dawning horror was evident on his face.

"I don't understand," I admitted, even as a clenching sensation started to grip my innards. "Wouldn't that cause a split?"

"Not if the change is small on a world scale. The enigmas— they pull out these hidden timelines, change which overshadows which without causing major changes. They effectively change which timelines are real," David continued. "Sometimes, timelines can be virtually identical, even if a specific person was never born."

"Wait, wait, hang on," I said, a horrible panic gripping me. "Are you saying that now, somehow, Quincy was never born? That's what you mean by she never existed?"

"That's just it," David replied coldly. "In this new version of the Aechrian timeline, Quincy was never born."

"No, no, no," Blake pleaded desperately. "Things can't be exactly the same *and* have someone missing."

"Don't you remember what being Timeless means?" Randy asked quietly.

I saw the question hit Blake like a brick. His brain would have, as always, immediately recalled that processed fact. But he couldn't stop from begging, "She said she was part of the Royal Guard. Someone had to be looking for the Princess at the Academy!"

"Someone probably was," David agreed. "But someone else now. Maybe someone else did everything Quincy did. Maybe several someone's at different points. Maybe her parents had a different daughter, who never became Royal Guard. Maybe a different Royal Guard recruit was assigned to Princess Sophia. Maybe—"

"But I remember her!" Blake interrupted. "I went to the ball with her! I know she existed!"

"We're Timeless," Randy reminded him. "We hop timelines."

"You felt the snap, right?" David asked, just as softly.

Blake nodded stiffly.

"That wasn't the enigma attacking us. That was us being snapped to the new timeline. A timeline without Quincy. She was clipped right out of Aechyr. But we couldn't be changed. We remember the old timeline, before it was clipped. Because we work on meta-time."

Blake stared blankly, blinking only occasionally.

"But someone else... If I asked Scarlett about...?" Blake suggested.

"She won't even know who Quincy is," David answered. "I don't know what Scarlett would say about tonight. I'd guess she'd say that you went alone. That would be the simplest timeline for the enigma to clip in."

Blake collapsed against the wall behind him and leaned his head against it. He looked pale, as if he was going to throw up. I didn't know how to react. It hurt me to see Blake like this. I didn't know how to act, though. I had never learned.

I gripped his uninjured shoulder with one hand. He didn't object. I willed some of my strength into him. Maybe I was just trying to make myself feel better.

David packed up the first aid kit. "You'll probably have a scar," he mumbled.

Randy whispered something to David, who nodded. Randy stepped around the corner, and I heard the bell of the diner door tinkle softly.

"But what even are these enigma things?" I asked David. "Is this Anarakia?"

"No," David said emphatically. "They're... well, they're their own thing. They sometimes appear around inactive future tech, like they're guarding it. Like a time gate without the power on. But they're hostile to anyone who approaches their territory. You won't find them if you look for them. They can disappear— slipping into spaces between timelines. Sometimes, they won't even appear when you slip into their territory. But when you do see them, there's almost nothing you can do. They can't be caught in an arena, and almost nothing breaks them. They're mysteries. Enigmas."

"So why was it here?" I asked.

David shrugged. "Maybe there's an arcane weapon buried under the basilica. Who knows?"

A silence descended on us. Nothing moved in the dark street. Everything from the buildings to the streetlights across the road seemed to be an illusion, a dream. And yet, they were also the only concrete thing I could know for sure. Everything had been shaken.

The door to the diner chimed again. Randy appeared, carrying four steaming drinks. He handed one to Blake first before giving out the others. I took a sip of the cream-filled coffee. It seemed to root me in the present a little more. Blake merely held his.

"Drink some," David suggested. "If you can stomach it. It'll help."

"Yeah, come on, man," I said feebly. "Randy did something nice for once."

Randy didn't comment. He stood behind David, watching with beady eyes.

Blake took a sip slowly. Eventually, a little color returned to his face.

"The data," he finally said. "You said this was related?"

"I'm willing to bet," David said, nodding. "I bet this drive wasn't just overlooked. I bet the enigma clipped someone who was supposed to go get it. In the new timeline, maybe a report was never filed."

"And that's when we came in," I concluded.

"That's right," David agreed.

"Then," Blake said tentatively, but with gaining strength, "let's see what we got for our trouble."

David nodded. He pulled the little black box and the universal data reader from his pockets. We gathered behind him as the screen sprang to life. He quickly located a file labelled "Alias Profile."

We held our breath as he opened it and scrolled through it. And there it was. The new name Sophia Tiscardia had chosen.

"I'll be damned," Randy declared.

X

The Lost Princess of Aechyr

The slender black figure approached the sleek car in the tunnel. The door opened instantly to her touch and she tossed her bag inside. Carefully, she checked that she had everything. When she was satisfied that she did, she straightened and looked back out the tunnel. It was as if she was taking in the view one last time.

A footstep in the dark behind her made her twist around suddenly, eyes wide.

"You lied to me," I announced. "Sophia."

Scarlett Foster's face darkened. I stepped into the light, so we could both see each other plainly. Her hair was now what I assumed was its natural color, a light ash brown. It had darkened from the blonde in her childhood photo. Some of her facial structure had changed, too. Her nose appeared thinner now, her face less rounded. The resemblance wasn't obvious, but still, I should have seen it.

She was clearly as on edge as I was. I couldn't say I wanted to meet her like this, but it seemed like our last chance. Sophia's eyes scanned the tunnel behind me. I raised my hands in an attempt to put her at ease. Naturally, it did very little.

"Can you blame me?" Sophia finally answered my earlier accusation. I couldn't tell if she was replying seriously or biding her time.

"About your identity? No," I replied. "I think we're even on that score. I meant you lied earlier tonight."

She narrowed her eyes. "About what?"

"You said you'd see me again," I answered, letting the edge melt from my voice. I nodded towards the car, and her pack inside. "It doesn't look like you're coming back."

She considered me for a moment. And I thought, perhaps, she did so more generously. "No, I'm not," she admitted. "How did you find me?"

"We were looking. Ironically, that's why I left early tonight. That's another one on me." She looked suspicious again, and I couldn't blame her. I tossed away as much of the subterfuge as I could, and I hoped it came through as I said, "Listen, Scarlett, or Sophia, whichever you prefer, I don't want to lie to you."

She made a skeptical noise.

"I'm serious," I said. "You know what it's like to have to hold things back. I didn't want to, but I had to. I didn't enjoy it. I don't want to be playing these games. If you ask me something, I won't lie."

Sophia considered me. "Are you alone?" she asked.

"Yes," I replied.

"Why did you come here?"

"Officially, just to pass on a message. I have it right here." I gestured towards the pocket of my jacket. "You take it and I'm gone."

"And what about unofficially?" she inquired.

I looked her straight in her eyes, and once again, I hated the sunglasses I was forced to wear. What I wouldn't give, at that moment, to have my eyes back, just for her.

Finally, her shoulders eased back and something softened in those icy eyes.

"You aren't lying," she said. It wasn't a question.

"No," I said emphatically.

"Sophia," she said.

"Huh?"

"You asked which I prefer. I prefer Sophia."

"Okay. Sophia," I said, trying it out. "Pleasure to meet you."

"You already have," she replied. The comment should have been accompanied by a little laugh, but she was somber. Almost worried.

I took a step forward. "Look, I'm tired of the lies. From all directions. From everyone. It feels like they're always there, like nothing's safe from them. I was hoping... that we could be."

She smiled mournfully. "Where do we begin?" A rueful chuckle slipped from between her lips as something occurred to her. "You're lucky you're such a bad liar."

I tried a lopsided smile, unsure of where we were headed. "Why's that?"

"Because it means I might just be able to trust you," she said, looking up at me. Now it was her turn to try pleading with her expression. "From now on, no more lies?"

"Not one," I immediately said. "I can't tell you everything—"

"Nor can I," she said abruptly. "But we can just say that. We're adults, aren't we?"

"I suppose we are," I said, finding the thought somehow odd. "From now on, I promise, only the truth."

"I promise, too," Sophia said. "So, can I ask who you're working for?"

"I can't say," I said painfully. "Orders. That's part of what the message is for."

"I take it your bosses won't do me, my mother, or Aechyr any harm, will they?"

"No," I said emphatically. "Not a chance."

"Right. You're not People's Front, then." She shook her head immediately after. "No, I shouldn't have asked."

"No," I again said emphatically. "No relation. Not Charmies, not—"

"Stop," Sophia said quickly.

"I'm not—"

"I know you're not lying," she said quickly. "But if you can't tell me, then let's not eliminate everyone you aren't. If you can't tell me, you can't tell me, right?"

I nodded, seeing what she was getting at. We couldn't let process of elimination sidestep our new rules. "The last thing I want to do," I said carefully, "is hurt you in any way."

"I know," she said. She thought for a moment, then asked cautiously, "Is Kennedy Frost your real name?"

"Yeah, actually," I replied.

She looked... not quite skeptical, but at least surprised. She seemed to debate whether to ask a follow-up question.

"I can't really explain," I said. "But strangely enough, it's true. It's always been my name."

She nodded.

"So then," Sophia said carefully, "that just leaves the big question."

"What question?" I asked.

"The real one you came to ask," she said. "Does this have to be goodbye?"

My heart leapt into my throat. I couldn't quite decide what to say. I wanted to shake my head, but I wanted her to continue. My head instead jerked slightly to the side and at an angle, tilting curiously.

"I might be breaking a hundred laws," she said slowly, as if unsure she should be saying anything at all, "but if you want, if you'll submit to security, maybe you could come with?"

I could hardly believe it. I didn't know what to say. Or more properly, how to say "yes" without leaping up exuberantly.

"Are you sure?" I heard myself ask instead.

"No," Sophia answered honestly. "No, I'm really not. I could be making the biggest mistake of my life. But I'd like to have someone I could trust."

I nodded. "I can do that."

"Promises, promises," she almost admonished, apparently still trying to talk herself out of this. Or into it. "I remember how you are with those."

"Before was because of the job. But that's out of the way," I said, holding up the drive with the message. "We found you. Now my promises are my own."

She smiled slightly. "Then get in."

I walked over, trying once again not to leap for joy. I slid into the passenger side as Sophia had indicated. I carefully took the bag she had placed there and turned to put it in the back, when I saw that she was sitting behind me. I tilted my head in confusion.

"I still have to be careful," she explained. "I want to trust you. But I have to be cautious for everyone counting on me."

"Okay, sure," I said, surprisingly okay with that sentiment, "but then who's driving?"

She nodded at the control panel in the middle. "It will. Preset one."

Surprised, I flicked the screen on and pressed the icon for preset she had indicated. The screen flickered for a moment, a blue box surrounding my fingerprint. I heard a blip from behind me as Sophia pressed something on her phone. The box around my finger blinked green, and text popped up reading "fingerprint accepted." The car hummed to life, and then, all by itself, it pulled carefully out of the tunnel.

I saw Sophia smile in the rearview mirror. "The title comes with a few perks," she said.

"Apparently," I replied. The car turned as a light changed green. Soon, the car was travelling through the side streets of Thysiopolis. Small strips of illumination shone through the darkened windows, which obscured the fact that no one was driving. The car was quiet, cool, isolated from the hustle and bustle of the last stragglers returning home after the party.

"Can I ask you something?" I said tentatively toward the back seat.

"I'll tell you if you can't," she replied.

"Why did you leave?" I asked. "The Crown, I mean."

"Mmm, the big question," she commented.

"You don't have to tell me," I added quickly.

"No, it's fine," she insisted. "It's just... it sounds stupid."

I let out a single chuckle. She glanced up, a spark of defensive anger in her eyes.

"No, it's not you," I hastily explained, dousing the fires. "I was thinking that sounded an awful lot like something I would say. About things I did."

"You didn't run away from a life of privilege because you were sad, did you?" she asked angrily. But she wasn't angry at me.

"No," I answered somberly. "I ran away because I didn't know how to deal with a bad situation."

Now she looked at me with surprised concern. "I'm sorry," she said.

"It wasn't that bad," I added quickly. "But I'm kind of an idiot when it comes to handling these things. If I had half the composure of David, of you, things would be different. But that's not how it worked out. I had my reasons, and you had yours. Yours were probably better." I looked back at her in the mirror. "Tell me."

She thought for a long moment. Slowly, she said, "Have you ever gotten stuck waiting for a bus?" she asked.

I looked back, a little surprised. A distinct memory flicked through my head, and for a second, I wondered if she could see into my mind.

"You know, long after it was supposed to arrive," she went on. "You keep waiting and waiting, but all the while you're not

sure if the bus is even going to come. You think maybe you should leave, maybe try another stop, but you're worried that the bus will arrive the moment you go."

I eased back a little, the similarity to a momentous memory of mine was just coincidence. I processed what she was saying.

"I know the feeling," I said slowly.

"Imagine that feeling, but worse. You've worked for weeks on a project you're supposed to present, but the teacher never shows up. You go to every practice, work your hardest, but in the game, you're always on the bench."

"You're saying that was what it was like as a princess?" I asked.

She nodded. "A lot of people are watching. You're expected to be a straight-A student, perfectly polite, a little insightful, up-to-date with current events, diplomatic, strategic, and ultimately, useless."

"Sit still and look pretty?" I suggested.

"No, that's not it," she said at once. "Not really. You have to be genuinely insightful. You really have to know a million different things; you can't fake it. It's not just a photo op. Not literally. Well, maybe metaphorically."

"Let me explain," she hurriedly added, unsure if she was making sense. "When a dignitary finally arranges a visit, you have to meet expectations. It's not just table manners or poise. You need those, but if you're in a conversation, you can tell if the other person is faking. You can tell if they really understand the subject or not. And the people who meet with my family aren't oblivious. Senators, judges, admirals—they are all brilliant in one way or another and couldn't have climbed to the top of their field without knowing when someone was obfuscating. You need to match wits with them. All of them."

"The monarchy is the heart of Aechyr," she emphasized seriously. "You absolutely cannot disappoint. But symbols aren't meant to breathe." After a moment, she laughed a little at herself. "Sorry, that sounds pompous."

Something occurred to me. "When was all of this expected?"

She gave a smile that was more of a shrug. "Now. It was expected I would be completely prepared by now. So to make sure, I started training when I was six."

"Six?"

"Maybe younger, really. But formal lessons started at six. It's not that bad. Just some extra school. And one of the perks of royalty is getting the best tutors you could ask for. They were smart, kind, caring, and patient enough to deal with a little girl who would rather be reliving a trip to neverland instead of memorizing pedantic details of a specific tradition. There was a lot to squeeze in, and it's not easy to focus as you're being shuffled from one fussy subject to the next. But if that was the price of a comfy life, so be it."

"I wanted to be who I was supposed to be," she said, almost defensively. The words started to trip over themselves as they flooded out. "If they wanted me to know why we had a particular ceremony, even if it seemed hopelessly outdated or pointless, I would make sure I could recite every iteration. If I needed to know the finer points of courtly fashion, then I would drill with aesthetic exercises to make sure I was right in line.

"I learned control. That's what I needed. No flights of fancy when we were hosting. No getting lost in thought during study time. What, was I going to waste some ludicrously expensive lesson plan tailor-made for me? Would I be that ungrateful? No, absolutely not. I would exceed everyone's expectations. I would be someone they wanted, someone they loved. If it's served to you on a silver platter, how can you turn it down? How can you spit in their faces? But then I would try to reach out to someone, and even when I did so adorned in the trappings of propriety, they wouldn't be answering me. They would be talking to the idea of me.

"And that's the trap. The image has to be more than an image. The symbol has to have some meaning to it. A princess can't just sit there and look pretty. There has to be substance behind the posturing, but it's still just a mold. And once you're squeezed into it, no one can see that. They see the symbol, even when they dig deeper. Because that's what they want. That's who they want something from. Meanwhile, I look into the mirror, and I don't recognize myself. What am I supposed to do? I did everything right! How can I tell them to stop loving me just because I hate my reflection?"

She came to a choking halt. She took three breaths, looking out the window as a moment of silence hung over the two of us. Glazed lights slid past the glass. The interior was a little pod quarantined from the world. It was a repository filling with disposed grief.

"But that wasn't what broke the camel's back," she went on, now passionlessly quiet. "That straw was when I realized that the person I was becoming would be entirely useless. When I was old enough to really start understanding what they were teaching me. The funny thing is, despite all of the controversy, the monarchy doesn't do much. We just sit there 99.9% of the time. Most of our counsel boils down to new and interesting ways to politely say, 'sorry, we can't help you.' The trick is to convince brilliant people that you helped them without saying anything. Even after they took me out of the spotlight, I was training as if I would become a savant, but I would never do anything with what they taught me. 'Please, Sophia, set aside who you are and be ready for the world to be placed squarely on your shoulders, but don't worry, you can't actually do anything after we put it there. Thank you kindly.'"

She sighed, emotion returning to her face like a campfire rekindling itself. "Sorry. I'm not really that resentful. It just all came out. My mother just wanted the best for me, and thought starting early was the way to do it. I know it was out of love."

"That doesn't mean you feel it," I said numbly. "That doesn't mean it comes through on the other end."

"Right, but you keep trying because you care, and you know your family has good intentions."

"Until you stop trying because you want to break the cycle. You want them to wake up, see that this isn't working."

"Except that never works. They think you don't care. And then, nothing you can do is enough anymore, because there's always that black mark on your record."

"It doesn't matter if six days out of the week you meet their high standards, that's not even a pat on the back. It's the seventh day they remember."

"And it's all so stupid. You feel like a child because all you had to do was talk to them about it—"

"Except that never works, either," I echoed. "And worst of all, it's not their fault it doesn't. You think you know what you want to say, but then you get there and, and..."

"It never comes out right," she concluded. "You sound ungrateful..."

"Or like an idiot..."

"...and so you must be wrong. It must be your fault. You were in the wrong all along."

Silence.

"You were thirteen, at least you have an excuse," I finally said.

"You didn't have the world at your feet," Sophia countered. "I'm the one without an excuse."

"No way," I said. I turned back at her, a fire in my gut. "Look at us, this is actually stupid. We don't have to keep dragging this around. Why are we doing this to ourselves?"

She chuckled slightly at the mild absurdity of our behavior. "I don't know," was all she said. I wanted her to throw off the lingering past, to rise defiantly to my challenge. That didn't happen. When I realized it wouldn't, I sat back in my seat. The fire slowly died in me, too.

After a moment of contemplation, staring out the side window, she added, "You know, sometimes I'm not sure if I ever stopped pretending. When you get so good at it—constantly thinking about your facial expressions, body language, intonation—you can't turn it off. Even if there wasn't a tutor around, I think I was always practicing. Even after leaving, I couldn't be sure how much of what I do isn't just training. And then, when I went to school… that was another act, wasn't it? Can't admit to being who I was. Had to put on another face. I was a transfer student, I was from another town, I was the dean's niece. Did I ever manage to turn it off? Have I lost something along the way? Am I—?"

"Sophie," I said, cutting her off. She jumped, as if she forgot she wasn't alone. Her eyes finally found mine in the rearview mirror.

"It's alright," I said.

She looked at me, perplexed. "What is?"

"It's alright," I repeated. "You're fine."

"I—" but something caught in her throat.

"I see you."

Sophia looked skeptical, but then tears appeared in her eyes. That broke the expression.

"Thank you," she said softly.

When we passed through the security checkpoints, Sophia mostly hid her face while I was exhaustively searched. When we arrived in the garage, we had to momentarily part ways as I was even more thoroughly looked over. Eventually, when the guards were satisfied, I was brought to a waiting room.

Sophia not only vouched for me, but she asked Blake and anyone else involved to be brought here as well. After a brief phone call, David seemed to think this was an opportunity, and the rest of Dark Eye Squadron was soon on the way.

"Excellent job, Kennedy," David said as he walked in with Randy and Blake. Blake nodded briefly when I glanced towards him. He was trying to say he was alright, but it wasn't convincing. He adjusted his bandages and took a seat against the wall as David clapped me on the back.

"I don't know about that," I admitted. "I just talked to her."

"He's just lucky our Princess lacks taste," Randy sneered. Maybe it was just my good mood, but I heard more good-natured ribbing than snide sniping in the statement.

"You did great," David emphasized. "This is an excellent first step for the organization."

I noticed his careful choice of words. There was a guard in the room, and no doubt others watching as well. Even though I had begun the opening moves of the diplomatic process, we still

had to maintain secrecy until the proper time. It was a strange tightrope act.

"Thanks, I guess," I said. I lowered my voice as I asked, "What do we do now?"

David lowered his tone as well, though it likely did little to prevent us from being overheard. "If Scarlett—that is, Sophia—has invited us here this quickly, she's probably hoping to bypass the experts and get to the heart of the matter herself. She might be thinking she'll get more information through us."

Because we don't know what we're doing, I thought. At least I didn't. They had chosen me specifically to deliver the message to Sophia on the grounds that we were familiar. Aside from that, I was told not to say much anything, and emphatically instructed not to screw it up. I didn't think that Sophia was just using us for information, but if she was, I had to be an easy mark, didn't I?

I had just started going over the conversation in the car again, a poisoned seed of doubt planted in my mind, when she returned.

"Hello again," she said formally. I could hear just a hint of nerves in her otherwise professional tone. "Blake, David, Randy. I suppose this is our official reintroduction. I'm Sophia Tiscardia."

"Blake Anthony. Pleased to meet you, Your Highness," Blake said, with a ridiculously low bow.

"No, please," Sophia said, raising her hands in embarrassed protest. "There's no need for that, Blake. I haven't been confirmed or anything. My title is basically hypothetical for now."

"For now," David agreed. "It's still an honor, Sophia."

He offered a hand, which she accepted gratefully.

"Your message said you represented a foreign organization?" she asked him. She had clearly identified him as the leader.

"International," David replied coolly. "It's a rather unique situation."

"And clandestine," Sophia noted.

"Certainly," David replied. "Hence the need for carefully arranged introductions."

"I see," she replied. She glanced towards me. "On that note, do you mind if I borrow Kennedy for a moment? My mother has requested to speak to him, as the one who delivered the message."

"Of course," David replied easily. "Might I offer my services, as team lead? I might be better able to answer any questions you may have."

"I'll pass along your offer," Sophia said pleasantly. "Kennedy?"

I glanced to David, who nodded almost imperceptibly. I turned back to Sophia, rising from my seat.

"Lead the way," I said.

It was only as we stepped into the hallway that it fully registered what was happening. Sophia's mother was, of course, none other than the Queen of Aechyr. And I was supposed to go talk to her. And potentially represent Time Peace. I was so the wrong person for this.

We reached the door to the hospital room, two guards on either side. Sophia glanced back and must've seen the obvious tension etched in my face. She leaned in and whispered, "Relax. I promise, there is nothing to worry about."

I really tried to believe her, but it wasn't easy.

Before anything more could be said, she opened the door and we stepped in. The first thing that struck me was how normal the room looked. There were piles of flowers and other tokens of goodwill, but otherwise, it was strikingly average. Well, maybe a bit warmer and cozier than an average hospital room, but it certainly wasn't lavish.

And laying on the bed, there she was. She looked startlingly old, but her eyes were alert. She smiled as we entered the room, and Sophia led me to a seat next to the bed. The Queen's kind expression eased some of my nerves, but plenty still remained.

I tried not to squirm in my seat as we finally got into position.

"You must be Kennedy," she said to me.

"Yes," I said, suddenly unsure if I should be adding a "Your Highness" or "Your Majesty" to the end of that sentence. If I had made a serious breach of protocol, it seemed neither Sophia nor her mother were going to mention it.

"It's good to meet you," she said. Glancing to daughter, she added, "An interesting choice, dear."

Sophia squirmed uncomfortably, but the Queen smiled.

"Well, Mr. Frost," she said to me, which took me by surprise, "what is it, exactly, that this organization of yours wishes to meet about?"

My mouth went dry. "I'm sorry, ma'am, I'm not supposed to discuss that."

"I'm sure," she replied calmly, "but you can give us an idea of what this is about. Is this some political matter? An economic affair?"

Her eyes were searching me, and I got the distinct impression that she could read me like a book.

“They told me not to—”

“I’m sure they did, as I’m sure you can understand that I’ll need to know who else should be present at these initial discussions,” the Queen said calmly, but forcefully. “This country isn’t run by any single individual, despite what some may claim. So tell me, should I be inviting my finance minister? Military advisors?”

“I—” I started to say. The Queen smiled patiently. “It’s more of an... you know, they really insisted that I don’t screw this up. I’m just a grunt. If you really need to know that sort of thing, David’s the one you should be talking to.”

The Queen nodded thoughtfully. “Well, at least he’s faithful to his cause. Thank you, Mr. Frost. I suppose we will just have to find out more for ourselves in this introduction. You can send our answer, we will meet with them.”

“Are you sure you’re up to this?” Sophia asked her, concerned.

“Of course,” she replied dismissively. “Besides, it won’t be only me there. Prime Minister Mattox, and some select senators. Harris, Tracey, Becker—”

“Becker?” I asked, ignoring decorum. “Charlie Becker?”

“Yes, dear,” the Queen said patiently. “He’s on several important senate committees, including several for national security. Of course he will be invited.”

“But he’s the guy—” I faltered, unsure of how to put it.

“I’m well aware of his political opinions, Mr. Frost,” the Queen said curtly, but calmly. “But he is still an elected representative of Aechyr, and we will treat him as such.”

“But—” I tried to think of some reason to protest other than “he’s partnered with Anarakia,” but nothing came to mind.

Sophia glared at me out of the corner of her eye, and I could tell that the slack they had been giving me had suddenly run out. I clamped my jaw shut and nodded jerkily.

"Thank you for this talk, Mr. Frost," the Queen said, more warmly once again. "It's been a pleasure meeting you. I'm sure I can call on you should we need you again."

I nodded again. "Yes, uh, Your Majesty."

She returned as slight nod and said, "You're excused."

Sophia whispered, "I'll catch up with you in a moment."

Back out in the hallway, I had to wait several yards away. Even then, the armed guards didn't look very pleased at my presence. Fortunately, I only had to wait a couple minutes before Sophia emerged once again.

"You can't really think having Charlie Becker at this meeting is a good idea," I said as she reached me. Immediately, her eyebrows raised at my brazen remark.

"I can't?" she repeated.

"You don't like him," I said, backpedaling slightly. "You said yourself that the Charmies are as good as garbage."

"I don't think I did," she replied mildly. "At least not that exact phrase. You're right, I don't like Becker. Of course I don't. I could say a lot about him, but that's not the point."

"Sophie," I said, holding her arm beseechingly, "you don't want him at this meeting. Trust me."

She stiffened slightly. "Are you going to tell me why?"

"You know I can't," I answered her.

"Then I'm sorry, Kennedy," she said. "It's not a matter of trust, this is business. And this is the one area that I need more than your word."

"You know he's connected to People's Front Nine, you—"

"Kennedy, drop it," she said angrily. "We *don't* know that. If we did, do you think he would be on those senate committees? We've considered it, and you heard my mother. Please, no offense, but you don't know what you're talking about here."

I know more than you think, I wanted to say. But I could tell there was no convincing her.

"I have to go back and talk to a few other people," she said, changing the subject abruptly. "Between this and the confirmation-slash-coronation... event, I'm getting pretty busy. But I can get away for some time this morning. You'll stick around, right?"

"Yeah, I'm not going anywhere," I said.

"Good," she replied, and cheered a little. "I'll see you soon. And this time, it's a promise."

She turned and left the other way, and I continued down the hall back towards the rest of the gang. I couldn't help but feel sulky. Even though I had been told not to interfere, or to negotiate, I felt I had an obligation to steer them away from Becker. No, it was more than an obligation, it was the right thing to do. Becker had that freak, Sainne, in his inner circle. There was no greater evidence of how twisted Becker could be then letting that creature skulk about around him. And the thought that Sainne would be one step away from the Queen, from Sophia—

A surge of anger nearly overtook me. Couldn't she see that this was important? I know I couldn't say anything directly, but surely she could tell from how I was talking that it was urgent. If only she would listen. I hated that I couldn't say anything, that my hands were tied.

With that heady mixture of helplessness and frustration, I bristled at the sight of a new man walking down the same hallway.

He was heading the opposite direction as me, towards the Queen's room. Instead of a doctor's coat or a guard's uniform, he had dark workman's overalls and a deep red shirt, heavy sleeves rolled up over deeply tanned forearms.

"Going somewhere?" I asked harshly.

He held up the thick tool bag. "Maintenance," he replied simply.

He looked pretty young for a repair man. His hair was thick, dark, and shaggy, sticking out from under his cap. His eyes were light brown, almost yellow, and his face was a little long, angular. Right now, it wore a bored expression. And yet, there was something in the way he held himself—the affected casualness—that set a deep alarm bell ringing. Whether primordial instinct or a half-learned diligence drilled into me, something told me the time to ask questions was over.

At the same moment as I came to that conclusion, the utility man seemed to read my mind. I was going for my watch, the only weapon I still had, but he was quicker. He let the bag drop as he pulled a silver gun from within simultaneously.

The bag fell away and he took aim.

A blue flash, and I collapsed to the floor. I had just unscrewed the crystal lens from my watch, and now it rolled uselessly down the hall. My body felt numb, save for a harsh tingling that ravaged up and down my arms and legs. A stun ray. An ATEP gun.

I felt tired, and everything began to blur. But just before my eyes unfocused entirely, I heard the young man speak, now serious and commanding.

"This is Trinity, we hit a slight bump. Move up the attack."

XI

Hang Time Duel

As blurry chunks of my vision returned, I struggled to remember just where I was. I seemed to be lying on a hard surface, my limbs stuck out at odd angles. My eyes focused, and I recognized the hallway of the Crown Royal Hospital. My memories suddenly snapped back into place.

I immediately pulled myself upright. My head ached, and my arms were slow and heavy. I barely noticed. Gunfire cracked through the silence, and the adrenaline pumping through my system doubled.

I sprang to my feet, head instantly clear. Before I could take my first step, I realized I was unarmed. I glanced around as the gunshots continued. Each shot was another spike of panic in my veins. As my anxiety ratcheted up again and again, I nearly missed it. The crystal lens for my watch had been kicked down the hallway, lodging itself in the entryway to a supply closet.

I heard a blood-curdling scream behind me. I hated to tear myself away from the sound of that shriek. My instinct was to run straight for it, diving in headlong. But I wasn't so stupid as to go in unarmed. I ran from the noise, leaning down to scoop up the lens, and then immediately turned on my heel.

I raced towards the sound of the battle. Horrible images flashed through my mind. Where was Sophia? Were they after her? For a horrible moment, I wished that this attack was aimed at the Queen, because then there was a chance Sophia might be safe. I hated myself for this thought, fleeting as it was.

I spun around the corner of yet another corridor. Almost immediately, the left side opened up into a wide passageway, forming a *T* with the hallway I was in. Standing around that corner, piled beds blocking their way in, men in black suits and helmets fired machine guns into the thinner hallway.

Someone grabbed my leg just as I was about to dive back around cover. I scrambled, raising my hand with the crystal lens as I collapsed.

"David!" I cried, seeing him crouched near the floor, still clutching at me. The body of one of the men in black lay next to him. At the intersection, next to the piled beds, two dead Royal Guards were splayed across the floor.

"Watch it or you're going to get your head blown off!" David yelled back.

He didn't have to tell me twice. I could see Blake across the opening, also hiding from the firing men and screwing in his own crystal lens. David made a slashing motion across his throat at him.

"They can't know!" he said loudly into his own watch. It hit me how poorly we were equipped for this. We had no backup communications, and no weapons apart from our crystal rays. Now David was telling us we didn't even have those.

"It's life or death!" Blake protested.

In reply, David grabbed a pistol from the dead attacker and slid it across the hall to Blake. Blake looked up, startled at the prospect.

"Where's Sophia?" I asked before we could be overrun.

"They went right for her," David shouted as he pulled a machine gun out from under one of the bodies. "Didn't even try for the Queen. Not that they could've made it."

"Which way?" I asked.

"That way," he said, nodding past Blake. "Towards the north entrance. We'll cover you."

He glanced towards Blake, who nodded, face pale.

"Hit 'em!" David shouted, and he and Blake turned the corner. David let out a spray of indiscriminate suppressing fire, Blake popping off after him. I sprinted across the opening, keeping low. I snagged a pistol from one of the Royal Guards and then put everything I had into my mad dash.

I hadn't been this way before. I desperately searched for every sign pointing toward an exit. I could hear bursts of fighting as I went along. I didn't bother trying to take cover. Sophia could be gone already. I couldn't wait. I just had to pray no one would take aim or get lucky.

If David and Blake tried to follow, I left them in the dust. Soon, I was far enough that even the sounds of fighting were dying down. I ran past a small cluster of nurses, who gasped and shrieked as some nutty kid with a gun dashed past. I kept running.

I skidded around a nurse's station, and all at once, a burst of gunfire exploded down the passageway. I let my feet fly out from under me. I landed on my shoulder as I raised my gun. I had so little time, I couldn't have thought about what I was doing. I fired. Someone swore and a gun clattered to the floor.

"Out now!" I heard in the voice of fake repairman.

"Red, you got a spare?" It took me longer than it should have to realize that I was Red. It took substantially less time to identify the speaker.

Randy was hunkered behind a pillar, unarmed.

"No. Sophia—where is she?" I shot back.

"Nearly gone," Randy snarled. "This is the rear guard. Let's grind 'em into the dirt."

I was already back on my feet, running towards the fleeing assailants. Randy quickly joined me.

We burst into the north entryway. From our vantage point on the second floor, we could see nearly everything. Across the right wall was a lengthy admissions desk behind a thick pane of glass. To our left were rows of chairs for visitors and those awaiting admission. Directly ahead were the rotating doors of the entrance itself, framed by square pillars, which parted the windows as well. But one of the panes on the right had been shattered by an ambulance, which sat in a pile of powdered glass halfway through the foyer.

If there was anything more on the ground floor, we couldn't see it. Large letters spelling out "CROWN ROYAL" mounted at the edge of this second-floor balcony obscured part of our view. I didn't even look for stairs but ran straight for the gaps between the words. I was going to jump it. With some help.

But the arena appeared before I had even reached my watch. Burning blue stars shone beyond the hospital windows, and I realized the lobby had become a battlefield.

And with a devastating crack, the floor fell out from under me.

Dust and smoke engulfed me as I fell. I tumbled and lost the horizon, which way was up, which way I was falling. The floor slammed into me, hard.

The light was hazed by the debris. I felt dizzy. A giant letter *N* was lying a few inches away from me. I was lucky I hadn't been crushed.

The gunfire sharpened my foggy mind. A burst came from above me, and another to the right. Two people were exchanging fire. Randy. Randy was above me. How had he gotten a gun?

Just then, a figure ran up through the dust, right arm bloodied, but left arm holding a knife. I had just an instant to take in the man. Young, like me. Asian heritage, sharp eyebrows, dark goatee, black eyes. He was small and lean but ran towards me with a fierce determination that amplified his presence tenfold.

I held up my hand defensively just before he stabbed into me. I pushed the attack aside just a few inches. Pain shot through my shoulder. If it weren't for my last-minute block, he would have hit my heart. Now it was pounding so fast I thought it might give out through sheer strain.

Knives stared right into me, eyes wide with intense drive as he dug the knife in deeper. I howled in pain, trying to push him off. I had no chance. I could only watch and wait for him to finish me.

I saw the time gauge. It was on my good arm, the one pushing back against my attacker.

I had only one shot. I pulled my left arm around. It felt as if I was tearing it off instead of performing a simple movement. But it didn't matter. Even if it did fall off, it wouldn't matter for long.

I clasped the crown on my watch. Knives' eyes darted to the watch, right as I pressed it in.

Time skipped backward several seconds. I was charging forward, toward the balcony, reaching for my watch again. My arm was whole once more. But I was running straight into danger.

Just as it had before, the balcony exploded behind me, and I fell with the front lip to the floor below. I had a split-second to brace. It hardly helped. The ground slapped me just as hard as last time, and the dazed pain returned. But I had to fight through it,

The gunfire sounded again from the two sources, though the pattern of bursts were slightly different. That was as good a cue as any. I forced myself to my knees and scanned for the gun. It had been ripped from my hand yet again in the intensity of the impact.

I found it. Only a few feet away. I grabbed at it, spun around, scanned desperately.

Sure enough, Knives was already in his berserker charge, nearly on me. I aimed the gun and pulled the trigger.

He stumbled and fell into me. He bowled me over, knife clattering aside. I felt something warm and sticky spreading onto my chest. Revulsion boiling up within me, I pushed him up off, and I saw his face.

A look of shock had spread across his previously intimidating features. Now, he looked even younger than me. Pitiable. Slowly, his eyes faded. They unfocused—went dull. I realized I was holding a corpse, still pushing it away in disgust. A dread horror crept over me as death visited so near. Horror and... guilt? Guilt at shoving away this victim as if he were a piece of refuse. Guilt at my own relief.

Fresh blood splattered my chest. I didn't feel the pain, so it took me a moment to realize this time it was my own.

I collapsed, about to join the dead man beside me. As my mind fogged, strange thoughts crept up inside. I felt confused, tired. But the horror and revulsion from before were gone. Now, I almost felt grateful. I would be going away. And maybe, when I got there, I could say sorry to the man I had just met.

Then reality snapped again. No more regrets. No horror. Only a little lingering guilt.

I was running towards the lip of the balcony again. I knew what was about to happen. I knew I had to do something different. I was closing with the letters.

I didn't have an idea, not exactly. It was more a quick flash of an image. The N lying on the floor, still mostly intact. With my last step, I abruptly threw my weight towards it.

The explosion knocked my feet out from under me just as I hit the back of the letter. The ground slid away. Slid. I wasn't falling nearly as fast. This side of the balcony was collapsing just a little slower than the rest.

But then it slipped away from me. My grip had been practically non-existent. There hadn't been enough time. The N hit a pile of debris, and I tumbled to the side. But I wasn't dazed, just aching and a little dizzy.

I stood up, glancing around for the gun. It wasn't where it had been. Of course not. I hadn't fallen like before. A flash of the horrifying look on Knives' face as I had shot him struck me out of nowhere. I abandoned the search, and instead rallied for his charge, looking at the precise spot Knives had charged from the last two times.

But he wasn't there.

I felt him a moment before he struck. I spun as the knife hit my bicep. Knives had come at me from behind, aiming for my right arm. He had gotten it.

I grabbed for his knife with my good hand. He was too quick. He pulled back and then slashed at me. He only got a

grazing slice across my chest as I backpedaled further into the open. Into the entryway. I kicked out and connected with his injured arm. He hardly winced, but he did step back.

I took a defensive stance, my eyes running over his wounded right hand, and that's when I realized the obvious. The other gun—the one Randy was firing—it had been Knives'. He had dropped it when I fired blindly around the corner and scored a lucky hit.

But in the realization, I had let myself get distracted.

Knives dove in. I blocked with my left arm. It was half-effective. Knives didn't get any vital organs, but he gave my forearm a nasty cut. I skipped the fancy maneuvers and grabbed his arm with my right, squeezing and twisting. I gripped as hard as I could, even as pain shot through me. I was intent on squeezing his arm into paste, or making him drop the knife, whichever came first.

He didn't make it easy. Just as his grip was weakening, he jutted his leg forward, wrapped it around the back of mine, and pulled. The back of my head hit the ground. A hollow pain blinded me for a moment. Only a moment. I was already scrambling backwards as my vision faded back in.

A bang and hiss from the admissions desk preceded the attack. I glanced aside just a moment, but that's all Knives had needed. He slashed forward at lightning speed. I clutched my throat. Knives raised his arm for a second blow. Sharp cracks, and then he fell backwards.

I rolled my eyes up and saw an injured Randy, clutching the machine gun and sliding down the rubble towards me. The admissions desk further back was engulfed in strange white smoke.

"Red!" he shouted at me. A shade of strain showed behind his anger. "Quit dragging us down!"

A burst of gunfire tore through him as the utility man strode across the entryway. Broken glass crunched under his feet as Randy fell. A waft of smoke followed his footsteps.

He looked over the three of us, eyes lingering on Knives. He hesitated, his face twisting. Finally, just as my vision was turning black, he reached over to his watch and hit the crown.

The balcony was about to explode. Get to the N, I told myself. It fell. I rode it down. I rolled to my feet, the gun still in my hand.

Knives. Where was he coming from? I held fast, preparing for the ambush.

I didn't have to wait long. The gunfire upstairs opened up just as Knives burst out from beneath the rubble. He leapt towards me, roaring a deep, guttural war cry to freeze blood.

I spun around, and he hit me in my gun arm again. I reacted just as I had before. My left hand shot out to grab his knife and missed. He slashed as he backpedaled, grazing my chest. Another repeat.

The rhythm of the fight came back as easily as a memory. I kicked and hit his injured arm. He backed off.

He had lured me into a familiar pattern. He was about to change it up, to go for my stomach. But this time, I had an advantage.

As soon as I had stepped back, I raised my gun and fired. It was hasty, with pain shooting through my arm. There was no way it would hit. I knew that. But Knives was startled, and suddenly glanced aside, looking for cover. That's all I needed. I sprinted backwards.

I could hear Randy and the utility man exchanging gunfire, but it sounded like Randy was getting off fewer shots. I just had to hope he was keeping the intruder busy.

The man with the knife held it up, poised to throw. I fired again, wildly, and he ducked back into the forest of chairs. For my part, I slid across the floor to the passenger side of the crashed ambulance, putting it between me and the utility man.

A huge bang echoed through the entryway, a hissing sound replacing it shortly after. I glanced towards the source—the admissions desk—and saw the utility man dive below as a fire extinguisher rocketed around, blanketing everything back there in white smoke. Still, a few muzzle flashes showed he was intent on keeping Randy suppressed.

"Gold, what's the play?" I asked into my wrist.

"Pierce has my number," Randy said flatly despite the moments bought by the billowing smoke. "He's too good. When we reset, you keep his attention, I'll take out Nergüi, then we hit Pierce together. Before he knows what hit him."

"Got it," I said, puzzling over the strange name "Ner-gwee," and how Randy could have known it. Or Pierce.

No time to ponder. Nergüi had popped up again, raising his knife to throw. I brought up my gun and pulled the trigger.

Click. Empty.

Nergüi smiled toothily and threw the knife on a straight course. Right between my eyes.

And then I was back at the beginning.

I turned on the spot, aiming for the *N* on the balcony.

The reset had happened so fast, I couldn't remember whether the knife hit, or if we snapped back before it could. All I could think about now was the plan Randy had hastily given me.

I slid down the collapsing rubble as the balcony exploded yet again. I rolled easily back to my feet, but this time, I didn't bother trying to locate Nergüi. I spun towards the admissions desk and fired once.

Pierce, or whatever the utility man was called, ducked below the desk as the glass spiderwebbed. I knew I only had one bullet left, but I had to somehow use this to keep Pierce down. At least until—

Randy slid down the rubble, firing two quick bursts. I didn't take my eyes off the desk, but I heard something large slump to the ground behind me.

Now, the fun part. The final blow. An evil electric thrill shot through me at the prospect of the end. My eyes dialed in. I tunnel visioned on that desk. The second Pierce would pop up, it would be over.

Movement. My finger tightened.

No. Wait. It was just a flock of papers taking to the air. A distraction. Pierce would pop up soon.

He didn't. Instead, a sudden burst of smoke engulfed the desk. It kept growing and growing. No, it was coming closer now. Pierce had grabbed the fire extinguisher and was using it to blind us. To close the distance.

I panicked and fired. It missed. Of course.

"Randy!" I shouted. He had already taken this in.

"Get down!" he hissed.

We hit the floor just as a burst of gunfire racked over our head, lancing out from the cloud of extinguisher smoke. And then the wave engulfed us. We were lost in a misty world of roiling white clouds. Pierce could be standing right next to me and I wouldn't see his legs.

I rose, crouching just below the line of fire. The smoke was thinner up here, but it still cast dark shadows as it rolled past. Any of these phantoms could be Pierce or Randy.

But then I heard them. No gunfire, but I could hear the quick scuffling of their struggle. There. Just ahead and to my left, I could see the smoke being churned up.

I rushed over to help, and the smoke slowly parted. Randy and Pierce exchanged blows in a flurry of motion. I could hardly follow. Randy was terrifying, swinging like an enraged beast, but with a primal control. He was constant motion, each strike setting up another, but always ready to turn on a dime. I caught a glimpse of his face, and it was pure concentrated fury.

Pierce was no less frightening but in a completely different way. His limbs snapped out, left and right, blocking Randy's strikes and lashing out like vipers. He ducked and weaved, sliding from one position to the next, sticking for a moment to power a fast and brutal opportunistic strike. He was a little more defensive, keeping his arms close in a tight guard, but switching up at a moment's notice. He was never quite what I anticipated, and yet he lured you into thinking he was predictable. Only Randy's constant adaptation and pressure seemed to keep him in the game.

And then it was all over. Randy moved to slam his fist across Pierce's face but swung wide. Pierce slipped in close and uppercut Randy's chin hard. I thought I heard something snap, but it could have been the crack of the shocking impact.

I stepped lightly, dashing at Pierce's back. I was going to slam my fist so hard into the back of his head that his nose would break on the ground. I was nearly on top of him when he spun on his heel and bowed out of the way.

I whiffed just as he drove his knee up into my stomach. The breath was driven from me as I tried to recover some control.

I stumbled away, nearly tumbling to the floor. But I wouldn't let myself fall to his mercy.

I heaved my body roughly upright again, planting my feet. But Pierce struck first. His fist crushed my nose. *Roll with it*, something said. I tried the best I could, stepping back as I allowed my head to twist with the impact.

Pierce didn't follow up immediately. His mistake. I knew it would have been over if he had. But maybe I had surprised him. Whatever the case, he had given me just enough time to get a grip on myself.

I was in bad shape. In two strikes, he had knocked the breath from my lungs and made me see stars. But I couldn't afford to let this slow me down.

Pierce struck out experimentally, testing my defenses. I took a lead from him, sliding out of the way rather than blocking. We were facing off for the first time; I wanted him to worry about how dangerous I could be. I wouldn't let him see what I was capable of. Little as that was right now.

This wouldn't be easy. His guard was solid, and he wasn't likely to give that up for a wild strike. We exchanged a couple probing attacks, but neither of us were making any real progress. I could tell his mind, like mine, was combing through several possibilities. Just as I wondered if using the nearby shattered glass was feasible, he glanced over as if he had the same exact idea.

I burst forward on instinct. It was a nice thought, but fun fact: you can move your eyes faster than the rest of your body. His had snapped back to me as I charged, aiming low. He split his attention, one arm pushing aside my strike, the other going for its own.

He hit my cheek, but I plowed forward. I latched onto him, wrestling him to the ground. Or I tried. He was slippery, tossing me aside. I stumbled to my feet, blocking his next blow, but he was

in a fierce, continuous assault. He kicked out, hit me in the stomach. I blocked the follow up strike, but painfully. The next one hit me in the throat, and I nearly choked, foolishly trying to take in a breath through a collapsed windpipe.

With my right arm hanging in front of my head in a weak block, I was an easy target for Pierce. He could have taken me apart. If it weren't for Randy.

Randy suddenly appeared behind him, slamming his hand into the side of Pierce's head, hard. Pierce stumbled, and Randy shot forward, burying his fist into his stomach. Pierce grabbed at Randy's hair in an uncharacteristically savage swipe. The two fell over onto the ground, exchanging brutal blows.

My throat cleared and I swallowed a huge lungful of air. My head became light for a moment with the sudden influx. I steadied my breathing, cleared my mind, stepped closer. Pierce rolled clear for a moment, and I raised my foot to slam down on him. Pierce caught it on the downstroke and pushed against me. He pushed himself off the ground as I fell.

My back hit the floor yet again, but this time I kept my head free from any damage. I rolled aside to get some distance before popping to my feet again. I had only just started to feel the sharp stabbing of the broken glass before I made it up. It crunched below my feet, and I immediately regretted my choice of positioning.

Randy was back up too, and he only spared a quick glance in my direction. The two of us formed a right angle with Pierce, who looked ready for both of us. With my unsteady footing, I couldn't push towards him aggressively. Randy didn't wait for Pierce to take advantage of that fact. He rushed in.

Pierce had anticipated the move. He blocked Randy's attack, got inside his guard, and smashed his knee. But Randy was an animal. He wouldn't be stopped so easily. He cracked his knuckles against Pierce's nose, tore at his chest and wrestled him back to the floor. Pierce toppled backwards and kicked desperately to get away from Randy's blind fury. He struck Randy on the forehead with his heel. Randy finally stopped. Just in time for me to slam into Pierce.

I fell onto his chest, focusing my weight into my falling elbow. Pierce gasped in pain. I had him. I struck him in the face to guarantee the victory. I wound back to do it again, just to be sure, and that's when it hit.

Pierce grabbed some of the broken glass and tossed it into my face. If it weren't for my glasses, I would have been blinded. But he didn't stop at that. The first handful of glass was just a distraction. He hit me with an opportunistic blow as he twisted out from under me. If he weren't mostly preoccupied with freeing himself, he might have done even more damage.

I fell away too. Simultaneously, we dragged ourselves to our feet. We were both in bad shape, but I didn't give myself even odds. Randy had been right, Pierce was good. If it was just him and me, even footing, I wasn't coming out on top.

I glanced towards Randy. He wasn't moving. I thought he was still alive. I wasn't sure. But I couldn't count on his help anymore. I looked back towards Pierce hurriedly, but it seemed he was doing something similar. His eyes had landed on Nergüi again, and his bloodied face paled.

He looked back to me and raised his watch arm just a little.

Our eyes locked as our thoughts paralleled each other's. It was all or nothing. Neither of us was leaving anyone behind. We stood there in mutual understanding and hatred for a moment before I nodded slightly. We never looked away as we carefully reached for the crowns on our watches, and pressed.

"Gold," I said into my watch just before the balcony exploded again.

"What?" Randy asked as I rolled back to my feet, landing on the first floor.

"We're not winning this. New plan."

I located Nergüi, fired once, and then dodged randomly, just giving myself time to talk.

"We break the arena."

"Dive straight through?"

"You got it."

"I'll cover you. Hit it."

I reached for my watch, relieved that Randy had immediately caught on to my thought process. I pushed the crown one last time as Nergüi's knife sank into me.

One last time, I turned halfway through my run off the balcony. One last time, the balcony exploded as I dived towards the *N*, riding the debris safely down.

Once more, Nergüi burst from the rubble, from the pocket of safety. But immediately, he was forced to duck back down into the debris. Randy had let out a burst in his direction, just enough to make him drop. I fired my two shots to keep Pierce down. I kept sprinting towards the doors as Randy picked up the suppression.

Now all that mattered was the door, and just beyond, the edge of the arena. I ignored the spinning doors and went straight for the ambulance and the shattered windows. I had to take a circuitous route, avoiding some of the shattered glass and the fall that would come if I rushed over it.

A moment later, and I nearly regretted that decision. Something told me that I was in danger. Maybe I heard something swishing through the air, maybe I saw a reflection in the windows that remained intact, but somehow, I knew. I ducked to the side just as Nergüi's knife flew past my ear. It embedded itself into the pillar next to the window I was aiming for, and for a second, I saw Nergüi's frustrated expression mirrored in the intact window opposite.

And then I leapt through the air, over the broken glass, and into the night outside. Three more steps and I was at the wall of the arena—the seemingly endless void of fiery blue stars.

I burst through, and the arena vanished, popping silently like a soap bubble. Real time returned, and I had to remind myself that only a few seconds had passed for the rest of the timeline. Hang time hadn't accumulated, and neither had my injuries. I had my full strength again, and I called on every ounce of it as I charged forward.

I could just see someone in the distance. Rushing towards a structure—the private parking garage—they were burdened with another figure slumped over their shoulder.

Sophie.

I had nothing else I could add to the chase. I was sprinting at full. My only consolation was that I wasn't carrying a load. I would gain on them either way.

Then I noticed another figure. Smaller than the man carrying Sophia. It was still far away, and I tried to make out if it had a weapon. Before I could, both intruders vanished into the garage.

The seconds ached by as the garage neared. I finally dashed through the entrance. It only took a second to locate the figures. A square ambulance was sitting there, running, side door open. Sophia and the first figure must have already been inside. Only the second figure remained. A woman with blonde hair tied into a braid.

I was out of the arena. I had a weapon that I could use. I tossed aside the gun and armed my crystal ray just as she hopped into the ambulance. She turned.

The shock stole a split second from me. Avery stared back, almost as surprised to see me as I was to see her. And then fury surged through my veins. I aimed my crystal ray just as she drew her gauge gun.

I fired, my shot going wide as I dodged hers. The tires squealed and the ambulance pulled away. I readied another shot, the back doors square in my sights. And I couldn't do it. I didn't know if I'd hit Sophia. I couldn't take the chance.

The ambulance pulled away. How could I let it end like this? How could I let them just get away? But I had finally reached my limit. There was no way I was chasing down a moving vehicle.

I looked around at the garage. There were few cars here, and I couldn't do anything with them. Except one.

I ran over as fast I could to Sophia's car. I yanked on the handle, but nothing happened. I tried again, but it was still locked. I saw a small black plate near the handle. On a hunch, I pressed my finger to it. The same finger I had pressed to the screen. The door clicked open.

I dived into the car and immediately looked for another plate near the ignition. I found it and the car hummed to life, the screen flickering on with it. I slammed the stick into reverse and peeled out.

Spinning around, I switched into drive and hammered my foot down on the gas. I flew out of the garage and onto the road. I caught a glimpse of the ambulance's taillights turning onto the long forest road skirting around the city. I sped after it, blowing past the vacant guard posts.

I raised my arm, crystal ray readied. I fired, blowing a hole in the windshield. It immediately spiderwebbed into a frost-like pattern obscuring everything except the empty hole. I tapped on the brake, suddenly fearing that I'd fly off the road.

I hunched over, staring out the little hole I had made. I could just see the ambulance. It would have to be my guide along the road. And then one of the back doors popped open, and a black-clad man aimed a gun towards me.

I ducked, trying to hold the wheel straight as the bullets ripped through the window. They let up a moment, and I glanced through the windshield hole. I yanked the wheel to the right before I hit the guardrail at the edge of the road.

There were a few fresh holes in the windshield, but it was otherwise as opaque as before.

They fired again, and I ducked. As soon as they let up again, I checked and realized I had overcorrected. I glanced towards the screen, looking for any help. It only showed a map, a few course options, and some self-driving modes. Including an "escort mode."

I clicked it, hurriedly pulling up a fresh set of options. There it was—a "follow" option. My fingers flew over the screen, pressing it, selecting the ambulance to follow, and clicking the emergency icon. I felt the controls slacken in my hands and the car straighten as it accelerated.

Another burst of gunfire hit the window, but I didn't care. I stayed low and dragged myself into the passenger seat. From my lying position, I fired upwards into the window several times, blasting a large hole in it.

They fired through that, and I pressed into my seat.

I couldn't sit up. I fired, trying to melt away through more glass, but this wasn't getting me anywhere. It would take too long to make a hole wide enough that they couldn't cover with a machine gun. I needed a new plan.

From my prone position, I couldn't see the ambulance. Just what was inside the car.

That could work.

I reached up and ripped off the rearview mirror, dropping back down just before another round of strafing fire. I lifted the mirror, angling it towards the back of the ambulance. I had just spotted it when it sharply rounded a corner. For a moment, my car seemed like it would continue on straight, but it abruptly cornered onto the new path, nearly missing it.

I twisted around, trying to avoid being slammed into a panel. The mirror rattled in my hand as the car straightened. I searched, trying to reacquire the ambulance. Its flashing lights guided me towards it at first, then became distracting.

I caught a glimpse. Just for a second, the mirror had angled perfectly. I saw into the back of the vehicle. The light hit just right, and I saw Sophia's face. She was lying, strapped to a gurney, laid low in the back, unconscious.

The gunman raised his weapon again. The ambulance hit a bump and he stumbled backwards. I popped up instantly and fired. The ray from my crystal struck the edge of the open door, burning a hole into it.

I ducked back down as he aimed again. I watched him from my mirror. It seemed they had changed tactics; Avery reached over and pulled the door shut. Except it wouldn't latch. I had burned through the handle, so it swung back open as soon as they rounded another corner.

Once again, my car took a moment before following suit. The city lights flashed past, a little less frequently now. The blades of a helicopter beat the air overhead. My time was running out. I had to derail the ambulance before it got to its destination, wherever that may be.

I popped up, but the gunman was back, and he had the same thought. He was showing no quarter, letting off burst after burst. I ground my teeth in frustration. I couldn't waste a second.

I pulled up the map on the screen, searching for a possible destination. The helicopter rotor still fluttered overhead. They had to be heading for somewhere it could land. We were at the outskirts of Thysiopolis, and I could bet we were heading out further still. I tried a few possible destinations, and as the computer traced the paths, I saw a turn coming up.

I knew what to do. I turned in my seat, facing the passenger door. I braced myself and kicked it open. I raised my arm, aiming in anticipation, readying for the turn.

Just as before, the ambulance turned, and the car continued forward for a second. In that moment, the ambulance was framed perfectly in my open door. I fired.

The intense beam exploded the tire as it rounded the bend. Its speed, the bursting tire, the turn—it all added up. As my car caught up with the action and spun around, the ambulance toppled to the side. I winced, but I was out of time.

The car ground to a halt and I leapt out the open door, charging towards the toppled rescue vehicle. The gunman stumbled out from the now-horizontal doors. I blasted him with the crystal ray, tossing him aside.

The side door, now facing the sky, burst open, and I saw Avery pop up, braid whipping back and forth in the wake of the helicopter. She raised her gauge gun. Too slow. My watch was already aimed at her.

A harsh ringing suddenly tore into my ears. Pain engulfed my mind. I grabbed at my head, stumbling. I tried to focus on my goal. The mission. Sophia. I tried to power through it. But it amplified and I couldn't. I fell to my knees.

My eyes watered as I tried to look up. The wind whipped past as the helicopter descended, ropes and ladders trailing down. A tall figure slipped from the ladder and strode towards Avery. Even through my watering eyes I recognized him immediately.

Director Sainne smiled contemptuously toward me, long white hair blowing around him, green eyes glowing in the darkness. He held that small orb, the Talhesian torture device. His black-gloved finger pressed firmly on a nearly imperceptible button on the silver surface.

He reached over with his long thin arm and helped Avery from the ambulance. His stick-like arm didn't so much as tremble as Avery leaned her weight on it. She grinned toothily as more black-clad figures swarmed around, either from the helicopter, or from the cab of the ambulance. They quickly hauled Sophia's gurney towards the chopper.

I stumbled forward, but the ringing was too much. My legs were like jelly and I stumbled aside. Avery said something, but I couldn't hear. Sainne replied calmly, amusedly. Avery laughed. Sainne released the button.

The ringing stopped and a deep exhaustion set in. Every muscle felt as if it had come undone, refusing to reply to my commands. And my mind was slowly fading.

"Oh, Kennedy," Avery said loudly over the beating rotors. "As I was saying, you're so earnest. It's cute, actually. But if you want to be a player here, do the rest of us a favor, and grow up first."

"Let's give him a chance, then," Sainne said dangerously.

"Excuse me?" Avery asked, suddenly taken aback.

"Take the Princess upstairs, dear," Sainne continued in the same tone, smiling more toothily.

Avery didn't move, eyes glued on Sainne as he waved one of the black figures forward. The Anarakian soldier dragged forward a man with a bag over his head. I groggily stared towards them, unsure of what to make of this. Avery looked more and more apprehensive.

Sainne stepped towards me.

"Kennedy, I can't tell you what a pleasure it is to finally have this opportunity for an up close and personal chat," he said, drawing ever nearer. Goosebumps rippled up and down my arms. He was exactly how I had remembered him. Worse, since now he was vivid reality. The tight skin stretching across the bones of his jaw as he spoke seemed waxy in the moonlight.

He kneeled down beside me, and I recoiled, but his long thin arm draped around me, grabbed my shoulder, and pulled me back. "I have to say I'm a bit unimpressed," he said thoughtfully, though his teeth were still bared in that wicked smile. "Oh, it took some talent to get here, I'm sure, don't take it the wrong way. But you see, I had higher expectations. I'm a little disappointed in myself as well, frankly, as I'm taking the time to waste my thoughts on you. Still, you could do me the courtesy of at least proving you have some nerve at this juncture."

Suddenly, I felt the cold metal of a gun placed in my hand, and the Anarakian trooper tore the bag from the prisoner's head. He had distinct gray streaks on the sides of his otherwise shiny black hair. Becker. Charles Becker.

"Sainne! What are you doing?" Avery screeched just as one of the Anarakians grabbed her from behind, pinning her arms behind her back.

"Hush now," Sainne chided gently, his green eyes never leaving me. I felt my arm, the one with the gun pressed into it, rise.

Sainne guided it, pointing it directly at Becker. The senator's face was pale, horrified.

"Sainne, what have you done?" he asked, still a trace of the confidence in it, but barely.

"This man, he's done a lot to you hasn't he?" Sainne whispered to my ear.

"Was that the Princess?" Becker asked, mortified, glancing around at the scene. "You've ruined us! You've—"

A gag was forced into his mouth. Sainne hardly seemed to have noticed.

"The mastermind behind the People's Front, we couldn't have even touched Sophia without the groundwork he laid out for us. Really, he rolled out the red carpet for Anarakia, didn't he?"

Sainne leaned a little closer, nearly touching my ear. I shuddered in disgust. "It's okay, Kennedy. You can kill him."

A little shot of adrenaline rushed through me again. I tried to struggle against his grip, but his unnatural strength kept me pinned. Though he couldn't hear us, Becker clearly realized what was happening. His eyes fixated on mine, calmly pleading. Avery was screaming something indistinct.

"He gave us the men who will be handling the Princess, you know," Sainne said, grinning. "They aren't the most stable of folk, but they have their uses. Of course, when they get their hands on her..."

He lowered his voice even further, and the smile vanished. I didn't look at him, but I could actually feel his eyes turn red. As the enjoyment drained, and only endless malice remained. A vacuum of hate that could only grow stronger. He whispered terrible things to me.

I twitched.

The gun went off, and Becker crumpled.

Sainne smiled and released me, standing up. Avery was screaming at him at the top of her lungs, still held firm by the soldier behind her. I looked to my hand, still clasping the gun, aghast. I hadn't meant to. I hadn't meant it this time. I couldn't have done this. I didn't.

I could still see the look of shock on Becker's face. It was Nergüi all over again. But this time it was irreversible.

My own shock turned to rage. I pointed the gun at the back of Sainne's billowing hair and pulled the trigger painfully tight. It clicked. Nothing happened.

He glanced back at me, eyes green again. The corner of his mouth twisted into a satisfied smile, and he turned back to Avery.

"You see," he said, his gloved hands held open casually to either side, "I kept my promise. Not a finger laid on him. Dear Kennedy will go down as a hero to Aechyr tonight, and Becker, a martyr to the Front. Now, let's bury the hero before he gets gun shy," he commanded.

The soldier released Avery, but it was clear she wasn't free to go. Sainne stared her down, still grinning. Tears started welling in her eyes as she unholstered her gauge gun. She didn't raise it, never pointed it at Sainne. Although it was obvious she wanted to, she couldn't. Two other soldiers were watching her as well.

She walked over to me instead. She spun the gear on the back of her gauge gun. I tried to pump thoughts through my clogged mind. She pointed it at my head, her watering eyes disrupting her aim. She tried blinking them away, and when they cleared, I saw she had as much hatred for me as she did Sainne.

She suddenly looked up as the sound of roaring engines sped towards us from behind me, headlights blinding her. I took

the chance, rolled to the side, then dashed for the rail at the side of the road.

Avery fired. My shoulder burned. I heaved myself over the rail as a second shot burned against the metal below me. Gunshots echoed through the night. The chopper's engines roared as I hit the grassy hill. I rolled down several times before settling, splayed out, face up several feet below the road.

I saw the helicopter rise into the air, two figures climbing upwards on the dangling ropes. The gunfire died out, and my vision faded.

XII

The Traitorous Trinity

When I first woke up, it was in one of the rooms at the Crown Royal Hospital. I was in a small room, bandages around my shoulder, monitors beeping periodically. The memories of what happened before didn't return in a rush or slowly trickle back to me. It was as if they had always been there, but the bits of my brain connecting the facts to any meaning had to be switched back on piece by piece. As much as the half-remembered events pressed on me, I was too tired for the surge of panic I had felt when first experiencing them. Instead, a dull worry rested in the bottom of my stomach.

And then it churned as I remembered Becker. I heaved while reliving the memory of my finger twitching. Of the gun recoiling. It hadn't been me, of course, I tried desperately to rationalize. It had just been a twitch after all. I had been disgusted at being so close to Sainne. At what he whispered. I heaved again, this time desperately reaching for a bucket. It all came up in waves.

Revulsion. Shame. Regret.

My experience got tangled after that. I wasn't sure how long passed. Whether it had been hours or days. But eventually, I knew that it was light out, and that I had slept a long time.

"Ken, how are you feeling?" Blake asked as he walked in. He looked about as tired as I felt.

"Like I just went through a spin cycle," I replied slowly, choosing to only speak for my physical state. "You in one piece?"

"Nothing new," he replied, though he looked tired, too. Better than the last time I had seen him, but weary. "David and I tried to follow you out, but we were playing it safe. Got pinned down a couple times. Maybe we should have been a bit more reckless. If we had gotten there sooner—"

I shook my head. The exhaustion had long since suffocated any potential resentment. "You'd probably be dead." I held my breath for a moment before asking, "I suppose I don't need to ask, but did…?"

Blake shook his head. "They got away. With the Princess."

I grimaced. "I figured as much. That backup—the guys who chased off Sainne—was that you two?"

"And some Royal Guard. And Randy. As soon as you broke the arena, it sounds like those Anarakia guys turned and ran. No doubt regrouping the rest. But there is good news."

I raised my eyebrow. Blake didn't look particularly pleased.

"We have Avery," he explained.

"No way," I exclaimed.

"Yeah. Sainne left without her. Hardly a glance back."

"Then we've got them," I declared, thinking we had a shot at getting Sophia back, too. A little of my energy returned as I thought about it. But I realized there was one major obstacle. "Is she talking?"

"They're working on it," Blake replied. "But it's a bit complicated."

"What is?" I asked.

"You remember how I said we pulled up with the Royal Guard?" he prompted.

"Yeah, so?"

"Well, there's a bit of a question as to who's in charge. The Aechrians think this is People's Front Nine—"

"Which it is."

"—which it is," Blake agreed. "But obviously, they don't know about Anarakia. The Hawk is trying to explain some of this Time Peace/Anarakia conflict without blowing their minds or locking us all up in a looney bin. Meanwhile, Aechyr's keeping this under wraps from the public, but internally... it sounds like a witch-hunt. They found Becker, so naturally, they're bringing in all of his associates for questioning. Of course, one is rather conspicuously absent."

"Sainne," I said, grinding my teeth. I peeled off the monitors on my arms and swung my legs over the bed. They had put me in a hospital gown, which felt uncomfortably light and exposed.

"Woah, where are you going?" Blake asked.

"It sounds like we need all hands on deck," I replied. "I'm doing no good here."

"You don't think you need rest?"

"I think there are bigger needs. But let's stop by the cafeteria on our way. I could use some food. And my clothes. What did they do with them?"

"I think they put a fresh set in the left cabinet," Blake replied. "We going to see David?"

"We're going to see David," I confirmed, pulling out my street clothes.

David, as it turned out, was near Avery's holding cell. Time Peace had set up a temporary headquarters in the woods alongside the hidden road to the hospital. Several enormous trailers, militarized hallways in all reality, occupied a set of clearings far from the road. David was standing next to a particularly large, armored one.

"Kennedy, should you be up and about?" he asked.

I slurped down a little more of my fruit smoothie, which was doing wonders to reinvigorate me. "Thought you needed some help," I replied, trying to sound more at ease than any of us actually were.

David nodded. "Things are moving fast. Let's try not to get in anyone's way."

I stepped to the side, making sure to leave the door clear as I asked, "What's the scoop, Green?"

"Prisoner exchange," he replied simply.

I choked a little. "Anarakia's going to trade a princess for Avery?"

"I had the same reaction," David replied somberly. "But it's not just for Avery. Sainne's also asking for a large ransom and a fairly random sampling of equipment."

"What kind of equipment?" Blake asked.

"Both Time Peace and Aechyr have their best people on it, trying to figure that out. You know, when they're not bickering about it. But the rumors aren't good. The rumors are this is stuff to hijack missiles."

"Missiles?" I asked, dread crawling up my back. I was remembering what David and Randy had told me about the other timelines. About how Anarakia had nuked two of them.

"But then, is this the flashpoint? Is Anarakia pushing it up?" Blake asked hesitantly.

David shrugged. "I don't know. But it's got everyone here on edge. The Aechrians are working on a plan, but they want to go through with the exchange. They think they can trick the People's Front, and they want Sophia back. Not everyone in Time Peace agrees. We're holding Bai—uh, Avery, for now. There's no telling what kind of damage she could do, what secrets she would spill, if we handed her right over to the Aechrians."

"So what about the rescue op?" I asked.

"Excuse me?" David replied.

"The rescue op," I insisted. "Someone around here has to have a Plan B. We find Princess Sophia and extract her. Avery will know where she's at."

David shook his head. "She's not talking."

"Have you been in there?"

"Better people than me have been in there," he replied flatly. "She's not going to talk. I guarantee it."

I narrowed my eyes. "You guarantee? You know something that I don't?"

"Yeah," he answered grimly, a faraway look in his eye. "I know her. You're not going to get anything."

"Greene!" Someone called from across the clearing. David nodded in reply, readying to set off. Before he did, he turned to me. "Don't do anything stupid," he instructed, and then walked off.

"Why do people insist on telling me that?" I muttered to Blake, half-jokingly.

"More importantly, how does he know Avery?" Blake wondered. "It sounded like he was going to call her something else."

"Yeah," I agreed. "It sounded like there was a lot more to it. Where's Randy?"

"I think he's back there," Blake pointed towards a handful of folding chairs near another vehicle. "You don't think—?"

"Yeah, I do," I said, and marched off towards the half-circle of chairs.

Randy was leaning back, though hardly relaxing. His left leg was tightly wrapped in bandages, and his expression looked slightly pained, though that may have been his usual surliness.

"Kennedy," he growled.

"They got you?" I asked, a bit concerned.

"Lucky shot," he replied sourly. "Pierce hit me just as you broke the arena. He and Nergüi got out of there in a hurry after that. But hey, if he hadn't hit my leg, they wouldn't have been so lucky."

"I'm sure," I said hastily. "I wanted to ask you about something else. David and Avery—"

"Bailey," he said.

"Huh?"

"Her name is Bailey," Randy corrected. He cocked his head to the side and said, "David's not sharing that, is he?"

"Not exactly," I replied.

"I'm not surprised," he commented. "I wouldn't volunteer that information either."

"But you'd volunteer someone else's?" Blake suggested optimistically.

"Your high opinion of me is inspiring," he snarled. "You wouldn't want to share why you were dumped into Dark Eye Squadron, would you?"

"I'm an impulsive runaway who calls his superiors liars," I immediately offered.

"I'm a package deal with him, apparently," Blake added, jabbing a thumb towards me.

Randy was surprised, but he hid it well.

"It's not my secret to tell," he finally grumbled.

"Come on, Randy," I said. "We're a unit. We may be the dysfunctional lost and found bin of Time Peace, but we're a team. You and I have died together, and we still came out of the arena in one piece. Mostly." I gestured towards our injuries. "Now this timeline might be at a flashpoint, and Avery, or Bailey, could be the key."

"Alright, alright, save it," Randy grumbled. "I'm skipping the gory details; you're going to have to pry those out of David. But I can tell you the big picture."

Blake and I sat down on either side of him, leaning in to catch every word. He rolled his eyes, but then lowered his voice as he began.

"Avery's real name is Bailey Morgan Walker. She's part of a team. You saw the other two members, Kennedy. The ones in the

arena with us. Pierce Elliot and Nergüi. Pierce Elliot is their team lead and tactician. Nergüi is a scout, a nimble infiltrator. Gearhead, too. And Bailey is their social engineer. She can hold her own in a fight, but she's best at gathering information and twisting people around her finger."

"Could have fooled me," Blake said. "As Avery, she wasn't exactly the friendliest."

"You didn't think she was Anarakia, though," Randy pointed out. "Didn't mention her to David, which would have been nice. More importantly, you let her get close. And that's what she wanted. She was watching you. Letting you do the work of finding your girl, Sophia. All she had to do was swoop in at the end."

"They followed us in," I realized, kicking myself. "Down the path to the hospital. That's how they snuck in!"

"Could be," Randy said, grimacing.

"But this team of theirs, what does that have to do with David?" Blake asked, bringing an end to the conversational roundabout.

"Simple, really," Randy continued. "Their little trinity wasn't always Anarakian. Just like us, they were once recruits for Time Peace. Bailey came from a very nasty timeline and jumped at the first chance to leave. But she got bored around here. I don't know the psychobabble, but I think she just wanted more missions. The fun kind. The ones that end in a bang. Nergüi's just a lapdog. He'll kill anyone who gets close to Bailey or Pierce. And then there was Pierce Elliot himself. Rising star. Aced his training, made Delta in record time, perfect record. They were the best team in years. Until this one rescue mission."

"They betrayed Time Peace because they failed?" I interrupted.

"No way," Randy replied, glaring at me. "They got the prisoner out. Right out from under Director Sainne's nose. Yeah, Kennedy, he was involved here, too. He was interrogating the guy. Anyway, Pierce and the others delivered the prisoner to the appropriate government in that timeline. And then the government locked him up themselves and left him to rot."

"They did what?" Blake asked, astonished. "Why?"

"Because he was a genius with revolutionary politics," Randy replied. "Turns out, not a lot of people in power like those types running around."

"And Time Peace was okay with this?" I asked.

"Obviously not," Randy shot back. "But remember what side you're on. Time Peace doesn't interfere with the timelines. Not unless we need to. Anarakia kidnapped the scientist, we freed him. Mission complete."

"And that's what turned Pierce," I said. I could almost understand. "But how could he join forces with someone like Sainne?"

"He probably didn't," Randy said, shrugging. "Anarakia has a lot of factions. Maybe the three of them joined someone else's. But then they got shifted around, and ta-da! Now their new boss is the Crypt-Keeper. But hey, Anarakia pays good, and if you think they'll come out on top in the end, you keep your mouth shut and roll with it."

"But then what does this have to do with David?" Blake pressed.

"Isn't it obvious?" Randy asked mildly. "They were a four-man team. David was number four."

I exchanged a surprised look with Blake. I couldn't picture David running with any of those three. And to think that he somehow didn't see their betrayal coming...

"Time Peace blamed him?" I asked.

"Blamed him? No way," Randy replied, shaking his head. "But it's a black mark on his record, for sure. It's hard to trust someone who missed all the warning signs."

"So they cast him off to Dark Eye Squadron," Blake mused. "That seems unfair."

"He's in charge of Dark Eye," Randy corrected. "They haven't given up on him. But try to tell him that sometime."

I thought back to his reaction when I first mentioned the name of our team. He only saw shame in this. He was probably desperate to make us Deltas just to prove his own worthiness. I felt a pang of sympathy. He didn't deserve this. He was the best of us. And now he was avoiding confronting Bailey just because of one mistake.

I was about to turn to go when I stopped to ask Randy one last question. "Don't suppose you want to tell us why you're in Dark Eye?"

"Fat chance," he replied.

"Fair enough. Come on," I said to Blake.

"Where are we going now?" he asked.

"We're getting David back in the game," I replied, striding off once Blake was on his feet. I marched determinedly back towards David, who had returned to his post outside the prison vehicle.

"David," I said. "You need to get in there."

"I do?" he asked in mild bemusement.

"You're great at this stuff," I continued on, unabashed. "You need to interrogate Bailey. If anyone can get her to talk, it's you."

He seemed surprised for a moment, then a little sour. "You talked to Randy?"

"Any history you have with her will just give you an edge," I insisted. "If you can handle me, then you can deal with her. You know this hostage exchange thing is dubious at best. You're our best shot at getting Sophia back intact."

He shook his head. "Aside from this being seriously unprofessional, you overestimate my abilities. I appreciate it, but you're just wrong here." I started to protest, but he interrupted me. "No, Kennedy. In case you forgot, I didn't actually 'handle' you. And I can't just make Bailey talk. She's smart and she's practiced. She's not going to give up Sophia's location."

"David, just because you made a mistake—"

"Kennedy, stop," he said, suddenly harsh. "You think because you heard my story you know me? I'm telling you I'm not going to get anything out of her. If you really do have respect for my abilities, then listen to my assessment. It's not happening."

"You can't just give up!" I insisted angrily. "The answer is right in there, and you're not even going to try!"

"Watch it, Kennedy."

"Do you have any idea of what is happening now, wherever Sophia is? Sainne has her! And you know he's not going to just hand her over. He's going to, going to…"

I choked on the horrific imagery coming to my mind, and the glowing green eyes of Sainne looming over it all, toothy smile just below.

"The Hawk won't let that happen," David assured me.

"Like how he stopped the trinity?" I asked harshly.

David's cheek twitched.

"I'm not going in," he said. But after a moment, he turned back to me. "You are."

"What?" I asked, caught completely off-guard.

"Bailey can exploit my weaknesses just as well as I could exploit hers," he continued. "But if you go in, I can coach you. Earpiece. My words, your mouth."

I took a moment to process, and then the anticipation shot through me. I slapped him on the back. "Let's do it," I said.

"Let's hope we can," he muttered.

I stepped into the little white room. Avery—Bailey—was leaning back with her chair legs up, feet on the tiny table. She gave me a casual glance as I entered, raising an eyebrow in emulated surprise.

"Start by getting her to open up," David had said to me before I went in. "She's planted herself into the Charmies for quite some time for this mission. I think it's more than a cover. I think she has an attachment there. Once we draw that out, we start squeezing."

"Bailey," I greeted her, starting slowly.

"Kennedy," she answered, grinning despite her predicament.

"So you were a spy too, huh?" I said, taking things slowly at first, getting my feet wet. "Guess ours was the class of liars."

"Everybody lies, Kennedy," she said casually. "It's not such a sin."

"Glad to see you're in such high spirits. You're taking Sainne leaving you behind well," I replied.

She laughed mirthlessly. "I'm all torn up inside. How could I ever handle the shock of betrayal?"

She put on a good act; it was just a silly one. I had been there as she screamed at Sainne.

"Right," I said calmly. "You're okay with him leaving the People's Front out to dry."

"Glad you know the score," she said.

"She's fishing," David informed me. "She wants to know our offer. Don't give it to her yet. Put on the pressure."

"Tell you the truth," I said instinctively, letting a little of my frustration seep into the words, "I'm a little jealous. Sainne will get all the fun of ripping into them. The Becker kill," what a horrible way to put it, "that wasn't me."

"I don't know what you're so excited about," she commented, still casual.

"Weak response," David advised through the earpiece. "We're on the right track. But you need to make it potent. Make it even more personal."

"What was his name again?" I mock-pondered to myself. "You know, the guy who couldn't handle a one-on-one fight. Brooks? I look forward to finding him back on campus and bringing him in for some private questioning."

"Ooh, fun. Go be a big manly man and fight it out," she suggested.

"I'm more of an eye-for-an-eye type," I replied ominously. "I think I'll get a few of my own friends when we go to chat. I'm sure Randy would like to get in on it."

"Glad to see Time Peace is as hypocritical as when I left it," she said, a little more coldly, trying to slip a knife into a weak spot.

"Glad to see you're still proud to be a traitor," I countered. It was getting annoying having to act serene while tossing out barbs. I wished she would just get angry already.

"Easy," David warned. "Let's offer her a lifeline."

I hesitated a moment. Bailey hardly looked like she was drowning. I wanted to shatter her calm exterior, make her desperate. But I had gone to David for a reason.

"Sainne doesn't care about them," I said bluntly, sticking to my strengths. "And you know that. Him or us, it ends up the same for the People's Front."

"Let me guess, you've got a magical third option?" she taunted.

It was like I was being heckled onstage. I tried to keep my composure, but as she called out my next move, it made it feel so scripted. Embarrassingly fake.

I pressed ahead anyway. "You give us the location of the Princess, and they can get out of the crossfire."

She laughed at me. "Boy, you actually think that's going to happen? You're going to ride to your princess' rescue? Get real. She's as good as dead already. And please, don't try to pull on any academy loyalty strings. If a spoiled brat gets what's coming to her, who am I to stand in the way?"

She smiled toothily at the last remark, and no doubt saw my jaw working.

"Keep it cool," David said. "They're trading away Sophia. Tell her that."

"What you did was kidnapping," I began.

She interrupted by slapping her hands against her cheeks in a parody of offense. "Come on, Kennedy, kidnapping is part of the game. On all sides. I know from experience."

"Well, I'm glad you know it's just a game," I shot back. "Because the Front are just rolling over and letting Sainne hand her back over. Kidnapping, not murder. Sorry if you thought they were serious."

"Kennedy," David warned.

"You think they're giving Sophia back?" Bailey asked incredulously before he could go on.

"No, she's not acting. She's really surprised," David corrected my assumption. "She's digging. Give her what she wants. And emphasize Sainne."

"Of course," I said as condescendingly as I could. "Sainne is doing you a big favor, actually. You get to come back to him and he'll give us Sophia. Congratulations, you get to go back and play with your friends. You know, those who aren't hunted down by the Royal Guard."

"Sainne's not trading Sophia for me," she said, but even I could tell the truth was sinking in.

"Yeah, he is," I replied, pounding it in further. "What? Did you really think he cares about some pawns like the Front? He's going to trade for you and enough equipment to play havoc with some missiles. He'll leave your friends, the whole timeline, blowing in the radioactive wind. Or he'll just make out with a tidy ransom for Anarakia."

"Sainne's not going to trade for me," she insisted, her eyes suddenly cold. "He's just buying time to have some fun."

"Don't let her steer the conversation," David immediately warned. "She's scared. Give her the chance to undermine Sainne."

"He doesn't have to get what he wants," I said, coldly. It wasn't the offer it should have been. "He has nothing without Sophia."

"All he wants is Sophia. He wants to split the timeline, duh," Bailey said, steamrolling over me. "Killing her is the easiest way to do that. One shot and it all changes."

"You don't have to play by his rules," I said, bulldozing the conversation myself. "You don't owe him anything. Not that loyalty ever meant much to you."

"Focus, Kennedy," David chided. "The lifeline."

"But of course, Sainne won't do it in one shot," Bailey pushed on. "That's no fun, and if Sainne likes anything, it's his fun."

"So you'll let him have his fun with the Charmies," I interjected, trying to find a thread in the conversation. Trying not to get distracted. To get worked up.

"He likes to play with his prey," she went on as if I hadn't said anything. "Poor wittle princess won't be going quietly."

"She's holding out for something," David mused. "Or she doesn't think this is her best shot."

"Unfortunately for Aechyr, there won't be any nice open casket ceremony, either," she crowed.

No words came to me.

"Trinity. She's thinking of the trinity," David concluded. "Tell her you killed Elliot."

The words shocked me. Bailey's lip twitched nastily as she thought she had scored.

"In fact, I doubt you'll have just one neat pine box," she gloated.

"Tell her you killed Pierce Elliot," David insisted.

I opened my mouth, but my mind flashed back to Nergüi. To Becker.

"Chances are, he'll be sending her back in several."

David was saying something in my earpiece. I didn't hear him.

"Although, he'll probably keep a souvenir. Maybe just a little of her face for his wall—"

I leapt over the table. She clutched at the lip, ripping off a jagged strip—a crude knife. She was far too slow. I had already grabbed her by the hair. I twisted the plastic out of her wrist and held it up. I aimed for her neck.

Someone caught my arm just before I could plunge it down. Someone else grabbed me around my waist and dragged me back. Bailey laughed harshly, though it was hollow, performed.

Blake and David shoved me to the floor outside the cell and slammed the door shut.

I swore loudly, tossing aside the jagged bit of plastic.

"I told you!" I shouted at David, though I was just as angry at myself.

"At ease!" I heard someone bellow from behind me.

I froze. I recognized that voice. I turned towards The Hawk.

"Going above and beyond, are we?" he asked, the barest hint of disappointment in his voice.

"Something like that," David admitted ruefully.

"I don't suppose you got the location of their base from her?" The Hawk continued, his voice perfectly calm, and all the more unnerving for it.

"No, sir," I replied.

"That's a shame, but not unexpected," he stated. "Take a seat, everyone. Sergeant," he said to the Theta next to him, "please

make sure our guest does not try to harm herself via more direct means."

The soldier nodded and immediately stepped into the small cell. He returned moments later with the table and chair, then re-entered with handcuffs and a second Theta. When they left, I saw on one of the observation monitors that Bailey had been completely restrained.

The Hawk grabbed a couple cups of coffee, placing one on the table we sat around in the corner of the vehicle.

"Kennedy," The Hawk said. "I hope you realize what just happened."

I remained silent. He didn't clarify. "Are you saying she was lying?" I asked, grasping at something to say.

"Almost certainly. But do you understand why?"

Blake was about to reply when The Hawk held up a finger to quiet him.

"No," I admitted.

"She was baiting you. She wanted you to hurt her, maybe even kill her," he explained.

I was baffled. "Why would she want that?"

"On the off-chance that it would sabotage the exchange," The Hawk replied simply. "If one of the prisoners has been mistreated, the trade is off."

"But that's..." I struggled for the right words to describe Bailey's plan. "Extreme," I finally said.

"Is it?" The Hawk asked.

"I know she hates Sainne," David said, unsure himself, "but to sabotage Anarakia? That's a big leap, isn't it?"

"You hit on it yourself earlier," The Hawk told David. "It seems Bailey Walker has finally found a home—a cause. She has chosen the Charmies and People's Front Nine. And now, she has just confirmed what I have been suspecting. She saw Sainne's true plan."

"Which is?" I asked.

"Sainne really is just using PF9," The Hawk continued. "His murder of Charles Becker is proof enough. He doesn't care about their goals at all. To him, they're merely a convenient tool. He's aiming higher. I'd wager he never put much stock in the plan to kill Sophia."

"Why not?" I demanded. "That would split the timeline, right? That's what Anarakia wants, isn't it?"

"Anarakia isn't a singular entity," The Hawk explained. "Many of their factions fight with each other as much as they fight with us. In theory, Anarakia could capitalize on two timelines with their superior numbers. But if they aren't prepared to do so, they could just as easily dilute their forces. And someone would have to share the glory. They have more numbers, but we have better coordination. Most of the time."

"So you think he's actually going to trade for Sophia?" I asked, dumbfounded.

"Yes, I do," he replied calmly. "Sainne understands the power of manipulation and subtlety. It's often more effective than outright force. Killing Sophia might create two timelines, or at least set up a future split, but no real avenue for Anarakia to exploit. Not as clearly, not as closely. I'm sure Bailey and many others think that the assassination is the best path, but I believe Sainne disagrees. No, I think he wants Sophia herself."

"What do you mean?" I asked, my mouth going dry.

"Sophia, as future Queen, holds a tremendous amount of latent power," he explained. "If he could find a weakness, or create one, he or an accomplice could manipulate her directly. For instance, if she were to develop an irrational hatred for a particular group within Aechyr—perhaps a political faction led by a charismatic leader—she could be easily swayed to abuse her power in rooting them out."

"Are you talking about the Charmies?" I asked, dumbstruck. The Hawk nodded.

"A Queen with a traumatic first-hand experience with the People's Front could be convinced to hunt down them and any so-called sympathizers. Never mind whether or not the supposed sympathizers had any true ties to PF9. Anyone with similar enough political beliefs, or seemingly similar beliefs, could be a target. They'd be another aspect of the same evil and would need to be rooted out. Perhaps freedom of speech needs to be suspended. After all, how can we allow them to promote their evil ideas? Perhaps you can't congregate without approval. We can't have terrorist cells forming, can we? Anyone and everyone should be watched. One missed opportunity and someone else will suffer as she has, won't they? Make no mistake, in a so-called emergency, a Queen could do this without any legal restrictions."

My blood ran cold. "Sophia would never do that, though," I said.

"Sainne thinks she would. If she had the right motivation. If something horrible happened to her. That's why he's taking so long to set up the exchange. But I think there is a way to avoid that outcome."

"You *think*?" I said hotly. My knuckles were growing white as I clenched my fists.

"I have a plan," he said. "We have arranged a meeting to ascertain whether Sophia is still in good health. It is a prerequisite for the trade. When that happens, we will provide her with tools to endure whatever may come. With that, and a convincing performance, Sainne will believe he is causing more harm than he truly is. He will go forward with the trade, convinced of his victory, and we can help Sophia with whatever trauma remains.”

“Whatever trauma remains?” I repeated indignantly. “So you’re leaving her to Sainne because you’re willing to bet he’s not too much of a sadist?”

“If Sainne’s plan is to work, she can’t be rendered incapable of leadership,” The Hawk replied, a forceful note in his voice now. “She has to appear stable, able to take the Crown. Only then can his agents take advantage of her power. He will be careful not to overdo anything. Subtlety is the watchword here.”

“If you’re even right about any of this in the first place!” I reminded him. “Sainne himself was one of Becker’s entourage! He’s on their side!”

“No, he’s not,” The Hawk stated. “Director Sainne works only for Anarakia, and even then, it’s more accurate to say that much of Anarakia works for him, not the other way around. He is not like Bailey. He has no sympathy for these people. He only sees opportunities. And here he has plenty.

“If we trade him the interference equipment, he can use that. If he can manipulate Princess Sophia, he can use her. And if he is forced to kill her, he can use the split at the flashpoint, though to a lesser degree. He has carefully arranged his hand so that he cannot lose. But I believe he is betting on one outcome above the others. When the Aechrians realized his demanded list of components could be assembled to interfere with missiles, naturally, panic set in. However, Sainne had demanded a couple of components without specifying an exact model. When a particularly devious engineer suggested giving him a semi-obscure variant, one which would sabotage any missile hijacking

assemblage, the Aechrians leapt on it. Sainne's lack of specificity was a serious oversight on his part. Or so they think. I do not.

"I believe Sainne has left these holes in his plan intentionally. To keep us focused on the terrifying possibility of nuclear war, however remote. But it is a tenuous plan at best. A hijacked missile is a disaster, but a cause for war? Hardly a certainty. No, I think Sainne would instead put more stock in manipulation than technology. He'll try to subtly corrupt Sophia. And then he'll play two sides of Aechyr against the middle. He won't throw away PF9. He'll keep them well supplied. After all, if there aren't at least a few valid targets, the hunt might seem futile. He'll keep a shell of PF9 around to stir up more hatred and provoke more crackdowns. Then he'll use the new power of the Crown for Anarakia's benefit. Or better yet, if PF9 somehow wins, his victory will be amplified. By backing both sides, Sainne will win either way."

During the entire speech, my blood was roiling, an outburst just waiting to erupt. As soon as The Hawk was finished, it did.

"You can't take that risk!" I shouted. "What if he does kill her?! I know him! He's going to do it!"

"No, Kennedy," The Hawk replied, as calm as I was hysterical. "*I* know him. Make no mistake—a sadist he may be, but above all else, he is controlled. He is careful to concoct the exact fear you are now feeling. But it is a calculation. He will not go further than he needs to. The real person you need to know is Princess Sophia. Do you know her?"

I stopped in my tirade a moment, but still felt the hot anger within me. The question had taken me aback a moment.

"Do you know her?" The Hawk repeated.

"I think so," I replied. "I mean, most of the time, I knew her as Scarlett, so take it with a grain of salt."

"But you know her as well as, perhaps better than, anyone else here, right?" he continued.

"Yeah, I guess I do," I replied.

"Then you will know," The Hawk stated with finality.

"Then I will know what?"

"When you meet her, you will know if she is well. If Sainne has hurt her, and if she can withstand him. If she can play her part, and if she can resist the manipulations that will come afterwards."

"When I meet her?" I asked, suddenly all anger forgotten.

"I said we have to arrange a meet to see if she is in good health," he repeated. "I need someone to evaluate her mental condition. An Aechrian doctor will be present as well, but it's a judgement call."

I hesitated. "Why aren't we planning a rescue? That would make all this moot."

"We are planning one," The Hawk replied. "But it's a Plan B, and a dubious one at that. For one, we still don't know where Anarakia is hiding. For another, Sainne still has a trump card. He can always fall back on an assassination. Under no circumstances can we let that happen. Any rescue attempt would have to be flawless or risk Sophia's life. This exchange is the best chance of getting her back alive."

"You're doing this to get in with the Aechrians," I accused softly.

"Kennedy!" David rebuked.

"Certainly," The Hawk said flatly. "That is indeed a benefit of this route."

"The Aechrians don't understand about the splitting timelines," I said, gathering steam. "They won't risk a rescue mission because they don't know what's at stake!"

"Sophia's life is at stake," The Hawk said quietly, insistently. "That is my first priority. Of course I am pleased that this will strengthen ties with Aechyr. But that is hardly the point. Even if getting her back alive would somehow damage relations with Aechyr, I would still do it."

"But sir," Blake chimed in. "Doesn't Kennedy have a point? If Sophia was killed, there are other royals who could be manipulated to overreact as well. Wouldn't killing Sophia both split the timeline *and* make it easy to manipulate the royals?"

"No, actually," The Hawk replied politely. "Good thinking, but your analysis overlooks one fact. Simon, the next in line after Sophia, is a sympathizer of the Charmies. No doubt he would be outraged at the death of his sister, but it would be a distant outrage. He hasn't seen her for five years. He would certainly find those responsible, and perhaps even persecute PF9. But he would eventually curtail himself. He would not be susceptible to the same blind passion. If the Charmies denounced the assassination, as they no doubt would, he would likely accept it and refuse to bring the full weight of the Crown down on innocent suspects. A compromise that would never satisfy Sainne or Anarakia."

"Oh," Blake said.

"Kennedy, I'm asking you to put your trust in Sophia, not in me," The Hawk continued. "I believe she has the talent and willpower to pull this off, to trick Sainne. I'm asking you to take a look for yourself. If I'm right, if she is well, believe in her and she will be the one to save us, not the other way around."

I sat, staring into his eyes for a long time. My breathing slowed and I considered every angle of what he had said. The thought of what Sainne was capable of still sickened me. The Hawk's arguments made a degree of sense, but it felt wrong. No, I just felt scared. I was absolutely terrified. If there was even the slightest chance that he would hurt her... but I couldn't let myself be overwhelmed. I had to think about what would have the best chance of getting her out. And The Hawk was right about one thing. Any direct rescue attempt might just provoke Sainne.

"Alright," I said finally. "When is the meet?"

"Tomorrow," The Hawk replied, showing no sign of relief at my answer. "Get some sleep. I want you ready."

I nodded, and he stood and left. I turned to Blake and David.

"This might work," Blake said, doubtfully.

"Trust him," David assured me. "The Hawk knows what he's doing. And he's right, people see what they want to. Including Sainne. If Sophia can act as if his plan is working, then we can get her back practically unscathed. And we know she can act."

"Please," I said, my leg trembling slightly below the table, "don't make me think of Sainne and Sophia trapped together."

"Sorry," David said. He gripped my shoulder. "We'll get her back."

I nodded and David too left the vehicle. I turned towards Blake.

"What do you think?" I asked.

"They're the experts here," he said, rubbing the back of his neck.

"Yeah," I said. "What do you think?"

He turned away, as if to hide the dark look that came across his face.

"It sounds too easy," he replied simply.

I snorted, trying to ignore the fresh wave of worried nausea sweeping over me. "If this is easy, then I'm a white rabbit."

XIII

Rendezvous at the Albatross Café

I eased back on the throttle of the motorcycle. I was still uneasy on the bike, but it kept me highly visible, which was the point. No one could accuse us of pulling any tricks when my entire body could be plainly seen.

"They've just confirmed the rendezvous," The Hawk said into my earpiece. "It's not much farther down the road."

"Okay, so where are we picking for the sit down?"

"Looking now, I'll send you a ping on your map when it's settled."

"Roger."

The line went silent, and I turned my attention to the road. Soon enough I would be at the meeting point where Sophia would be waiting. As the negotiations went on between Sainne and The Hawk, we had agreed on selecting two points for the meet. First, Anarakia would pick a spot to hand Sophia over to us.

Well, to one of us. Namely, me. As we'd ride out, Anarakia would be right behind, capable of overpowering me if Time Peace tried anything. Then, The Hawk would select the second point—the place for the actual negotiations. The thinking was that if Anarakia concealed the first point until the last minute, Time Peace couldn't pick the second point in advance. And that meant Time Peace couldn't prepare an ambush. Neither could Anarakia. It was all very complicated and ludicrously paranoid. Welcome to the Eternal War, right?

I approached a gentle bend in the road, and along the side there was a parting in the trees. A lone figure stood in the clearing. My heart leapt and I steered closer, slowing to a coast. I tried another crooked smile as I pulled up and removed my helmet.

"Need a ride?" I asked.

"Kennedy? They sent you?" Sophia asked, with an astonished expression. I was overwhelmingly relieved to see that she looked perfectly fine, save for a little exhaustion in her eyes.

"It's complicated," I said, scratching the back of my head. "But I'm not alone. There's a lot of people waiting for you at the rendezvous. What do you say? Think we should swing by?"

"You know," she replied, cracking a smile, "we probably shouldn't disappoint."

"Then hop on," I said. As she walked towards the bike, I glanced around, trying to find the Anarakian agents who were surely watching even as we spoke. But they were evidently experts, as I didn't spot a single one of them.

Sophia slipped her arms around my waist and I felt an electric tingle, and a surge of relief. I glanced back to see her head, now helmeted, near mine.

"Do you know what you're doing on this thing?" she asked.

"Uh, you've got me in a predicament," I said jovially. "See, either I have to keep my promise to be honest or, hypothetically, I'd have to admit to the future Queen that I don't have a license."

"Tell you what, as long as you don't crash, we'll waive the ticket."

"I can work with that," I replied, and revved the engine. Sophia let out a surprised squeal and held on tighter.

"Frost, the rendezvous will be three miles back down the road at a diner called the Albatross Café," The Hawk informed me over Sophia's nervous laughter. I acknowledged under my breath, so only the Hawk could hear.

"Here we go," I said more loudly. Grinning, I accelerated back onto the road.

And we rode down the street, all the tension, all the complications slipping away for just a moment. Rays of sun swept over us through the leaves above, touching our smiling faces, and we were gone.

The Albatross Café was a white-and-red-walled little diner slightly yellowed by years of unenthusiastic care. It was an off-the-beaten-path little place that was seeing the most exciting moment of its life, which in and of itself, didn't appear that impressive. Despite having agents from Time Peace, Royal Guard, Anarakia, and the People's Front Nine, no one was bustling about or trying to kill each other. One agent was standing behind the counter, another half-dozen in various seats. I had forgotten which were which at this point and wondered if that was by design. Maybe everyone was dressed in plain suits and sunglasses to provoke that confusion. The employees and two customers that had been here had been shuffled out, and the only remnant of normal business was the folksy song still playing overhead. In the rays of a sun on its downward slope, the afternoon was as warm and sleepy as any other. And it smelled slightly of fish.

"...and lastly," the man with a thin beard sitting next to me said, "how would you rate your own feelings of anxiety on a scale of one to ten?"

"Six," Sophia replied calmly. Personally, I thought that had to be a low estimate, even if it didn't show on her face. I knew that if it had been me, I would probably be at an eight, maybe a seven at the absolute minimum. The Aechrian psychologist nodded. If Sophia's answer conflicted with the other hundred or so answers she had given, it didn't seem to concern him. He briefly flicked through the stack of papers so thick it strained the clip on the board. He glanced back up at both of us from under thick gray eyebrows.

"I have to say, unless for some bizarre reason Her Highness has been misleading me, her... hosts, shall we say, have been quite accommodating, relatively speaking. From what I can gather here, I'd give Her Highness a clean bill of health, though I'm sure I'd surprise no one by recommending bed rest." Sophia inclined her head towards him graciously. "May such a time come sooner rather than later," the psychologist said, and bowed his head as he stood to leave. "Your Highness."

He walked carefully away, making sure the hand without the clipboard swung freely to the side, clearly within view.

I turned to Sophie. "Are you really okay?"

"They haven't done anything, if that's what you're asking," she replied with a tired sigh.

"That's partly what I'm asking."

"No, I'm not really okay," she admitted. "How could I be? Are you okay?"

"This is the most okay I've been since the hospital," I answered truthfully. "And that's not saying much."

She smiled slightly. "If it means anything, I think you're doing fine. Considering how we met, I'm a little impressed you haven't started something here."

"I was tempted," I said, trying to roll with the spirit of the light ribbing. "Right now, I'm regretting not getting a few more blows in on those Charmies."

I abruptly stopped, remembering the dangerous waters Sainne was hoping to steer Sophia into. I slipped into that sort of thinking so easily. Would she do the same?

"No, forget that," I hastily added just as she opened her mouth. She blinked.

"What, afraid you're going to get in trouble?" she asked, mildly amused.

"No, not that. It's just—" I lowered my voice further. The annoyingly amplified music would hopefully be enough to cover up our words. "We think we know what An—the People's Front want from you."

The mirth drained from her face. In an equally quiet tone, barely audible even to me, she whispered, "I knew there was more to this than a simple ransom."

"Yeah, there is," I confirmed. "Sainne—that's Becker's one advisor—"

"White hair, green eyes, looks like death's chauffer?" she asked.

"That's the one," I replied.

"He makes my skin crawl. Even when he just looks at me, I want to find the deepest darkest pit, and jump to the very bottom. Just to get out of his sight."

"Don't take your eyes off him," I urged. "He's easily the worst of them."

"You say that like you know him," she noted, the question implied.

"Yeah, I do," I said gravely. "We met briefly. That's all that I needed."

She waited, eyes scanning my face. She seemed to be deciding whether or not to push further. I took the burden from her.

"He did this to me," I confessed, and slowly removed my sunglasses. The white void returned to my world, and she vanished from my sight. After a moment, I felt her fingers brush against my hand resting on the table. Fumblingly, I accepted her grasp.

"I understand," she told me.

I was relieved to hear this, but too busy to properly show it. My hand with the sunglasses carefully, subtly, pried a small pill from the temple. Sophia had unintentionally given me the perfect opportunity. I gently placed the sunglasses on the table and stretched out, grabbing her hand with both of mine now. I had done it a little too quickly, and I could feel a twitch of surprise, but she said nothing.

"Sainne has made some interesting requests," I whispered, slipping the little chip into her hand, pressing it into her palm. She gave a short squeeze of acknowledgement. "He's requested several pieces of sophisticated equipment and the release of a prisoner. The equipment is a semi-random bunch, probably bits are red herrings. But most of it can be used for calculating trajectories and other rocketry stuff. Our guess is they're planning to hijack the upcoming missile tests. The People's Front would love the excuse to get the country militarized. And Sainne is probably hoping you have some secrets to divulge to further his plan."

"I think he'll be disappointed," Sophia mused.

"Either way, he'll try," I emphasized. "But..." I imitated an unsure hesitation. "even if he did get something, we know enough to stop him. We can disrupt his plan either way."

"Are you saying there's something I should tell him?" She asked, and I could picture her incredulous expression, though I couldn't see it.

I released her hand and slowly picked up my sunglasses and slipped them back over my eyes. Once more, the lackluster café came into focus.

"I'm saying," I said, adjusting my gaze to look into her eyes properly. "No, I'm asking that you take care of yourself first."

She looked at me oddly. I thought perhaps she was evaluating my suggestion. But I wasn't sure. Maybe I was just hoping to see what I wanted to, but for a second, I thought there was a glint of understanding in her eyes.

"So, I'm really going back with them," she observed with the first real hint of fear I had seen yet. It was a twinge in my gut. I kept it in check. I wasn't done yet.

"Yeah," I replied grimly. "Sainne wants to check that our prisoner is unharmed as well. He's taking his sweet time about it."

"How fun for me," she said stiffly. The knuckles of her hand, the one with the chip, went white.

I jerked my head in a semblance of a nod and leaned back a little in the seat. Slowly, with one hand, I removed a package of lozenges, set it on the table, and removed one for myself.

After holding it my mouth for a second, I muttered, "I'd offer you one, but I don't think they'd appreciate that," jerking my head towards the Anarakian or PF9 men watching us.

"No, I doubt they would," she agreed. "It would stand out. And they're waiting like crows, picking the bones clean."

"You wouldn't think we'd be that interesting to look at us," I said, trying to lighten the mood while mentally imploring her to get the message.

"Not fun being in the spotlight, is it?" she replied.

"No," I agreed. *Come on, Sophie...*

"So I'm going back," she repeated.

"It's not exactly my first choice," I stated. "I hate the idea. I hate it as much as you do."

She considered me carefully. *Come on, Sophia, it's in your hand! Did you miss the hint?* Did I have to repeat it? Would that be too obvious? I hated this subterfuge. There was so much uncertainty.

"I doubt it," she said. "Can I ask you something?"

"Yeah, of course," I said, staring at her hand from behind my sunglasses.

"How do you really feel about me?"

I looked up, startled. She stared straight at me.

"You know what I think," I mumbled.

"Indulge me," she said, a little more forcefully this time.

"Here?"

"Kennedy..."

"Are you trying to make this worse?" I asked, more sharply than I should have. I quickly added in a calmer voice, "Look, back at the hospital, as soon as I saw something was wrong, all I could think about was making sure you were safe. I did everything in my power to get to you. I was right behind you. If I had just—"

"Thanks," she said simply. She hadn't cut me off so much as let me off the hook. Some of the edginess around her had softened, a little worry removed. "That's what I needed to hear."

Her simple response was a salve to my frayed nerves. Sophia had a way of speaking that, despite being short and direct, communicated volumes of worth of reassurance.

"I suppose there isn't much option for what to do," she sighed.

"We could bust our way out, guns blazing," I suggested.

She chuckled appreciatively. Then caught my expression. "You were joking, weren't you?"

I leaned back, smiling faintly. "Yeah, of course I was."

"Kennedy," she said. "You remember—"

"No, I wasn't joking," I admitted. I met her eyes again. "But I'll follow your lead."

"Then I suppose let's stick to what will work." Despite her pensive demeanor, I was sure I could see resolve in her eyes.

Then she rested her chin in her hand. Her right hand. Her curled fingers just covering part of her lips. *Yes!* I could barely tell, but she slipped the tiny pill into her mouth as she appeared to stare off, thinking.

"When this is all over, I expect you to be there," she said.

"Count on it," I replied immediately.

"Try not to get into any more trouble while I'm not around to bail you out."

"Me? I can handle myself just fine. You're the one who needs to watch her back."

She snorted. Men from both sides of the diner were approaching now. Time was up. They reached our booth, and the

Time Peace agent placed a hand on the back of my seat, while the Anarakian trooper placed his on Sophia's shoulder. We took the cue and slid from the booth. Before she could be shuffled off, I turned to her one more time.

"I'll see you soon," I said.

Her response was muffled by the shifting of bodies as they escorted her away. It stung to see her vanish behind the crowd of faceless figures, which slowly exited on one side. I was led to the other by our own mass of suits.

"Well?" one agent, wearing a Delta pin, asked me.

"She's alright," I replied, keeping it as short as possible.

He nodded and we walked out into the orange glow of the afternoon sun. The bustling agents slowly scattered from the building in opposite directions, like rats fleeing a sinking ship. I hopped back onto the motorcycle, glancing back once more towards the Anarakian side, but only two men remained visible. Most of the vehicles were long gone. The forested highway was returning to its silent seclusion. At last, I turned back gloomily and drove off, too, returning the Albatross Café to its anonymous rest.

I stood behind The Hawk's platform. He and the techs were raised two steps above the rest of us, their eyes glued to the large monitor. On it, a blue dot traversed the Aechrian landscape. One of the technicians sitting in front of the screen twisted a dial and the map adjusted its position and zoom.

"The signal's still strong," he said.

I still held my breath. It seemed The Hawk was doing the same. The small clear capsule I had given to Sophia was still transmitting, but for how much longer, we didn't know. It wasn't the most powerful transmitter that existed; that wasn't the point. Still, I hoped the signal would hold. The techs weren't anticipating it.

No sooner had I gone over this point in my head than the blue dot flickered. A second later, it vanished completely.

"We're losing it," the technician said.

"Send a ping," The Hawk ordered. "Push it a little if you need to, but let's not give the game away entirely."

"Trying, sir," he replied. But after a few seconds, the map remained dot-free. "No use, sir, it's interference. They're blocking the signal. Nothing we can do."

"Understood," The Hawk replied evenly. "Gentlemen, we knew this was likely. Our Plan A is still intact. This is not a setback, but merely a missed opportunity, and an unlikely one at that. Now we all have jobs to do, and the mission will not complete itself. Let's get to work."

The small crowd that had gathered dispersed, and a low buzz of activity returned to the oversized compartment. I stared at the screen a moment longer, even as it flicked to a feed of some unfamiliar data. Blake nudged me from behind.

My eyes lingered a moment longer before I tore them away and looked to the rest of Dark Eye Squadron. David gestured toward a little table in in the back where Randy was already leaning against the wall in his chair. We joined him.

"The mnemonic neutralizer was working when we lost contact. It'll still be going strong," David assured us. "We already know Sainne won't use torture. Similarly, he can't do anything too mentally scarring or else she won't be put on the throne. His best bet was to use another Talhesian device to implant suggestions or cover up whatever psychological tricks he would try. To falsify her memories as best as he could. The mnemonic neutralizer will protect her from that."

"But if it stops Sainne from editing her memory, how will she know to play along?" Blake asked. "Like if he tries to remove a memory, how can she pretend it's gone?"

"She'll know," David answered. "Any edits Sainne tries to make will flash briefly before her eyes. It's very intuitive. And any fake memories he adds will have an obvious fog or haze over them. She'll know the details, but it will be clear that it's not her memory."

"And as soon as that starts happening, she'll understand what Sainne's game is," Blake realized.

"Then we hope she figures out that she's supposed to act just scared enough for Sainne to be satisfied," I noted.

"She will," David declared. "The clues are all there for her, and she's smart. Every time I spoke to her as Scarlett, I could tell that she had a knack for understanding others and what they wanted."

"Right," I said. Actually, I was somewhat mollified. David's intuition was usually spot on, but coils of worry still wrapped tightly around my chest. "So how come you didn't see through Avery?"

"I never met Avery," David replied coolly.

"You didn't?" Blake asked, surprised, though I could see the gears clicking in his head. Even before David answered, the dawning comprehension was evident by his expression.

"No," David said. "We never crossed paths. I guarantee that was part of her plan. Obviously, she changed her name in case you mentioned her to me, or I stumbled on an enrollment list."

"We met her just outside the Box," I mused aloud. "I know you weren't there that time, but you never saw her hanging around?"

David was surprised. "No. She didn't go into the west building, did she?"

"I don't think so," I replied, searching my memory. "She was on the east side if I remember right. Why?"

"There were some suspected PF9 agents spotted in the west building," David elaborated. "We searched around but didn't find anything."

"That can't be a coincidence," I said.

"Like I said, we didn't find anything, and we definitely didn't spot Bailey sneaking around there. Not that they stuck around long enough to meet."

"Then they left a message," I suggested.

David considered that. "That's possible. But the People's Front agents must have taken it with them. We didn't find anything left behind."

"Not necessarily," Blake put in. "They could have left a message in a code, or in invisible ink, or some other hidden medium."

"You don't think one's still there, do you?" I asked. "Bailey never came back from the Crown Royal mission, maybe there's something she didn't clean up."

"You're stretching," David reproved gently, but was already standing up and putting on his jacket. "But what good are we doing here? Let's take a look."

I was on my feet in a flash.

***

Back at the Box, we could see David hadn't exaggerated. There wasn't a hint of anything suspicious. I'd say there was nothing out of place, but the Box and the rooms looking into it were already plenty messy. Most of the rooms weren't used for anything more than "storage," a.k.a., "we're not quite ready to throw this into a dumpster, so instead we'll throw it in here."

Randy swept his flashlight across each of the rooms we checked, but he was getting lazier and lazier with each one. It was hard to blame him. It was getting late, and there were no signs or clues anywhere. And worse, it was becoming apparent that we couldn't do anything close to a thorough search. There were simply too many rooms to check. If we took more than a few minutes with each one, we'd be there until dawn.

"How do we know if this thing is even here?" Randy asked, yawning deeply as he hobbled along.

"We don't," David said. "But it's worth checking."

"Checking for what?" Randy pressed. "This message could be literally anything."

"Almost," David admitted. "For now, just look for anything out of place. Blake, did you find something? Blake?"

I turned, and I saw Blake staring out the window, across the Box, to the buildings on the other side.

"They wrote on the sunglasses..." Blake murmured.

"What'd you say?" I asked.

But Blake suddenly turned to Randy.

"Toss me the light," he ordered.

Randy raised a sardonic eyebrow but lobbed the flashlight into Blake's open arms. Blake caught it and pointed it out the window. The beam hit the windows on the other side.

"What's up?" David asked, but Blake was still lost in his own thought processes.

"That window is tinted," he observed.

"So?" I asked.

Suddenly, Blake turned and ran for the door, announcing, "I have to check something."

"Wait up!" I shouted back and chased him as he ran through the hallway. "You've got an idea."

"Yeah, you remember that Charmy who wrote on your glasses?"

"Hard to forget. But what does that have to do with this?"

"I think that marker he used is the key!"

"But that wasn't secret. That wasn't invisible ink. You could see it," I pointed out as we burst into the night air. Blake immediately set off towards the building on the other side of the Box.

"That's because your glasses are polarized!" he announced.

I tried to put the pieces together as we burst into the building, but what Blake was implying seemed way too simple. "Are you saying this ink can only be seen through polarized glass? Hate to break it to you, but of all the special attributes in my sunglasses, polarization isn't all that special. Half the sunglasses out there are polarized. If this is their secret code, well, it could be seen by just about anyone."

"No, it's not seen through polarized glass," Blake said, running into a room facing the Box and examining the window. "Which this isn't," he added, and then ran towards the next room. I had to suddenly skid to a stop and reverse. "No, I think the ink only reflects polarized light!"

"Wait, hang on," I said, following his path, though not his train of thought.

Blake pumped his fist in the air triumphantly in front of the shaded window. "This is it! This has a polarized screen on it!"

David and Randy ran into the room behind us. "What is this idea of yours?" David asked.

"Polarized light!" Blake exclaimed. "When light goes through a polarized screen, it only lets through the light that vibrates in one direction. Basically. Like a bunch of vertical blinds that only let through vertically vibrating light."

"Well, obviously," Randy said sarcastically, clearly uninterested.

"How does this make a secret message?" David asked.

"I think, somehow, Anarakia has this ink that only reflects polarized light," Blake continued. "So, if you shined a light through a polarized screen, like Kennedy's sunglasses, and then the light hits this ink, it would bounce back. And you only see things that bounce light off of them. But if the light isn't polarized, it wouldn't bounce off the ink."

"In normal light, you wouldn't see anything," David said, working through the explanation. "It's only if you shined a polarized light on it that you would see the ink?"

"Exactly!" Blake said.

"But, Blake," I reminded him, "my sunglasses were in broad daylight. Normal, unpolarized light."

"But that's the key!" Blake replied excitedly. "Remember, he wrote on the *inside* of your glasses!"

I nodded, remembering the strange detail.

"That always seemed odd to me. This tinted window reminded me of it," Blake continued. "But here's the thing. Because

the ink was on the inside of your sunglasses, it was reflecting polarized light! The sunlight would go through your glasses lens, become polarized, and then bounce off the ink on the inside! Then, because it's polarized, it could bounce right back out! Meaning, we could see the ink!"

"So how does that help them pass secret codes?" I asked.

"If I'm right," Blake began, raising the flashlight to the window. He pointed it to one of the windows across the Box, revealing an empty room beyond. "If I'm right, all you would have to do is shine a light through this polarized screen." He moved the flashlight to the next window, where again, nothing unusual was revealed. "A message in this ink would be written on one of the other windows," he moved the light again, and again nothing. "Then, that ink would reflect the light back, and suddenly..."

He slid the light to the next window, one diagonal to ours. Glistening silvery letters suddenly appeared.

"They become visible," Blake concluded, satisfied.

"Yes! Nicely done, man," I said, clapping him on the back.

"Good thinking," David congratulated. "Let's see what it says."

The lettering was clumsy, a couple letters reversed. I quickly realized that was because the messenger, Bailey, was writing from the inside of the room. She had to write backwards to make it look right from this vantage point.

But once we got used to the eccentricities, it was easy enough to read. "Princess found. Operation going forward. When complete, will abandon post. Backup point is Cloister Cove if need me."

"Cloister Cove," David said, triumphant. "Looks like Bailey did get a bit too attached. Couldn't help but give her companions a place to run to if things got dicey."

"Hey, I'm not complaining," I said. "You know where this Cloister Cove is?"

"No, but I bet we can find out," David replied.

"Then let's tell The Hawk," I declared. "The rescue is back on the table."

"It's definitely on the table," David agreed, taking out a phone. "But let's see if it changes the calculus."

He stepped out into the hallway as a complicated series of dial tones sounded through the phone speaker. I bounced on the balls of my feet anxiously waiting for David's return. My patience quickly ran out, and I turned towards Randy.

"What's the play, you think?" I asked.

He snorted. "Why are you asking me? That's The Hawk's decision, isn't it?"

"Yeah, but you've been around the block a couple times, haven't you?" I said. "You have an idea of how this is going to go down, right?"

He looked me over, his eyes narrowed slightly. "This is purely professional curiosity, right?" he said without the sneer I was anticipating.

"It's anticipation," I replied.

After a moment, he shrugged. "Sainne's meeting with Bailey tomorrow to see if she's alright before the exchange the day after. I'd say if you could scout out their forces and make a plan quickly enough, you'd want to hit them tomorrow while they're out. And I'd still want to be quick and quiet about it. If you're seen, the rear guard would hit the Princess. An open fight is the last thing you'd want. Beyond that, I can't say anything until I see what we're dealing with. Without any intel, forget about it."

"Right," I acknowledged, thinking that all made sense, but was unfortunately vague. I was starving for information.

David walked back in, pocketing his phone. "The Hawk is scrambling people to work on a rescue plan. But," he added, cutting off my exultation before it could escape my mouth, "it's still a Plan B. Too much risk to put it into action. He wants to feel out Anarakia tomorrow before making a call, and the trade still looks better."

"Hang on, isn't tomorrow the perfect window for a rescue?" I protested. "Shouldn't we decide now?"

"What did I just say about intel?" Randy asked, with just a hint of the usual growl. "That's what The Hawk is after with the check-in on Bailey."

"Sure," I said, reining myself in a little. "But a rescue could still get her out entirely unharmed. You really can't think it's a good idea to give Sainne more time with her?"

"The Hawk trusts her, what's your problem?" Randy retorted.

"It's not a matter of trust," I insisted as calmly as I could. "Sainne could have some sort of device—"

"That's why we gave Sophia the mnemonic neutralizer," David put in.

"Okay, okay, fair enough," I allowed, "I'm just worried that Sophia isn't going to come out of this unscathed."

"No one comes out of this unscathed," Randy replied cruelly.

"You sound a lot like Bailey," I retorted. Springs were coiling in my back. I took a deep breath of cool air.

"Do you think I would let any harm come to Sophia if I could help it?" David interjected.

"No, of course not," I answered hastily.

"And I'm telling you it won't," David stated forcefully, yet evenly.

"None that you can help," I noted as the coils tightened. "I get it, I get it," I added before the argument could begin again, "I'm being difficult. I just hate sitting here, and I hate that Time Peace is doing nothing."

"You know that's not what—" David began.

"You'd rather Anarakia keep her?" Randy shot back.

"Of course I don't!" I exploded at him, composure shattering in a single instant. Everything that I had been holding back suddenly rushed out, stampeding over my tattered restraint.

"Woah, Kennedy, cool it, Randy's not worth the anger," Blake said, pushing me away from him.

"I'm trying to rescue her, what do you think?" I yelled at him. He snorted, amused. "What? Do you actually think you're helping here? Do you ever have anything useful to say or do you just get excited whenever someone gets hurt?"

"Shut up," David interjected. "Kennedy, Randy, shut up. We're tired. It's late. Kennedy, I know you want to help. Randy, you aren't. Call it a night. We accomplished something here, we discovered a crucial bit of information. That's the note we should leave with. Forget this argument ever happened. Agreed?"

"Agreed," I said, exhaling some of my built-up tension. Blake released me, and I shook my arms out before letting them fall limp, trying to make my muscles relax.

Randy grinned toothily. "Yeah, sure, boss."

"Randy," David warned.

"Fine, fine," he said, dropping some of the tone. "I agree. I take back what I said."

He sounded half-serious, which meant about nothing to me. Blake steered me towards the doorway. "Let's go," he said, and I let him guide me. David and Randy left shortly after, and I could hear David chewing him out in his ever-even tone. I also caught a snippet from Randy that sounded an awful lot like "...who the real princess is..."

As we walked back towards our dorms—it felt like years since we had slept there last—Blake kept looking up towards the night sky, as if trying to pick out the few stars still visible. Halfway back, I turned to him.

"I'm not being crazy, am I?" I asked.

He glanced back down, blinking as his eyes adjusted to the view back on Earth. "Probably a little," he replied simply.

I sighed. "I just don't need Randy being..."

"Randy?" he suggested

"Yeah, being Randy right now," I concluded.

I took a couple more steps. "I don't like this plan, Blake. I've got this gut feeling that something terrible is going to happen."

"Do you *think* something bad is going to happen, or *feel* something bad is going to happen?" he asked slowly.

"Feel," I replied immediately.

"That doesn't necessarily mean anything," he explained carefully.

"Trusting my gut has kept me alive this far," I countered.

"In a fight, maybe," he admitted. "But then, this isn't some hectic life-and-death situation where you don't have time to think it over. It's not like you have to trust that your brain has noticed something and is trying to tell you—"

"Isn't it?" I countered.

"I don't think so," he replied, shaking his head. "In a fight, you don't have time to consciously process everything you're sensing. But right now, you've got too much time. Your brain might be telling you something, or you might just be feeling anxious because of course you would! I feel anxious about this too. I think everyone does. Even Randy, but he only has one strategy for processing his emotions. No matter which emotion it is."

"Happy? Sarcasm. Sad? Sarcasm. Angry? Sarcasm," I noted, chuckling slightly at the chance for levity. "Love? Sarcasm. I'd hate to be the target of his affection."

"I don't know, I think he's found a very efficient way of dealing with his feelings," Blake joked. "One size fits all makes for a very quick processing time. I bet he's great at poker."

"If he doesn't flip the table first," I laughed.

After a moment, I returned to the subject. "So you don't think we've missed anything?"

"I can't see what it would be," Blake admitted.

"Earlier you thought this plan sounded too easy," I reminded him.

"Yeah, I did," he agreed. "But I heard your reports, saw the footage of your meeting with Princess Sophia. Everything lined up 100% with what The Hawk was getting at. I think it was a slick move. And I seriously think she knows what's going on and how to play the game. I mean, this is way outside of my comfort zone, but if I were in her shoes, I would not be remotely calm and collected. It was impressive. And Anarakia's actually holding up their end of the bargain so far."

"That doesn't mean they will continue to do so," I said half-heartedly. "They're holding onto her for a while."

"As The Hawk predicted," Blake reminded me.

"It doesn't mean everything will work out. It's a lot of time for something to go wrong."

"It is," he conceded.

"You know," I began hesitantly, "we really don't have to take the risk of waiting it out."

"The Hawk's already made his decision, hasn't he?" Blake replied.

"That's not what I meant by 'we,'" I said carefully. Comprehension dawned in Blake's eyes. "We know that she's being held in the Cloister Cove," I added hurriedly. "Randy said it himself, stealth is the best approach. If we could get in and get out—"

"Now you are being crazy," Blake said.

"Blake," I said seriously, stopping in my tracks. "What if it was someone else? What if you had the chance to undo what happened to Quincy?"

Something odd happened. I saw a flicker of determination briefly in his eyes, despite his grim expression.

"I think I still do," he said quietly.

"Huh?"

"That enigma just changed probabilities," Blake said, looking at his clenched fist intently. "With all this arcane technology around, the time gauges, the time gates, with techniques like hang time, there are always possibilities. There's a way to use these, a combination to maximize their potential, I just know it. Somehow, it could work. Someday."

He looked back at me. "But that's the thing. It's not going to come down to a single moment, I think. I think it's the long game that matters. Same here. Sainne knows that, and that's why he wants to corrupt Princess Sophia, not kill her. I know it seems clearer to just go in and rescue her, but I don't think that's what we need. I think it's the healing that will be more powerful in the end. And that can't happen if we risk her life by running in without a plan."

I looked at him, stunned. It wasn't at all what I had expected. Neither Blake nor I were ever that... eloquent. I was a little hurt, too. Why hadn't he taken my side? That's what friends were supposed to do, a very childish part of me said.

"So even if you were in my shoes, and Quincy—or someone else—was in Sophia's place...?" I asked, choking a little in sudden rueful disappointment.

"Even if it were someone I loved," Blake said firmly. "Then it would be all the more important to find the optimal solution. To think. It would be harder, but that's why I'd have to try—"

"I am thinking!" I hissed at him. "I'm thinking of what could happen if we do nothing!"

"Are you?" Blake asked, nonplussed at my outburst.

He looked utterly unbothered. That same calm, curious demeanor he had had since childhood when contemplating a difficult math problem. Slowly, I deflated.

"Come on, Blake," I finally said, pleading. "Can't we at least try?"

He shook his head slowly. "Kennedy, you know I would do anything to help. I followed you when we left home. I followed you beyond time. I don't regret any of it, but this time, I'm not going. I would do anything to help, but this won't help."

My eyes fell to the ground.

"You're right," I said softly. "I'm just being stupid."

"Nah," Blake said, suddenly casual again. "You're just having a hard time."

That night, the dreams returned. The smell of the sea mixed with the smell of blood and gunpowder as I lay once more on the beach, the rocky hills rising before me, taunting me as I lay there helpless. I had to reach them. I had to. Tommy and the others would be diving into the enemy encampment by now. Why wasn't I there? Why wasn't I in those caves? Why was I on the beach being rocked by the shells of the defenders?

As if my futile fury had reshaped the dream around me, I was suddenly flying towards burning caves. The warmth grew, both inside and out as I grew closer. Flames begged to be released from the mountain, to swallow the prey laying at its maw.

The woman stirred. I shot towards her, over the shattered beach. She pulled herself off the rocky surface. Strange. She didn't have her gear.

The flickering in the cave intensified. The beast was about to breathe on her. I rushed towards the small figure. I would swoop in like a protective cloak. If I could only get there. For some reason, even though I rushed over the sand, I didn't seem to be getting any closer.

But I could feel the heat rising.

She rose. But it wasn't Claire. It was Scarlett—Sophia. She looked back towards the beach—towards me.

And the flames rose. They engulfed her.

I flew forward, but I couldn't reach her.

I could only fall into the fire. It rose and scorched me, burned through my flesh. The world turned white as I entered the inferno.

And as the blaze burned out my eyes, I heard Sainne cackling in the distance.

I shot up from pillow. Everything was still white and for a moment I panicked, thinking the dream had caught me like a spider's web. But as the sweat cooled around me, I slowly came to realize, despite my mounting fear, that this was reality. That I was awake.

I groped for my sunglasses.

I would owe a lot of people apologies for this. I might even regret it. But I couldn't simply wait anymore. I couldn't make it through another night of dreams. I found the go-bag, I found my gauge gun, and I found my time gauge. Lastly, I found the keys to the motorcycle.

I left a short message on my bed, and then I just left.

"I guess this is my resignation," it read.

XIV

Return to Crucible Cove

When I arrived, the sun had just risen over the horizon, coating the landscape in a golden radiance. I could smell the sea salt from my spot on the road, but the ocean was only visible through skeletal trees. They had shed nearly all of their crimson leaves, covering the graying grass below. The cove itself was hidden just beyond a rise.

I glanced at the GPS. I had gotten as close as I could from the street. I found a patch of scrubby brush and marched the bike over. Doing so confirmed a fear that had developed since I first scanned the environment. The dead leaves crunched loudly under my feet, giving away my presence. I'd have to go slow and hope for the best.

I covered up the motorcycle and slowly crept my way towards the sound of the waves. As I approached, some of my fear was alleviated. Each step would bring me closer to those waves, covering up the sound of my steps. Better yet, as the trees began to thin, the ground became clearer and clearer.

I crested a ridge and got my first real glimpse of the cove. My heart stopped, and for a second, I questioned whether or not I was still trapped in my dreams. Cloister Cove, it turned out, had been my crucible. It was the beach I had nearly died on a lifetime ago.

It was exactly the same yet utterly different in the daylight. I was at the top of the same rocky cliff face that had taunted me in my dreams. I could look out across and to my left and see the network of caves where the defenders and their guns had lain in wait. But today, it was entirely silent, and I was far from the sands below. I was removed, up and to the side, hiding at the edge of what had once and never been a battlefield. It was eerily different, and yet, I thought for sure I could smell the scent of blood on the sea spray.

The sound of cawing birds pulled me from my petrified reverie. Near the pinnacle of a rocky spire to the right, a handful of crows circled ominously. Crows. Hadn't Sophia said something about crows back at the Albatross Café? Had she been trying to tell me something with that? Had I really missed this clue? Or was this merely a coincidence?

I didn't have any other ideas of where to begin. I might as well try out this hunch. I carefully crawled along the lip of the rocks towards the little spire. As I approached, I could see several slots looking out from a tiny chamber carved within this miniature mountain. There would be just enough room for a single guard, but it seemed empty now. Still, I was cautious.

I crept up extremely slowly, looking for any signs of electronic eyes or ears. Finally, when I was at the very base of the spire, I looked up into the room and saw something embedded into the ceiling. I took out my gauge gun. The device didn't look like a camera—I couldn't quite tell what it was. It might have already detected me. Maybe I should just shoot it and hope for the best.

But as I considered, I realized something was off about the small circular device. Wires trailed from it to the wall, and then down below. But near the device itself, they looked frayed. Even cut.

I rose slightly, moving to get a closer look, and a startled crow flapped and flew into the air from just around the rocky watchtower. A thought suddenly occurred to me. Perhaps these crows would show up on whatever sensor this was. They might provide me some cover.

I found a larger opening into the small room, and I squeezed through it. Inside, I glanced up at the sensor, and could easily see that for some reason, the wires had been slashed through. I couldn't quite fathom why someone would sabotage their own security. I stepped closer to look when I heard a crunching under my foot. I looked down to see an empty chip wrapper. In fact, there were several discarded wrappers up here.

On a hunch, I glanced out one of the slits in the guard post. Discarded remains of other snacks and meals sat between a couple of crows. The rocks were slightly discolored, as if they had been stained by hundreds of tossed coffees. Only wrappers and bits of plastic litter remained, the actual food items having long since been devoured by the scavenging birds.

A picture began to form in my head. For one reason or another, the Anarakian guards were tossing their trash up here, which had led the crows to frequent this spot as their own little cafeteria. The crows probably had set off the sensor, and as they became fed up with the false alarms, the guards disabled it rather than changing their habits. Lucky for me.

I glanced back towards the ground, at the small round hatch taking up half the narrow floor. Placing my feet carefully, I pulled open the heavy trap door. The distant sounds of human activity wafted up from below. I had my way in.

I didn't hear anyone immediately beneath me, so I lowered myself onto the rungs embedded into the stone and climbed down, lowering the hatch behind me. I found myself in a small alcove off a longer hallway. It was still mostly quiet, no hints of nearby guards. Just in case, I lowered myself to a crouching position and retrieved a small mirror from my pocket. Holding it low, I turned it until I could see around the corner and into the hallway beyond. Empty. It was entirely empty.

There was a series of doors along the hall, and at the far end, I could see it take a sharp turn. In this moment, I had a clear shot. I decided to take it. I slipped down the corridor, keeping low to the ground at first. I glanced into one of the windows embedded in the doors. Inside was a cell. But an empty one, only a hard slab sticking out from the wall—presumably a bunk. I checked the next door. Another cell, just as vacant.

I was desperately checking each room when I heard the footsteps.

"Heading to the breakroom?" A voice asked in the distance, barely audible around the corner. Someone was about to round it. I instantly searched the corridor for a hiding spot, but I was too far to get to the alcove, and the rest of the passageway was completely flat.

"You know it," a second voice replied. "Can't relax with them always looking over my shoulder."

I looked back at the door next to me. I twisted at the handle. It turned.

"You mean they won't let you smoke in here," the first voice said mockingly.

The second merely grunted. I pulled the door open, slipped inside and closed it as fast as I could without making a sound. It had just latched shut when I heard the footsteps turn the corner. I pressed myself against the wall, watching the window as best I could from my shallow angle.

A dark form slipped past it for just a moment. I only caught a glimpse of the back of his head. He just kept on walking. A few moments later I heard his footsteps in the corridor replaced by boots clinking against the rungs of the same ladder I had used.

When I heard the hatch close, I exhaled in relief. The hallway was silent once more. I pulled myself from my spot against the wall and turned the handle. It stuck. I tried again, but nothing happened. It had locked on me.

I swore at myself internally for overlooking this possibility. After a moment, I calmed down and took stock of what I had. I had my gauge gun, my time gauge, a knife, a mirror, a short length of climbing cable, a flashlight, a few marbles, and a lockpick set. Too bad the door was sealed with an electronic keypad. I could always blast the door open, but that would make a lot of noise. Unless...

I pulled out the gauge gun. I spun the dial down to the lowest power setting and pointed it at the lock. I pulled the trigger and only heard a very slight whoosh from the expelled energy. Pulling the gun aside, I checked the damage. It didn't seem to have done anything to the pad.

I had started far too low. I took an educated guess and spun the wheel back up a bit. Pointing it back at the lock, I fired once more. The hum of released power was louder this time but shouldn't have travelled beyond the hallway. I glanced at the lock again, but it was still intact. And working, based on a quick test.

I had hoped to short it out, but obviously this wasn't working. I considered cranking up the dial further but wasn't optimistic. Even if I fried the electronics, that didn't mean the door would open. Maybe I needed a different approach.

I put away the gun and twisted the crystal lens from my time gauge. Pulling the strap around my thumb, I connected the lens by pressing it into my palm. I turned the dial that had been hidden under the lens, setting the power low to start with. I aimed at the lock and fired.

A bright flare of light and a louder rush of air met me as I did so. I shrank to the side, once more fearing I would be caught. But once more, no one came. I glanced to the lock. It seemed unchanged.

Looking closer, though, I could see it glowing slightly. It might have been my imagination, but the metal seemed to have drooped a bit as well, like it had started to melt away. I increased power slightly and repeated the process. The second and third shots didn't break through the lock either, but the melting effect was becoming more pronounced. I cranked up the power and tried again.

I wasn't quick enough when the metal plate suddenly fell and clattered to the floor. I winced as the first trickles of adrenaline shot through my system. For a moment, I didn't dare to do anything, convinced someone was about to come running around the corner in response to the noise. But no one did.

I leaned over to pick up the metal plate, and then thought better of it. With my fingers just an inch from its surface, I could feel the heat radiating off it. Maybe it was best I hadn't caught it after all. I slid it aside with my shoe and then pulled the door open. It didn't budge easily, but with a little strength it freed itself from its threshold.

I stepped out and closed it behind me. Glancing back, I could see that I had a problem. The lock had melted on this side as well. Maybe if the returning guard was really oblivious, he

wouldn't notice, but I didn't have the luxury of taking that chance. My rescue mission now had a ticking clock.

I ran quickly but quietly to the end of the hall and turned the corner. Another short hallway and then everything opened up into a huge cavern. I crept forward, listening intently, but there weren't any more footsteps. I reached the end of the hallway, glanced to make sure there wasn't anyone on either side of the opening, and then slipped out.

The cavern was massive. I had just stepped out onto a catwalk which ran the perimeter of the enclave, three stories up from sea level. I could see doorways and hallways along the second and first level walkways, and a large, square watchtower standing on a stilt-like framework towards one corner. A couple cranes and other pieces of equipment were scattered about, dotted here and there across the scaffolding, surrounding the centerpiece of it all.

Suspended three feet from the water was a huge craft. Two large metal shafts descended side-by-side from the roof of the cave and into the middle of the vessel, holding it steadily aloft. It looked less like a boat or a ship, and more like a tank. The green armor plating enclosed the rather boxy profile, and there were two large blister shapes running along the bottom on either side. They must have been pontoons, or something similar. A vaguely cone-like protrusion poked up and ahead like the head of a canine. That had to be the cockpit, I decided. And the whole thing could have fit two cars comfortably side-by-side within, judging by the size. It wasn't pretty—it was sturdy.

My gaze drifted towards the people. On every level, men in black uniforms walked around rather casually. It seemed that this place was secret enough that no one was really on guard. Then again, most of them had submachine guns, so I couldn't be too relieved.

Unlike when I had seen them during the attack on Crown Royal, almost none of them were wearing full helmets. A couple had hardhats on, but most were going bare headed, another sign of complacency or comfort. It was strange looking at all of them. They weren't hideously scarred or otherwise cruel looking. Most of them looked like normal people, albeit in tip-top shape.

I checked my watch. By this point, the check-in with Bailey should have just begun. This was Anarakia with their guard down. And still, it wasn't comforting. There were plenty of soldiers left to get in my way. But I didn't have time to contemplate my bad fortune.

I scanned the room once more, trying to find signs of where they might be holding Sophia. Nothing stood out to me, and there were far too many hallways to search. Then I glanced down. Through the grated floor. One level below, almost directly beneath me, two soldiers stood guard on either side of a hallway entrance. It was the only guarded hall that I could see.

That had to be it.

Of course, this was still an obstacle. Somehow, I had to get into that corridor without their noticing. I considered trying to steal a uniform like in the movies, but aside from the difficulty of finding one that would fit me, it seemed customary to go without the face-coverings in here. While I didn't expect anyone would recognize me, I also couldn't expect to go unchallenged while wearing my sunglasses. I would stick out like a sore thumb, sure to draw attention to myself

So, the question remained. How could I get down there? And how could I avoid being seen? I took a careful step back into the hallway as I considered my options. Then something astoundingly obvious occurred to me. All I had to do was go down.

I crept back quietly into the cell whose lock I had burned off. I adjusted the crystal ray again, switching it to a low power setting and pointing my hand at the floor. I had to hope that there was a cell below, and that like these, it was empty. I fired several times in a row, hitting the same point on the ground.

The stone glowed faintly but seemed mostly unchanged. With a surge of recklessness, I cranked up the power and started shooting again. Cracks started forming after each shot, surrounded by a glowing circular area. Heat radiated into my skin. This had to be a bad idea, but I didn't see any better ones.

I fired another half dozen times, trying to carve out a crevice I could work on. But before I anticipated, a patch of rock collapsed and clattered into the cell below.

"Who's there?" A voice called. It was the second guard. The one who had gone up for a smoke break. I hadn't heard the sound of the hatch opening over the firing of my crystal ray. I cursed myself and held still. As if that would do anything. The heat and missing lock would be impossible to miss if he got anywhere near this cell.

I grabbed the gauge gun and inched towards the door. I hastily switched out the watch crystal for the silver pistol as I approached. I strained to hear the sounds of the guard's footsteps, but he was being careful, too. I couldn't make out anything over the ambient activity in the large cavern. I couldn't just burst out through the door. He would have a split-second more to react to my sudden appearance while I had to rush out and acquire him.

I reached into my pocket and grabbed one of the marbles. I flicked a switch on my gauge gun, then reached out with that same hand to grasp the door handle. With my left hand, I carefully aimed the marble, looking through the hole where the lock had been. I listened.

I heard nothing. My heart beat faster. Then, I saw the start of his black-clad form.

I threw the marble hard. My aim was perfect. It shot through the little hole in the door and struck the wall on the other side at an angle. It clattered behind the guard and he twisted in surprise.

I yanked at the door. As soon as it flung open, I let go and raised my gauge gun. The guard was already spinning back around, raising his own weapon. I was just a hair faster.

The blue bolt shot into him and he collapsed into a heap, his weapon clattering to the ground. I cringed, glancing around, but it seemed my luck had returned. No one called out, none of the ambient noise changed.

I pulled the man and his weapon into my little cell, closing the door as best as I could behind us. I had no idea how long any of this would last. I felt my pulse continue to pound through my veins, a clock ticking away, each second bringing discovery nearer.

Perhaps fueled by this panic, I let off several more shots into the floor around the hole, and I heard more crumbling stone. I let it settle as I plopped the guard on the stone bed. I took the opportunity to steal his uniform. At least it gave me a potential for camouflage, though it didn't fit particularly well. As I pulled it on, I was already second-guessing my choice. It hung off me, a few sizes too big. But I couldn't waste any time.

Looking through the hole I had made, I saw a cell identical to the one I was in. I had a big enough hole, but the floor glowed around it in a large disk. I was already sweltering from the heat. I couldn't even think about touching it.

The guard began to stir behind me. I switched back to my gauge gun and fired into him again. There wasn't a set time limit to how long someone would stay stunned. Maybe it would be best to simply set it to lethal...

My stomach churned. I couldn't do it. Not in cold blood.

I turned my attention back to the hole I had made. Below was now a pile of jagged and glowing rock, right where I would land.

I cursed myself for not realizing the obvious. I couldn't wait for this to cool, especially not now that I had a stunned guard in my cell. I paced around the hole, trying to find a solution to the problem I had made for myself. I couldn't just use a cable without the burning rock melting through it. Not that I had any great places to attach it. That left me with one idea.

I zapped the guard one more time just to be sure and then replaced the crystal on my time gauge. I looked it over, but there were only the vaguest hints as to the size of the arena it might project. I thought that was a serious design flaw. If I had been returning to Time Peace after all this, I would have been sure to file a complaint. As it was, I just had to hope, which was becoming an unhealthy habit.

I pushed in the crown and a small arena appeared. I saw the hallway beyond the door blacken, and red whisps of strange comets fly past. I looked down and was relieved to see that the cell below had also been brought with me into the arena. Now for the hard part.

I took a short running start and then leapt feet first into the hole in the ground. I misjudged badly, hit the edge, and felt it burn through my clothing. I forced myself not to scream and was already hitting the reset button just as I slammed into the ground.

I was standing once more, contemplating the hole. I tried another leap, cleared the hole, but didn't get enough momentum. My legs collapsed from under me, and I tumbled back. I landed in the burning hot rock behind me, feeling it as it stabbed through the stolen uniform. I hit the reset button so fast that the pain had barely time to set in.

I rubbed the back of my head where it had slammed into the floor, now a little hesitant to try again. But I had to. There wasn't another way. I ran forward once more, hardly thinking about it this time, and instead trusting my instincts. I leapt, sliding downwards feet first, hitting the ground hard at an angle, but rolling to the side.

I popped up immediately and checked myself. I didn't feel anything other than the beginning of the aches and pains from hitting the ground. My stolen uniform wasn't burned or cut. I was fine. I had done it. I pulled the crown and collapsed the arena.

After listening for a moment and not hearing any guards reacting to this from down the hall, I pulled the same trick on the lock of this door, melting through it, though more carefully this time. I heated it until it was pliable enough to be pulled apart with my knife. I was genuinely surprised that the guards didn't hear any of this, but I supposed that was because of how far down the hallway I was. Between that and the crashing waves outside, I must have had just enough cover.

I slipped out of the cell and checked that the metal handle looked fine on the outside. It did, but there was a pile of spiked rocks in the middle of the cell. You would have to look into the cell to see it, but it was another clue waiting for someone to find it. Speed was becoming more essential every second.

I glanced down the hallway, and immediately saw a large door at the end that had to belong to the most secure cell. I raced quietly towards it and was relieved to find that it, too, opened when I turned the handle.

When I slipped inside, I didn't let the heavy metal door close behind me. Holding it open just a crack, I heated the latch until it glowed. Then, with my knife, I peeled the protruding molten metal from its place, casually flicking it aside in the cell. I chipped away at it like this until there was almost nothing left to click into place and hold the door shut. What remained I pressed back into the lock mechanism to cool into a useless mess. Only then did I let the door fully close.

I turned into the cell, expecting to see Sophia on one of the slab beds. Instead, I saw a large dirty metal box. It was just a little taller than me, raised on a pedestal, and had several tubes running down into it. There was a complicated electronic lock on an even heavier door, and my heart sank. There was no way to blast through that without cooking whoever was inside.

I approached slowly, unsure of what to do, and dreading what would come of my indecision. But I was so close. Sophia had to be inside, didn't she?

I tapped on the side of the box. I couldn't tell if it would be audible inside, but I thought the large metal thing must amplify my every tap. I waited for a response. None came.

I tried to put myself in Sophia's position. I had to assume she was inside, otherwise everything I had done so far was a complete waste, and soon I would be captured as well. If I was her, stuck inside, and someone was tapping on the box... well, I'd assume it was some sort of taunt. I had to tell her that it was me somehow.

Some of the codes David had taught us flashed through my head. No good. Sophia probably didn't know any of them. No, I needed something that only she and I would know. But we hadn't shared any secret ways of communicating. The closest we had come was putting on masks, and that couldn't be communicated by taps.

Masks. Masks couldn't, but it reminded me of the masquerade. Of the ball—the dance. I tapped out the beats of a waltz—a more archaic dance that she nonetheless had enjoyed teaching me. *One*, two, three, *one*, two, three. Emphasis on the first beat. The three beats were different from most modern dance music, she had told me. I couldn't put it as well as she did, but I could feel the difference.

After a couple of repetitions, I let up. Please understand. Please be there.

Tap, tap, tap.

The same pattern tapped back at me. My heart soared into my throat. Yes! I was sure I had found her! Now I just had to figure out...

The tapping repeated, but it wasn't against the wall this time. It was coming from a point higher up, from the top of the box. I immediately understood that she was trying to tell me something. I glanced around the room, but there wasn't anything I could use for a boost. I would have to do this the hard way.

I clicked on the arena again, which was limited to the room this time. I wouldn't be hurting myself this go around, but I couldn't afford the muscle strain. I grabbed the top edge and heaved myself up. It took a couple of tries and a couple of resets, but I heaved myself onto the roof of the prison.

I shut off the arena and tapped the waltz again on the roof. It was answered by an identical beat a little to the side. Right next to a hose that led down into the box from the ceiling.

Perfect, I thought, and took out my knife, which had been slightly warped from the heat of the melted door latch. Despite that, it was enough to cut a ragged slice into the tubing.

"Sophie?" I whispered into the black void. I could see nothing through the little tear I had made in the piping.

"Kennedy?" she answered.

A wave of purest relief washed over me. I hadn't realized until that moment that I had even doubted it was her inside this contraption, but the reassurance was overwhelming.

"I can't see you," I whispered.

"It's completely dark in here," she explained. "I can just barely see you. What happened? I thought the exchange was going through."

"Change of plans," I muttered. There would be time for explanations later. "We need to get out of here, fast."

"I don't know the code to the lock," she replied.

"Well, that makes two of us," I admitted.

"Kennedy," she asked worriedly, "what's the plan?"

"This time might really be guns blazing," I said, trying desperately to come up with a real solution. I still had the gauge gun, so I could stun the guards at the end of the hall, but after that... We had to get out quick.

"Kennedy," she began again, a little scorn mixed in with her anxiety now.

"You know that ship they have?"

"The sea skimmer?" she asked.

"Yeah. We get to that quickly and quietly, and then we run."

I could practically hear her biting her lip in worried contemplation.

"Leave the hard stuff to me," I said, trying to push the anxiety out of my own voice. "As long as we're quick and quiet, we—"

Voices drifted down the corridor and through the door.

"I was never here," I whispered through the tear in the piping and slid off the metal chamber, landing around back just as the metal door was pushed open.

"And you would rather let them get away with it?" A vaguely familiar voice demanded.

"No, of course not," a second voice replied hotly. It was a low, kind of raspy voice that I didn't recognize. "If they lay a single finger on Bailey, they'll lose it, and a lot more."

And all at once, it hit me where I had heard the first voice before. It was the voice of the Utility Man. Of Pierce Elliot.

"Nergüi," Pierce said more softly, but still with some of the ice of before, "I'm not just worried about what *they'll* do."

"I don't follow," Nergüi admitted.

"You know how Bailey is with these Aechrians," Pierce reminded his comrade. "If she knows she's being traded for the Princess, and knowing her, she does…"

"Imbecile!" Nergüi declared at no one in particular. "You don't think she's gone that native, do you? She wouldn't sabotage this just for their sake?"

"It's Bailey," Pierce replied grimly. "She's a sucker for a paramilitary man in uniform."

Nergüi didn't laugh at the joke. "Okay, how does it go down?"

"We take custody of the Princess. We take her to the sea skimmer. We head off somewhere secure and contact Sainne. We make sure we're at the exchange, and that he knows there won't be any if Bailey doesn't come back in one piece."

"Got it," Nergüi said. "We'll still be defying an Anarak. I hope you have cover for that."

"There's more than one Anarak who will pay for our services," Pierce reminded him. "Even Sainne won't openly defy the Supreme Commander. Not yet."

There was a pause, and shortly after, I heard several beeps and then a loud click.

"Your Highness," Pierce said mockingly. "I thought you might like a change of scenery."

"How thoughtful," Sophia replied with equal scorn. "Did your master have the same thought, or doesn't he know that you've slipped your leash?"

"Young lady," Pierce replied coolly, "I have no master. Only financiers."

"And yet somehow, I get the feeling you won't listen to a counteroffer."

"People pay based on reputation, Your Highness. And my patrons rarely look kindly on incomplete contracts."

"I doubt you have many patrons. What do you call mercenaries with only one client?"

"An oversimplification, I assure you," Pierce said in an imitation-suave voice. "But if it helps, think of us as privateers. And so, we're taking to the sea. Try to make this easy. Our clients would prefer you alive and in one piece, but let me assure you that they will settle for much less if it comes to it."

Sophia didn't respond, but based on the series of steps I heard, there was a small back and forth as Pierce and Nergüi got into position to escort her. I had to think quick. In one way, this worked perfectly with my plan. The traitors would bring Sophia onto the sea skimmer, right where I wanted her. The only problem was that I wouldn't be there with her. They would. Still, it might be best if I let them proceed for now. I just needed to figure out a way onto the ship myself. No small task.

I heard the door open, and a few seconds later, shut again. I immediately dashed out from around the metal box and went for it. I slipped through carefully. Pierce and Nergüi were already at the end of the hallway, discussing something with the guards there.

I slid slowly and carefully down the hall, hoping they were distracted enough not to notice. It was an absurd risk. But soon, the two traitors were escorting Sophia off, apparently having satisfied the guards. In fact, they turned and left their post, apparently no longer having anything to guard with Sophia gone.

I straightened and rushed to the end of the hallway. Glancing out, the enclave had suddenly become a bustle of activity. It seemed Pierce's orders had really stirred things up. I could see many of the black-suited men rushing to different stations, especially the brick-like watchtower. A squad jogged in formation into one of the hallways across the cavern. It suddenly hit me that Pierce and Nergüi weren't going to go on their little trip alone. Some of these men were loyal enough to them to come with. Considering Sainne was willing to sacrifice the PF9 members here, whereas Bailey had lived with them, that made a disturbing amount of sense.

I decided to move fast. One of the many tips David had drilled into us was how confidence could camouflage as equally as shadows or patterned uniforms. Sometimes better, if you believed him.

I strode out into the open as if I was just another Anarakian. My disguise, as ill-fitting as it was, would have to be enough. With all the commotion around, who would notice one more person striding to their duty station? And mine, as assigned by me, was aboard that sea skimmer.

I crossed the thin catwalk towards its hatch and pulled it open. No one even gave me a second glance. I dropped below, and as I closed the door behind me, I was engulfed in a world of silence.

Suddenly, I had a very bad feeling. The hull so stifled all outside noise that my entrance couldn't have gone unnoticed.

And as soon as I had that thought, the arena dropped. The few rays of sun that had streaked in through the portholes in the slanted walls were suddenly extinguished. Pale comets, breaking apart into a million fragile whisps, like dandelion seeds, soared overhead, rippling into fizz or foam before bubbling apart.

My luck had finally run out.

I didn't have time to take in the sights. Pierce rounded on me and the sound of a shot echoed harshly off the walls. I stumbled to the left in shock, dropping to a knee.

Reset. Reset now! An authoritative voice bellowed at me in my head.

Pierce took aim at my head as I grasped at my watch.

I hit the crown and I was standing again. And again, I had just dropped into the skimmer. Adrenaline pushed me forward. I couldn't lean back, and I couldn't dodge to the side. Straight ahead was my only option.

I leapt forward, towards the inner wall, and turned towards the front of the craft. The wall I was leaping towards bulged where the metal pillars holding up the ship must have connected. Further up, there was a ramp, also on the inner wall. It led to a hatch that must have gone to the cockpit, or bridge, or helm, or whatever it was called on a sea skimmer. Along the starboard outer wall, the one I had just leapt away from, were ridges partitioning the hallway like ribs. Behind one, only partly secured, was Nergüi. And worse, Sophia. Nergüi's left hand was clamped tightly over her mouth, and his right was holding a gun. And as he took aim, I saw Pierce. He was peeling himself from the other side of the same ridge I had landed next to. And he had been waiting for me.

I don't know whose bullet hit me first. All I know is that after the first, I scrambled for the reset. I don't know how I reached it that time, but I did.

I was back behind the rib next to the hatch. I needed to think of a plan. But I didn't have the time. I grabbed the time gauge and jumped out into the corridor at an odd angle. They hit me again, as I had anticipated, but I was ready for the reset. Seeing them again, it helped me process. And the jump back in time bought me one extra second to think.

As I snapped back, one thought burned through my mind. *Pierce is too close.*

I went in low, diving around the ridge, charging straight for him. He hadn't anticipated it. He shouldn't have let himself become used to my wild leaps forward. I hit him low, but my real target was his gun. My arms shot up, I grabbed it, and twisted it around.

I seized the gun and spun towards Nergüi, hoping against hope that I could line up the shot. But he was playing dirty. He knew now that I didn't have backup. He hadn't aimed for me this time. He had changed strategies. He smiled evilly as the gun pressed against Sophia's temple.

The knife slipped in, right between my ribs. I had underestimated Pierce. A stupid, stupid mistake. I dropped the gun and went straight for my watch. But his free hand had already grabbed it. He pushed me against the inner wall, pushing me down as my fingers tore at his, desperately trying to get to the watch.

"Where are the others?" Pierce demanded.

A hideous screech rang throughout the hull. Both Pierce and I looked towards the others just as the gun went off. My blood ran cold. My heart stopped. Sophia's face was covered in blood, and she was slumped to the side, lifeless.

Nergüi was shouting something, but all I processed was a ringing in my ears.

Pierce was yelling at him. They were arguing. I couldn't tear my eyes from the horrible sight of Sophia, lying motionless.

Get up, I pleaded. *Get up.*

She didn't. She couldn't. Never again.

Nergüi made a motion that I barely paid attention to. I should have.

Suddenly, I was back at the hatch, completely whole.

"Don't do it, Kennedy!" I heard Nergüi shout. Too late, I was already in motion. I couldn't let that iteration repeat.

My brain barely processed Pierce rounding the corner. He had been prepared for my move. I had just enough time and sense to try to repeat my ducking charge, and it saved my life. Pierce's aim was just a little off. I hit his legs but grabbed for the gun.

"I'll shoot her!" Nergüi shouted. I ignored him. We were playing with time. I could beat them. There had to be a way.

I saw the knife just as Nergüi screamed again. I disengaged suddenly from Pierce. Before he could line up a shot, my hand was already at my watch. I pushed the crown just as Nergüi's gunshot rang out again, but it was abruptly cut short.

We shot back to the opening moves. I dived around the rib again, making it appear as if I was going for the gun. Pierce almost had me this time. I could actually feel the bullet whiz past my ear. We were moving too fast for it to sink in that I had almost been ended.

I knocked aside his gun arm, as he anticipated. He didn't anticipate my other arm reaching towards his belt and seizing the knife. I slashed upwards viciously, catching his throat. I wasted precious moments grabbing his gun from his dying hands.

When I looked up, Nergüi wasn't looking at me, but glaring at Sophia.

"If you do that again, I'll—" he began just as Sophia bit down hard on his finger. A spurt of blood and a hideous crack later, and the finger popped from its socket.

He pulled the trigger at the same time as I did. Both he and Sophia collapsed, instantly dead. I screamed a futile, primal scream. I looked down towards my watch. There was an easy fix, of course.

I looked down at Pierce, who was bleeding profusely from his neck. He was still alive. Our eyes met. His yellowish, wolf-like gaze dared me to do it.

I reached up and hit the reset.

I plunged in again, just as I had last time, but faster. Except he wasn't trying to shoot me now. Pierce had taken half a step back, pulled his knife, and as soon as I rounded to face him, he cut me down.

The knife burrowed into my shoulder as I heard Sophia bite off Nergüi's finger again. Why was she doing the same thing over and over? The three of us were constantly adjusting, why wasn't she?

No time to think about it. Pierce raised his gun. My reflex to hit the reset, firmly burned into me now, was all that saved me.

Hang time looped back around, and I realized how stupid I had been. I grabbed my gauge gun. I didn't dive forward this time, but leapt to the side, aiming it towards Nergüi. Pierce had his knife raised, hoping to bait me into the same move. Nergüi was the threat, but he didn't expect my new maneuver.

My finger was on the trigger when a panicked thought hit me. I remembered clicking the gun over to stun to deal with the guard. If I fired in this mode, I would be stuck in a real loop.

I shouldn't have hesitated. Nergüi re-aimed, and I instinctively went for my watch. The bullet hit my leg just as I

gripped the crown. I realized how futile this iteration had been even as I hit the reset. I caught a glimpse of the slider. The gauge gun had automatically switched off of stun. A safety feature that activated as soon as an arena dropped. *Idiot!*

Nergüi was quick on the uptake. As I leapt around the corner, he didn't point the gun at me. He didn't waste time trying to predict my course.

As I dove out, I saw Sophia's body hit the deck, the gunshot still ringing in the hull.

"She's dead. Surrender," Nergüi ordered.

I ignored his words. I easily shot blue energy into both of their chests. They hadn't even tried to defend themselves. Because they knew they had leverage. Sophia was lying there again. I couldn't look. I pressed the reset just before I could be sick.

The gunshot went off again.

"I can do this all day," Nergüi said.

I reset immediately.

Another gunshot.

"Why don't you try talking?" Pierce suggested.

I pushed the reset. Another gunshot.

"Enough, Kennedy!" Pierce shouted. Somehow, as if it were a command, it made me hesitate.

"Let's talk before you hit the reset again," he demanded.

"What is there to talk about?" I hissed back furiously.

"Neither of us want Sophia dead," he replied. "But we can settle for it. You can't. So why don't we work together to keep her alive?"

"Sure, hand her over," I spat.

"Don't be stupid, Kennedy," Pierce said evenly. "Simple demand. You surrender, we reset. Sophia lives, so do you. I'll even trade you back in the exchange. It doesn't make a difference to me. You and Sophia go home."

"I can't trust you to do that," I replied. In truth, I had no idea whether or not Pierce could be counted on to go through with that deal. But I absolutely could not trust Sainne to hand me over. He had taken a perverse pleasure at forcing my hand with Becker. He had sought me out in a previous meta-timeline. There was a reason. As soon as he found out that Pierce had me, he would want to play. And frankly, I didn't believe Pierce could convince Anarakia to hand me over. I didn't believe he would have the motivation to. Not if Sainne leaned on him.

"You don't have much choice," Pierce replied. "We hold all the cards here. We can play this game until the end of eternity."

I thought about how right they were. I pushed the crown on the time gauge in desperation. I turned and fired. I missed. They shot her again.

"Kennedy, it's over," Pierce said gravely as I ducked back behind cover. "Don't make us do it again."

"Getting tired of murdering her?" I shot back.

"Are you?" Nergüi asked in return. "You will tire long before I do."

The icy venom in his voice left no doubt in my mind. They were far more merciless than I was. Mercenary. That's what Sophia had said. That distance, that perspective, it gave them power here. I cared. And that was killing me.

"There's no situation where you win this," Pierce said.

Maybe I was desperate. Maybe I just couldn't help but take such a statement as a challenge. Maybe I was just looking at the right place at the right time. But my eyes fell on the bulge where the metal shafts held the sea skimmer above the waves.

There was just a second where Nergüi had to adjust his aim. When hang time started, he would be pointing the gun towards me, having anticipated a larger force invading their ship when the arena first dropped. Of course, the heartbeat it took for me to round the corner and point my weapon at him was just enough time for him to aim at Sophia and fire. More than enough time, really. But it was a moment, nonetheless.

I didn't need to waste it. Not to change everything.

"Yeah, we'll see about that," I said and hit the reset one more time.

This time, I didn't charge around the corner, or make any move other than to slip the crystal lens into the palm of my hand. Into the waiting black strap, where the gauge gun had just been. It was clumsy at first, far too slow, so I reset and tried again, and again, and again, until I could do it in a heartbeat.

In a single moment.

And in that moment, in the time between heartbeats, I pointed it towards the metal shaft and fired.

XV

One in a Million

David had warned us not to fire our crystal rays in hang time, and for good reason. You can't create an arena inside an arena. The crystal rays worked on the same principles as our fight had. If it didn't work, reset. Except the ray goes way further than we ever could.

As power is channeled to it, the weapon in the time gauge usually just sparked, or created a beam too weak to do anything. It would be a pretty pathetic weapon under most circumstances. It was the arena tech that made it special. By creating a mini-arena around itself and the beginning of the beam, it could reset as many times as necessary until it got the big boom the wielder asked for.

But my time gauge didn't have a mini-arena to reset. It couldn't create one. At best, if the safety was removed, it would reset the big one. I removed the safety, and so it did.

I watched it spark for a split-second, then skip back. It sparked, fired a thin trail of light, sparked, sparked again, fired something that looked like a beam but did nothing, then sparked once more. Over and over, the same handful of milliseconds replayed themselves. Each time, only a shadow of the proper beam emerged from my crystal.

We hung there between heartbeats. Neither Pierce nor Nergüi had time to do anything. My hand was firmly pressed on my watch's fire button as it failed over and over to do so. We couldn't speak, there wasn't even enough time to get more than a grunt past our lips. Soon, it felt as if the others didn't even exist.

Everything around me was a slightly shifting painting. My body slightly tilting to the side, a motion I hadn't even noticed when I first fired. My fingers extended just a bit as my hand opened to receive the crystal. There was a small movement out of the corner of my eye, perhaps Pierce trying to round towards me. After a while, it didn't matter. It was just an illusion.

All that mattered was me and the ray. And the non-existent beam that I kept hoping would spring into existence before me. It was maddening. Each time, I felt a little rush of hope, but it never came. Eventually, the tiny spikes of anticipation shrank and shrank and finally melted away.

I was stuck in this cycle. But that was okay. It was painful, it was annoying, but even that was okay. My mind flew off on a tangent as it relived this moment over and over and over again. A sporadic series of thoughts and memories appeared and vanished at light speed. Blake holding out a hand in the rain. Scarlett—Sophia—angrily holding back tears at the Crystal Ball. Raising a shard of sharpened plastic at Bailey. David, at Iterant Point, ashamed to admit what Dark Eye Squadron meant. Randy, near the Box, grinning maliciously, but with something else in his eyes. Somehow, the discordant notes came together in a lost song in my mind.

I thought of Quincy, of the enigma. The enigma. That unstoppable machine. But there had to be a way. Blake said there had to be a way. *He was right*, I thought. *There must be a way*. Even as I was trapped in this singular moment, there always were possibilities.

The split-second clicked back again and again painfully. Reality resetting itself, and the crystal ray failing to fire. A couple times, it seemed like it was going to go off, but it never did. How I wanted it to. How I wanted it just to end.

And yet, this is where I was supposed to be. Or had to be. All of the previous moments since I had landed in Aechyr had led me here. I had chosen this path. This is where I was always going to end up, where I should have ended up. It was a sort of penance. Or maybe not. Maybe just a natural conclusion.

I thought of everyone again. Of how I had wronged them. I had disappointed David, marred his record by resigning when he didn't deserve that. I had betrayed my word to The Hawk. I didn't think I had betrayed Randy. I didn't think we had any bond to betray. But perhaps there was a missed opportunity. We had fought together in the arena. There was a possibility of friendship. I hadn't fostered that. He didn't make it easy, but I could have done more.

And then there was Blake. He still wouldn't admit it, and maybe he didn't even see it, but I had wronged him worst of all. We shouldn't have been in Aechyr. But I had allowed him to follow along. No, that wasn't right. He had chosen to follow, but I knew he would. The truth was much more painful. I should have never run in the first place. Even if I was meant to be there, even if I had arrived in other meta-timelines, I shouldn't have run. If it was meant to be, they would have found me some other way. I couldn't run now.

The beam fired.

It actually fired. I didn't know how long I had been in that loop. Had it repeated hundreds of times? Thousands? I had no sense of time anymore. But it fired. A brilliant white beam shot from the crystal ray. It all happened slowly before my eyes.

The beam was as wide as my fist and headed straight for the metal pylon. It was over. The endless repetition was over.

But it's not enough, a part of me said. The beam wasn't wide enough. It wouldn't shatter the pillar.

Every part of me, having been given the opportunity to escape the moment, screamed that it didn't matter. The moment was over. My heart would beat and I would live again. I could move freely, I could think normally. I would return to the real world instead of this hell between moments.

But it's not enough.

I needed to destroy that pylon. I needed to free the ship. I needed to save Sophia. I needed to live on after the beam hit. I had to try again. I couldn't try again.

I felt the firing button start to release. All I had to do was let it switch off, and everything would end. I didn't even need to do anything. I just needed to let go. Let it all go. I had done enough. I could rest.

No.

No, there was no rest for me.

Even as my finger lifted from the button, a terrible, horrible, wracking sense of purpose welled up within me. Blake in the rain. Scarlett in the basilica. Bailey in the interrogation room. *No. No. No.*

Just let go.

But I needed more. MORE.

If I had the time to scream, I would have bellowed. The purpose, tearing at every instinct in my body, roared into life, exploding beyond my very being. *I am beyond this*, it said. *I will go on*, it roared. I will try again. *Even as every fiber of my physical form falls apart, I won't give in.* I just had to press that button back down.

For such a simple action, it was the hardest of my life. And I did it. I wouldn't let it be otherwise. I ripped my mind, screaming as it was, back into the suspended moment between heartbeats. I pressed the button back down.

The first half dozen sparks from the time gauge weren't even disappointing. I was still raging internally. *Yes!* I would do this. No matter the cost. Even as everything else was a blurred painting around me, this wasn't about me. I had made the mess, yes, but now I did this for everyone else. It was no recompense, but it was the beginning. And that was what mattered, I told myself. It seemed so obvious now. Painful, but obvious. That the first step mattered.

In that moment, that moment between moments, even something as simple sounding as that platitude carried weight enough to move the cosmos. It wasn't complicated. It's not mind-blowing. It's insultingly, grossly simple. But right then, for me, it was wisdom unrivalled. It was the truth that kept me going through millions of permutations. Each step was a new first step. And that was the most important thing of all. Each time the time gauge reset the arena, I was choosing to do that. That's how it felt, and it might as well have been real.

I plunged through an eternity of these moments with such single-minded determination that nothing seemed real. I couldn't have counted them if I had wanted to. And it didn't matter. These infinite instants were one and the same. It was the first step. And it was the first step again. It didn't matter how many times; each one was the first again. And I would do it right. This time, I would do it right.

I don't know when it happened. I don't know if it had happened before and I simply pressed on in my absolute plunge through infinity. But at some point, it happened. I was present enough to recognize when the crystal ray shot out the largest beam I could remember.

It exploded from my palm, nearly burning off the tips of my fingers as it burst outward. It engulfed everything before me. The pylon would be vaporized. It actually went further than I had asked. The power reading overshot the dial setting. That was fine. It would do what I wanted. I could accept this iteration. I just had to remove my hand, and it would be real.

But I didn't want to. I had found such clarity. I knew I had been wrong, and I was doing right by going through the infinities. *I should just let the watch correct itself. Continue to reset until it got the beam just right. It's what I deserve.*

No.

Not anymore. I was telling myself that because I wanted to stay. I wanted to hold onto that apparent clarity, the shocking wisdom, the ascended consciousness. I could be there forever. But to step back out? To actually join the world again? To face what I had done?

It was another first step, I told myself. A real one this time. And it was always painful. But I had done it once before.

I pulled my hand from my watch, letting the fire button click back once again. The pylon vaporized, and the sea skimmer fell.

The ground fell away. My stomach leapt. I heard a cry of surprise from one of the others, and then that shriek of pain, freshly renewed from Nergüi. It brought me back in an instant. I was there.

The sea skimmer hit the water and shuddered with the splash. The arena broke as the waves ripped through it, or as the sea skimmer hit the bottom. Either way, it was over. I saw Pierce fall over when the boat shuddered with the impact. I had braced just in time, without thinking.

I quickly swapped out the crystal lens for my gauge gun and spun around the corner as Nergüi fired. But he missed. I knew it before I had seen it. The landing had ruined his aim. Now he was pulling his free hand away from Sophia, his middle finger missing, and trying to adjust his aim for another shot at Sophia. He didn't get the chance.

Nergüi collapsed as the stun beam hit him. Pierce didn't even get that far. He had just started to push himself upright when I hit him. I ran past him, straight for Sophia. She was suddenly real again. Blood trickled from her mouth, but she was beautifully, gloriously alive.

"Kennedy," she said shakily, "What just happened? What was that?"

"Ask me later," I suggested, and before she could say another word, I scooped her up and ran up the ramp.

She made a surprised sound, but quickly recovered. "Do you know how to drive this thing?" she asked as I sat her down into one of the two chairs in the conical cockpit.

"No, sorry," I said even as I scanned the controls.

"Don't apologize," she commanded as she too looked over the buttons and levers. "Just try. It's last-ditch effort time."

"I think," I said flicking a few switches and gripping what I hoped was the throttle, "we're pleasantly beyond that."

I shoved it forward, and the sea skimmer rumbled to life. We were off, slowly gathering speed as ahead, the mouth of the cave slowly grew and the morning sun welcomed us to the sea.

"Are you... okay?" Sophia asked strangely. "You seem..."

"Different?" I suggested. "Adrenaline. I think. See if it sticks, then ask me. For now, let's just say I had a hell of a fight."

She looked at me even more strangely. But before she could ask further, the sea skimmer rocked violently.

Several things slammed into the hull. We rocked dangerously, and our speed abruptly decreased. And I felt the cockpit tilt upwards as something shuddered behind us.

"They're shooting us!" Sophia shouted in total shock. "We're sinking!"

I slammed my fists into the control panel, the calm that had carried over from my bizarre infinity suddenly gone. "I should have known! Of course there are more guns. I had seen them!"

"You can beat yourself up later," Sophia declared, unstrapping herself from her seat. "I'm not about to go quietly."

"Right," I said, regaining some of my composure. "Forget that. We're out of here."

I could feel the skimmer tilting backwards now. Water was greedily sucking up the dry inner space, pulling us under. We had a minute at most to get out. Both Sophia and I rushed to the first hatch, just behind the cockpit. She pushed it open.

Suddenly, the noise of battle filled my ears. There were machine guns firing and the occasional heavy thud of artillery. They had really doubled down on Plan B.

Sophia stood in the threshold, suddenly unsure of her own suggestion. I grabbed her arm. She turned, the fear evident, though suppressed, in her eyes.

"We go straight across, right angle to the ship," I instructed firmly. "Dive as far as you can and keep swimming in that direction. Do not surface until the last moment. Do that and they can't touch you."

She didn't admonish me for lying. She just nodded, steeling herself. We both turned to the water, coming ever nearer to the foaming waves as the ship lowered itself to the sandy bottom below. As another huge shell ripped through the air like thunder, I couldn't blame her for the fear. It was rattling through me as well. It was one final gamble.

And then a cacophony of new firepower crackled through the cove. Instinctively, I cringed and looked around. And then I saw them. Three helicopters, bristling with guns and missiles falling from the sky and unloading into the cave. I clutched my hands to either side of my head as my eardrums took a beating from explosion after explosion. I couldn't tell, but I thought after a moment that the guns within the cavern were going silent.

Missiles streaked into the mouth of the giant cave, and it was over. The entire thing collapsed in an avalanche of rock. The roof, and half of the cove, collapsed and rolled into the sea. And then everything was quiet, save for the beating of the rotors above us.

A rope ladder suddenly appeared before us.

"Climb up, hurry!" someone ordered. We didn't need to be told twice. I gestured towards Sophia. She was about to protest, so I picked her up and put her on the ladder. She glared back angrily, but now she either had to climb or block me from following.

The water was lapping at my ankles when I took the rungs, but it didn't matter. With the cave imploded, there wasn't any immediate risk. I could have let myself sink into the ocean and simply tread water until they could bring me up. Besides, Sophia was safe, and that had always been the primary objective. Maybe the only objective to me.

As I reached the helicopter, a large hand clasped my arm and pulled me in as if I were a ragdoll. I collapsed on a small open section of floor, suddenly feeling exhausted. Everything had finally

caught up with me. I glanced up at my rescuer and I felt another shock.

"Tommy?" I asked, gaping at the big black man with the Theta symbol on his collar.

"Have we met?" he asked gruffly. "I don't remember running with any small fry like yourself. And if you had pulled a stunt like that in my unit..." He shook his head grimly, but I could see a little bit of the old twinkle in his eye.

"You would have me flayed alive," I finished for him.

"So we have met?" he asked, unsure, but open to convincing.

"In another time," I answered in the most straightforward way I could. "In another life."

They unloaded us right at the top of the cove and immediately set about checking on us. The second helicopter that touched down unloaded an all-too-familiar figure. The sharp outline of The Hawk marched towards Sophia and me. Just as he was about to address her, she stood, pushing the protesting medic back, and stumbled several paces away.

I tried to pull myself up to go to her, but my medic was quicker on the draw, and far less gentle with me. He shoved me back down as Sophia came to a stop at a point overlooking what remained of Cloister Cove, uncomfortably close to the cliff's edge.

She stuck two fingers into her mouth, and for a horrifying moment, I thought she was going to bite them off as she had Nergüi's. But no, she was reaching to the back of her throat. She gagged violently, heaving from her stomach. It nauseated me just to watch. And then it horrified me.

Something was falling from her mouth. A black, segmented snake-like object. I had seen enough strange things to recognize it as a machine, but it was one of the most disturbing machines I had ever seen. Little hair-like tendrils poked out at right angles every so often along its body, and they wriggled even as Sophia puked it up.

Finally, it fell to her feet, twitching uselessly. Sophia hacked once more, before pulling herself up a little straighter and viciously stomping on it over and over until it broke into a million pieces.

I was utterly horrified. Was this the pill we had fed her? If I had known, I would have never, ever—

Sophia walked towards The Hawk, eyes tired, hair blowing messily in the wind and hands pulling the blanket tight around herself. Nevertheless, she looked determinedly up at The Hawk as she spoke.

"I'm sure I speak for my mother when I say you have the Crown's thanks for your timely assistance," she said sternly, "but you will understand my concern at a foreign power conducting military actions on sovereign Aechrian soil. I thank you for everything you've done, but I must insist that you cease any ongoing operations immediately."

Surprisingly, The Hawk smiled. He bowed his head. "Certainly, Your Highness. I apologize for our rash presumption but can assure you that we wish nothing but cooperation with your government. To that end, you have my word as a gentleman and an officer that no further military operation will take place on Aechrian soil without prior approval or oversight directly from the Crown. Save perhaps a flight back to the capitol?" he suggested.

"That is acceptable," Sophia said stiffly. The Hawk bowed again, and I thought it slightly comical. Here he was in his crisp

black uniform, surrounded by his marines, and yet he was bowing to this young woman, half his size, exhausted and bleary-eyed, and almost all alone. And yet, there was no mockery in his gesture.

"If you'll excuse me, there's just one other matter I must address before we take off," The Hawk said. Sophia nodded in a dismissal she had no way to enforce. Nonetheless, The Hawk left at her signal, and made his way towards me.

I didn't bow my head in shame. I just steeled myself for what had to be done.

"If you're taking me to court martial or something," I said, "I'll go quietly."

"Stick to a report for now," he said grimly.

I told him everything that happened, as clearly as I could remember without being too pedantic. His expression never wavered. Not once, though I thought for a moment I saw something in his eyes when I told him how I had activated the crystal ray inside the arena. But no, it was gone. I continued with the story until I got to the moment he arrived.

"I didn't expect reinforcements," I said lamely.

"Thank your friend David for that," The Hawk replied. "He found your note. Not only did he immediately report it, but he was instrumental in organizing our response. If it weren't for him, we wouldn't have been here so soon. But either way, you really forced our hand."

"That wasn't my intention," I said, finally dropping my gaze.

"No, I expect it wasn't," The Hawk said. He considered me for a long time. "You're lucky Sophia isn't a Timeless. Forcing her through all those recursions might have given Anarakia exactly what they wanted."

I looked up in panic, glancing towards the far helicopter, where Happy and Claire were carefully lifting her, despite her weak protests, into a chair in the back. I looked to The Hawk. He raised a reassuring hand, the first friendly gesture he had given me.

"I said she *wasn't* a Timeless. She's fine," he said. "To her, she just saw the final version of events. She didn't have to relive those endless resets. She was in no danger of mental harm, not from that."

I let that sink in. To her, she had just seen me fire a single huge energy blast. No fighting with Pierce and Nergüi, no million-recursion nightmare trying to get it to fire in the first place. Clean and simple.

"What about that thing?" I asked, gesturing towards the destroyed remnant of the snake thing.

"I confess, I didn't think Anarakia had any synapse slicers in this timeline. They are quite rare, and hard to carry around secretly. Nevertheless, the capsule we gave Sophia would have blocked most of the damage."

"Most?" I asked, suddenly defiant again.

He stared back at me, and slowly, I let the fire die just a little.

"Speaking of mental damage," he finally said, changing the subject. "Until I accept your resignation, your orders are to return to Square One Medical Center for a full psychological workup. Few have gone through what you have. Fewer still have come out the other side in one piece."

I nodded. It was the right thing to do, of course.

I glanced towards Sophia's helicopter.

"Psi first," The Hawk ordered, clearly following my gaze. "Then we'll talk about your future."

I nodded again, and was soon being loaded into my own chopper, a very mixed feeling about said future cloying at my chest.

When I arrived back at Square One, Kate, the receptionist on the fourth floor with the very curly hair and bubblegum habit looked at me with exasperation. That reaction was a bit confusing, considering this was the first time we had spoken. Then again, Kate's continually glassy expression suggested this might be her default with patients.

"You the guy who got himself looped?" She asked in a thick Brooklyn accent when I introduced myself.

"Yeah, I guess so," I had replied with a weak smile.

The truth was, I was feeling alright about the whole ordeal, save for a bit of a twitch in my left hand. I had been so anxious about coming here, though, that by now I wasn't sure if that was an actual symptom of my experience, or if I had induced this in myself by constantly focusing on that hand. Maybe getting looped by using the crystal ray instead of the gauge gun had fewer side effects because there was less motion involved. All I had done was hold down a button.

Ah, who was I kidding? I knew the real side effects wouldn't be in my hands, but in my head.

When I actually went back for the sessions, it was a lot less intimidating than I had feared. I had expected a long series of questions like those that had been asked of Sophia, but it wasn't like that at all. Dr. Emmaline Zita Abraham was patient and attentive, never firm with me, though I had the impression that she could be if she wanted to. But no, she was always understanding, and if she coaxed me in any direction, it was only to get me to say what I was already thinking, and even in that she didn't use a heavy hand.

We sat for hours in her little office. It was just big enough to avoid inducing claustrophobia. We sat across from each other on the creaky—yet fluffy—furniture. The couch could only be described as belonging in a grandma's house, and I suppose that fit. Dr. Abraham (she preferred I address her as Emmaline, but I wasn't ready for that) wasn't quite elderly, but was past middle age. Her eyes crinkled at the corners and her hair, hung from either side of her face in loops, was graying, but her movements conveyed a youthful strength and vigor. She was a solid presence, but never an intimidating one. She was an everlasting rock, impervious to erosion even from the constant waves of my unstable psyche.

I just talked. For hours on end, though it never felt like it. Even after weeks, each session seemed to end just after it started. Everything that I had gone through since stepping through the time gate, and some of what happened before that, all came out slowly, but it became increasingly easy the more I talked. I didn't always like who I was when I recounted the story. But it was the truth. Dr. Abraham made it all seem okay, even if I had made the wrong choice. Not that what I had done was okay or would be swept under the rug, but she recognized the reasons for my actions, and encouraged me to reflect on them. That little gesture was heartbreakingly comforting. Just being able to acknowledge that it had been real. That everything I had experienced had been real.

But the one knot that couldn't begin to be undone with just the two of us was my decision to return to the cove. It was stupid, it was rash, and I knew I wouldn't have done anything differently. But I couldn't forgive myself for instigating that disaster. The simple fact was that if The Hawk hadn't arrived just in time, I would be dead, and Sophia probably would have been too. I needed to know what was going to happen because of it all.

And then one day, I got my wish.

"Well, Kennedy," Dr. Abraham said after one of our sessions, "I've learned a lot from our talks. You know, of course, that I work for Time Peace, and while none of what you told me has left this room, you are aware that I was asked to perform a psychological evaluation, is that right?"

"Right," I said, with a bad feeling of what that report would mean.

"If you don't mind, I would like you to stick around as I deliver the results to the War Marshall."

It took me a moment to remember that was The Hawk's official rank. Come to think of it, I had never heard Dr. Abraham refer to him as "The Hawk" like the rest of us.

I nodded. "Okay, sure," I said tentatively.

"If you're ready, he should be standing just outside. Shall I invite him in?" she asked.

I thought it was utterly bizarre that she was asking me if the Hawk could come in. "Yeah," I answered awkwardly. I certainly wasn't going to deny him entry to a part of his own base.

Emmaline Zita Abraham nodded and strode over to her door. She spoke a couple of words I couldn't quite hear, and then re-entered, The Hawk behind her. He looked rather strange with his pristine black uniform, single gold bar, and a tiny floral teacup in his hand. While Dr. Abraham took her seat, he looked around the office for a place to sit, and she gestured towards my couch.

I was about to rise to attention, but The Hawk waved me aside and instead sunk into the cushion next to me. In my little motion, I may have unconsciously shifted a little further from him. He looked up, absurdly sunk into the brown patterned couch with his little teacup, but gestured for Dr. Abraham to continue as if he were prompting a subordinate to explain the strategic situation.

"As I just explained to Kennedy, I have completed his psychological workup," Dr. Abraham said calmly, almost casually as she handed The Hawk a few thin sheets of paper on top of a manilla envelope. "Kennedy has been through a great ordeal, and it is no surprise that the event has left its mark on him. What is surprising is the resiliency that he's displayed. He has displayed no major side effects from the loop, nor developed any incapacitating conditions. Perhaps he has been extraordinarily lucky, perhaps he simply is more resistant to this type of psychological damage. Regardless, it is my opinion that this event has not impeded his ability to perform in the field.

"Additionally," she added, and the cautious optimism that had started to rise in my chest fluttered uncomfortably. "Kennedy has demonstrated to me an ability and willingness to reflect on his past actions, identify mistakes, and make strides to correct them. In many ways, compared to the preliminary evaluation done at recruitment, he appears to be healthier, if not happier. Obviously, growing and healing is never complete, certainly not in the little time we have had, and much of the difficult work still lies ahead, but I have to say I have been very impressed at his maturity. So long as you don't throw him into any war zones, I am optimistic about his future."

The Hawk carefully considered the papers, seeming to take in every word, but betraying nothing on his face. Finally, he looked up. "Thank you, Emmaline," he said politely. "Would you mind if I borrowed your office a moment to speak with Mr. Frost?"

"Of course not," she said, examining him carefully with piercing eyes. I had the sense they had discussed this before.

"In just a moment," The Hawk said, getting up before Dr. Abraham could. "There is something I would like to collect first."

She nodded, then turned to me. "Would you mind waiting here?"

"No. Not at all," I said at once. I had grown very comfortable in this office. I far preferred waiting there for The Hawk's ominously looming conversation than anywhere else.

They left for a moment as I contemplated my fate. Dr. Abraham's words had surprised me a lot. I didn't think that they'd change anything, though. I wondered if Time Peace had a prison. If I would be locked up. Was I traitor? Did they execute traitors?

The Hawk interrupted that uncomfortable thought by opening the door and stepping back in. And then, throwing me for yet another loop, White Rabbit walked in right behind him. A sarcastic smile tugged at the corners of her mouth, but she didn't say anything. Instead, she flopped down into the spot on the couch where The Hawk had just been sitting. She stretched out her legs, nearly taking up the entire floor as she managed an impressive feat of relaxed slumping that turned her sitting position into a near-lying one. The Hawk sat much more professionally in the chair Dr. Abraham usually occupied.

He stared at me for several seconds. My discomfort welled up more and more, but I didn't say anything.

"You've put me in an awkward position," The Hawk began. I didn't protest. I didn't deny it. He continued, "I suppose some would call that karmic."

Unprepared, I didn't catch the meaning of his words.

"It's time I laid all my cards on the table," he said. He took a deep breath, glancing to the side, and for the first time, seeming to doubt himself. "I admit, I had never intended to tell you this. Especially after Cloister Cove. While at first, I had intended to hide it for practical reasons, after the cove, I intended to do so because, frankly, I didn't want you to gain an undue sense of self-importance. Most people in your situation, especially at your age would. However," and he paused here again, returning his gaze to mine, "I trust Emmaline's judgment. While it is her job to sympathize with all our agents and operatives, and she does her job quite well, she is rarely impressed. So I am substituting her judgement for my own in this case. Don't disappoint me."

"I'd say I won't," I began slowly, "but, sir, I have no idea what you're talking about."

He smiled thinly. "No, and that's the point. Let's change that."

He sat a little straighter and folded his hands in front of himself. When he began to talk next, his tone was much more formal and precise. "You were quite correct that your dreams were, in part, from a previous meta-timeline. Many of the details are incorrect, some likely fabricated by your subconscious. But you were recruited by Time Peace in that previous meta-timeline. Perhaps a meta-timeline before that as well. Perhaps many, many times before. Regardless, you were recruited, and you served with our Thetas as a marine. In those meta-timelines, the battle for Aechyr's soul played out much differently. The details are unimportant, but you and a team of Thetas stormed Cloister Cove which then, as now, was an Anarakian outpost. However, while you were likely wounded in this assault, you were not killed, nor assaulted by Director Sainne."

I sat up much straighter.

"But sir, my dreams always ended with—" I began. He held up a hand.

"All in good time," he promised. "You see, in this meta-timeline, your career continued. I am reliably informed that it wasn't particularly spectacular, but certainly up to standard. You were a good marine but didn't stand out from the pack. Until the end."

For a second, I thought I saw a mischievous glint in The Hawk's eye, much like one found in White Rabbit's, but it was gone a second later.

"In this meta-timeline, Time Peace was utterly defeated," he continued. "Anarakia rallied its forces and crushed us. A single organized campaign, as we always knew it would be, was more than enough to defeat us utterly."

"If I may," I began, and when The Hawk didn't object, continued, "I was under the impression that Anarakia fought with itself too much for that sort of thing. I mean, I thought the only one who could unite them was..." I faltered a moment. I wasn't sure if it was acceptable to speak of the Ashen Phoenix, whose existence was officially denied, in front of The Hawk.

"The Ashen Phoenix," The Hawk stated plainly. My eyes widened in interest, and I kept silent, willing him to go on. "Officially, I will deny having said any of this, of course," The Hawk continued lightly, "but yes, the rumors are quite correct. The man known as the Ashen Phoenix exists, and it is only he who can channel the full might of Anarakia. And he did.

"It was a terrible power that Time Peace was woefully incapable of matching. In the last climactic battle, he destroyed us in a series of expertly executed maneuvers. Our command and control was disrupted, our time gates seized, our forces captured or killed."

"But you know his moves now," I suddenly blurted. "You can prevent all that from happening again."

"Possibly," The Hawk said. "More likely, his forces would still be more than enough to defeat ours. But that was never my goal. I never intended to undo our defeat."

"But—" He cut me off with a raise of a single finger.

"I wasn't finished with the story," The Hawk reproved. "You see, while the Ashen Phoenix had defeated all of Time Peace's organized resistance, there are always pockets. Not everyone surrenders just because their commander is taken out. Especially not particularly stubborn marines who never learned any common sense."

It suddenly occurred to me where this was going.

"It seems that a freak occurrence happened at this point in our story," The Hawk continued, a hint of triumph in his voice. "The Ashen Phoenix himself saw to the destruction of one of these resisting platoons. But in doing so, he was met with a surprise. Through sheer dumb luck, an otherwise unexceptional fighter managed to pierce his armor and kill him." He pointed towards me now. "Somehow, Kennedy, you managed to score the killing blow."

"How?" I asked, more baffled than impressed. His declaration didn't feel real. It seemed more like a weight that was pressing down on my shoulders, growing heavier and heavier with each passing moment.

The Hawk shook his head sadly. "That we unfortunately don't know."

"Okay, so what does this mean?" I said, trying to see if there were any connections with my experiences in this meta-timeline. "Are you saying I'm going to kill the Ashen Phoenix?"

"No," The Hawk sighed deeply. "That unfortunately, is now definitively off the table."

"Why's that?" I said. The weight of responsibility that had begun to settle on me suddenly turned to worry.

"Because Sainne was quicker than I was," White Rabbit said casually. I turned to her. She still was trying to affect an apathetic demeanor, but she couldn't quite keep the same cool expression. She seemed to realize this and sat up just a little.

"Anarakia almost immediately started eating itself," she explained. "It's like you said, the Ashen Phoenix was the only one holding all of them together. Oh, sure, they had loyalists that would carry on the fight, but with a dozen other splinter factions nipping at their heels, they were guaranteed to fall apart. The tiny remnants of Time Peace, and more importantly, the forces of the various timelines Anarakia had invaded would be enough to chip away at them until nothing was left. Victory for the good guys!" She raised her hands in a rock-n-roll gesture.

"So what went wrong?" I prompted.

"Sainne," she repeated. "As soon as he saw what was happening, he realized what I was going to do. I'm a white rabbit, duh. It's my job to head back down the meta-timeline should something go horribly wrong, or in this case, horribly right."

"I'm missing something," I said.

"It's simple really," White Rabbit continued. "We didn't have assets ready to capitalize on this victory, so all that I needed to do was go back in meta-time, set up a few reserves in the right positions, and repeat the whole process exactly the same. Anarakia wins, or thinks they do, only for you to take out the Ashen Phoenix. But this time, we'd be ready. A few strike groups to take out potential leaders and stop their own rabbit holes, and we're golden. Checkmate. V-day. Game over."

"But Sainne beat you to it," I realized.

She grimaced. "Yeah, he did. He didn't let himself get bogged down in the chaos and infighting. He went straight for a rabbit hole. I went in right behind him, but it was too late."

"That's when he blinded me," I realized. "So I couldn't kill the Ashen Phoenix!"

"That's our theory," The Hawk agreed.

"Well, I didn't know he was going to use some fancy new Talhesian torture device," White Rabbit grumbled. "I figured he was just going to kill you. So I thought to myself, no problem, I'll just create another rabbit hole and jump further back in meta-time to make sure you're recruited safely."

"So you are the real White Rabbit?" I asked.

"We're all the real White Rabbit, dude," she laughed. "But I am the one you met that rainy day at the bus stop. White Rabbit the Thirteenth."

"What was the name—?"

"Mirabelle," she answered immediately. "I also referenced *It's a Wonderful Life*, which you still haven't seen."

"No," I admitted sheepishly, though with a smile. I was relieved. The curtain was finally being lifted on everything. It wasn't the prettiest picture, but it was the truth. Clarity.

"Well, as we discovered," she continued less enthusiastically, "Sainne somehow corrupted your identifying information. Any version of you that stepped into a time gate to become a Timeless would inherit the blindness he inflicted. It's a truly nasty trick. If only I knew how he did it. Shoot, the device may have even told him that a previous version of himself corrupted you he knew it could do a number on you when you were chasing down Bailey."

"So, that's it, then? No way this can happen again, like it did before?" I asked, repeating White Rabbit's words back to her.

"For a while, I thought it might be possible," The Hawk said dolefully. "When Thirteen here came to me and told me everything, I couldn't just throw away such an opportunity."

"Even with me blinded?" I asked. "I mean, why not try to come up with something that doesn't end up with all of Time

Peace getting killed? Especially if the meta-timeline's already different?"

"Because, Kennedy, it was a chance for the end." The words seemed to pain the War Marshall as they left his mouth. "This is called the Eternal War for a reason, remember. We've fought this war for so long, and each time one side nearly defeats the other, the faction on the losing end simply creates a rabbit hole to start it all again. There are some limits as to when we can use one, but certainly not enough to make an end to the war seem plausible. And we've learned from each other so well that the thought of being able to defeat each other has become nearly unthinkable. We know each other's strategies, and there are none left effective and devastating enough to achieve victory. And then this fell into my lap.

"A freak occurrence, a stroke of luck," he said wistfully. "It couldn't be planned for, it couldn't be prevented, because Anarakia would be blinded by their victory. Only then, with their guard down, could we guarantee success. It was perfect. A final way out. But you see, I was the one ultimately blinded by the prospect of victory. I wanted that outcome so badly that even when it was clear this meta-timeline was deviating from the last, I tried to stay the course, hoping in vain that it would right itself. That Time Peace could still seize that final victory in the end.

"And so I decided to try to treat you as any other recruit. After all, that is what I had done in the victorious meta-timeline. But it was a futile effort. I simply couldn't. You had been blinded and needed special care. Plus, you were hot-headed and had something to prove. But I had to pretend as if I had no foreknowledge. What would I have done if I didn't anticipate you to become our accidental savior? Naturally, I would assign you to the remedial Dark Eye Squadron. So I did. After all, there was a chance I had done so in the last meta-timeline as well. But I overlooked David's eagerness to prove himself. I didn't expect him to begin training you as a Delta, or for you to latch onto that idea. I didn't expect him to lead you in a search for the missing Princess. And I didn't expect him to unwittingly feed your conviction that you were something special."

I hung my head in shame.

"I should have realized my error then, but I pressed ahead. I tried to squash your ambition with White Rabbit the Twelfth, and a bribe. I thought perhaps you could still be led back to your place as a Theta later, that something could be salvaged. But this was foolish, wishful thinking. It was at that point that I should have either told you the truth or dismissed you. But instead, I asked for your trust while deceiving you."

"Sir, I was in the wrong," I said hastily. "I was so angry and frustrated that I ignored my duty, what I had agreed to when I signed up. I should have—"

The Hawk raised his hand.

"That is probably true," he agreed. "But make no mistake; it should never have come to that. I knew what you were like when you were recruited. I knew you had dreams of a past meta-timeline. I knew you wanted answers and you would be tenacious in seeking them out. Yes, you disobeyed orders and behaved in an unbecoming manner. However, I had betrayed the trust that is given to a superior officer. Not anticipating an obvious problem with personnel is a failure in leadership as much as, and perhaps more than, a failure of the subordinate.

"Needless to say," he forged on before I could speak again, "when it was revealed that you had discovered Princess Sophia, and in fact had become quite close to her, my plan had utterly failed. In the previous meta-timeline, you had been a mere foot soldier. Little to distinguish you from the many others, save for your typically tenacious attitude. Now, you had inextricably involved yourself with a potential flashpoint in the Aechrian

timeline. Nothing could ever be the same again. Only my own stubbornness, and in fairness to myself, the other more immediate concerns regarding the Princess' kidnapping, kept me from revealing the truth then and there.

"And so, finally, that brings us back to your resignation, and activities at Cloister Cove," he concluded.

I shuffled my feet anxiously. "What are you going to do with me?" I asked softly.

"I've been placed in an awkward situation once again," The Hawk replied. "On the one hand, regardless of the surrounding context, you betrayed your word to me, violated orders, and risked the future of an entire timeline on a misguided whim. On the other, you rescued Princess Sophia, allowed a decisive victory over Anarakia, and even gave us a reason to continue holding onto a valuable prisoner. So which am I to weigh more? Your intentions, or your results?"

I didn't speak. I didn't like the correct answer.

"Then there's this," The Hawk added, and produced the folder Dr. Abraham had given him. "An almost glowing recommendation from my top psychologist. Despite her noting some 'typical teenage flaws,' she has all but told me you would make an exceptional agent. She also notes a lot of genuine remorse. But is that enough for a field agent? What do you think?"

I stared at my toes for a several seconds before answering meekly. "I think you should decide based on how you expect a recruit to behave in the future, sir."

"I agree," he said gravely. "And while your feats at Cloister Cove were undeniably impressive, some of them seem like the same dumb luck that led you to victory in a previous meta-timeline. But I don't recruit based on luck. Let's assume you get one lucky win per meta-timeline, and you've just used this one's up.

"But even so," he continued, "your experiences in the loop, the perseverance you displayed, that is far from luck, I think. That suggests potential. So does self-reflection."

I looked up, not willing to believe what he was saying.

"I told you that you were a savior of a previous timeline," he continued seriously. "Don't let that go to your head. You won't be again. You were merely in the right place at the right time. From this point forward, if you want to make a difference, you have to earn it. You are not special. But you could be useful."

He carefully placed two objects on a table beside and between us. I recognized both immediately but could hardly believe I was seeing them. One was a brass metal bar divided into five small sections, and the other was a pin shaped into a triangular symbol. A Delta.

"Despite everything, you're granting me a tab?" I asked incredulously.

"I seem to recall that you chose to resign," The Hawk replied. "If that decision stands, then my offer is irrelevant. But if perhaps that message was left in error, they are there for you. Believe me," he added, as I was about to protest further, "this is hardly an easy decision on my part. There are plenty of good reasons not to offer this to you, as you no doubt were about to enumerate. Your record is shoddy, your future in question. I am making a judgement call based on a professional assessment of your renewed character and your potential. You will not be getting special treatment. You will be watched carefully, and now that everything is in the open, you have no excuses for insubordination. All I will need is one reason. One reason to dump you in some godforsaken timeline and forget I ever laid eyes on you.

"But you need not accept your commission," he added. "You can maintain your resignation and simply walk out of here.

I'm sure with your connection to the Crown Princess of Aechyr, you could find a happy life in that timeline. Or perhaps in a different one. You can simply walk out of here and leave this life behind." He stood and straightened his uniform. "Believe me, Mr. Frost, it would be much easier for both of us if you simply took that life."

It would be a good life, too, I reflected. No doubt peaceful. Happy. Really the greatest thing that could have happened to me was meeting Sophia. And to stay with her if I could? Even if she wasn't royalty, that would have been wonderful. I could picture a bright future unfolding before me, a wondrous adventure. I could be someone there.

I could have been.

"Take your time and think about it," The Hawk was saying, but I had already stood and grabbed the tab and the pin.

"I don't need to, sir," I replied simply. I knew what I could do. I knew what I could be. And I knew that there was a war going on out there. If I could help, I couldn't just let myself relax on a comfortable timeline. I had to go. Even with what it meant leaving behind.

"This cat's crazy," White Rabbit said, shaking her head. I had forgotten she was there.

The Hawk grimaced to me, ignoring her. "I knew you would do that," he sighed. "Well, as I said, you will not be without plentiful supervision."

"I understand, sir."

"For one, you will be immediately remanded to a remedial unit. I believe Dark Eye Squadron is notoriously short of personnel," he said without a hint of a smile. Thankfully, he didn't reprimand me for mine.

"Additionally," he added hastily, "Dark Eye is to be sent on a rather dull assignment for routine and thorough reconnaissance. I will be expecting detailed and precise reports submitted in a timely manner. The work will be mundane and tedious, and I will nevertheless expect you to behave as if the timeline depended on it."

"Understood, sir," I replied crisply.

"Lastly," he continued, "considering recent events, Dark Eye Squadron will be further supervised by a Theta unit. You will answer directly to them, and do whatever they instruct, no matter what. If they tell you to polish their boots, I better be able to see my reflection in them. The unit you will be assigned to will be led by one Thomas Madding. I believe you met briefly."

"Yes, sir," I said, elated at the thought of working with Tommy again, even if he didn't know me in this meta-timeline.

"I want to make it clear that their supervision will be strict," The Hawk emphasized, deflating some of my enthusiasm. "You are in a probationary unit, and you specifically are on notice. Any infractions, and I mean any, that the Thetas report will lead to your immediate dismissal. No strikes, no do-overs, no leeway. I will only accept a spotless report."

I swallowed, but nodded.

"Oh, one more thing," he said. His tone got even more serious. "If you do choose to continue your commission, you won't be coming back to Aechyr. Not for a long time. Think of it as removing temptation. Maybe, when I think you're ready, you can come back. But until then, you'll be staying far away. Do you still want to sign back up?"

I swallowed. No, I didn't really want to accept those terms. That was the last thing I wanted to agree to. But it was fair. I desperately wanted to say no, but this was my flashpoint. I knew the right answer was the painful one.

"Yes, sir, I do," I answered.

"Good," The Hawk concluded. "Then report to Dark Eye Squadron Leader. You have one last assignment before shipping out with the Thetas."

"Yes, sir!" I replied, saluting.

He dismissed me and I exited the room as White Rabbit made some lighthearted comment about "what kind of circus we're running here. We've clearly got enough clowns."

As I left, I heard Blake call my name from down the hall. Catching up with him, he proudly showed me his own identical rank tab and Delta pin. He nodded to me, leaving a lot unsaid in the motion. It wasn't as ecstatic as he had sounded when he had called me over, but was still proud. I returned the gesture.

"Pipe down," Randy growled. "You'd think you won the lottery or something instead of a brand-new workload."

"Easy there, Randy," David told him as he turned the corner carrying four shirts in his arms.

"What do you got there?" Blake asked, already taking in every angle.

David handed him one. It was a long-sleeved, high-necked jacket with a white torso, but colored sleeves and shoulders. The one he handed to Blake was blue.

"Call it an unofficial uniform," he said. "You need something to put those pins on until the real ones come in."

He tossed the red one to me and the yellow—excuse me, *gold*—one to Randy. Blake was already halfway done putting his on. As I pulled my arms through the sleeves, Randy started complaining again.

"No way am I wearing some cheerleading outfit," he complained.

"Put on the damn shirt, Randy," David ordered flatly.

Randy muttered something nasty under his breath but complied. Soon, we were all standing there with our team uniforms, each with the appropriate color. Blake had been the first to place his pin and tab, and I quickly followed suit. When I had finished and looked up, I noticed that while Randy's was identical to Blake's and mine, David's tab was slightly different. He only had three bars, and the gold one was slightly longer than the one on Blake's or my tab.

"Hey, what gives?" Blake asked, gesturing towards it.

"Team lead," David replied simply.

"But you have access to Class 3 information? That's two above us! That's what? Threats? Why do you need to know Threat Assessments?"

"If I told you, I would have to kill you," David replied dryly.

"That's not funny," Blake said.

"It's not funny because you're the butt of the joke," Randy retorted.

"It's not funny either way. What's the real scoop, David?" Blake pressed.

"That's for me to know, and you to find out. Or not," he said.

Blake groaned and continued to pester him as my mind wandered off. I thought back to everything The Hawk had told me. While he had said he would deny it all, I wondered what level of information that bit about the previous meta-timeline, or about the Ashen Phoenix was. Surely, it was at least part of Threat Assessments. And yet, he had implied not even David had known about it. Was it Class 2—Temporal Factors?

Whatever it was, he hadn't given me clearance, or instruction on what to do about it. I suspected that was intentional. I had a gut feeling he expected that I would tell Blake, even if it might not be technically permitted. After all, I hadn't officially heard any of that. I might need to share some of this "speculation." I don't think he would mind if I just kept it to Blake.

"What do you think, Kennedy?" Blake asked, bringing me out of my reverie.

"Huh, what?" I asked.

"I said we should all get sunglasses for the Dark Eye Squadron theme, to go with the jackets," he explained. By the tone of his voice, I could tell he was asking my permission, making sure it didn't offend me.

I cracked a big smile. "Yeah, sure," I said. "But they have to be mandatory. Randy can't go without. It would ruin the team look."

"You're living on another planet," Randy snarled.

"Technically, we've been to another Earth," Blake pointed out.

"No, it's the same Earth, different timeline," Randy shot back, stubbornly. "And I'm still not wearing any stupid sunglasses."

"Actually," David said, suppressing a smile, "for our next assignment, they *are* kind of mandatory."

"Ha!" Blake said.

Randy scowled.

"And speaking of," David continued. "Sophia has been in contact. Since she is rejoining the royal family officially, there is going to be a big ceremony, and she's given us an in. So pack your bags. We're going to back to Aechyr one last time."

XVI

The Coronation

"Your girlfriend has a real sense of humor," Blake muttered to me.

"She's not—we're—" I stuttered before giving up and grumbling, "I'll be sure to tell her. If I get the chance."

David, Blake, Randy, and I were standing in a booth far above and removed from the ceremony, stuffed into suits and shades and standing guard. While hundreds of VIPs flooded into the courtyard in front of Capitol Castle, awaiting the moment when Princess Sophia would be confirmed as heir, we were guarding a glorified light post. There were four raised booths like ours, each draping cables suspending bright lanterns over the temporary amphitheater. The dancing orange lights made a thinly woven canopy above the guests, warming the proceedings below. And while the elaborately dressed audience bustled about in refined excitement below, we were stuck up apart from everything, as far as possible from the stage.

"What are you whining about? I still don't get what the big deal even is," Randy said. "It's a coronation, but it's not a coronation—it's all meaningless. Who would even want to be here?"

"It's a confirmation of Sophia as Crown Princess," David explained. "It's not a typical ceremony but considering her absence from the national stage for years at this point, it's very necessary. Legally, it means nothing, but the monarchy here has always been as much symbolic as political, especially in recent history."

"Translation: it's a meaningless made-up production to keep a bunch of old farts from having a heart attack at the slightest change in the status quo," Randy proclaimed.

"I'm not a fan of this kind of thing either," Blake commented, "but I'd rather be in the party than on-duty."

"You would rather be in the middle of all of this?" Randy scoffed.

"Rather not be working," Blake countered.

"Rather be supporting a friend," I added.

Randy smirked. "What, guard duty isn't supportive? Thought you were all about that kind of noble protector thing."

"Do you want to, or shall I?" Blake asked me.

"Go right ahead," I replied.

"Shut up, Randy," he said. Randy just continued to smirk.

"We need a better team motto," David sighed.

When the ceremony finally, slowly, began, we were already getting stiff standing in the same little box, with only some wiring for company. In theory, we had a bird's eye view of any potential threats. In reality, we were a minor backup for the Royal Guard and even military personnel who had this place fully covered. As the ceremony ground on, one of us would switch out just so we didn't have to stay on our feet the whole time. Three of us were more than capable of keeping an eye on things.

And of us all, I was the one paying the most attention. When Sophia finally appeared before everyone, there was a great sigh of approval from the crowd. I cringed at the thought of all those eyes focusing on me. Even as she smiled gratefully at the crowd, I could practically feel her doing the same. But on the outside, she was perfectly composed. The only clue to Sophia's discomfort at the occasion was her choice to introduce herself in a particularly plain deep blue dress. Even by the conservative tastes of the monarchy, it was especially unadorned. At least, that's what I thought. I didn't really know anything about fashion, and that made me second guess myself. From up there, I really couldn't see Sophie's expression. She seemed so far away.

Randy yawned loudly. It was his turn off his feet, and he was hardly treating the occasion with any solemnity.

"It's not naptime," David warned him. "No movement on the southeast corner," he reported.

"Clear on the west," Blake replied.

After a moment, I added my own voice, "North is clear."

The prime minister, a short, heavy guy named Mattox, was speaking, going on a lengthy sermon before the small silver circlet would be finally placed on Sophia's head. If I wasn't mistaken, this too was created rather recently just for the occasion. Honestly, I didn't think Randy was too far off with his assessment of the ceremony.

"Ever since Prince Alexander the First tamed the island, we have been blessed with a series of leaders who have upheld the highest traditions of..." the prime minister was saying.

Something shuffled behind us.

"Hey Randy, could you keep it down?" Blake asked, glancing back, and then his jaw dropped open. I turned just as he pulled out his gauge gun.

Randy was already choking out the second intruder, pointing his gun at the third. He fired the stun beam at the same time as Blake, and the last two collapsed.

"What the—?" I asked, still processing the appearance of four armed intruders in our little compartment.

"Sentinel three to all posts, intruders in the lookout," David was saying rapidly into the radio. No one replied. "Sentinel three to all posts, please acknowledge." Silence again.

"These are professionals," Randy noted.

"Agreed," David replied, and raised his watch to his lips. "Keeper, this is Dark Eye, we have intruders."

When no reply came, a cold tingle dripped down my spine. "Anarakia," I realized.

"Who else could jam arcane tech?" David affirmed. "We have to—"

A series of short cracks outside cut him short. I immediately spun back to the scene outside, but it was already too late. The crowd was gasping, panicking, as masked figures with red armbands took the stage. The prime minister was knocked to the floor as Sophia leapt to her feet.

But they were coming from both directions. One of the intruders grabbed her from behind and stuck a gun in her back. Instinctively, I raised my own gun, but before I could fire, a new sight took me by surprise.

Director Sainne took to the stage as one of his accomplices brazenly fired into the air, attempting to silence the crowd. That didn't happen. Not until Sainne scooped up the prime minister's dropped microphone.

"Ladies and gentlemen, my distinguished compatriots," Sainne sneered, strutting across the stage, "I apologize for interrupting this lovely occasion, but a serious crime needs to be addressed, and your dear royal family is responsible. I speak of nothing less than the murder of Senator Charles Becker."

Sophia stiffened, then tried to stomp at her captor's foot, but missed. He pressed his gun more forcefully into her back.

After a second, my peripheral vision returned, and I realized David, Blake, and Randy were all staring at me apprehensively. David might have just said something, I wasn't sure. I lowered my gun.

"Any chance we could snipe him? Stun him?" I asked, stepping away from the window to reduce the chances of being seen. It seemed we were the only security left, and I wasn't about to give that fact away.

"I wouldn't trust the accuracy of an ATEP stun at this range with that target area," David replied professionally. The rest of the team's tension seemed to ease slightly, their energy suddenly channeled into solving the problem.

"Even if we hit Sophia, we'll just stun her, right?" Blake asked. "Should we go for it?"

"No, no," I quickly replied. "Stun her and we provoke the guy in the mask, he'd go right in for the kill if someone was shooting his way."

"If the gun can use a mini-arena to find the perfect stun setting, you would hope it could use a mini-arena to find its target," Blake muttered.

"Sorry, not how it works. Besides, it couldn't distinguish between Sophia and the trooper," David replied.

"Wait a moment, wait a moment," Blake said, inspiration flashing across his face. "The stun setting—that's just energy, right? Electricity?"

"Not exactly, but close," David corrected.

"Would it conduct like electricity?" Blake asked. "If he's holding onto Sophia, could the energy jump to him and stun them both?"

"No," David replied, but was already prying open a latch on his gauge gun. "Not without some modification. We're talking a highly specific beam configuration."

"Both of them—as a unit—that would be an easy target," I noted.

"Even with the ray's accuracy," David agreed as he fiddled with the interior of the silver gun and a setting on his watch.

"That's a nice science project," Randy cut in, "but don't you think the rest of them will notice?"

"The Royal Guard will open fire," David confirmed.

"The Anarakians are closer," I realized. "They could get to her before the Guard could. Randy might have a point. We could use a distraction."

"Forget distraction," Blake replied, "let's go for blackout. I bet I can kill these lights—distract and deny them a clear view of what's going on."

"That works double," I pointed out. "Anarakia won't know what hit them, and the Guard won't either, so they might be more cautious."

"Once again, you're forgetting the Anarakians will have time to react," Randy hissed.

"Not if we do it simultaneously," I replied. "Line up the shot, then fire just as the lights flare out."

"Already on it," Blake noted, pulling open a metal panel and carefully examining the wires. "I might need to do some guess work," he admitted.

"We only get one shot at this," Randy reminded us unhelpfully.

"No problem," I replied. "We arena this."

"Hey, genius," Randy shot back, "The arena would have automatically deployed with Sainne so close. He's got a watch too. But there's too much going on, too many people that would immediately break it. We can't make an arena around everything."

"We won't," I explained quickly. "I'll create an arena just around our box up here, Blake will give some of those wires a try. If it's wrong, I reset within a second, before anything can break the arena. We do it again and again until we find the right combination."

"In case you forgot," Randy retorted, "you were going to use a gauge gun at the same time. It may be no big deal to you, but the rest of us would like to avoid looping, if at all possible."

"I know," I said calmly. "We will. Once Blake's found the correct wires, we'll reset again to do the same thing, only this time, I'll shut down the arena right away. Then David takes the shot."

"I'll need to take aim before the arena goes up," David noted. "We better hope they don't move."

"It'll only be a second," I promised.

"Good. That'll work," David assured us.

"Anarakia will recover quick," Randy warned, but he was clearly warming to the plan.

"Blake, will these wires be hot when you're done?" I asked.

"Ice cold," he replied. "Why are you—oh. That's pretty nuts."

"You think they'll hold?" I asked, already pulling off my suitcoat.

"I'd put good odds on it," he replied.

"If you're going straight for the Princess, you'll need some cover," Randy declared.

"Thought you'd be in position by now," I retorted.

"Give me thirty seconds," Randy said. "Don't bother looking, you won't see me. Neither will they."

"Better not." I glanced back up to add something else, but he was already gone.

"Twenty-six and counting," David announced, re-sealing the gun casing. He popped the weapon over the edge and took aim. "Let's hope I remembered enough of my arcane tech."

"You have the target?" I asked, looping my jacket over one of the wires, catching both sleeves with one hand, and being extra careful not to touch the cable.

"Dead center," David replied. "Twenty and counting."

"...unrestrained force these unaccountable monarchs are capable of," Sainne continued down below. He was still strutting across the stage, lapping up the expressions of fear below in a cartoonish display that sucked any sincerity from his words.

"Blake?" I asked, readying my watch.

"I've got a good guess, but I'm glad I'm getting some extra chances," he replied.

"Don't sweat it," I said.

"Agreed," David echoed. "You have all the tries you need. You will get this."

"I got ya," Blake answered.

"Tonight, we answer with the same force," Sainne said in a sickeningly sweet sort of voice, speaking directly to Sophia. A single bony finger stroked her cheek, and her composure broke for a moment as she turned away in pure revulsion. Sainne lowered the microphone for just a moment, which prevented his laughter from being amplified tenfold. It still managed to waft to my ears, but I held onto my cool.

"Six seconds," David announced. "Five..."

I readied to push the crown on my watch.

Sainne turned, stepped away from Sophia, raising the mic again.

"Four..."

Blake stiffened. I scanned the crowd for Randy. He had kept his word, he was invisible.

"When they retell of what happened here tonight," Sainne continued.

"Three..."

"...remind them that we only do..."

"Two..."

Sophia and her captor weren't moving.

"...what was done to us."

"One. Hit it!"

I pressed in the crown, and the mystical space descended around our upper room. Blake started pulling cables. When the lantern inside the barrier of the arena didn't flicker out, I pushed the reset. Blake, in his hurry, pulled the same wires, and again the lantern stayed on.

"Relax," David ordered as I reset again. "We have time, just get the rhythm."

I reset again, and this time Blake tried a different set. A fourth reset, and he tried the second combination again, but I realized why. He was taking the time to decide what to try next rather than pulling randomly. He was using the time we had. And David had said we couldn't make more time.

Blake's third guess was right on the money. The orange lantern flickered out, and I reset immediately while crying, "That's it!"

Blake repeated the same move. "This one?" he asked.

"That's the one. David, you tell me when to drop the arena," I said, performing yet another reset, and Blake keeping up.

David didn't answer as we tried twice more, our rhythm tightening up, Blake yanking the correct cables sooner and sooner after each reset.

"In three," David commanded. This time he didn't give the countdown, but we were all thinking it in our heads.

Three, two, pull.

The arena fell, and as the lights over the frightened audience flashed brilliantly, David fired. By the time the bulbs had all burnt out, and the courtyard had become much darker and colder, his blaster bolt had already struck dead center. Sophia and her captor dropped to the floor, like puppets without strings.

Another panicked uproar from the crowd greeted me as I stepped onto the ledge. A couple gunshots could be heard, but far fewer than I had anticipated. I didn't look to see what was happening, but instead grabbed one of the sleeves with my other arm, and before I could think about it, leapt into the air.

The cable slid neatly under my jacket, and for a terrifying moment, I thought I was falling to the ground. But the slack tightened, and I was soaring over the fleeing bodies of the guests, the night air whipping around me. I was a part of the insane scene now, no box keeping me safely apart. The stage rushed towards me, and I locked my eyes on Sophie's collapsed form. Another couple of gunshots rang out, but I couldn't do anything about it now.

A moment before the stage rushed below my feet, I let go. I twisted around, readying myself to roll as I hit it, hard. I tumbled to the side, absorbing much of the blow. When this was all over, I would be aching pretty badly, but my pumping blood swept that sensation away for now.

I glanced up, saw where Sophie lay, and sprang to my feet. I picked up her limp form and slid off the stage, falling just below the lip of the platform and crouching there. Only then, when we were both in some semblance of cover, did I glance back around.

Three of the assailants at stage right had collapsed, and I just got a glimpse of pointed red hair darting behind cover, the gleam of a silver gun with him. *Nicely done, Randy.*

Sainne was fleeing, striding quickly on his long legs to two remaining troopers at the left end of the stage. He passed by just overhead, and I was tempted to leap out and fire, but with Sophie in my arms, I needed to stay hidden. I didn't breathe, hoping he wouldn't notice me. And of course, in all the commotion, he didn't.

But the Royal Guard did. I heard some shouting and glanced up to see one of the captains in a similar sort of federal agent suit as mine pointing towards me. Two more guards ran in my direction.

I glanced back over my shoulder, over the lip of the stage, just in time to see Sainne's long white hair whip around as he vanished into the castle. The two Anarakian agents moved to follow, but one was cut down by gunfire before he could make it into cover.

The Royal Guard arrived, guns pointed downwards and thankfully not at me, though they hardly looked friendly.

"She's alive," I quickly told them. "She's fine, just unconscious."

They didn't reply, but one just nodded and started to take her from me. Then I heard an all-too-familiar sound of rotors beating the air. A single thought electrified my mind. *He's going to get away again.*

Sophia's weight lifted from my arms and I leapt onto the stage. One of the guards shouted something, but I didn't hear it. I had tunnel-visioned again. I ran straight for the door Sainne had entered—a small service entrance added to the palatial castle. It was seated at the bottom of the thin, pointed tower. Though it was a utilitarian aspect of the otherwise decorative building, efforts had nonetheless been made to make it fit with the fantastical architecture of the monument.

I burst through the door and quickly located the stairs Sainne had taken. The last of his troopers was almost out of sight, rounding the bend of the spiral staircase. I was quicker. The shot from my gauge gun hit him, and he collapsed, tumbling back down the stairs, stunned.

I leapt over him and dashed up the stairs. I could just hear the clatter of Sainne's boots ahead of me around the bend.

"Sainne!" I shouted, as if by doing so I might get him to stop to listen.

He didn't. Instead, a cold laugh hit my ears, echoing hollowly back down the stone structure.

"Is that you, Kennedy?" he asked, mockingly.

"Turn around and find out!" I shouted back. Thin, arched windows whipped past as I continued to run as fast as I could up the tower.

"You are pathetically persistent, you know that?" he taunted.

"You started this," I countered. "You blinded me!"

"Oh, Kennedy, I did much more than that," I could practically hear the sinister smile, baring more teeth than should be humanly possible. "Don't tell me they haven't told you yet. Of your lost fate?"

"That's not going to work, Sainne," I bellowed. "They told me everything, and I don't care! This is much more basic."

"Truly, I'm shocked," he replied in faux surprise. "Your grasp of the big picture is surely one of your most admirable traits."

"And what's yours?" I called out, starting to breathe hard from running up the seemingly endless stairs. I stumbled a little with the effort. "Torturing the innocent?"

He laughed again, but more cruelly this time. "It's decidedly humiliating to think that someone as dense as you could have so much as annoyed Anarakia. No, you simpleton, my area of expertise, as you will soon discover, is influence. Why do you think I made an appearance tonight?"

"Because we burned out your base," I huffed. "You're desperate—this was your last grasp!"

"How simplistic," he replied coolly. "Do you honestly believe there was no more to it than that? That I would risk my men in such a foolhardy, spiteful move? No, young man, it is because even now the gears are turning, and the pawns are falling into place."

I stumbled again. This tower was a lot taller than I had thought.

"You see, Aechyr wants so desperately to hide what happened to their dear Princess, so I had to force the issue. The following of the late Charles Becker is far from dead, and to them, he is a martyr. Or at least, that's all the public needs to think. And how they will believe it. That's all they ever needed to set loose the rabid dogs. It's all I ever needed."

"You're being run out of the country!" I said, but a more subtle fear was creeping into my chest.

"And? You think in such simple terms. You think my hand needs to be directly upon the pieces? No, Kennedy, they've already fallen into place. Momentum will do the rest. The weak heartstrings of the human soul have made this country's upper echelons my agents, ready to do 'what must be done.' They are simply waiting for their opportunity—the chance to whisper into dear Sophie's ear. And while they do, you're here, chasing down a ghost."

I stumbled again, perhaps from the shock. I quickly recovered but hesitated for a brief moment on the stairs near a window. An oddly dark window. With strange, purplish starbursts pulsing just outside...

I hadn't stumbled because I was tired. I had stumbled because Sainne had reset the arena while I was mid-stride. The arena I hadn't even noticed.

He must have heard my footsteps suddenly stop because he laughed madly as he clambered up further. The echoing cackle ignited the fear within me into a rage and I charged off, only after fishing out a small marble and tossing it through the window to break the arena.

"Oh, and Kennedy," he said distantly as I barreled up the stairs.

I saw a door swing shut just a few feet ahead. I raced ahead, tore it open, and dashed out onto the balcony—

And then my head exploded in pain, and I collapsed right in front of Sainne, who was already seated in the helicopter hovering precariously close to the top of the tower.

"Have a seat," he said, grinning, while two men at his sides were already stepping towards me. "How about we help you feel closer to sweet Sophia?"

They stepped from the helicopter as the pain blocked out nearly all thought. Sainne was holding that Talhesian torture device in one hand, and a golden pocket watch in the other. A time gauge.

I fumbled for my gun but dropped it in my agony. Just as the agents reached out towards me, I tried something incredibly stupid. I threw myself over the edge.

Sainne and his minions would have seen me tumble over the balcony, bounce and tumble off several obstacles, and finally land surprisingly softly on the ground. Some protruding stonework, a convenient balcony, dead lighting cables, and a taut awning all miraculously broke my fall. If it weren't for these unlikely obstructions catching me, I would have been dead.

Of course, my experience had been much worse. Because not only did I have to go through that fall, I had to go through the dozens of others inside of the arena before I figured out how to slow my fall enough to feel confident in tumbling out of it. I had flicked on the arena as soon as I went over the lip and then reset time and again before I hit the ground. Finding things to bounce off was a little trickier, mostly because my psyche resisted my commands to fling myself into painful collisions. But I did it. Over and over again until I could survive the trip down.

When I rejoined the timeline, I was battered, but miraculously alive and shockingly whole. Somehow, aside from a few ribs, I hadn't even broken any bones. I was getting really good at doing really stupid things.

A fresh patter of gunfire signaled Sainne's helicopter to take off, and soon, it was once more flying into the night.

David, Randy, Blake and I pushed through the teeming crowd of reporters just inside the doors of the castle. I was still very, very sore from everything that had happened just hours before, but it was about time to do something. The media vultures hadn't let up, and instead seemed to be getting worse. If I was going to get a chance to speak to Sophia before we had to head out, it would have to be now.

"Any chance we're going to get an extension?" Blake asked over his shoulder as a pair of cameramen suddenly closed off the opening he was aiming for.

"The Hawk still wants us shipping out tomorrow," David shouted over the collective noise of everyone there. If he was worried about anyone overhearing, he wasn't showing it. Then again, no one could really interpret what we were saying.

"Don't suppose we could convince him I'm a good point of contact?" I asked, squeezing behind a woman who was practically leaping off the ground as she shouted questions.

"Call it an uphill battle," David replied. Yeah, that's about what I figured. Well, I'd just have to try to prove it.

"Forget this," Randy said irritably, as he was smacked in the face by an elbow. He hooked his leg around that of a rather large cameraman and shoved. Even as the cameraman tumbled into a crowd of journalists with notepads, Randy had already vanished behind a mass of people. The sudden pile of collapsed men and women caught everyone's attention, and the general volume increased for a moment or two, but the knots towards the front loosened slightly.

"You don't think that was a bit much?" I just barely heard Blake say chidingly towards the back of the crowd.

"Kennedy wanted in, didn't he?" Randy retorted.

"We didn't need to sabotage a diplomatic engagement," David observed.

"Is that what we're calling it?" Randy scoffed, amused. "Whatever, if this is how Kennedy wants to spend his off-time, fine. Meanwhile, I'll settle for something real. Like burgers. How do burgers sound?"

"You are such an idiot," David said, and the rest was drowned out as I made my way to the line of Royal Guards.

One of them stopped me short, holding up a hand, ready to restrain me if necessary. The onslaught of reporters clearly had frayed some of his patience. But a display of my temporary security clearance was enough for him to call a superior, who then approved my access.

Once behind the linked row of guards and the podium where a spokeswoman was trying to restore order, things were much easier. I crossed to the stairway, had my security clearance checked again, walked up the stairs, had it checked yet again, and finally entered the warm room two stories above.

The scene in the secured chamber was almost as chaotic as the one I had just left downstairs. Sophia was at the center, looking quite composed for someone who had been stunned not long before. She was the calm eye of the storm, with the advisors around her the furious hurricane. Or hurricanes—plural—by the sounds of it.

"—kind of statement is inappropriate for the situation," one was shouting.

Another, right beside the first, insisted, "The public needs an immediate reassurance that something is being done."

A third, apparently on the side of the second advisor, seemed to lose his last bit of composure and practically screamed, "Your Highness, we have traitors within the military! The Royal Guard could be next!"

Sophia's expression became irritated as this was shouted almost directly in her ear.

"Is this confirmed? I thought this was just rumor," the first man asked pointedly.

"We just got the report from the Guard," the angry advisor announced. "People's Front sympathizers. In the military! They crippled the Guard tonight! Who knows what else they've infiltrated?"

"Sophie!" A new voice shouted, and I was battered to the side. A kid—he couldn't have been older than sixteen—had burst into the room, pushing past the huddled dignitaries without regard. He was wearing a white suit with several elaborate pins on his chest, and his curly blonde hair had been styled so thoroughly that I was practically choking on the hairspray wafting off of it.

"Simon!" Sophia said in surprise, as her brother rushed up and nearly crushed her in a tight hug.

"Thank heavens you're alright," he said. "When the lights went out and you disappeared, I thought, I thought... But you're okay. Thank heavens!"

"Yes, yes, I'm fine," Sophia stuttered, patting him on the back awkwardly. Clearly the years of separation weren't as easy to forget for her as they were for him.

He finally pulled away, and his face became serious. "We can't let anything like this happen again. To think of what they almost did to you."

"But they didn't. I'm alright," Sophia tried once again to reassure him.

"They infiltrated the military. They infiltrated the Guard! Nowhere is safe anymore. We have to weed them out. They humiliated us. Our family. Our country!"

"Simon, calm down," Sophia tried to say, but he only became more agitated.

"There is no time for debate. We can't let anything like this ever happen again. We have to hit them. We have a proposal. Prime Minister Mattox and I have a plan. You can help. How can Sophia help, Minister Mattox?" he asked of the squat, but broad-shouldered, mustached man.

"In addition to a public appearance to reassure the people you are unharmed," Mattox replied instantly, "we should make a denunciation of these terrorists, and issue a warning that men like these may yet pose a danger. The followers of the late Charles Becker, as we've seen tonight, pose a serious security risk and we should prepare the nation for any action that may need to be taken against them."

"No! You can't do that!" I interrupted. A dozen pairs of eyes swiveled around towards me, all questioning just who I was and why I thought I could speak here. All but one pair. When Sophia looked towards me, she showed the same anger as she had at the bickering advisors.

"And who exactly are you?" Minister Mattox asked irritably.

"Minister Mattox," Sophia cut across him, "I think the real question here is just who do you think I am to give such a proclamation."

"Your Highness, I—" but she cut him off.

"I will remind you that I am merely a member of the royal family," she said firmly, the last fragments of calm straining in her voice. "Yes, I said 'merely.' Actually, due to the events of tonight, I am not even confirmed as Crown Princess. But even if I was, the decision on how to handle such a crisis would not be up to me. If you're seeking royal approval, then you should be speaking to my mother. Otherwise, you could declare a state of emergency yourself, prime minister. Or are you so unsure of your own position that you need the public support of an eighteen-year-old girl?"

"Your Highness," Mattox replied in an abruptly calm manner, "I'm afraid your inexperience in the realm of politics has betrayed you in this regard."

"Then we are agreed that you don't need such a statement from someone so inexperienced," Sophia said swiftly.

"Sophie," Simon said soothingly, "you're right. Let's go talk to Mother. She should know what has happened, and together, we can make her realize that the country has become far more dangerous than she remembers. We can't let this betrayal stand when it happened right in our backyard."

A betrayal. *That was the sting, wasn't it?* I thought. Simon, the scumbag, wasn't actually worried that Sophia might have been hurt. He was mad that his buddies had pulled this stunt under his nose, without his approval. It got too close. And, as he said, embarrassed him.

I might have voiced this opinion, or otherwise berated the Prince for this, but I didn't need to. Far from convincing her, the last comment made Sophia look at her brother with disgust.

"I think you should leave," she said coldly. And before anyone could respond, she repeated in a louder voice, "Unless you have a medical degree or are a personal guest, everyone here can leave the room."

There was a general grumbling, but the intense, dangerously tired look on Sophia's face convinced any lingerers that it was best to leave. Simon needed his own dirty glare to understand that "personal guest" didn't apply to him. He didn't even give me a second glance as he skulked out. The doctor, standing out in his white coat, merely whispered something to her, and after she nodded her acknowledgement, turned and left as well. I stood to the side as everyone bustled out.

As the last man exited, I asked, "Did I make the cut?"

"If you're going to start telling me how to do my job, then we're going to have problems," she replied, still fuming.

"So, I didn't make the cut?"

"Out of everyone, you have the least grounds to try to lecture me on politics."

"I did make the cut," I stated, grinning slightly.

She closed her eyes, sighed deeply, but when she shook her head, she was holding back a smile. "Fine. You made the cut."

"That's a relief," I said, and plopped down beside her on the couch. "I'm kind of worried someone's going to realize they made a horrible mistake giving me a security clearance."

"Are you saying I made a mistake?" Sophia asked, faux-indignantly.

"No way," I replied. "But if I were in charge of security, I would think it's the biggest mistake of my life to let someone like me anywhere near you. I'm a very bad influence."

She laughed. "You still can't pull off the bad boy thing."

I shrugged. "It was worth a shot. Joking aside, how are you doing?"

Sophia pushed a stray lock of hair from her face as she sunk deeper into the couch. "Just tired. Really, really, tired. Mattox is right that there's something to worry about with the Charmies. I've barely stepped into the spotlight and they've gone after me twice."

"No, Sophia, you can't," I said, feeling a sudden sense of panic. It was as if Sainne had stepped into the room with just the two of us.

"I can't what?" she asked. It was the same automatic defiance that welled up in me countless times before.

"You can't just crack down on them. That's what... uh, they would want," I concluded lamely. The flame flickered back to life behind Sophia's eyes again.

"This coming from the man who punched one of them out. And what do you mean what 'they' want? The Charmies want to be hunted down?"

"That's not... I mean..." I had nothing. I was already nearly blowing it.

"But really, since when have you cared about politics?" she asked again.

Thinking fast, I said, "It's just, that doesn't sound right. You told me the monarchy is supposed to be a symbol of what was right and all, or something like that. I just don't think that would be what you'd want."

Something changed in her expression. The anger had more or less vanished, but the emotion that had replaced it was much harder to define. A strange half-smile formed on her lips, even as her eyes seemed to harden.

"You heard me say I'm *just* a princess, right?" she asked in a strange tone.

"Well, yeah. Of course," I replied, feeling suddenly confused. "But it's like you said, you don't need to support someone like that Mattox—"

"Where did you come from?" she asked.

I was taken aback. "Where did I come from?" I repeated.

"You ran away, right?" she asked, that same strange smile on her face.

"Yeah," I said, rubbing the back of my neck. The subject, which had never been comfortable, seemed even less so after the events of Cloister Cove.

"Where did you run away from?" she asked again.

"Like the state?" I asked, really unsure why she was suddenly curious, and yet, I had a bad feeling in my gut.

"Who do you work for?" she asked abruptly.

"Okay, hang on now," I said, really uncomfortable. "I can't tell you. You know that."

"Kennedy. The truth," she insisted. Her eyes softened for just a moment. I felt like someone was pulling a trick on me. My instincts were running in two very different directions, pulling me just as firmly towards either end.

"I thought we weren't supposed to use that for business," I said, almost pleading.

"You brought business into it first," she replied. "You suddenly started talking politics. Now I'm asking. Kennedy, tell me. Who do you work for?"

I looked long and hard into her eyes. I knew that strictly speaking, I shouldn't give her the answer. But I couldn't lie to her. And I couldn't deny her an answer either. If she was going to find out later, anyway, then what was the harm?

"Okay," I said slowly. "Okay, I'll tell you. But it's going to sound a little crazy. A lot crazy."

She didn't say anything. She just kept her eyes fixed on me.

"Okay, so I work for a group called Time Peace," I said, unsure of where exactly to start. "It's kind of weird. But they have these things called time gates—big white rings that glow in the center—that's not important. What's important is that if you walk through one of these, you go to another timeline."

Her eyes hardened again and I started to panic.

"It's like this," I said, blurting out the words. "When something important happens, time like splits in two. But it has to be a really important event, but also it has to happen fast. Because it's not like every important event and not every moment makes a split. It's just sometimes. And this has happened a bunch before, so there's a bunch of these timelines. I, uh, I actually come from a different timeline. Only in my timeline there's no Aechyr."

"Right," Sophia said coldly.

"Sophia, I swear, I know it's crazy, but I'm not lying. Time Peace works across all these timelines to fight Anarakia—which is like this big evil organization that funds all sorts of people like the Charmies, and Sainne works for them—"

"Oh how convenient," she said scathingly. Her voice cut like a knife into the soft underbelly of my panic.

"Convenient?" I asked, dumbfounded.

"The anti-royalist is part of some grand evil conspiracy," she said. She was suddenly on her feet, pacing angrily. "I'm not an idiot, you know."

"No, of course you're not," I said, quickly losing track of the conversation. "I know it's crazy, but it's true. It's—"

"Stop it," she ordered. "Stop it, Kennedy, or whoever you really are. I always suspected the Guard would send someone into the Academy to keep an eye on me, but somehow, I didn't think they'd be so underhanded as to... as to exploit me like this."

The Guard? The Royal Guard? She was right, of course, there had been someone following her in the Academy. Quincy had—oh. Quincy. Quincy had been wiped from existence, but the timeline had been changed as little as possible. Sophia's suspicions apparently, had been kept intact. And here I was. Someone who dropped into the Academy out of nowhere, discovered her secret identity, and fought to protect her.

"Okay," I said as calmly as I could. "I understand why you think that. But, Sophie, I—"

"Don't call me that," she spat, recoiling as I stood up. She curled in on herself in a corner, brooding. "This is why I left in the first place. All anyone cares about is the image. Tell me something, is that why they sent you? To make sure I fit the proper role? So I don't say anything outrageous?"

"No! That's not it at all!" I said earnestly.

"Right, you're just a time traveler," she mocked. "And just when I started to think there was more to the symbolism than just lies and appearances. Thank you. And tell Simon thank you as well. Thank you both for reminding me of what it's really like."

I was really panicking now. Not just for myself. Not just for the hurt I was causing her, though that was probably the most painful. But for how I was sabotaging Time Peace and their future relations with Aechyr. For everything I was ruining.

"Please, Sophia," I said desperately, running a hand through my hair distractedly as I tried to come up with a strategy. But as usual, this wasn't my area of expertise. I had nothing. "Forget I said anything, it was stupid."

"Yes, it was," she agreed nastily.

"Please," I begged. "I only have one night before I have to leave. I ship out tomorrow, and—"

"Get out," she hissed from the corner.

"I—"

"Get. Out," she repeated, cold hatred in her eyes. They were nearly as terrifying as Sainne's. They certainly hurt more. Far more.

I knew there was nothing I could say. Nothing right now, and right now was all I had. I nodded, then turned towards the door.

I slumped down the stairs, reflecting that the rank I had barely earned would soon be stripped away. I should have just refused when she had asked. The damage I had done would be irreparable. I could have dealt with it if I had just sabotaged my career with Time Peace. I could have even dealt with it if I had just sabotaged my relationship with Sophia. But to have done both? Once again, I would be drifting aimlessly through life.

I stepped out into the marble entrance hall of the castle. Where just minutes before, reporters had been trampling over each other in here, now it was nearly silent. Apparently, everyone had been evicted, as now some staff were moving the podium. Only they and a handful of Royal Guard remained, who insisted, once again, on checking my credentials.

As they did, I glanced around the strangely empty high-ceilinged room. There were several hallways branching from it, and a couple stairways sinking into the floor, leading into the subterranean floors. One was cordoned off.

"What, did you shove all the reporters down there?" I tried to joke to the guard. It didn't sound funny to me, either, but that could have been my joyless voice.

The guard's eyes glanced towards the cordons around the sunken staircase. "General caution," he grunted. "Nothing down there, but rumor has it's unsafe."

"Rumor?" I asked, thinking it sounded odd that a Royal Guard would cite rumor.

He shrugged. "No one goes down there. It's always been off-limits."

"No one?" A wild, crazy thought flitted through my mind briefly. "And you say nothing's down there?"

"Nope, nothing," the guard confirmed, handing me back my credentials. "You're all clear."

"If it's not a security risk, you wouldn't mind if I had a look, would you?" I asked.

He immediately looked at me suspiciously, but after a long moment, he nodded. "You're clear. Like I said, nothing down there. Just don't get yourself hurt."

"Thanks," I said, and briskly walked towards the stairway, tucked almost completely out of the way. It was to the side and just within one of the branching hallways. Coming into the castle, you would definitely miss it.

I ducked under the cordon, and my shoes clacked against the hard steps. Despite that, no one paid me any attention as I descended down into the dark underground. Soon, I was swallowed, the light from the entrance hall above failing to pierce the impenetrable black. I fumbled in my pocket until I drew a flashlight and flicked it on. It did little to push back the dark. The cold stone seemed to reflect less light than normal, but it caught on the dust I kicked up with each step.

The stairway continued down for a long, long while. It felt like I had descended two or three stories before I came to a heavy door. I fumblingly tried the handle, but to my relief, it swung open. It was another dark corridor, but I pressed on. The silence weighed on me more than ever before, but I rushed ahead. It was clear no one had been in here in decades. The dust was thick, the stone was cracked. Maybe no one had been here since the castle had been built. My heart raced.

I pushed through another door. It led into a chamber of rough rock, a cave or a tunnel that obviously clashed with the once-polished stone corridor it was connected to. My excitement mounted as my insane theory seemed more and more likely. Of course they wouldn't have built further in from here!

I walked quickly through the tunnel. The only thing that kept me from running was the unknown. My flashlight cast long shadows on the rocks, presenting many tripping hazards. But after a few minutes, these became less and less pronounced. The cave seemed to smooth, with jagged rocks becoming less frequent, less prominent.

When I saw part of the tunnel give way to a strange, flat, ceramic-like surface, my heart leapt into my throat. I ran forward. The ground became level. I was running down a hallway again. This one wasn't broken by the shapes of stones, but only by a few thin black lines.

I reached a metal door and pushed through it hurriedly. It fell open too, as if it had been just waiting for someone to try. The chamber within was as black as everything behind me, but I could tell at once from the sound of the door echoing around that it was much bigger. When I raised my flashlight, this was confirmed, as was my desperate theory.

Standing in the center of the artificial cavern, raised on a podium, and with several large tubes surrounding it and leading to various control panels, was a time gate. Its architecture blended perfectly with the rest of the room, which had yet more artificial tunnels running deeper into the mountain, into the island. Because, I realized, this was the island. This is why Aechyr wasn't on the other timelines. It was all one massive time gate complex. Maybe there were even more deeper within.

"Yes!" I cried in sheer joy. "Yes! I told you!"

All I could think of was what Sophia would say when she discovered that all of this ran underneath the Capitol. Absolute proof that I wasn't lying. A real time gate, right before her eyes. But I had to take care of the danger first.

There was a reason, of course, that no one had come down this way to discover it. Or rather, that no one existed anymore to tell of the secret. Lurking somewhere, perhaps deeper in those tunnels, would be enigmas. These tunnels may even connect to the Bridgehead Borough Basilica, I mused. It would certainly explain the presence of an enigma there.

I raced to one of the control panels. The switch to turn on the power was obvious enough. A light next to it blinked a dull amber, telling me the machine was just waiting to be awakened. I flipped it, having to push with some force to pry it from its stuck position. The room glowed softly turquoise, strange runes on the walls flickering with internal light. The time gate itself whirred briefly. The intersecting rings moved forward once, then back, as if stretching after a long sleep. A cover on the control panel slid open, and a dial appeared. And then everything became still. The gate didn't fill or glow. It just sat there, revealing an open tunnel behind it.

I could only guess, but I thought it must have been some kind of standby mode. I glanced over the controls again. I was pretty sure the new dial would fully activate the time gate. I reached towards it, then hesitated. I didn't have to turn it on. Connecting it to the network might actually complicate things. No need to have Time Peace or Anarakia immediately trying to come through or capture it. Even in standby, it would hold off the enigmas. I could just leave it like this.

I searched my pockets for something to write with but came up empty. I glanced around, and the answer became clear immediately. I stepped over to a spot just in front of the time gate. I bent over and started writing in the dust.

"To Sophia,

I leave this choice to you.

—K"

I stood back, saw that it was clearly legible and took in the waiting time gate one last time. It wasn't going to be so awful after all. I would still be shipping out, and I didn't know when I would see Sophie again, but it would be alright. For the first time in years, I knew everything would work out in the end.

Epilogue

Commander Fia Florentine shuffled the large stack of papers she was carrying as she walked through the command center at Iterant Point. As the second-in-command, she was always extremely busy attending to the details The Hawk couldn't oversee personally. It was a very tedious job that left little room for frivolity, and Commander Florentine excelled in such a role. Even if the War Marshall made it difficult on occasion.

Now was one such occasion.

"War Marshall," she said, demanding his attention as she dropped her papers on his desk. Any other subordinate who tried such a thing would hardly last long, but The Hawk had long since adopted a unique attitude towards his pent-up second-in-command.

"Fia, come in," he said mildly as the door swung closed behind her.

She didn't seat herself, instead continuing to lean over the desk. "What is this Dark Eye situation?" she demanded.

"You're going to have to be more specific," he said, taking a sip of tea. "I know you've never been a fan of that group—"

"I'm talking about Frost," she interrupted quietly. While she was granted a lot of leeway with The Hawk, she knew yelling would overstep her bounds.

"I thought for sure you were going to tell me again why the whole group should be done away with," The Hawk replied, sounding almost relieved.

"I stand by my arguments," she replied more evenly. "Any agents who need remedial training can do so without being in the field. I also would point out the shoddy record of Dark Eye Squadron in general, but by now I'm sure you know it as well as I do."

"You've practically made me memorize it just from your own recitation," The Hawk replied, wincing slightly. "But I stand by my arguments as well. We're always short of manpower, and Dark Eye Squadron has produced as many success stories as failures. But as for the current line-up...?"

"I have to voice my vehement protests at continuing to field Frost. In this unit or any," Commander Florentine said flatly.

"I can understand that," The Hawk conceded. "He's not my first choice by any means. But you saw Emmaline's report. She's convinced he's stable. I also spoke to him myself. Say it's a judgement call."

Commander Florentine didn't say anything. She wouldn't outwardly question his "judgement calls," but...

"You're still worried about it," The Hawk noted.

"His history isn't encouraging. It was one thing when we had reason to suspect he would win us the war. But now..."

"Consider him an investment. He's handled the arena quite well. Even when he was looped, he came out the other side nearly unscathed. He's not particularly impressive outside of combat, but he's made good use of hang time. He's got a mind for it, I think. I could use someone like that in some of our projects, so long as he can prove himself reliable."

"I see," the commander said, clearly unconvinced. "You're thinking of the Lambda project?"

"It's definitely a possibility," The Hawk said. "But there's a lot to be seen before it could be seriously considered. I'd like to see him expand his talents first. And of course, his friend, Blake Anthony, is another promising one. I suspect that if we want to keep him around, we may have to keep Frost."

"And we're short on manpower," the commander guessed.

"As always," The Hawk confirmed.

Commander Florentine scanned him thoughtfully for a bit. "This has nothing to do with the white rabbit or the previous timeline?"

"I think we've missed the opportunity on that one," The Hawk replied simply.

"You think? This seems like a pretty cut and dry case to me," the commander said, suddenly suspicious that she had caught on to the real reason.

"No," The Hawk said firmly. "It's not what you're thinking."

"But there's a chance."

"An infinitesimal chance. I don't make plans based on such chances."

"Did the white rabbit give you a full report?" Florentine asked. "Did she confirm that it will happen?"

"After it became clear that we couldn't depend on a repeat of Frost's lucky performance, yes, I had a complete debriefing with White Rabbit the Thirteenth."

"And?"

"Sit down, Fia. We have a lot to discuss."

I strode across the sunny deck. The sky was clear, the ocean was a deep blue, and for early winter, it was a beautiful day. Normally, the bustling activity and incessant noise of the amphibious assault ship's flight deck would be an ugly stain on my good mood, but nothing could bring me down. Even now, I was still riding high on the thought of what I was leaving behind on Aechyr.

The report had gone over extremely well, but I didn't much care about that at the moment. I was happy enough that I wasn't immediately fired for blurting out the truth to Sophia. It seemed that I had managed to even out my screw-ups again. But what I really couldn't stop thinking about was what might happen when I returned. Whenever that might be.

And then, while I was mid-stride, it happened. The deck of the ship shook, and a roaring sound burst out behind me. I stumbled and spun to see a pillar of smoke and flame shooting up on the deck. The crew were scrambling, alarms were blaring, and the air was wrought with panic.

And yet, I felt a strange sense of calm. The panic didn't phase me. I just felt a strangely familiar feeling, one that had elements of adrenaline and fear, but not enough to overtake me.

"Kennedy!" Blake called. "Get over here, quick! We got trouble!"

Yes, it was a strange, but calm sensation. One that demanded only that I act.

I turned and ran towards Blake's voice, straight into danger.

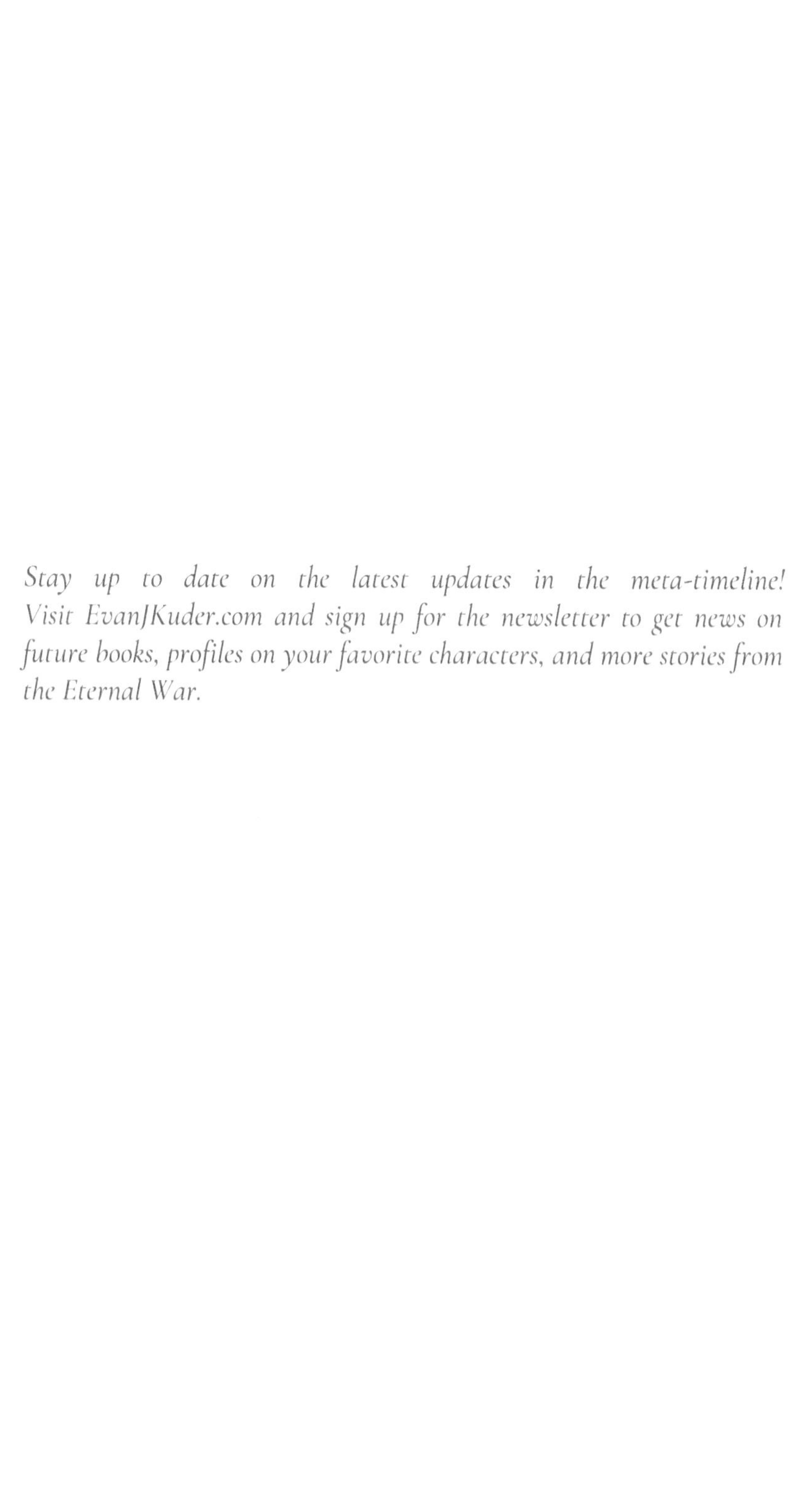

Stay up to date on the latest updates in the meta-timeline! Visit EvanJKuder.com and sign up for the newsletter to get news on future books, profiles on your favorite characters, and more stories from the Eternal War.

About the Author

I hate writing about myself. The parts of my life that would make the best bullet points are the parts I'm least interested in writing about, and the things I'm most interested in writing about... aren't about me. So let's compromise, and I'll tell you about how this book came to be.

For most of my life I've lived around the Twin Cities, MN. But I wasn't much for hunting, fishing, or tromping around the woods. I spent most of my time reading, catching re-runs on TV, or watching movies. That, or emulating (read: blatantly copying) these stories in my own. When I was very young I drew picture books. When I was a little older, I drew comics. And when I was a little older still, I wrote a couple chapters of a book, procrastinated on the rest, decided to re-write what I had made, got stuck... well, you get the picture.

It was about then that Kennedy and Blake first came to be. They were always best friends, but they weren't the same Kennedy and Blake in the pages of this book. They weren't time travelers, and they weren't runaways. They were ordinary suburban kids of about 13 or 14. In other words, they were just like me. Back then, they were recruited to become spies for... someone. I quickly realized I didn't know how to write espionage, so that story never made it past the premise.

But it was always escapism. Because real life just wasn't that exciting. In retrospect, I'm not complaining, but the most common foe younger me ever had to face was boredom. So I preferred the exciting fictional lives of characters on TV or in books. Naturally, Kennedy and Blake reflected that. So time travel, a favorite story device of mine, had to work its way into their adventures. Their escapades became grandiose timeline-hopping affairs. At least, they were in my head. On the page, well, there weren't many pages to speak of. A year would pass and I might write a chapter, or tweak what I had. Or more likely, get caught up in another project that never left the ground. "Artists," am I right?

Well, as I grew up and figured out what to do with my life, it became increasingly apparent that starship captain, superhero, and secret agent weren't terribly realistic career options. That just left the boring options. So I'd make my own entertainment. Literally.

Eventually, I studied film at the University of Wisconsin-Milwaukee and made quite a number of silly short films. They were great fun to create, but I learned my technical skills weren't all that sharp. My writing, however, kept getting honed.

Cut to the Real World and a Real Job. And of course, the pandemic. And me, in a deep depression. Aside from the general stress of lockdown, I was unhappy with myself and where I was. I realized I needed to do something. So what could I do? Write, of course.

And so, once more, I turned to Kennedy and Blake. They had never really gone away, but now I needed to bring them to life once and for all. I spent most of my free time writing. Actually writing, not just idly dreaming. And slowly, Ascension at Aechyr started to emerge. Kennedy and Blake were no longer children, but 18, which saved a lot of headaches over moral quandaries. I settled on the timeline mechanics, created a plot, and furiously edited for errors and inconsistencies.

All said, it took a couple years of figuring out what I was doing, but here it is. And I don't think anything has been as frightening or gratifying as finally finishing this particular project. Or rather, this first step. One way or another, Kennedy and Blake are going to have their adventure—their full adventure across 10 books. It all begins with a single step. This one.

And so, dear reader, I hope this has come full circle. I hope Kennedy, Blake, David, Randy, Sophia, Avery, Quincy, Director Sainne, White Rabbit, and the Hawk have relieved you of your boredom, your troubles, or your worries just for a bit.

Until next time, when all this might just happen again.